EMBEDDED

"Dan Abnett is the master of war."
SFX

"Rips across the page like a blast wave from a barrage of low orbit launched kinetic impactors. Abnett makes hard bitten, high concept mil-fic fun again."
John Birmingham

Embedded, by Dan Abnett, isn't war the way Robert Heinlein wrote it. It's war the way it's fought now, brought to us by embedded journalists. *Embedded* offers an intriguing glimpse of what it might look like through the lens of the present."
SF Signal

With a firm grasp of character and a superior ability to convey action... Abnett delivers a great, readable science fiction novel and earns his comparisons to an a Bernard Cornwell."
Wertzone

A great story, a dangerously more-ish mix of corporate engineering and boneshaking action. It feels fresh, it's accessible to everyone and permeated with the vivid and immersive action that's become Dan's trademark. Lovely stuff."
My Favourite Books

"*Embedded* is gripping and near-impossible to put down, and you will find yourself compelled to keep reading, well into the night, until you reach the satisfying

D0243013

ALSO BY DAN ABNETT

Triumff: Her Majesty's Hero

Doctor Who: The Story of Martha
Doctor Who: The Silent Stars Go By
Torchwood: Border Princes
Primeval: Extinction Event

WARHAMMER 40,000 NOVELS
The Gaunt's Ghosts series
The Eisenhorn Trilogy
The Ravenor Trilogy
Horus Rising
Legion
Prospero Burns

ORIGINAL AUDIO ADVENTURES
Doctor Who: The Forever Trap
Torchwood: Everyone Says Hello

COMIC COLLECTIONS
Nova
Guardians of the Galaxy
Legion of Superheroes
Kingdom
Sinister Dexter

DAN ABNETT

EMBEDDED

ANGRY
ROBOT

ANGRY ROBOT

A member of the Osprey Group
Midland House, West Way
Botley, Oxford
OX2 0PH
UK

www.angryrobotbooks.com
Tarfu

Originally published by Angry Robot 2011
This paperback edition 2012
1

A catalogue record for this book is available
from the British Library.

ISBN: 978-0-85766-151-7
EBook ISBN: 978-0-85766-092-3

Set in Meridien and Swisz by THL Design.

Printed and bound by CPI Group (UK) Ltd, Croydon, CR0 4YY

For Adélie and Cal, and thirty years

ONE

The digital brooch at the throat of his regulation unitard read *Fanciman, Major Gene Gillard, S.O.M.D.*, but from the handshake and greeting it was clear that the major affected a more mannered pronunciation of his surname, something along the lines of *Funsmun*.

He suggested the chair Falk should occupy with a *su casa* wave, then resumed his seat at the desk. As he sat down, he pinched the thighs of his unitard to hoist up the slack in the legs.

"When did you get here?" he asked.

"Last night," Falk replied. "I came in by spinrad a month ago, but I've been in acclimation out on the Cape for twenty days."

"You won't have seen much of Eighty-Six yet, then. You'll discover it's fine country, Mr Falk. Beautiful country."

"Country worth fighting over?" Falk asked. He meant it lightly.

Major Fanciman favoured him with an expression of distaste, as though Falk had just skilfully farted the first few bars of the Settlement Anthem.

"Did I say something wrong?" asked Falk.

Fanciman prepared and lit a smile, slowly and expertly, like it was a Corona Grande.

"We are very conscious of vocabulary, Mr Falk. The word you used has negative connotations. It's, uhm, sensitivity-adverse. I'm not blaming you, God knows. You only just got here, and you haven't had time to digest all of our guideline document packet."

"Sorry," Falk lied. There hadn't been much else to do during the adjustment quarantine. The guidelines had run to several hundred thousand words, and had been remarkably informative. They had made it abundantly clear to Falk just how much stonewalling was going on.

Major Fanciman was keeping his smile alight, tending it to make sure it didn't go out.

"There is a message, Mr Falk," he said, "and we like to stay on it. We like all our sponsored correspondents to stay on it too. We are a mature species, and we no longer find it necessary to resort to crude practices such as fighting."

Falk leaned forward slightly.

"I understand, Major," he said, "but isn't this entire situation military in nature?"

"Undeniably. We have five brigades of the Settlement Office Military Directorate boots dusty here in Shaverton itself. Their role is entirely one of safeguard. Public safeguard."

"But let's just say," said Falk, "if the public was placed in immediate threat, their role of safeguard might require the SOMD to use its weapons?"

"True."

"And wouldn't that be fighting?"

"I can see why you came so highly recommended," Fanciman said, opening a file on his desk. "Probing questions. Incisive. Agile mind. I like it."

"Oh good," said Falk.

"Where are you staying, sir?" asked the driver who Major Fanciman had summoned for Falk.

"Doesn't matter. Where can you get a drink?"

"A bar?" the driver replied with a little halt in his voice that suggested he thought there might be a trick in the question.

"Where do *you* get a drink?" Falk asked.

"The mess, or the Cape Club sometimes."

"Either will be fine," Falk smiled. He closed the vehicle door and grinned at the driver encouragingly.

"They're both serving," the driver replied. He seemed uncomfortable.

"Good. I don't want to go to a bar that isn't serving," Falk said.

"No, I mean they're both reserved for serving personnel. You people use the Embassy or the Holiday Inn or the GEO."

"Me people?" asked Falk.

"Press," said the driver. "There's a list of clubs and bars that correspondents can use, provided you've got accreditation."

Falk had accreditation. It was one of the few things he was certain of. Most of everything else was a fuzz. It was hard to peg time of day. His body wasn't telling him. He reflected that he hadn't had a steady diurnal rhythm in about five years, and the stay on Fiwol with its frantic, twenty-minute days had utterly fucked his bioclock.

It looked like it was late afternoon. The sky over Shaverton's glass masts, blocks and pylons looked like a late afternoon sky. It was the colour of lemon Turkish Delight with an icing sugar dust of clouds.

He didn't know how long the day/night cycle was on Eighty-Six. It wasn't that he'd rushed his presearch, he just wasn't much interested in the physical ecosystem. He'd learn that by living in it. During acclimation, and the trip in-system on the gradually decelerating spinrad driver, he'd studied the political, military and social content of the briefing packet, and any other documents he could access. The SO was doing a more than usually extravagant job of redacting material and neutering news outlets, even the big networks and authorised broadcasters.

His meeting with Major Fanciman had been designed to deliver a specific message. The message was: Lex Falk, you are an acclaimed correspondent with several agency awards to your name and a reputation for hard facts and pene-trating coverage, therefore the SO is very pleased to welcome you to Settlement Eighty-Six, and to validate your accreditation. Having you here proves to the public back home that, despite reports of open conflict, the Settlement Office has nothing to conceal on Eighty-Six, and your reportage will be received as unvarnished and credible.

You will, of course, report only what we permit you to report.

That had been pretty much it. Fanciman had told him all of that without expressly using any of those actual words. Falk needed to understand it, and needed to make it clear he understood it. If necessary, the message could be rein-forced through further meetings with SO execs more senior than Fanciman. If really necessary, an accommodation might be reached where the SO surrendered some juicy nugget to Falk, something that would lend any correspon-dence he filed the bat-squeak of raw truth. One hand washes the other.

Falk sat back in the bodymould seat as the driver turned west onto Equestrian and accelerated towards the hazy megastructure of the Terminal. It amused him to think that the Settlement Office had precisely fuck all idea how uninterested he was in any of it. He was bone-light and lagged from too many years riding drivers, he was having trouble finding anything he actually engaged with any more, and he'd only agreed to the Eighty-Six commission because the fee-with-expenses was generous by any network standards, and the whole thing smelled just like another Pulitzer. He had issues. He had a few things he should have taken care of long since, things he couldn't really work up the enthusiasm to tackle head-on. He had a vague plan (which he'd share with anybody who asked because it made him sound layered) of going home, rebuilding his health and leasing some place on the ocean for a year while he switched gears and wrote That Novel. The addendum he didn't share was that he was no longer sure what That Novel was about, or that the prospect really didn't get him all that fucking thrilled, though living beside the ocean sounded nice.

Falk hadn't warmed to Eighty-Six much. The climate of the Shaverton region, at whatever time of whatever year it was, nudged at the comfort limits of hot and humid. It was one of those places – and Falk had been to a few – that wasn't a natural fit for occupation. It was a tiny margin of variation, almost a nuance thing, but just because the atmosphere wasn't technically inimical to human life, it didn't naturally follow that people ought to live there. Outdoors, it was too hot in an odd way, and too bright. There was an odd saturation to colours.

Indoors, everything was too cold. Everything smelled of air-con and a ubiquitous, lemon-scented twang of Insect-Aside.

The driver took him to the GEO. It was the name of both the corp and the serious glass mast the corp occupied in the land skirts of the massive Terminal. From the executive offices, employees of Geoplanitia Enabling Operator could see the heavy-hipped ferries banging up and down out of the arrestor silos on the Cape, serving the vast drivers lurking invisibly, upstairs at the edge of space.

There was a bar in the basement, flushed with sickly lighting, piped music and a funk of bug spray, and fitted out with Early Settlement Era furniture, undoubtedly repro, woven from wicker-effect polymer lattice. The place made up in business what it lacked in soul. There were distinct currents separating the crowd: non-local correspondents and affiliates, sorted by old acquaintance or network loyalty; GEO employees; locals work-ing the room, shilling everything from sources to sex in order to leverage a little network expense account action.

Falk got talking to a GEO exec at the rail of the marble-effect bar. The exec was ordering a tray of drinks. It was a colleague's birthday. As the barman filled the order, a casual question or two got the exec to admit that the mood was downtrend among GEO staffers. The dispute (even after two beer-effect drinks, the exec was on-message enough not to refer to the situation as a "war" or even a "conflict") was having non-advantageous outcomes for the corporation. Development contracts were overrunning or remaining unfulfilled, SO grants were being withheld and GEO's share price had dipped badly on the home market because of public perception. GEO had substantial holdings on Eighty-Six.

"Our share value is in the shitter," the exec said, "and our corporate rep is floating there right beside it. The public thinks we're driving this dispute through corporate greed. It's like Sixty all over again."

"Except," said Falk, "this isn't a big post-global company

taking the blame for what turned out to be fundamentalists terror-bombing settlement pharms."

"Fuck you know about it?" the exec asked.

"I was there."

"On Sixty?"

"At the end, yeah."

The exec nodded, and folded his mouth down in a shape that indicated he was quite impressed.

"Big pharm got the blame on Sixty until it finally came out that there was some pretty nasty activism going on. That's not the case here, is it? This dispute has been triggered by the aggressive policies of corps like GEO. Please don't compare it to Sixty unless you know what the fuck you're talking about."

The exec offered to buy Falk a drink and took him to meet his colleagues. They were a sallow bunch who plainly spent too much time indoors in the tailored environment of their corporate glass mast. Falk had never understood that. He looked like shit because he spent too much time aboard drivers where there was no outside to step into. But if you've gone to live and work on another planet for a five- or ten-year rotation, or forever, why the fuck didn't you ever go outside? Why the fuck do you stay inside your mast? You might as well be on a driver. You might as well have stayed in Beijing.

They wanted to know about Sixty. He gave them a short but embellished version, romanticising his own hardline newsman cred. They all oohed and aahed in all the right places, like they knew from bullshit. They all nodded sagely at his tough yet sentimental verdicts.

Three of them were due to leave in a week, six years shy of their contracted finish. Two more were going the following month. There were, he learned, whole floors of the mast unoccupied. Some had emptied since the start of the dispute, as GEO reposted staff to other, less controversial settlements. Others had never been filled. The GEO glass mast had been standing for just twenty years. There was a real possibility that it would be closed and sold off before the corporation that had paid for its construction had properly inhabited it.

Falk listened to them rabbit. It was automatic, just warming up his journo muscles. They weren't saying much that was interesting beyond the state of the mast. They were worried about their futures, about their careers. They were fretting about where they might get posted, and what the bad press was doing to their stocks and bonuses.

His Scotch-effect drink was crappy but welcome after the abstinence of transit and acclimation. He got a little buzz cooking and felt good about himself. He arranged his face so it looked like he was interested.

He kept an eye on a nearby table where some network boys had clustered. One of the faces looked familiar, like a very old, careworn version of a man he had once known, an older brother, a father.

"Falk? Is that you?"

He recognised her voice, but not her face when he turned to look at it. She was carrying a lot of mass, even more than she had when he'd last seen her. Like her voice, her smile hadn't changed.

"Cleesh."

He got up and hugged her. His hands didn't meet. She smelled of nutrition bars and the sugar-plastic aftertaste of diet control packs. There were little flesh-match patches covering the constellations of surgical plug excisions dotting her scalp, the side of her throat and her slabby upper arms where they showed beyond the sleeves of her *Cola* tee.

Falk hadn't seen her since Seventy-Seven, and even then only on screen.

"How are you?" he asked.

"I'm wealthy. Really wealthy," she laughed.

"Look at you. You unhooked."

"Had to," she replied, looking him up and down. "Doctors said I had to. Can't circle forever. Freeks® you up. I needed grav time."

"But circling's what you do, Cleesh," he said.

"I know. I'm not an in-person person. But it was that or die, so I thought I'd spend a little time in the company of normal gravity, drop a gazillion sizes, make sure I don't go cardio-pop."

She eyed him head to toe again and grinned.

"Look at you, though, Falk. You're like a bird. We're like the pedia entry for sublime and ridiculous."

"Hey, I'm at my fucking physical peak," he objected.

"You look like shit. But shit that I'm pleased to see," she replied. "Buy me a drink."

He'd known her for years, but the core of their relationship was a sixteen month assignment to Seventy-Seven. Cleesh was a data wet nurse, feeding, supplying and managing the newslines from a can station circling at twenty-nine miles. She was the most able and clued-in editor-engineer he'd ever worked with. They'd become friends, but he'd never met her in the flesh. She never unhooked from the plug network and left her no-grav home. Prolonged no-grav fucked you up, sooner or later. It made you bone-light or flesh-heavy, sometimes both. No matter how well sunlight, clean air, fresh water and food were simulated, they were still simulated, and it poisoned you eventually. Diabetes, SAD, muscle wastage, organ failure, obesity, eczema, there was always some kind of price.

They talked. He became aware of how twig-scrawny his wrists were compared to hers. Perhaps he had been riding the drivers too long.

"You're here to cover the thing that isn't a war?" she asked.

"Of course."

"You got an in? They're freeking® tight about the press free-associating with servicemen."

"I've got a hot ticket pass," he said. He took a sip of his Scotch-effect. "Settlement Office accreditation. Access."

"Of course you have," she smiled. It was the friendly, reassuring smile he'd seen via hi-res boxes a million times.

"They've arranged some visits for me. I saw some SOMD desker." He brushed his palms together, lit up the tiny screen of his celf and opened the document Fanciman had posted him.

"Two days' time, a look at Mitre Sands, then a visit to Marblehead." He showed her the celf's little display in the cup of his hand.

Cleesh pursed her lips and wobbled her head from side to side.

"What?" he asked.

"That'll just be handled PR stuff. Mitre Sands is a pretend camp they use to show everyone."

"It's not pretend."

Cleesh was drinking a tall glass of NoCal-Cola. She turned the glass by the rim with her thumb and fingers like she was cracking a safe.

"Okay, but it's a stores dump, dressed up to make people feel like they're visiting something authentic. Marblehead, that was hot, just not any more. It's tourism, Falk. They'll show you a wall with hard-round holes in it. They show it to everyone. Four days' time, you'll be sitting here telling me how they showed you the wall with the hard-round holes in it."

"That's always how it works," he replied. "You follow their tours around at the beginning while you find your feet, then you give the guide the slip. You know that."

"Tougher here," she said. "Freeking® tough."

"You've come here to report?"

"Yeah. Makes a change. I thought, if Falk can do it, how hard can it be? They're not letting anyone close to the good stuff. There's a lot of people doing a lot of graft on the down low to get access."

"A lot of people including you?"

"But of course."

"Have you got something, Cleesh?"

She gave him her stern look.

"I've been here three months, Falk. I've worked something out and it could be good. It's almost in the bag. I might share it with you, except you'll probably be here three minutes and get something better."

"Come on, Cleesh."

"Be patient. Work your magic. What I've got isn't guaranteed or anything. And if it boils over, it could get me rescinded forever."

"It's that dodgy?"

She shrugged. "I will spend the rest of my years teaching elementary ling to grade school settlementeers. Or in jail."

"Give me something," he said. "What do you know? Is the Bloc really involved in this, or is it just a corporate shooting match?"

She dropped her voice and leaned forward.

"It might actually be the Bloc this time, Falk," she said.

TWO

He was a good boy. He stayed in Shaverton for the next two days, and didn't step off. He walked boulevards that were so prosaically planned their designer's lack of imagination was as plain as the rows of palm-effect trees. He drank iced tea and NoCal-Cola under the glare shades of terrace diners, and watched the flitters and bugs droning through the sunlight. The biggest bugs were known as blurds. They were about the size of sparrows, and extremely common. They fluttered about like delicate pieces of folded paper engineering.

On the second day, he had lunch with Cleesh at a ProFood outlet on the north end of the Cape road. They sat near a big plastic statue of Booster Rooster. She brought a couple of people with her: a woman called Sylvane who was a stringer from NetWorth, and a nondescript man that Cleesh claimed worked for SO Logistics. Falk wondered if the man was her contact, and tried to open him up a little, but he was singularly dull and unforthcoming, and spent most of the time talking to Sylvane about import tariffs.

"You know they named Seventy-Seven?" Cleesh asked Falk.

"Officially? I hadn't heard that."

"Yup. They called it Fronteria."

"That makes it what? A settlement? A full state?"

"A full state."

"Wow."

"One hundred and thirteenth state of the Union," she said.

"It'll always be Seventy-Seven to me," he said. "Who the fuck thought of *Fronteria*?"

"I know," she agreed, "it's a freeking® awful name, right?"

"What's with this 'freeking' thing?" he asked, putting down his wrap.

"Sponsored expletive," said Sylvane.

"It's what?"

Sylvane was good-looking enough, but it was camera-ready attractive. There was no depth to her appeal. It was all shopped and cosmetic.

"The SO wants to control bad language on all broadcasts," Sylvane said, "especially if stuff is going to the US networks free-feed. They were going to patch in a bleep-mask to cover any cussing."

"Then NoCal-Cola stepped up and offered to sponsor an expletive for use in the zone," said Cleesh. "Freek® Like in NoCal Freek®, the lime-flavoured hi-caff one. Didn't they offer to patch you when you got here?"

"No," said Falk.

"I told you he was special," Cleesh said to the others.

"They actually plugged it into you?" Falk asked, uneasy.

"Ling patch," said Cleesh. "It's a permit requirement for anyone from Associated or the indies. Keeping it clean across the networks."

"That's how you're making that little sound at the end of the word?" Falk asked.

"It's freeking® amazing, isn't it?" said Cleesh, doing it deliberately, with relish. "I spent the first few days swearing my freeking® ass off, and I can't say freek® all except the sponsored word."

"None of you can actually curse any more?" Falk asked, laughing.

"Nope," Cleesh replied. Sylvane shook her head.

"Say *fuck*!" he demanded.

"Freek®!" said Cleesh.

"I don't want to," said Sylvane.

"No one patched me," said the man from Logistics. "I think harsh language is the mark of a limited imagination."

"Screw that," said Falk. "Whatever happened to free speech?"

"This is free speech," said Cleesh. "I didn't have to pay for the patch."

"I meant your constitutional right as a citizen of the United Status," said Falk.

"That's what I'm freeking® talking about, baby," she said.

On the morning of his first arranged tour, he was required to report to the depot at Camp Lasky on Shaverton's south shore two hours before dawn. He got transport down and arrived in good time, but he felt like crap. He couldn't sync to the day/night cycle. Lag had got him. He was wide awake in the middle of the night, and hungry for something he couldn't specifically identify. He had spent too much of the previous evening sinking Scotch-effect at the GEO bar in an attempt to feel drowsy while trying to talk Sylvane into bed. The latter was a purely academic exercise. He didn't especially want to sleep with her. He wanted to sleep with somebody. He wasn't that fussy. It was part of his hunger. He let her say the no he was expecting, and told himself it was useful sparring to get himself back in the ring.

Wake-up felt disgustingly early. Falk felt as though someone had folded the night in half. He'd managed to catch about half an hour's sleep in the end, and his head was raw from too much Scotch-effect. It never got much better, despite some pills and a bottle of water.

The transport dropped him and two other correspondents at the gate, under the blue-white floods. Blurds were battering themselves insensible against the mesh covers on the lamps.

The other two correspondents looked refreshed and well equipped. He felt shoddy and rough. He wondered if they could smell his breath. Fuck them if they could.

Two SOMD shaveheads in tundra-pattern kit checked their credentials and let them in through the barrier to a waiting area beside the loading docks. A female warrant officer called Tedders came to find them. She checked their credentials again, and made them bag their celf plugs and any other transmitting devices. The poly bags, labelled and signed for, went into lockers.

"You're going to be embedded for the sweep tour from Mitre Sands," she said. "We can't have an unsecured live signal coming off any of you." One of the other two produced a pen tablet and asked her if that was okay. She spent a moment checking it over. She was small and robust, with sleeves folded up to her elbows and her hair in a tight bun as small and hard as a grenade.

"How are you today, sir?" she asked when it was Falk's turn to be swept.

"I'm wealthy, thank you," he replied. He got his game face on, notched up the charm.

"Good to hear," she said. There was a look in her eyes, the way she regarded him, that suggested he was special-handling cargo she'd had notice of.

"You've been told to expect me, haven't you?" he asked.

"I do my job, sir. I read my presearch. I see I'm going to

be hosting a guy who's got press awards over his fireplace, I take it seriously."

"I don't bite," he said.

"I don't get bitten," she replied. Her smile was firm, non-negotiable. Then her expression changed slightly, became more agreeable. "Sit out the debrief if you like. I'm sure we won't be telling the likes of you anything new."

"The likes of me would like to hear it anyway," he said. "It's part of the embedding experience. Besides, I don't want them resenting me for getting special treatment."

He nodded his head in the direction of the other two correspondents.

"Okay then," Tedders said.

Four other agency reps had already assembled in the office space behind the waiting area. Like the two who'd come in with Falk, they looked packet-fresh and eager. He wanted tea, maybe some variety of baked goods, and twenty minutes by himself in a clean latrine. He felt like an old, notorious uncle who'd turned up at a wedding.

"Major Selton," Tedders announced. Selton stepped up, fronting the room. She was a she too, a long-wheelbase Amazon compared to the portable, compact Tedders. Her fatigues had creases that could draw blood. Her hair was a black lawn, mown short. The overhead lights, unflatteringly hard, glinted off the digital brooch at her throat.

"Welcome to Lasky," she said, "I hope you're all good and wealthy this morning. The SOMD wants to make your visit comfortable and safe, but I want to make sure you've all signed your permission waivers. My colleague, Warrant Officer Tedders, will have been through the prechecks, but I want to stress again that if you're carrying anything that transmits, you need to turn it in now. All our connections need to be secure. If you don't know, if you're uncertain, be safe and ask."

She moved closer to the large wall box, and the proximity of her brooch woke it up. A test pattern colour card came up first, then the SOMD crest logo against a blue background. She was still talking.

"Settlement Eighty-Six was first developed one hundred ten years ago during the Second Expansion. It has always been a high-productivity location, with specialisms that include agriculture, mineral sourcing, bulk manufacture and orbital assembly. Notable in-system resources include Eighty-Six's second moon, 86/b, locally known as 'Fred'. Page three of your packs. Fred has the third highest concentration of extro-transition elements in settled territory."

The wall box opened a complex, rotating plan of Eighty-Six and the mechanism of the stellar system that supported it. Fred was highlighted.

"Forty-four years ago," Selton continued, "the Settlement Office formally declared all Northern Territories of Eighty-Six as the jurisdiction of the United Status, acknowledging the US's claims of sustained investment in, and support of, the Northern Territory settlements. This was ratified two years later. Nineteen small territorial parcels in the southern and subpolar zones remain outside United Status dominion. Seven are independent commercial outsearch stations. The others are agricultural fiefs of the Central Bloc."

Topographs and geopolitical sat-maps of Eighty-Six rolled across the wall box, with little hot, bright data-markers appearing and disappearing very fast, each one shooting a tag spear down to some surface detail before it vanished. Selton slowed the map rotation with a hand stroke.

"The Northern Territories appealed for full statehood a decade ago. We're in work with the usual long, slow programme of discovery and interest-conflict assessment.

The SO has supported the claim, and expects that Eighty-Six will be approved for full state status within five years."

"Presumably unless this war gets in the way?" asked a correspondent in the front row.

Oooh! Don't interrupt her! Falk winced. *And don't say war!*

Selton didn't miss a beat. She looked at the correspondent, a girl in a puffy, green litex hiking jacket, and fired off a ground-to-air laser-led public relations smile. Falk felt the girl incinerate.

"The situation here on Eighty-Six may force a revision of that estimate," Selton said smoothly. "It does not, however, have direct relevance to the pending statehood process."

"But surely–" the girl continued.

Fuck me, learn to drop it! Falk thought. *In God's name, stop baiting her!*

He stuck his hand up.

"That will make Eighty-Six the what?" he asked. "The one hundred and fourteenth state of the Union?"

"One-fourteen or one-fifteen," Selton replied, acknowledging him with an agreeable smile. "It depends whether Sixty-Six fast-tracks its statehood legislation or not."

"What will Eighty-Six be called?" Falk asked.

"We don't know. That hasn't yet been decided."

"But formal naming usually accompanies the declaration of statehood."

"Of course. I mean, we're not in the loop. I believe some names are being audience-tested for a shortlist. That's not my bailiwick. You'd have to ask the SO direct."

"Thanks," said Falk, and pretended to make a note. The girl in the green hiker definitely owed him big for easing the heat off her.

"We expect to be out for about fourteen hours today. The weather's looking clear along the seaboard, so we should make good time into the mountain zone. We transfer from hopter to ground roller for the last leg. I'm going to buddy each one of you up with a member of the sweep unit. You can ask them questions, but you will, and I stress will, follow their instructions at all times. This is a potential fire-zone, so there is a present danger of death. Follow instructions. Do not deviate. We do not expect trouble, but if trouble starts, we cannot have you making it worse."

"Don't mention it," Falk said.

The girl in the green hiker looked at him.

"Mention what?" she asked.

"Me taking that bullet for you."

"What are you talking about?" she asked. She clearly wasn't amused or impressed. Irritation creases bunched at the bridge of her nose.

They were outside, doing up their jackets and spraying on Insect-Aside, waiting for the unit. The sun was coming up.

"Selton was going to scorch you," said Falk.

"I asked a legitimate question," the girl replied.

"That was what it was, was it?" He laughed.

"Who the fuck are you?" she asked.

"Falk," he said.

"I know what the fuck I'm doing, *Falk*," she said.

"How many days of subtlety school did you miss, growing up?" he asked.

"Fuck!" she said, backing away. "I don't know what this is. Are you coming on to me? You're being weird."

She walked away.

"Smooth," said Tedders. She was standing right there beside him.

"Some people don't know when you're doing them a favour," he said.

"I hear you," said Tedders.

"Who is she?" he asked. She consulted her celf.

"Noma Berlin. Affiliated Dispersal. Says she's got a short-term contract with Data-Scatter."

"Rookie," he murmured.

"She's young, she'll learn," said Tedders.

"What's that supposed to mean?" Falk asked.

"The 'she'll learn' part?" asked Tedders. "Or the 'she's young' part?"

He shook his head like it was all a joke and he didn't care. The compact, portable smile didn't leave Tedders' lips.

"Are you coming with us, Tedders?" he asked.

"Today?" she replied. "No. Thank fuck."

Selton called everyone to order. The rising sun was already notching the heat up, and the air was swirling with tiny bugs. She ran through a few more pointers, took a question or two and then led them across to the hangars.

In the interval since the brief, she'd strapped on body armour plates and a torso harness the colour of putty. There was some kind of short-action sidearm holster-packed on her left hip.

The hangars were vast, airy spaces out of the heat. A row of big, matt-grey transport hopters sat facing the north doors. C440s, bleeding-edge machines, intended to impress. The blades of their turbofans were neatly folded like the buds of photonastic flowers waiting for the sun.

Beside each hopter, groups of SOMD servicemen were suiting up from kit sets laid out on the deck in identical patterns. They were all big guys, even the ones that were girls. They wore the same style tundra-pattern field dress and armour harness rigs as Selton. They were intimidatingly clean and precise. Each kit layout included a principal weapon, reverentially resting on a ground sheet. The most common issue was the heavy, black M3A Hardlaser (beam) Emitter, known as the pipe or piper, though some mission specialists carried more compact PAP 20s loading 2mil SOMD Standard Caseless in stock-lock clips. Falk could smell gun oil and anti-dust lube.

"Falk?"

One of the specialists had approached him. He was seriously tall, and bulked out by his harness plates. The high and tight made his head seem over-large.

"You Falk?" he asked.

"Yes."

The specialist held out his hand.

"Renn Lukes, payload specialist. I'm going to be your buddy."

THREE

The hopters blatted downcountry, low and determined, riding the rush of their howling chop-wash.

Through the open side door, Falk watched their shadow chasing them across the terrain, matching them in a perfect parallel trajectory, sometimes big, as volcanic crags thrust up, sometimes flickering in the salt-gorse, sometimes abruptly small and distant as low dune basins dropped away.

Lukes re-checked Falk's harness.

"Don't want you falling out," he said. His voice, half-drowned by the fan-jets, echoed itself with a tinny delay via the com-plug in Falk's left ear. The payload specialist's voice was being chased by its own fuzzy shadow, just like the hopter.

There were eight other SOMD servicemen in the hold space, and two other correspondents. One was a technology reporter from thInc, a beardy little nuisance called Jeanot. The other was green hiker girl.

Lukes finished another stow check, and crossed the deck with the spread gait of a man inured to swell and pitch. He used overhead grip rails with unconscious ease, strap-hanging like a commuter.

"What can I tell you?" he asked.

Falk shrugged.

Lukes buckled in beside him.

"Major Selton says we should answer all your questions, demonstrate practice, give you the talk-around."

"That's why we're here," said Falk.

Lukes smiled and pinched his fingers and thumb together gently like they were an adjustable wrench.

"You don't have to shout," he said. "I can hear you fine."

"Sorry."

"You want to know about the bird?" Lukes offered. "Standard SOMD gunship and workhorse. We call them Boomers."

"C440 Avery Boreal," Jeanot cut in from his seat nearby. "Quad-engined utility and assault lifters, affectionately known as 'Boomers' or 'Boombirds', a basic retool of the long-serving C400 platform with new-generation instrumentation packages and dermetic-weave six-ply fuselage sheathing. Fabricated by GEO and Lowmann-Escaper Systems under licence from Avery Daimler Eiser. Forty thousand pound capacity. Top speed two hundred seventy-five knots."

Lukes laughed heartily.

"There's almost no point you being here," Falk said to Jeanot.

"You know your stuff," said Lukes, still amused.

"Test me," Jeanot laughed back. "What else do you want to know? Range is nine-thirty nmi, rate of climb is twenty-two hundred feet per minute, disc loading is sixteen pounds per square foot. All home-standard figures, of course. This is the Egress variant with the boosted–"

"No," said Falk.

They both looked at him.

"It's the Echo version. Those aren't Lycoming plants. The nacelles are too bulked up. They're T490 Northrop cold fusion units."

"Good eye," said Lukes, laughing again.

"Good engines," said Falk.

"You were hiding your inner nerd," chuckled Lukes.

"Unlike some," said Falk. He returned Jeanot's toxic glare and mouthed *fuck you*.

Outside, it was hard to see far. The sky was the colour and texture of steel wool, and it felt like they were swathed in dusty heat. You could see how hot the day was, how close.

You could see how dreary and endless the land was under the skipping, flickering shadow in mindless pursuit.

They set down at Mitre Sands, on a mesa above the camp strip. As the jets whined down to rotor stall, they de-bussed with their heads down.

Scarves of dust trailed the air. The sky was diffused heat and sour light, too hot, too bland. Falk slipped out his glares and put them on. He keyed the *snapshot* function on the left arm so that he could blink-record photo notes as and when.

The light felt abrasive on his face. There was a prickle of storm static that he could taste on top of the grit in his mouth. The sky over the flat hill was simultaneously too big and too close. It was intimidating them with a ski mask on. He wanted to cough and spit to clear the dust from his throat, but felt self-conscious. Spitting somehow seemed too provocative and disrespectful. Falk decided it was the bullying sky he was cowed by, not the virile SOMD servicemen.

Desert blurds, white as bleached bone and as big as his hand, chittered by. He brushed himself down, hoisted his carrypack, and blinked off a few of shots while everybody caught up. He got a couple of nice snaps of the boomers

parked in a row, and two of green hiker girl bending over
to do up her laces. The saved images stayed on the inside
of his glare lenses for a moment before fading.

They went down the slope into the camp. It was a village
of crate-and-create box huts and reflatable hardskin store
domes. Dust blow had scuffed all the surface paint. SOMD
staffers were waiting to greet them. Falk could see a row of
Fargos and other roller rides parked beyond the genny shed
and the uplink masts. At the defensive points of the camp
strip, SOMD gunners manned autohunt gun carriages. Falk
watched one reposition, plodding on its stocky tortoise legs.
The fat muzzle shrouds of its four mated pipers had been
painted white to reduce their profile against the sky.

Selton went to meet the camp rep and they started to
chat. Another officer directed the media party and their
SOMD buddies towards a sideless aluminium frame hut
where materiel boxes were stacked under netting.

"Time to plate you," Lukes said to Falk. "What do you
wear? A thirty-six?"

"Forty, forty-two," said Falk. Did Lukes think he was
some kind of shrimp?

Lukes looked at him. "Maybe we start with a thirty-eight.
It's got to fit tight, or it won't stop a freeking® thing."

The servicemen started to unpack body armour and torso
rigs from the boxes. The kit was putty coloured the same
as theirs, but it had "PRESS" printed in giant block white
across the chests and shoulder blades. Falk wondered if they
should have just cut to the chase and printed on the words
"aim here" instead. Lukes helped him strap up.

"Marblehead really a firezone, or is this to lend authentic
flavour?" Falk asked as he adjusted the waist fasteners.

"It can be lively," Lukes replied. "Probably won't be, but
returning media observers to Lasky with sucking chest

wounds because we didn't insist they wear rigs doesn't play well."

"Has that happened?"

"No, because we insist they wear rigs."

"You're US, right?"

Lukes nodded.

"How far into your SO attachment are you?"

"Year two of a four-year tour. Most of us are US, but there's a great Chinese brigade up at Thompson Ten."

"I wondered if we would get any Bloc forces in our escort."

Lukes grinned.

"It's always a possibility," he said.

"But?"

"The possibility is technical. In practice, certain unspoken policies apply."

"Bloc forces on SO attachment would not supply cover for US media on Eighty-Six?"

"I said the policies were unspoken. I don't make them. I don't speak them."

"Is this a fight against Bloc forces?" Falk asked.

Lukes took back the gloves he'd just passed to Falk and exchanged them for a smaller pair.

"Anti-corporate paramilitary forces are staging armed resistance to the territorial interests of the United Status," he said. "The Settlement Office Military Directorate has been engaged to police and contain the dispute."

"That sounds like something you read off a prompter."

"Ain't it a bitch when the truth comes as no surprise?" Lukes replied. He slapped Falk on the back. "You're done."

Falk flexed his shoulders and circled his arms.

"Good," he said. "I told you. Forty-two."

"That's a thirty-six," said Lukes.

• • • •

The rollers had their engines running ready, throbbing idle revs into the morning heat. Most of the rides were big six-wheel Fargo models spray-jobbed with tundra paint mottle, but there were two small Smartkart All-ways that would act as follow cars. Lukes led Falk to the front Fargo and showed him his seat. The specialist was carrying his M3A on a mesh sling over his right shoulder. The weapon seemed to sport an unnecessarily complex cluster of tactical optics on the top rail. The muzzle shroud covering the emitter's tube looked grotesquely wide, like a section of black plastic drainpipe.

Falk discovered he had been placed behind Major Selton, who was strapped into the centreline command seat.

"The general wisdom seems to be that the paramilitaries are landgrabbers," he remarked.

"It's a time-worn story, and Eighty-Six isn't the first settlement to experience the problem," she replied. "It won't be the last."

"What is it? Independence? Rejection of US dominion? Territorial ethics? Legal right to worship?"

"That's quite a list," she said over her shoulder, busy listening to her com-plug while she addressed her drop-down tactical display.

"It could be longer," said Falk. "A source told me that the Reserve Bank had reneged on the agreed scale for parcel subsidies for first- and second-generation settlers."

"Not true," she said.

"I also heard that mineral rights had been revised and cut to a one hundred and one year review."

"That is true," she said, "but hardly material. The chances of any parcel tenant losing their mineral rights after review is very small. The review period has really just been reset to assist with the SO's ongoing resource audit. The only circumstances in which a parcel tenant would forfeit their mineral rights at point of review would be if the lode involved fell within the remit of a Strategic Significance Order."

"Well, I also heard–" he began.

"How long does this list get, Mr Falk?" she asked him, smiling. "Just so I can block out my afternoon."

He held her look.

"I guess it'll get longer and longer all the while the specific nature of the dispute remains vague. Speculation grows wild, especially since this is the first full-scale shooting war to take place post-globally since settlement began. That comes with the words big deal stamped on it."

"If this is what a full-scale shooting war looks like," said Selton, "we haven't got much to worry about. This is a minor armed dispute. I don't think it's the big story you think it is. We've got it contained. It'll be over in a couple of months."

"You don't think it's the big story I think it is, or you don't think it's the big story us media types think it is?"

"I meant the latter, Mr Falk," she replied. "Why, is your imagination particularly feverish?"

Something crackled in her ear. She signalled the driver up front and they started to roll. The Fargo immediately began to lurch and rumble over the rough terrain. It felt and sounded like every single one of the fat tyres had blown and shredded.

"Everyone always wonders about the Central Bloc," Falk said.

Selton shot him a glance. He couldn't tell if it was a nervous look or a pitying one.

"The Cold War's been cold for nearly three hundred years, Falk. As we move out and expand, all it ever does is get colder and colder. Hard space sucks all the warmth out of it. We were at close quarters when it started, sharing one world, and still it started cold. It must be approaching heat death by now."

"Poetic. Can I quote you?"

"Sure. We've put plenty of space between us, Falk. Literally. The US, the Bloc, the Chinese, everyone's got room to breathe, to develop. No one's treading on anyone else's toes any more. No one gets to seem like a bad neighbour. There's no reason for war, cold or otherwise."

"But you'd agree," said Falk, "if we suddenly found one, that would be a huge hairy deal?"

"None hairier," she replied, flashing her eyebrows at him. "But that is not the situation on Eighty-Six. It's a local settlement dispute with disaffected paramilitaries."

"Where do the paramilitaries get their arms from?" asked green hiker girl from the bucket seat behind Falk. Falk hadn't realised she'd been listening.

Selton said something in reply, then turned to check something on her display's terrain scanner.

"What did she say?" green hiker girl asked over the thunder of the engines.

"I think she said 'that's not material'," Falk replied.

FOUR

A short distance out of Mitre Sands, on the open track, the Fargos rose up on their suspension and went what Lukes called "long-legged". Lifting the hull and broadening the chassis frame made for superior clearance and weight distribution, and the extended footprint boosted stability. The ride got appreciably smoother.

Through the dust-worn side window, Falk watched the All-ways riding out wide alongside them across the stone scrub, lifting plumes of dust like foam wakes. The chase cars were light and fast. Sunlight flashed off the glares of the shavehead manning the heavy-gauge pintle mount.

Mountains sulked to the west of them like a grey barn wall. For an hour, the cloudcover came and went like time-lapse footage: cloud boil, sharp sun breaks, cloud boil again. Over the shared com system, Selton drew their attention to a pair of the big, rare tundra grazers, turning on the thermals, but Falk didn't get to the window in time and all he saw were sun dogs.

He was uncomfortable in his seat. It was tight, and the hard form-mould transmitted every bump and vibration to his ass. His back and his right hip began to ache.

Green hiker girl was writing something on a clutch tablet.

"This your first zone posting?" he asked her, trying to reboot things.

"I'm thirty-one," she replied.

He gave her "quizzical".

"Are we playing Respond To One Question With The Answer To Another?" he asked.

"I'm not playing anything with you, period," she replied. She returned to her work.

"The longer I spend with you," he said, "the more I sense I'm getting to know the real you."

She looked up at him again. He considered himself thick-skinned, but the contempt in her eyes came as a surprise.

"I have a horrible feeling," she said, "that someone once told you that you were charming, and you believed them."

Marblehead was an ore town that had been seeded about fifty years before. The first-gen pop, according to Selton, had been mostly Chinese and Portuguese, though that had diluted as the town's prosperity had grown. The place had secured major contracts to supply ore for the construction industry, mainly blue metal aggregate for precast concrete mixes, though it also quarried quality materials for facing and dressing. The extractors of Marblehead had made a significant contribution to the rise of Shaverton.

Marblehead had been one of the flashpoints in the early phase of the dispute. Production had cut back as the SOMD restricted transport and conveyance. A lot of the pop had drained out in the previous nine months.

Selton told them that the op profile was to meet with a Forward Patrol Group, conduct a security appraisal and then extract before nightfall. Falk was pretty sure that was just a bunch of rugged-sounding terms that actually meant a pretend wargame exercise with added show-and-tell.

Approaching the town, now driving on a hardpan roadway, they dropped their profile again, and ran low. The All-ways tucked in close. One zipped ahead, taking point.

"Stay buttoned up," Selton said into her mic. Their speed had decreased. "Authority given for weapons live. Commence standard sweep and target sampling."

There was a disconcerting noise of motor gearing in the roof above them. The autohunt turret mount on the Fargo's cabin top activated and began to traverse.

They entered a long incline, a winding ribbon road that followed the side of a valley down to the town limits. The place looked nondescript, dirty and dead, not so much a township as row after row of ugly precast buildings dumped on waste ground waiting to be shipped out on flatbeds to permanent homes. Places were shuttered and boarded, screened by chainlink and mesh sheeting, painted with pollution, stained by sunlight and finished off with the fine detail of graffiti scrawled by the bored, the indolent, the dispossessed, the township youth, the out-of-a-job migrants, the contract-less miners. East of the town were the vast land scars of the open-cast mines and the quarries, lunar landscapes of step-sided pits like negative spaces created by pressing ziggurats tip-down into soft clay. Each pit was big enough to hold the town itself. Spoil heaps and outfill had formed new mountains. Rusty orange bulk excavators, dump trucks and mass conveyer assemblies made it look like a sand box abandoned by children for fear of rain. The quarries were barer, their sides scraped back to pale, grained rock, like exposed bone.

North of the town lay the precast plants, the curing works and the functionally ugly blast furnaces used to process byproduct. Near to these monstrosities sprawled the loading docks and the immense shipping parks where bulk road-liners that hadn't made the coast highway run regularly for almost two years slumbered under grimy weather wraps.

"Seems delightful," said Falk.

"I've been looking to summer here," said Lukes.

They reached the edge of town and followed the road through three or more sets of wire gates that were wide open and seemed to have no purpose beyond the sculptural. Fuel drums weighted with set concrete dotted the roadlane, along with other trash like fence posts and some buckled signage, a makeshift slalom course to slow the advance of anything short of an MBT. The convoy steered around the obstructions, keeping line, bleeding little speed.

"Where is everyone?" asked Jeanot, peering out and recording footage with a tablet.

"There's a curfew," replied Selton, her attention primarily focused on her displays.

"It's late morning," said green hiker girl.

"It's a strict curfew," said Falk.

Something on Selton's display pinged. For a second, Falk felt himself tense up instinctively.

"Contact signal," said Selton, and typed something into a text pane.

Fucking dope, Falk admonished himself. *You actually bought into it.*

The FPG was coming out to meet them.

The members of the Forward Patrol Group were driving in Fargos of their own, and they had a fat, armoured Longpig gunbus as the centrepiece of their motorcade. The vehicles, and the SOMD troopers riding in them, were caked in air-blown dirt. Their kit was a little bit more personalised and

non-reg than the *fresh-on-this-morning* look being worked
by Selton and her unit. Their rollers came to a halt, engines
running, in a little fan behind the rumbling self-propelled,
laid out like playing cards wiped across a table. Troopers
with pipers and RPG thumpers dismounted and locked off
the thoroughfare, shoulders tight to stocks, cheeks to top
rails, eyes to optics, fingers resting ready on trigger guards.
The gunbus, twice the size of a Fargo, reminded Falk of
some creature from a bestiary, a traveller's excited fabula-
tion of a rhinoceros or a warthog. It was broad and fat,
lethargic and ill-tempered. It sat heavily on its broad treads
with anti-rocket armour skirts hanging down around its
wheel hubs. It was almost black with grime. The M190
howitzer slanted at the sky like a unicorn's horn, vulgarly
big, rendered preposterous by the massive, fluted, vented
muzzle brake at the end of the barrel. The brake lent the
whole machine an unpleas-ant fetishistic air.

The commander of the column was an SOMD major
called LaRue. He and Selton chatted for a while, then he
ambled over to greet the media crew. He seemed real to
Falk, genuine. Falk wondered if he might actually have
cynically overestimated the show-and-tell factor. He got the
tingle of tension back, the feeling that he was actually in
some fucker's crosshairs after all. LaRue looked like
someone who'd been leading an FPG in the field for six
weeks. He spoke like it. His body language was unman-
nered and tired. There was nothing scripted or autocued
about what he said.

He told them that the FPG was about to conduct a room-
by-room of Number Two Blast Furnace, following a tip-off
from one of the labour watch teams. A forced entry overnight
had lit a red light on the site foreman's security display.
Selton's unit and the correspondents were welcome to

accompany the FPG for the duration of the operation, provided that they followed FPG instructions explicitly and didn't get in what LaRue gently described as "the fucking way".

Unpatched, thought Falk. Unreconstructed.

Dropping the pitch of his voice, LaRue issued a bald statement about the risks. Shots might be fired. There might be full-on contact. Their lives would be in danger, despite the body-plate and the SOMD presence. Even if they followed every syllable, every letter of the instructions, there was still a chance that any one of them could get scorched. LaRue wanted them to know that. He didn't want anyone operating under the illusion that this wasn't the real deal. The real fucking deal, as he put it.

Anyone could duck out, no problem. They could stay under guard with the rollers, or be taken to a strongpoint to wait for the others. No one would be judged.

"Think about it for a minute," he said. "To be honest, I'd be happier if none of you came. It makes our job easier. But I will accommodate you. Think about it, then have a word with my staff sergeant here if you want to be included."

Falk felt an odd heat rising inside him. Tension and fear, a blend he hadn't tasted in a long time. Of course he was going to get himself included. Things had just got interesting. The most interesting thing of all was his unbidden response. He was excited. He was scared. He felt cynicism peeling off him like onion skin. He didn't want to get shot. Now there was a chance he could. He felt sore from the ride, nauseous from the night before and sick with trepidation. He was amazed at how upbeat these crappy physiological responses made him feel.

"Oh, there's something I want to show you," LaRue added. "Crazy. You'll love it. It'll give you a little perspective while you're making up your minds."

Escorted by a bunch of troopers carrying their primary weapons ready across their chests, LaRue walked the media correspondents a little way back down the roadway, and then off onto the dirt, into the yard behind a derelict construction works.

"There," he said. He said it with pride, like he was a breeder parading a prize-winning steer, or the patriarch at a bris.

He was showing them a wall. It was peppered with hard-round holes from small-arms fire.

"Un-freeking-believable," murmured Falk.

FIVE

She wasn't at the GEO bar. When he called her on his celf, she told him she was at Hyatt Shaverton and he should come and meet her there.

"Why are you acting so freeking® pissed off about it?" she asked. "I told you that's what they'd do. Bullet holes. I told you."

Cleesh had been having dinner with the nondescript man from SO Logistics, and another guy Falk didn't know. They'd had chicken-effect parmigiana, and pushed the plates into the centre of the table when they were done. Falk wondered about ordering some food for himself, but the service in the Hyatt was clearly terrible.

"I'm acting pissed off because I am pissed off."

"That I told you so?"

He sniffed.

"The SO thinks we're stupid. It treats us like we're idiots."

"You must have had that kind of shit before," said the man Falk didn't know.

"Have we met?" Falk asked him. He didn't feel like making a terribly big effort, socially.

"No," the man said. "But I know who you are. I was on Seventy-Seven for a work contract. Used to read your stuff. Enjoyed it."

"Thanks," said Falk.

The man stuck out his hand.

"Bari Apfel," he said.

Falk shook. "What do you do?" he asked.

"Consultancy work. I used to be with Liitz, then Norfolk-Zumin. Now I'm doing a short-term consult with GEO."

"What sort of consultancy?" asked Falk.

"Dull stuff. Corporate image, PR. I'm pretty good at what I do."

"He is," said Cleesh.

"GEO needs all the help it can hire right now," said Apfel.

A hearing- and vision-impaired waiter went by, ignoring Falk's waggling finger.

"The service blows," said the SO Logistics man.

"Why are you eating here?" asked Falk.

Cleesh and her friends exchanged a brief, awkward look. Falk was so busy jonesing for a Scotch-effect he barely cared. It had to be something to do with the big-deal secret thing she was working out.

"It just made a change," said Apfel. "We go to the GEO all the time."

Falk scraped his chair back.

"I'm going to get drinks from the bar. If I wait for these fucking idiots, I'll die of thirst. Get anybody anything?"

He could. He made a mental note and went over to the bar. His hip was still hurting from the ride in the Fargo, a dull, sore pain. He wondered if he should get a medical report and then use it to sue the SOMD.

The bar was up a few steps from the bistro in a corner alcove with vast windows. They were on the mast's fortieth floor. Outside, the night hung there as black and heavy as a theatre's safety curtain. Coloured blurds banged against the outside of the glass and left dusty splashes of wing scales.

The moon was out, a headlamp disk, small and high up. Down below, the lights of Shaverton twinkled like guttering votive candles at a kerbside vigil. In the western sky, three quick meteorites sketched lightpen tracks and vanished.

Falk ordered a Scotch-effect, and drank it while the barman was making another and filling the rest of the order. Gulping, Falk scanned the bistro. More of the ubiquitous Early Settlement Era furniture, repro and still shabby and worn. Corporate employees with over-loud voices and cosmetic laughs. The lemon stink of Insect-Aside. Falk turned three-sixty, took in the view again. He suddenly saw the familiar face he'd seen that first night at the GEO, the old, careworn version of a man he had once known.

He realised it was his own reflection. It must have been his reflection back at the chrome-and-glass GEO too. He felt heavy, deflated. He didn't want that medical report now, not even to sue the SOMD. He didn't want to know what was wrong with his sore hip. He didn't want to know what else it would turn up.

He didn't want to know how fucked up he'd got riding drivers and living poorly. He didn't look the way he assumed he looked any more. He wondered how long he hadn't.

"I need another Scotch-effect here," he told the barman.

"Want a hand with those?" asked Bari Apfel, appearing at his shoulder. "We thought you'd been kidnapped."

"Sorry," said Falk. "Deep in thought."

"Come to any interesting conclusions?"

"You know, I came here because it seemed like an easy score. Notch up some expenses, do some basic coverage. I knew the SO wouldn't play along. I knew it would be media tourism. I knew before Cleesh had to tell me. I didn't care."

"You didn't?"

"It was just the next thing to do. The next excuse not to do something else."

"Displacement activity?" Apfel asked.

"Yeah. I don't give a fuck about what's happening here on Eighty-Six."

"But now, what? You've had a rethink?"

"God, no," said Falk. "I still don't give a fuck. But I do give a fuck about being treated like an idiot. I don't want to know the story, but now I want to get it, just so I can ram it up the SO's backside. There's something you should never give a tired old hack like me."

"A third drink?"

Falk grinned.

"Yeah, that. I was going to say a challenge."

"I know you were," said Apfel.

"The SO's sheer mindless attitude just engaged me in a way a thousand decent stories never could. Not any more."

"You going to stick it to the man, Falk?"

"I'm going to find something," said Falk. "I'm going to work some angle. If the SO had thrown me a bone, I'd have been gone inside a month. Now I'm going to stay on, and worry at this until I get something, however small, that I can slap in their faces."

"How far are you prepared to go?" asked Apfel.

"I'm not familiar with the concept of *too far*," said Falk.

"Man, are you pissed off tonight."

Falk nodded and took a drink.

"I think that's what it's all about, by the way, if you're interested."

Falk looked where Apfel was pointing.

"The moon?"

"Yeah," said Apfel. "God knows, you won't care what some corporate consultant whore thinks–"

"Say it anyway."

"Fred," said Apfel. "The second moon."

"Notable in-system resource 86/b, locally known as 'Fred'. Third highest concentration of extro-transition elements in settled territory."

"Exactly."

"Fine. You're suggesting... this isn't a land-grab fight about Eighty-Six. It's a fight to secure Eighty-Six because of its moon?"

Apfel smiled, lifted his glass off the tray and sipped.

"It makes a certain amount of sense," he said. "Since settlement began, we haven't seen fit to actually, properly go to war with anybody over land, because there's always plenty of it, *worlds* of it, at a time. It's got to be something pretty big to make us do it here."

"If that's what's happening," said Falk. "I just got shown some holes in a wall."

"Oh, it's happening."

'How do you know?"

"I've been here eight months. You hear stuff. Nothing you could use, but stuff that's still got substance to it. The Central Bloc is involved."

"You subscribe to that theory?"

"I think so. The rumour's just too persistent. If Eighty-Six is going to US dominion, that'll shut off the Bloc's development access to Fred. If you look over the SO reports, the last nine big extro-transition element sources all ended up in United Status ownership. The Bloc's got territory, but it's getting hungry for a slice of the more lucrative pies."

Falk thought about it.

"I never did find out why it was called Fred," he said.

"Named after Frederick Shaver, captain of the first pioneer mission," Apfel said. "The first moon's called Ginger, after his wife. That's the story I heard anyway."

"I should not be talking to you," said Tedders.

"You look nice," said Falk. "Out of uniform. Not out like naked. I mean not *in* uniform."

"Smooth," she said. "I have a weekend pass. I'm wasting one dinnertime of that with you, even though it's not a date, and an understanding of that condition was a strict requirement for me saying yes."

"I know. Plus, I asked nicely."

"But you don't assume this is some kind of date arranged via a reverse 'not a date' code?"

"No. This is just a correspondent buying an SOMD officer dinner so they can have a nice, informal chat."

Tedders looked at their surroundings dubiously. Falk had chosen a small, family-run restaurant just off Equestrian.

"Why here?" Tedders asked.

"I heard the chicken-effect parmigiana was better than the Hyatt's."

"It's chicken-effect parmigiana," said Tedders. "Define 'better'."

"It arrives during your lifetime," he said.

A waitress brought wine and a warm dish of re-baked bread rolls.

"I don't know what you expect me to be able to do for you," Tedders said.

"Just talk."

"Seriously, Falk, if your complaint is that the SO isn't giving you the access you need, the best I'm going to be able to do is listen and nod sympathetically."

"That was a pointless excursion we went on," he said.

"Yeah, it was. Isn't it always?" She stared across the table at him. "It always surprises me when the media is shocked that the Office can manage its own message. It's like you think that because we wear uniforms and drive tanks we must be too dense to know about subtext and nuance. The SOMD looks like a modern army should, but it's just a very, very slick PR company with added guns."

He didn't answer. He was waiting to hear what she said next.

"Someone once told me that back in the day, the Queen of England used to think that the world smelled of fresh paint, because everywhere she went a team of workers had been there the day before pimping the place up for her. That's all we do, Falk. We paint over the rough patches and make everything user-friendly."

He split a roll with his bread knife.

"Sometimes, that's not in the public interest," he said.

"Not your call to make," she replied. "Really, not in this day and age, not in situations on this magnitude."

"Let me ask you this," he said. "Just for my own interest. Do you personally know something and are just not telling me, or do they keep you in the dark too."

She smiled a quick version of her compact, portable smile.

"Need to know, and I don't need to," she said.

"Listen, I never thought you'd be able to do anything for me or tell me anything," said Falk, "but I wanted to cover all the bases. You're going to urge me, advise me, to go through official channels and see what extra cooperation I can coax, and I am going to do that. Really, I am. I am absolutely going to do this the way a correspondent should. But, and I'm not being defeatist here, I have a feeling it's not going to work, and after a month or two, I'll be right back here, scratching around to find an unofficial channel.

I just thought I'd try and save myself a little time and set both things in motion at once. Start both balls rolling."

"And?"

"If you suddenly change your mind, or your conscience suddenly gets the better of you–"

She laughed.

"Or you run across something, or someone, you think it wouldn't hurt to pass my way, please do. It can just be general background, colour stuff, anything. Your name won't be in it. There won't be any comeback."

"You say that. There always is."

"You've done this before then?"

"No. But once or twice I've seen SO people like me lose their jobs because they've been dumb enough to develop relationships with the wrong people. People they thought they could trust. People they thought they could relax and be off the record with."

"That's not me. I promise. Won't happen."

"It can't," she said.

"Why?"

"This weekend pass. I got given it because next Friday I rotate into the field for six months. Routing orders. Active detachment."

"Where to?"

"Yeah, I'll tell you that and point to it on a map."

"Okay. Damn. Okay."

"Sorry," she said. "You look all sad now. Like I've scored a dinner on false pretences."

"Are you kidding? Anyway, look."

The chicken-effect had arrived.

SIX

On Seventy-Seven, he'd lived on the coast for a few months, in a fabric house on the point near Beakes. At night, the ocean would crash against the foreshore, a hard boom followed by a long, clattering hiss of withdrawing surf dragging shingle back with it. The crash and draw punctuated his work and his sleep. He'd wake up to a chime on his celf, another link or edit from Cleesh, and lie there, listening.

The ocean had woken him, sudden, sharply. The dream he'd been having snapped like a wishbone, and he was awake, eyes open, knowing he'd been disturbed.

He was miles from the beach. He was in the small apartment he had rented on Parmingale Street in Shaverton. There was a city and a deep stretch of wild coastal foreland between him and the sea. There was the city and the night.

Falk got up. It was long after midnight. The windows of the apartment faced north and, beyond the soft amber freckles of the city lights, he thought he could see another glow, something softer and more diffuse, far away towards the north-west. The harder he looked at it, the more he couldn't see it.

He turned on the apartment's box, but there was nothing on the news. He lit his celf. There were messages, mostly junk, two from Cleesh that he'd return later. He got a glass of water. It was too early to get up and too late to sleep. The moment he turned the night stand light on, blurds began to patter against the windows.

He took another sip of water. Even the water was threaded with the lemony tang of Insect-Aside.

Sleep seemed the only sensible recourse, but he couldn't shake that half-dreamt oceanic boom, the crash and draw. He ran a few last searches on his celf.

A minor news hub, unaffiliated and unsupported by any network or SO mandate, had a story. An accident in northwest Shaverton. An explosion in the Letts district. No details.

He waited thirty seconds. Suddenly, his celf began to chime repeatedly as all the query searches he'd launched on waking up began to return positive matches for his parameters. Small news hubs first, then quick responses from the associateds, then a flurry of independent correspondents who were monitoring the main links. An accident in Letts. An explosion. No details. Unconfirmed.

Then the first main newsfeed carried it as a breaking story. At almost the same moment that his celf pinged it, the news channel playing on his box switched to developments in Letts. An explosion had occurred at 2.09. That was ten minutes earlier.

Falk had been awake for ten minutes.

The world caught up. In another minute it went from no stories to almost forty items. He tried calling Cleesh to see what she had, but there was no answer from her celf or her rental.

He felt slight agitation. He put on some coffee and pulled on trousers and a shirt while the filter sputtered. Sixty-six items now. The first unsubstantiated details. A major explosion in a derelict industrial site on Letts, north of Landmark Hill, in a non-residential zone sandwiched between District Through and the Cape Highway. Two reports said unstable chemicals, oil condensates, improperly stored in an abandoned warehouse. Another said a meteor strike. No mention of casualties.

The filter sputtered. He went back to the window and looked out at a flat, glazed night that wished to make no official comment at this time. Was that a fuzz of light in the north-west? A radiance? A fire? If the blast had been enough to wake him, it must have been big.

He tried Cleesh again. Nothing. He tried two other correspondents he'd got to know. On the box, an SO spokesperson appeared on a live feed, talking calmly and solemnly. Behind her, the unfocused yellow glare of a significant fire, the silhouettes of emergency teams moving against it.

Falk put the sound up. The spokesperson was live in Letts. She was explaining that meteor impacts were a rare but very present fact of life on Eighty-Six. Everyone had seen the shooting stars. The majority by far were atmosphere grazers or too minuscule to matter. Most bolides weren't significant enough to cause damage or hypervelocity impacts. The Letts district had been unlucky. Still no word on any casualties. City rescue was containing the incident.

It was too early for the city's overground rail system, and cabs had become extinct. A driver in the ProFood luncheonette down the street from Falk's apartment told Falk he was off duty, hence the breakfast, and besides the SO had closed north-west routes in the city. There was an advisory.

Falk went back into the empty street. It was dark grey and barren. The main window of the ProFood glowed like a giant box, an aquarium, an Edward Hopper. Falk contemplated stepping back out of the twilight into the warm, vivid world of the ProFood's interior and offering the cab driver a chunk of change, but the man was clearly committed to his sausage and egg. He watched him eat for a while through the chicken-in-a-spacesuit logo of ProFood's Booster Rooster® etched on the glass.

He went back up the street to his apartment, woke the night manager, who was chin-on-his-chest comatose at his back-office desk in front of looping situation operas on a portable box, and negotiated the temporary hire of the manager's transport.

The manager's ride was a scuffed little Shifty two-seater, pearlescent blue with an interior that smelled of fish-sticks. A Madonna bobbled from the mirror.

It had been a long time since Falk had driven anything anywhere, even a toy car like the Shifty with its auto-touch controls, safety sensors and road-reader nav. Under his hands, the wheel felt like it was fighting him. The car slowed down when he wanted to speed up along a clearway, took junctions he hadn't intended to take. When he reached the edge of the advisory cone, just outside Letts on District Through, the ride parked and stopped dead. A dashboard window explained that the Shifty would not operate in an advisory area, and function could only be enabled if the vehicle was steered out of the cone.

Falk give it a frank opinion of its performance. He couldn't set it to manual because he didn't know the duty manager's code.

He walked up into Letts, through the industrial underpasses and vacant streets. His hip still hurt from the ride in the damn Fargo. His celf was collecting news hits, sorting and filing. Details were still scant, but meteor strike was the official story. As he walked, he left a message for Cleesh to call him.

He became aware of others. A few vehicles went past, some of them city transports with hazard lights. There was a murmur of voices and activity, and a dry smell in the air. The darkness had enfolded and hidden the light of the fire, but the paling sky of the morning could not disguise the shabby trail of smoke.

He long-stepped over a deep gutter choked with trash and turned a corner. The street ahead of him was suddenly full of people and vehicles, so many of them it was almost shocking. Letts was not a densely populated part of town, but crowds had gathered: locals, derelicts, watchmen site wardens, and shift workers. SOMD troopers and civil defence officers were keeping them back from the emergency vehicles, SO transports and rescue wagons packed in along the kerb. The press had gathered too. As he limped up to the edge of the mob, Falk saw several well-paid cabs loitering for return runs.

Beyond the line and the clustered vehicles, beyond the red and blue lamps firing strobe blinks in the thin dawn light, a large acreage of warehousing was on fire. Significant sections had been levelled. It was burning fiercely in some places. In others, smouldering metal frames made a charcoal diagram of where buildings had previously stood. Falk could smell soot and cinders, chemical retardant, damp concrete, smoke. He could hear distant, shouted instructions cutting over the crowd's murmur.

He nosed his way through the crowd towards the boundary of the incident zone. Three, maybe four blocks had gone. He could see the debris, some of it fused and flaked or blackened, scattered on the road, the pavement and flat roofs. A curl of burned roofing felt hung from a street sign. Pools of shattered glass lay under every road lamp. Ash residue had frosted every surface, and flecks of it tumbled in the air like grey snow. Oil-sheened run-off thick with curds of retardant foam drooled along the gutters and stood on the road surface.

"Back behind the barrier, please," said a middle-aged man wearing the high-vis vest of civil defence.

Falk didn't blink.

"No, I'm going to my ambulance," he said.

The man hesitated, but regarded Falk's lack of med-crew uniform dubiously.

"Is that rain-top regulation?" Falk asked, gesturing to the garment the man was wearing under his vest.

"I was in a hurry," said the man.

"My point exactly," said Falk, and pushed past him with a confidence born of fifteen years of being an arrogant dick.

He walked up the pavement, past a foam bowser and a trio of emergency transporters. The hatch ports to the carry-bay and equipment lockers were wide open on all three. He leaned in as he walked by one of them, and helped himself to a high-vis vest from a locker hook, clipping it on around his body as he moved on. The heat from the fires wafted to him with each swell of wind. He could hear emergency cutters. Civil defence workers passed him, going the other way, talking emphatically into their celfs. A hopter droned overhead, thrumming the air, lost and found in the rising smoke.

Falk wiped the lenses of his glares and slipped them on, selecting *snapshot*. He started to blink off shots for general ref. He rounded a corner, got a wall of heat in the face, and saw a crowd of rescue workers engaged in urgent activity. He stepped back. They were SO staff, firefighters, paramedics. Some were shouting, others were running up with carry-kits from the transports. There were bodies on the ground. Falk couldn't get a good view, or blink off more than general shots, but there were definitely bodies. Three or four, wound in plastic blankets, surrounded by kneeling medics.

He wanted a better look, and considered fronting his way into the huddle, but there was a difference between bluffing your way past a police line and obstructing life-saving procedures that even a fifteen-year arrogant dick could recognise.

He moved around, and approached firefighters working a gutting blaze with pressure jets, but the sheer heatwash turned him away. He found quieter space for a moment, a storehouse section that had been knocked down but not burned by the blast. He wiped the dirt, sweat and spray off his face with the tail of his shirt, and polished his glares.

"You shouldn't be here," she said, coming up behind him.

Green hiker girl was carrying a first aid box, and wearing a luminous SO armband and a sly smile.

"Neither should you," he replied.

"I don't care about me," she said.

"Neither do I," said Falk, "so go away and I'll pretend I didn't see you."

She kept showing him the odd little smile, and he found that curious.

"You saw it newsflagged?" she asked.

"I heard the blast."

"Me too," she said. She looked at the vest he was wearing.

"That's deep cover, huh?"

"Obviously nothing like as well researched as an armband and a medi-pack," he replied.

She showed him the digital brooch she was also wearing, pinned to her collar.

"Slightly more authentic," she said.

"And a really bad idea," he told her. He began to walk away. She followed him.

"Why?" she asked.

He considered explaining, then decided he didn't care enough and had better things to do, like losing her. It was a little disconcerting she was suddenly being so coy with him when she hadn't wanted a bar of him during the trip out to Mitre Sands.

Then he got it, and felt stupid it had taken him so long.

"You looked me up," he said.

"I'm sorry, what?"

"You looked me up, didn't you? After the tour. Now you know who I am."

She grinned.

"So what?"

"So nothing," he said.

"Yes, I didn't know who you were. I didn't know you'd won all those sparkly press awards. So what?"

"So suddenly I'm interesting, am I?"

"Oh, get over yourself. It just amuses me that the great Lex Falk has turned up here tonight. Makes me think I must be right to think this is very off. This whole thing. Plus, the great Lex Falk faked his way inside the perimeter the same way I did."

"No, I didn't," he replied.

"You so did. You lifted a few props from the paramedic transports."

He didn't answer her. He'd seen something.

"You know who I am," she said, following him again.

"I don't think so. I can't remember."

"Yes you can."

"You're some newbie from Affiliated Dispersal."

"You deliberately checked my name out. I heard you do it."

"Yeah, maybe I did. I was bored. I don't remember it now."

"Noma Berlin. I'm with Data-Scatter. Do you always do

this? Play hard to shake off, and then hard to get? It's undertractive."

He turned and looked straight at her.

"I didn't come here to have a conversation with you," he said.

Her grin came out again.

"What's so interesting over there?" she asked. She nodded in the direction he had been heading.

Falk hesitated, then said, "Look at those guys. No, not the ones with the drills. Those two on the far side of that collapsed roof. See what they're holding?"

Through the haze, they could plainly see the two men playing small drumstick wands over the smoking rubble.

"Sniffers," she said.

"Yup."

"That'd be pretty standard, wouldn't it? Scanning everything."

"If this is a bolide strike, why are they sweeping for traces of explosives?"

"They could be sweeping for anything. All sorts of things could've been spilled or released or burned off. Toxins. Public health, you know. That's all."

"Or they could be sweeping for traces of explosives. Munitions of some kind. There's more to this than has been newsflagged. There are casualties, for starters."

"I saw," she said, losing the smile for a second. "Five, I think. I heard they were derelicts."

"Who told you that?"

"One of the firefighters. He said they were bringing out bodies of derelicts who had been living in the warehouses."

"I don't think so," Falk said.

"Why not?"

"I got a look at one."

"They were all badly burned."

"Yeah, but the one I saw, I could tell he was clean-shaven. He'd had a haircut."

"Derelicts get haircuts."

"What are you," he asked, "Little Miss The Glass Is Half Crazy?"

"I'm just saying it's hardly proof of anything."

"That's why I'd like you to shut up and go away so I can keep doing my job."

She was about to reply when someone shouted at them. They turned. An SOMD trooper was jogging towards them. He was in body-plate, and carrying a weapon.

"You two," he called. "I want to see some credentials. Now."

"Lose the brooch," Falk hissed.

"What?"

"Lose the fucking brooch, you silly bitch. Fast!"

The SOMD guy came right up to them. He was in full rig, harness and plate. The gun strapped across his front was a PAP 20, common, standard issue, a bullpup-format carbine. *Personal [weapon] All Purpose*. As he came close, the PAP seemed to become alarmingly, extravagantly big.

"You know you're not supposed to be in this area," the trooper said. He sounded weary, with a little edge of stress. It was immediately clear to Falk that there was going to be no mileage in trying to front it. The trooper wasn't in the mood to play a game. He hadn't even bothered to question the vest or the armband.

"Sorry," said Falk.

"You're just making our work more difficult," the trooper said. "Where's your freeking® self-respect? There's freeking® people scorched over there. You're getting in the freeking® way."

"Sorry," Falk repeated.

"Press?" asked the trooper.

"Yeah," said Falk.

"Well, better than you being freeking® rubbernecks, I suppose. Creds."

Falk fished his out of his pocket quickly, with an exaggerated show to demonstrate he wasn't reaching for anything else.

"I've got an SO validation," he said quickly, before green hiker girl could say anything or produce any papers of her own. "She's my researcher."

He willed green hiker girl not to say anything, not to contradict him.

The trooper looked at Falk's ID.

"Your researcher?"

"Yes."

"Uh-huh."

"I brought her in with me. This is on me. She seriously didn't want to cross the picket line."

The trooper looked at her.

"I didn't," she said, a little slowly, trying to follow what Falk was attempting. "I told him I didn't."

"I should've listened to her," said Falk.

The trooper's Mil-issue glares had scanned Falk's ID at the same time the trooper had. Falk saw a little ice-blue backlight behind the lenses as a secure processed response came back from SOMD Operations.

"Okay, that checks," said the trooper. "You're going to have to leave the area. I'll escort you. There may not be a follow-up, but I have to advise you that you may get a fine, or even some suspension of your validation privileges."

"Okay," said Falk.

"That's just how it works."

"I know," said Falk. "I was chancing my arm. I'm sorry."

"Let's get you to the line," said the trooper. They started walking. "Do me a favour and go home. I don't want to hear about you trying to get back in here."

"Sure, no problem," said Falk. "You stay wealthy. Thanks for being okay about it. It was a dumb stunt. But I had to try, right? How many meteor hit stories do you get?"

The trooper waved them across the barrier line.

"Almost none," he conceded.

They left the high-vis vest, the armband and the medical kit on the open tailgate of a paramedic roller. Several entrepreneurial types from the North End had turned up with food carts and mobile kiosks, supplying refreshment to the early morning crowd of sightseers and the crews on rest-breaks. Falk bought two teas from an electric barrow with a chrome urn.

"Why'd you do that?" asked green hiker girl.

"It was the best way out," Falk replied.

She took the cup he offered her.

"You didn't want him looking at my ID," she said.

"I've got SO validation," said Falk. "And I'm Lex Falk. My accreditation can soak it up. If I get a fine, I can wash it through expenses. They'll probably waive a penalty if I keep my nose clean. You're only affiliated, so you're not half as flameproof."

"So you took the fall for the two of us because you're such a great fucking person?"

"I took the fall for the two of us because I was taking the fall anyway, and taking it for two wasn't going to hurt any worse."

He took a long sip of tea.

"And I took the fall for the two of us because of that fuck-ass brooch. Where is it?"

She took it out of her pocket. He took it, and looked at it.

"It's not a fake," he said.

"No," she replied. "It was in the door pocket of the transport I lifted the first aid kit from."

Falk stared at her.

"Do you not get it?" he asked. "You get caught bluffing in a secured zone, you get kicked out, fined, full marks for trying. Slap on the wrist, naughty correspondent person. You get caught in a secured zone with a fake or stolen SOMD ident, that's impersonating the Office, and that comes under martial regs. That's a whole avalanche of crap right there. They'd yank your accreditation for starters, forever. In fact, they'd probably boot you upstairs to catch the next driver home."

"I guess," she said.

"No, no, it's not guesswork," he snapped. "It's fucking what happens. You have to know these things. You have to know them, so you don't do something so fucking stupid it ends your career."

He bent his arm and threw the brooch over a fence into a marshalling yard.

"Wow," she said. "It's almost like you care what happens to me. Or you want to jump me."

"Neither," said Falk. "I was standing right beside you. If he'd found the brooch, the fan sprays that shit a long way."

SEVEN

Cleesh had been calling him. When he finally got hold of her, she sounded upset for some reason.

"I need you to come and meet some people," she said.

"Who?"

"Just come and meet them."

"Where?" Falk asked.

She told him.

"Can you make it this afternoon? Four-ish?"

"Okay," he said. He didn't want to, and he was growing increasingly less interested in whatever it was Cleesh was into.

But it was Cleesh, and she sounded upset, and he had some fucked-up notion he owed her.

He had stuff to do. His hip still hurt. It hurt a lot. He tried to make himself comfortable in his apartment by adding cushions to the chair at the desk, but it was easier to stand up. He decided he could head to the SO Library in Furth, and work there. They had leather-effect banquettes. He could sprawl.

His celf lit.

"It's me," she said.

"Who?"

"Noma."

He let it hang for a moment, just so she'd know how little room she took up in his headspace.

"Oh. Right. What's up?"

"I've got something."

"Now that's being generous," he replied. "If you work hard for another five years, and exploit your sources ruthlessly, then maybe–"

"Hah hah hah, so funny. I've got something. I think you'll want to see it."

"Why?"

"Because it's cool, Falk."

"No," he said. "Why are you calling me? If you've got something and it's actually, properly good, then why are you calling me? Why aren't you just running with it?"

"Do you want the convincing answer?" she asked.

"Okay."

"Because you got me out of harm's way this morning in Letts, and I'm trying to say thank you. One-time gesture, no repeats, take it or leave it."

"Okay, that is quite convincing. What's the real reason?"

"Because this thing I've got," she said, "I don't know what the fuck I should do with it."

She lived in a cubicle hotel in South Site, the oldest part of Shaverton. Another twenty years, the area would catch a dose of Early Settlement chic, and incomers would pour money into the narrow streets, the depots and store sheds, the weatherboard and cinderblock businesses. People would buy into that pioneer/prospector vibe, and heritage plaques would appear on the facades of the counting house and the weights-and-measures office.

Until then, South Site would remain a hole reserved for low-rest accommodation, migrant temporaries, murky enterprises and ballast markets. There was a smell of rancid soap in the air from the big drain outfalls, and a river-stink of decaying tar and stagnant water. There were cooking smells too, smoking hot and over-spiced, from the immigrant food stalls in the market walks and row streets. Vendors shouted their bills of fare, but the cooking smells shouted louder. Disguise recipes. Heavy peppers and flavour enhancers, copious spices, rubs, marinades. Cooking designed to mask the substitutions made for chicken, pork and beef. Not even chicken, pork or beef, in truth. These stands were working without chicken, pork or beef *effect*.

The buildings in South Site were caked in rust, or wet with lime seep. Some displayed the vague apparitions of their old, first-generation, hand-done sign boards. Paint withered and flaked, losing its colours before it lost itself into the inshore wind entirely. Blurds tapped around Chinese lanterns and bare bulbs. The streets were so tight and busy, Falk buttoned up his coat and dug his hands into his pockets.

He'd taken a cab from his place. The city had looked drab and lightless. Smoke cover from the Letts incident had formed a huge anvilhead of darkness in the north-west, and stolen all the colour. There was a gritty haze in the air. Even the majestic glass masts looked like they'd been sandblasted to a matt finish in the afternoon gloom.

Falk didn't like South Site much. The opportunities for something criminal and unfortunate to happen seemed high. But at least the place had some colour. Coloured lights and lanterns, colourful awnings, stainless-steel trays of vibrantly coloured food, brightly coloured flames from stall burners, colour-dyed cloth, colourful smells in the air.

He walked past wire baskets of brightly coloured rubber shoes at the edge of the ballast market, then more bins of cheap toys, knock-off sports caps, mops and brooms, kitchenware, each bin staked with a wire loop holding up the handwritten price card. Fashion glares hung like fruit from drying rails, their paper price tickets twitching in the wind. Men with trays like the olden-time concession girls presented celfs that came without packaging or paperwork.

Green hiker girl was waiting for him on the front steps of her cubicle dorm. She had no room to invite him into, no space where they could sit and talk. She said she knew a place.

She was actually wearing her green litex hiker, but he was beginning to think of her as Noma.

"How are you?" she asked cheerfully as they walked through the market.

"I'm wealthy," he said. She had her clutch tablet tucked into the breast of her hiker, and she kept touching it to make sure it hadn't gone anywhere.

She took him to a ProFood outlet on the west corner of the market space. She ordered two bottles of NoCal-Cola, because they could verify the tamper seal on the caps to tell if they were refills. Falk got a fistful of napkins from a dispenser, and some straws in individual paper sleeves. She ordered some food for herself. It was a franchise place. They still had the old Bill Berry Astronut logo on the napkins, rather than the slick, modern Booster Rooster rebrand.

They sat out of the way at a table in the back. There were sticky rings on the plastic tabletop. She offered him a bite of her food, a greaseproof cone full of what seemed to be grilled meat on skewers. He shook his head.

"The food around here isn't actually bad," she said.

"Neither's basejumping, but I'm not attempting that either."

She gnawed a lump off one of the skewers.

"I think there's a fair bit of reprocessed blurd in it, mind," she added.

"Really selling me on basejumping," he replied.

She grinned, chewing.

"So what's this about?" he asked.

"In such a hurry. Can't we just continue our conflirtation?"

"What's this about?" he repeated.

She took one of the napkins, wiped the tabletop, and then put her tablet down and slid it over to him. Upside down, she woke it, rotated an image, expanded it.

"What's this?" he asked.

"Play it. Watch."

He let the clip run. There was about forty seconds worth. He paused when it had ended, then touched replay and watched it again.

"Where did this come from?" he asked.

"Friends. High places. You know."

He glared at her. She shrugged.

"Eighty-Six is prone to meteoritic strikes. Fact of life. Risk small, but real. That's the official line. Letts got unlucky on the bolide lottery. Oh, the humanity! Zero warning. Impact values so high, so fast, nothing tracked it, not ground-based, not orbital. Nothing. Official line, on the feeds just an hour ago. Nothing. Forget we've got, let's think, *the Terminal* out there on the Cape. Nothing detected it until it impacted."

She touched replay on the clutch tablet clip again. Looking up, she met his eyes, and seemed amused to find him looking at her rather than the playback.

"And did you know," she asked, "there are currently eight drivers geo-stationary upstairs? Eight drivers parked directly over Shaverton."

"With their detector arrays on downsweep," said Falk.

"Yes, to monitor cargo traffic. And that, Mr Lex Falk, is a direct lift from the array archive of the spinrad driver *Manchurian*."

The clip, heavy with informatic overlays and subsidiary data, was an orbital view of northwest Shaverton. Night. Thermal capture. A city plan with a gentle drift to it. Twenty-eight seconds in, a white-hot flare blooms in Letts.

"No track," said Falk.

"No track. Not even eye-invisible. Nothing on instrumentation. It wasn't a strike."

"How did you get this?"

"The *Manchurian* was the driver I came in on. A reasonably senior crewperson decided it was better to source the clip for me than have me write about the non-regulation relationship he conducted with a passenger on the trip in-system."

"Dirty pool," he said, almost in admiration.

"It wasn't even something I was keeping in my back pocket," she replied. "It was just expedient. You said to me they'd boot me upstairs to catch the next driver home, and it got me thinking about drivers. Just in time."

"What do you mean?"

"There was a guy on one of the general networks this lunchtime interviewing an SO rep. He asked straight out if anything parked or circling had got a view of the strike, and the rep told him categorically that all sources had been checked and there was nothing."

"It's been redacted already."

"Uh-huh."

Falk tapped his fingers on the tabletop beside the tablet. He felt hot, and the plastic seat was hurting his hip. He unwrapped his straw, uncapped the Cola bottle and took a drink.

"I can see why you were conflicted," he said.

"I thought you might have some ideas."

He reached over and helped himself to a skewer from her greaseproof cone. He was experiencing something like a caffeine rush, and he needed to be steady. He needed some carbs and protein. It actually tasted okay. Crunchy. Like pork-flavoured peanut brittle.

"The explosive sniffers have slightly more significance now," he said.

"They do."

"If we're going to 'do' anything with this, we need to be sure what we're 'doing'."

"Go on."

"If we're going to expose something, we need to know what we're exposing. What's going on that they needed to say it was a bolide strike? Did whatever it was happen in Letts randomly, or because of what was in Letts?"

"Okay. How do we find that out?"

"Let me work on it. Let's meet up again tonight."

She nodded.

"Can I take this?"

"No."

"A copy?"

"No."

"But I can trust you to look after it?"

"Yes."

"And not do anything stupid with it?"

"Yes," she said.

Cleesh had been crying.

"You're late," she said.

"It's a little out of my way," he replied. He looked at her and narrowed his eyes.

"Have you been crying?"

"My eyes have been playing up," she said. "I told you about it the other day. Tear duct, humidity thing. I was up in a can for too long. I told you."

He remembered her saying something. It wasn't the first time he'd seen her with pink puffiness around the eyes. He was beginning to realise that he didn't know her that well, in person. He didn't know if she suffered from allergies, if she was prone to tearfulness, if pink puffiness was a normal look.

The six foot tall aluminium cut-outs mounted along the concrete forecourt spelled PIONEER USEUM, because the first M in museum had been mysteriously removed by hands unknown. The site was just off Equestrian, in an area earmarked for parks and memorials by city planners. At some point, three decades or more in the past, someone had got militant about the investment of serious capital in a museum to celebrate the settlement of Eighty-Six, when there were still so many aspects of Eighty-Six's infrastructure in need of funds. The project had been frozen. It wasn't the first world Falk had visited where a grand scheme of commemoration had been mothballed.

Weeds had inveigled their way between the pavers in the concourse, the coloured gravel in the beds, the layout of paths. Nothing ornamental had ever been planted, so the weeds had filled in there too, and supplanted the lawns where the grass hadn't gone wild and hippy. The museum structure was a vast shed, like a boat dock or a bulk hangar. Construction had halted a week or two before it had reached the tipping point of being weatherproof. Guttering had slumped. Stained skylights in the immense roof had fallen in. Last winter's dead leaves and seed cases had blown in through the half-open main doors in huge, gritty drifts. Blurds had nested in the rafters. In places they were swirling madly, almost angrily, around their homes, as if a selective vortex had relaunched some of the dead leaves.

Falk followed Cleesh inside. The museum would have been magnificent, airy, light. Even from the half-finished and neglected evidence, the architect had known his business.

It was a museum of vacancies and empty spaces, a commemoration of voids. Plinths and displays had never been filled, description plaques never printed or placed. White stone blocks and elegant metal trestles supported nothing whatsoever for public inspection.

The only palpable exhibits were the three crude man-rated bulk landers that filled the main space of the shed, each one resting in a cast-stone cradle. Their pitted hulls of maraging steel were flecked and discoloured, carbon-scorched and seared by entry burns, but it was still possible to see the black and white paint scheme, the foiled silver of the thrusters and couplers, the bold red of the United Status and SOE identifiers. These titanic metal drums had brought the first settlers down. Fred Shaver had been aboard one. His wife Ginger too, presumably.

"Why here?" Falk asked.

She kept going. Sometimes he forgot the bulk of her and what an effort it was for her to walk.

"No one comes here," she said.

"Should I have worn a raincoat with the collar up?" he asked. She didn't laugh.

"Just come on. There's a degree of privacy. This whole park area is unlinked."

He'd taken an electric tram up Equestrian and walked the rest of the way. He presumed she had done the same thing, because there had been no sign of a vehicle out front. She led him down the length of the cavernous shed, their footsteps trailing small echoes. He craned his neck to admire the giant landers as they went.

"So the thing in Letts," he said, by way of conversation.

"Yeah. Something else."

"What are you hearing about that?"

"Same as everyone. Meteor slamdunk."

"I can't help noticing you're not your usual cheery self," he said.

She spared him a quick backward glance. He noticed that she'd been scratching at the surgical plug excisions in her throat.

"Stuff's going on," she said. "That's mainly why you're here."

"Have I done something to piss you off, Cleesh?"

"Yes. You're Lex Falk and I'm me."

"What?" he asked.

She stopped walking and turned to face him. Some brief emotion that was hard to define passed across her face, like an interaction between clouds and sunlight.

She surprised him by walking back to where he was standing and embracing him. Her mass swallowed him up.

"Sorry," she said. "That was bitchy. I don't mean it. I've had a few setbacks. A few gut punches to my confidence."

"You?"

"Teasing isn't going to help, Falk. Everything was fine and wealthy when I was an omnipotent voice in a circling can. Life sucks in grav time."

"It's a matter of adjustment," he said, secretly hoping she'd let him go soon but not wanting to pull away. "Everything will be wealthy again soon, you'll see."

"No," she said. "It freeks® you up, circling. Freeks® you completely up. I've blown a lot of my choices forever, and that holes your confidence behind the heatshield."

She released him from the bearhug and smiled down at him.

"I don't blame you for being you, and look – you get to take full advantage of my setback."

"How?"

"You'll see."

They started walking again.

"About Letts. It wasn't a strike."

"We know," she said.

"Who's 'we'?"

"The strike is just a cover story."

"Who's 'we'?" he repeated.

Beneath large picture windows at the rear of the museum hulk there was a raised viewing platform that had been built to allow visitors the chance to peer down into the anatomically sectioned hull of the third lander. Bari Apfel was waiting for them on the platform. He was wearing a dark suit, an exec's suit, under a brown litex coat.

"Hello, Falk," he said. He shook Falk's hand.

"So, what is this?" asked Falk. "Legit GEO biz, or something on the side?"

"Can't it be both?" asked Apfel.

"I don't know," said Falk. "Can it?"

Apfel kept smiling and made a little "let's see" shrug.

"Geoplanitia Enabling Operator has me on a short-term contract," he said. "My brief is corporate image."

"You told me that," said Falk.

"My remit is broad, and part of it is deliberately woolly. There are aspects of my function that haven't been put on record so as to facilitate deniability in the event of blowback."

Falk chuckled.

"I love the way you people talk," he said.

"I'm sure you do," said Apfel. "We frame our terms with the same care as media whores like you people."

Apfel turned to gaze at the third lander.

"The downside of this job," he said, "is that I'm a vague contract number buried in the non-specific end of the GEO books. My working brief is spectacularly nebulous, and GEO can cut me loose and deny me at any moment in the interests of corporate integrity."

He glanced a smile Falk's way.

"The plus side is resources."

"Black budget?"

"Grey, actually. But extensive. The personal remuneration scale's great, of course, and far in excess of anything a contractor of my apparent significance ought to warrant. But the working capital. The access. The possibilities. I've got a free hand to use pretty much anything I want, including the development and deployment of some of GEO's most conjectural properties. Provided I return some decent results, the GEO top floor is happy to invest and turn a blind eye. They'd prefer not to know what I'm actually doing."

"Should you be telling me any of this?" asked Falk. "I'm a media whore. Who knows what I'll do? You leak me stories like this, it sort of subverts the whole deniability thing."

"Hear him out," said Cleesh.

"I'm quite happy to sell you some line if needs be, Falk," said Apfel, "but I've always believed in the policy of not lying unless I have to. Fewer pieces of crap to remember. Makes life less complicated. And lies, when they occur, more valuable. I'm telling you about my interests because I'm pretty sure they're about to become mutual, so you'll be guarding them too. Cleesh agrees, don't you Cleesh?"

"I suggested you when we realised we'd need another person, Falk," said Cleesh.

Apfel tipped his head to suggest a direction he wanted them to walk. They went down the concrete steps off the platform.

"GEO's interests on Eighty-Six are suffering badly because of the situation."

"Well known," said Falk. "And GEO's not the only corp in trouble."

"True, but we don't care about the others. The problems on Eighty-Six are actually beginning to impact GEO's position on the home market and across the General Settlement. It's ugly and it's going to get worse. The main problem is perception. It's generally held that GEO is responsible for its difficulties on Eighty-Six."

"You're going to tell me this is like Sixty after all, Bari? A poor little post-global giant taking it in the nutsack for somebody else?"

"Is that so hard to imagine?" Apfel asked. "The sheer scale of the post-globals make it so easy to believe they are insensitive and faceless and responsible for all society's evils. But on Sixty, it wasn't big pharm. Big pharm got serious shit thrown at it, and it wasn't them. You know that. Of all people."

"Interesting choice of phrase."

"You were there. You speak about it quite plainly, in open defence of big pharm and the way it was treated."

"You know a lot about me," said Falk.

"I told him stuff," said Cleesh from behind them, a tone of apology in her voice.

"If you can't be bothered to do proper presearch on a man you intend to do business with," said Apfel, "you might as well get the fuck out of Dodge."

"So who's not playing nice here?"

"The United Status has got itself into a pickle on Eighty-Six,"

Apfel replied. "They're messing with the Bloc. Things have gone hot for the first time ever."

"This is over Fred?"

"It's over Fred and all sorts of other shit. We don't even know the half of it, but it all seems to be resource-based. Strategic Significance Orders. Mineral lodes. Comes, quite literally, with the territory. Because the US and the Bloc are going at it, the SO is sucked in."

"But not GEO?"

"When GEO first came to Eighty-Six and started to invest, it played it very safe and smart. Standard operating practice. GEO's got strong US ties, I won't pretend otherwise, but it's not an exclusive relationship. It built itself up so that no matter who came out on top here, no matter who ended up holding the reins, GEO was in place, with the right infrastructure, ready to benefit."

Apfel looked at Falk. They had reached a large, grubby loading dock at the side of the shed, where concrete steps led down to a closed shutter. A silt of dead leaves had gathered in the step well.

"Are you getting the picture?" Apfel asked.

"The Settlement Office is enforcing a media blackout on the dispute between the Bloc and the US, and as a consequence GEO is soaking up hits because it appears to be the aggressor?"

"Pretty much."

"So how would you change that? If you'd been employed on a woolly contract to rescue GEO's corporate reputation, I mean."

"You tell the truth and shame the devil," said Apfel.

"Meaning?"

"You get more of the real story out there, into circulation, so that people start to get a more realistic picture of GEO's involvement. Re-information, Falk."

"And how does that work?" Falk asked.

Apfel bent down and got hold of the handle at the bottom of the battered shutter. He stood up again, clattering the shutter up and away into its over-door drum. Daylight streamed in on them.

"You find yourself some high-quality correspondents," he said, "and you embed them in the warzone."

EIGHT

"The SO won't wear that," said Falk. "I mean, they flat-out won't."

"I know," said Apfel.

"Then you can't do it. You can't do it without their full cooperation."

"Turns out he can," said Cleesh.

They walked out into the open air across a weed-choked patch of ground in the lea of the museum shed. Blurds buzzed by. Falk felt microbugs alighting on his skin, and wished he'd bothered to top up his spray. It was an occupational regime that hadn't quite become second nature yet.

A cinder path had been laid across the tract of scrub and, beyond it, an object had been put on display under a stand of tall, straight, ivory trees that were either dead or leafless. The object was about the size of a detached house, and it was reclining, three-quarter length, on a patch of pink gravel. Weeds had invaded the path, the gravel plot and the cavities of the dented, battered metal. Lichen had begun to coat the underside where the sunlight was never direct.

"The original surveyor probe," said Apfel, "launched from a Settlement Advance driver. First man-made object to touch Eighty-Six. They dug it out of an endorheic basin a thousand miles east of Marblehead. Buried there, sending back informatics that changed this world."

"Oh, it's so symbolic, I may have to kill myself," said Falk.

"You think I'm that cheesy?" asked Apfel, amused.

"You are that cheesy," said Cleesh.

"I am, but still," said Apfel. "We were only coming this way to reach the truck."

They followed the path around the mangled lump of the probe and past the trees, and the truck came into view. It was a medium cargo roller, pale blue, no insignia, parked on the rough slip of the park's slope. Coming out of the museum via the loading dock, the probe had kept it hidden from sight.

Apfel knocked casually on the truck's cargo door, and then led the way up when it opened from inside. Falk followed him. Cleesh had to brace herself on the door frame, get a foot on the drop-step, and haul herself in. She was puffing from the walk.

The truck interior was well-lit. The cargo module had been spray-lined with matt-white, shock-absorbent rubber, and then fitted out with frame-mounted data systems, all lit and busy. The rear of the space, nearest to the cab, looking like a miniature dental surgery, with medical tools and scanners racked around a floor-mounted recliner under adjustable lamps.

There were three people inside waiting for them: a good-looking black kid in coveralls, a middle-aged woman who was dressed like she ran a veterinary practice on an agrarian settlement, and the nondescript man Falk had met in Cleesh's company several times, most recently at the Hyatt.

"He's SO Logistics," said Falk.

"Yes, he is," said Apfel.

"Alarm bells?"

"He's paid for," said Apfel. "We need people inside, in several key roles. We've very carefully presearched and recruited the right people."

"You happy for him to talk about you like that?" Falk asked the nondescript man.

"I know what I'm doing," the man answered, without much emotion. "I don't agree with the US or SO position on this, and this is my way of lodging an objection."

"This is Ayoob, this is Underwood," Apfel said, introducing the kid and the woman. The kid grinned broadly and stuck out his hand. Falk shook it.

"We'd like to get you in the chair," said the woman, Underwood. She had a handsome but weatherbeaten face, outdoorsy, and her hair was fine and blonde. Her clothes were litex and functional man-mades.

"We've only just been introduced," replied Falk.

"Underwood is one of my medical consultants," said Apfel, "She needs to check you over. A basic bill of health. We can't go anywhere with you until we're happy there are no underlying conditions that will jeopardise the procedure."

"You haven't told me where we're going or what the procedure is yet," said Falk.

"And I won't, until we're sure you're viable," replied Apfel. "It'd be a waste of your time and ours. If it turns out to be a no-go, the less you know, the less you'll be burdened with."

"You've told me plenty already," said Falk.

"He's barely started," said Cleesh. She was clearing her nose into a tissue. Falk saw that her cheeks were flushed. Quietly, she'd started crying again. She hadn't passed the test. He saw it now. She'd been on Apfel's list, but she'd failed the medical minimum. That was why she was upset. That was why she'd brought him in.

But there was a tension too. A time factor, he was sure of it. Something had cranked the clock forward, eaten up all the lead time and built-in overrun margins.

Falk let Underwood lead him over to the recliner. At her instruction, he stripped off his celf, his coat and his shirt, and sat down in the seat under the lamps. The plastic upholstery was cold against his back. He became abruptly aware of how white and hollow his chest looked, how skinny his arms.

"You've been riding drivers a while?" asked Underwood, preparing some swabs.

"Yeah. A lot of travel in my line of work."

She started to do some skin and saliva wipes, then took a little blood and ran various scanning wands over him. She asked a few questions about his health, his diet, made notes on a tablet.

"It's Letts, isn't it?" Falk asked Apfel over her shoulder.

"What do you mean?"

"What happened last night in Letts. It's forcing you to step things up."

"Our window has closed considerably," said the nondescript man.

"What happened in Letts?" Falk asked.

Cleesh and the kid both looked at Apfel. Apfel nodded at the kid.

"The site in Letts was an unlisted operations centre for the SOMD," said Ayoob. "Strategic, Special Focus. Very high-value asset. We believe the Bloc scorched it with some form of autoguided surface-to-surface munition device."

"They walked a drone bomb onto an SOMD Special Focus base?"

"You saw the size of the hole," said Apfel. "They just walked a drone bomb into the general vicinity."

"Why?" asked Falk.

"Best guess," Apfel replied, "is that the SOMD had got their hands on something. Data of some sort. They'd sent it to their Special Focus centre for processing or unpacking. And the Bloc did not want that information shared."

He looked at Underwood.

"Well?"

"I need to wait for a few results," she said, "and I have some concerns about a few things. Bone density, for one. Renal function. A few additional items. I wish I had a week or two to process him and–"

"You don't," said Apfel.

"On the basis of this, then, he's reasonably sound."

"Thanks for the glowing reference," said Falk.

"You can put your shirt back on," Underwood said.

"So I'm in?" asked Falk.

"We'll work on that assumption," said Apfel.

"So tell me about the procedure."

"You ever seen a Jung tank?" Ayoob asked.

"A what?"

"A Jung tank," said Apfel. "It's a theoretical concept."

"Funny, I don't see many of those."

"It's a theoretical concept everywhere outside of the GEO actualisation division," said Ayoob. "Very much conjectural technology. It's based on some of the breakthrough telepresence tech GEO evolved back in the Early, mixed up with some realtime sensory reposition hardware we've been tooling around for about a decade. We've repurposed stuff designed to help pilot drone probes in ultra-hostile environments."

"What does it do?" asked Falk. "Allows for remote viewing?"

"Sort of," said Ayoob.

Falk stood up, slipped on his shirt and then relinked his celf. He buttoned up his shirt, and tucked it in, all the while looking at Apfel.

"So what, Bari?" he said. "Are you proposing to jack a pirate feed off a Mil-secure signal to let me look through the glares-cam of some poor SOMD shavehead? I've seen that sort of shit before, and it blows. It's all novelty. The feed quality is generally fuck-awful, and the POV is lousy. You're always looking at completely the wrong thing. I'm really not interested. In fact, I can't think of a single credible network that would take anything like that, unless you managed to scoop some stand-out clip by accident. They wouldn't carry it for the news content. I mean they wouldn't take it for the solid, message-related reasons you'd want them to take it. They'd buy six seconds of exclusive explosion on camera. They wouldn't buy a story."

"I know," said Apfel. "This isn't a pirate feed to let you see through some joker's glares."

"Really?"

"This lets you see through his eyes, Falk," said Cleesh. "This lets you *be* someone. This lets you go in *inside* someone's freeking® head."

NINE

It was getting dark by the time he got off the tram downtown. Lights were shining in the windows of the commercial properties, and the streetpost bug zappers had started to glow. Over the roofline, a purple silhouette, the glass masts were lit up like neon ladders.

Neon ladders with many rungs missing.

Falk felt pretty good. His response qualified as excitement, despite various misgivings. A really inviting possibility had opened up, and even if it turned out to be hollow, it was going to make for a very saleable story.

He walked down the street as trams hummed past. Street boxes trailed the latest headlines about the Letts incident. There was talk of a publicly funded meteor defence programme.

Classic misdirection.

He stepped into a ProFood, and ordered a coffee. While he waited for it, he stared out of the front windows into the darkening street and considered his misgivings. Poplite trilled in the background.

He felt an uncomfortable measure of guilt and responsibility towards Cleesh. That wasn't like him. He didn't like

85

seeing her so low, and even though she'd put him in the frame for this, it felt like he was stealing something that should have been hers.

He'd always been wary of playing in corporate grey areas, and this was certainly a bad neighbourhood, but that was precisely why the story was interesting.

If the SO rumbled them, he would be rescinded. It could be a massive career wound he'd never recover from.

The procedure sounded harebrained. If anyone could do it, it was GEO, but he fully anticipated an outright failure, or at least a truly pathetic realisation of the wonders Ayoob had been boasting about. Then again, that was the story too: the corporate machinations, the misadventure, the schadenfreude.

He realised what was souring his excitement the most was the way Underwood had looked at his scrawny white torso when he'd taken his shirt off. The tone in her voice as she'd listed his deficiencies to Apfel. Contempt he could have handled. Disdain too.

It had been pity.

He reached his rental building, and unlocked the door under a porch light clicked against by orbiting blurds. The stairwell smelled of cooking, and his apartment was cold. He was on his second Scotch-effect when the buzzer went. It wasn't green hiker girl. The carry-out meal had arrived first: plycard punnets of Vietnamese from a half-decent hotel kitchen further up the street.

Noma arrived about ten minutes later, grinning. She brought a bottle of sparkling wine.

"What have you done?" he asked.

"Nothing," she insisted.

"You'd really better not have done anything."

She wandered around his apartment.

"Cosy," she said.

He was about to tell her it was a hole and he was actively searching for somewhere better, when he remembered what she was living in.

She took a glass of the sparkling wine. It was wine-effect, but the foil stopper wrap and the cork were at least real.

"When do we move with this?" she asked.

"I told you we'd have to wait, and we'd have to box clever."

"So you've done nothing all day?"

"It's going to take longer than a day," he replied. He began to split open the carry-out punnets. Warm food smells permeated the room, robbing away the aura of damp carpet and cold plaster.

"I've actually begun to get somewhere," he said, "so there's all the more reason to keep a lid on this. It's a great story, and it could open up an even greater one. We do not want to crap on our own leads."

She picked up a bowl and started to eat.

"So tell me all about it," she said.

"I can't just yet."

"You're going to thieve this away from me, aren't you, you bastard?"

"No," he said. "I was making a few very discreet enquiries this afternoon, and they led me to a very interesting place. You need to leave it with me for another few days. A week, maybe."

"A week? Are you kidding me?"

"A week isn't long. Not for something this good."

"How good?" she asked.

"It's either good good or bad good, but either way, we'll both walk away looking very pretty indeed. Just leave it with me. It's delicate. We mustn't jeopardise it."

Fork rocking thoughtfully in her hand, she studied him.

He felt as though he was being measured. He wasn't sure if it was for a new suit or a coffin.

"I will cut you in," he insisted. "Full share. It's the kind of story that will need two POVs. We'll clean up. The bolide story *and* where it goes."

"Tell me."

"I can't."

She took a deep breath.

"I can place the story," she said.

"What do you mean?"

"I spoke to some contacts."

"For fuck's sake!" he said, and got up, dropping his bowl on the counter. "What did I tell you? One simple thing! What did I tell you?"

"Oh, relax. I'm not stupid, Falk. I didn't tell anyone what the story was. I just touched base with some feature editors, sounded out things in theory. Jill Versailles at Reuters is very keen. Just in principle."

"Jill Versailles is good," he admitted.

"See? I'm not fucking about. Just a little careful ground-work. I didn't cross any line. I *am* trusting you."

He nodded, but he could see it in her eyes. No matter how careful she'd been, how discreet, she'd got a whiff of the interest from Versailles, and from others, no doubt. A whiff of their hunger, a whiff of the money. She wanted that payday fast now it was in sight. A week was an eternity. She wanted the payday of the cash, the celebrity, the sudden ballistic ascent of her rep.

A week was an eternity. She was going to get sloppy, cut corners to shorten that time. She was going to do anything necessary to punt the story into the back of the net. The thought, the very idea, that someone else might beat her to the punch, hurt like a physical injury. She could not allow it.

"A week," he said quietly. "Just a week, and this will be better than you can possibly imagine."

"Do you promise, Lex Falk?"

His celf chimed. He turned away from the girl to take the call. It was Cleesh, blunt and unemotional, saying she might need to talk to him later. She cut off quickly. He looked around to see where Noma had gone.

The problem with giving someone a nickname based on an item of clothing was that it became less and less appropriate the better you got to know them. Her name was already starting to eclipse his tag for her.

He realised he could never really think of her as green hiker girl again now that he'd seen her naked.

It was an inducement. It was her way of keeping him onside. He woke up in the middle of the night still riding the tail-end of the endorphin wave, but he was already getting head-spin sick from too much fizz and Scotch-effect. The buzz would soon wear off completely, and he'd be left more aware than ever before of his aches and deficiencies. What would abide would not be a memory of her pliant, stripped enthusiasm, but rather the look in her eyes. Pity, same as Underwood's. She'd been good at minimising it, but she hadn't been able to hide it altogether. He was a means to an end, just as others had been the means to his ends in the past. It probably wasn't for the first time, but it was the first time he'd known about it.

She was asleep. Unsteady, he got up and caught his reflection in the window. A guy like the one standing in the city lights did not get a girl like the one lying on the bed without there being something in it for the girl.

He found his glass and drank some Scotch-effect to try to restore his postcoital high, but it was far too late. This is a moment, he thought, this is one of those moments of self-realisation that you get four, maybe five times in a lifetime, that changes your world view, and shows you that you're not the person you used to be, and proves that you never can be again, and leaves you broken in a ditch beside the highway.

He was washed-up and no kind of catch. He was a long way past being the good-looking guy who could charm the pants off anyone, and his way into any story. The idea that he was still using those moves, making himself look like a total asshole, made him feel nauseous.

His celf rang.

He realised it must have rung already. That was what had woken him. He went into the bathroom so he wouldn't disturb her. Some bleary-eyed, haggard old fucker looked back at him out of the bathroom mirror.

"What?"

"Lex, it's Cleesh."

"What time is it?"

"It doesn't matter."

"What?"

"It doesn't matter, Falk. It's got to be now. You've got to come now."

"Fuck that," he replied. His hip throbbed. He was fairly sure he was going to hurl. "Call me in the morning. We'll set up a time to–"

"It's got to be now, Falk. Things are moving too fast. If you want to be part of this, get here now."

TEN

"Here" was a suite on the thirty-eighth floor of the Hyatt Shaverton.

"Why not the GEO mast?" Falk asked Apfel when he came to meet him at the elevator.

"Plausible deniability," said Apfel with a smile that suggested he thought the concept actually carried some currency.

"So it's not the chicken-effect parmigiana?"

"That's just an added bonus," said Apfel. They walked down a carpeted hall with high, backlit glass brick walls. Piped musak was being used in some insane effort to counteract the smell of Insect-Aside, like the mutually annihilating collision of shit and anti-shit.

Apfel ushered him into the first big room of the suite. Double-height ceiling. Falk could smell machines, the scent of warm plastic and electricals. There was also a dash of pine disinfectant and salt. He could hear the hum of fans venting warm air. Outside, through the one-way windows, floor-to-ceiling deep, Shaverton lay under cover of an amber night, studded with lights and striped with the luminous needles of other glass masts.

The carpets had been removed, and replaced with the rubberised matting that Falk had seen in SOMD field hospitals. The walls had been spray-lined with matt-white rubber like the inside of the truck in the park. The configuration of the internal walls and the light fitments had been altered. One side of the suite was a raised platform facing a wall of boxes and high-end informatic consoles. The screens of all the boxes were busy, flickering, scrolling: text, data spreads, multi-views. Cleesh was sitting in a specially adapted roller chair, sliding up and down the consoles, making adjustments. She looked over her shoulder at him, but said nothing and allowed her face no expression. She adjusted her headset and turned back to her job.

Behind the platform was a large medical space, some big floor-mounted modules that looked like repurposed military hardware, and a set of shutters into the next part of the area. The nondescript man from SO Logistics was standing near the modules, talking to two people Falk didn't know. Underwood was working in the medical area.

"You look like death warmed up," she said.

"I'm wealthy, thanks," Falk said. "Entirely wealthy."

Underwood shot a raised eyebrow at Apfel. She was wearing a surgical smock so box-fresh it smelled of clean.

"If we could just—" she started to say, but Falk walked past her towards the shutter.

"Falk?" Apfel called.

"Tell me all about it," Falk replied, over his shoulder.

"I will," said Apfel, coming after him. "Just sit down and we can catch up."

Falk slid the shutter open. Over-warm air flooded out. It felt like a steam room. The levels of light were much lower. Falk was reminded of a deep-sea aquarium. Four large metal pods sat in a scaffolding frame. They were dull grey and shaped like eggs. Cables and feeder tubes spooled off them like hair matting from coconuts and connected to overhead arrays. Ayoob was halfway up one on a walkway, checking a side panel.

"He's here?" Ayoob called down to Apfel. "Is he ready?"

"Not yet," Apfel replied. "Mr Falk is showing himself around. Falk?"

"That's a Jung tank, is it?" Falk asked.

"Yes," said Apfel. "Can we get you back to the med area? Time is tight."

"Why is time tight, Bari? You told me the Letts incident had moved the timing up, but you implied there were still a few days to play with."

"It's got to be tonight."

"I'm not ready. I've got things to put in place, and–"

"Explain them to Cleesh," said Apfel. For the first time in Falk's experience, he sounded impatient. "She can handle whatever you need. The whole Letts thing has escalated everything. We have to move while our Jung Guns are still accessible."

"Your what?"

"That was me," said Ayoob. He had come down from the tank side to join them. He shrugged apologetically. "I kind of came up with it. A joke. It sounds pretty stupid now everything's so serious."

"Ayoob's referring to the subjects selected for the embed process," said Bari. He looked over a data display that had just been sent to his celf. "They're all SOMD, of course. We recruited carefully, quietly approached a few suitable candidates who seemed prepared to make a little extra money on the side. We have contracts, agreements to provide in the event of injury or dismissal."

"How many candidates?" asked Falk.

"Nine," said the SO Logistics man. His role in the whole thing was becoming clearer.

"He's your finder? Your talent scout?"

"Yeah," said Apfel.

"Nine ground troopers?" Falk mused.

"Yes."

"How will mine be selected? When do I meet him?"

"The match is based on a number of variables," Underwood began. "There's a bunch of biological issues, synaptic patterning being the–"

Apfel cut her off.

"Actually, right now, it's about availability. And you don't get to meet him."

"Now wait–"

"Thanks to Letts, the SOMD is mobilising a major taskforce response. Just about everything's shipping out. Every single one of our nine possibles will be in the field by lunchtime tomorrow, and embedding will be impossible. It would take us weeks to presearch and shortlist replacements. Unless we move right now, we can forget being operational for at least six months."

Falk walked over to one of the medical couches and sat down. He leant his elbows on his knees and rubbed his face with the flats of his hands, eyes and mouth wide. His head was rushing so much, he barely felt the pain in his hip.

"What's his name?" he asked.

Apfel looked at Underwood and nodded. She took up a folder from the cart beside her, opened the cover and searched for the answer.

"Bloom," she said. "Nestor Bloom, private first class. Age twenty-six."

"Is he ready?" asked Falk.

"We've got him prepped in a mobile just outside Camp Lasky," said Ayoob. "Another forty-five minutes, and he's expected to report for mobilisation. That's all that's left of our window. We miss this, we miss him."

"Okay, okay," whispered Falk.

He sat for a moment, as Underwood began to strip the plastic and paper sleeves off various sterile tools and clips, and lay them out on a tray. He suddenly became aware that Cleesh was standing over him.

"It'll be all right," she said. "It'll be freeking® amazing."

"What happens once I'm in?"

"Not sure really."

"You've beta-tested this, right? Cleesh, you have beta-tested this?"

"Not as much as we'd like," she replied. She patted his arm. "It'll be great."

"But I want to know what happens once I'm in," he said. He felt a slight seam of panic in his core, a sense of sliding past a point of control. A sense of being unable to stop himself making a bad decision.

"I want to know too," Cleesh said. "We'll find out together. We'll improvise. We'll figure it out as we go along."

"I don't know, Cleesh."

"I'll be with you every step of the way," she promised.

The Jung tank was heated. The metal shell of it was warm, almost like skin. He thought it was metal, but when he came to touch it, he realised it was some kind of ceramic. He could hear Ayoob and Apfel talking nearby, and he knew he ought to feel odd just standing there, buck-naked apart from the external plumbing of the intravenous tubes and sensor wires Underwood had fixed all over his body.

But he didn't. His head was swimming. She'd shot him

with several doses of stuff, including some premed-type anaesthetic and muscle relaxants.

Ayoob and Underwood helped him up onto the step plate beside the tank's open top hatch. The smell of disinfectant and salt was stronger. There was steam heat coming out of the hatch. He peered inside. It was full of dark water, or dark fluid at least, barely rippling, carrying enough warmth to waft steam from its surface in the dank chamber.

He murmured something.

"Sensory deprivation," said Ayoob, as though Falk had asked him a question. Perhaps he had. "Pretty old-school tech, basically, but that's just the medium to suspend you in. We find it gives the best results for the embeddee in terms of feedback and response. It helps to sustain the reposition too."

Underwood was clipping lines and tubes from the tank array to some of the drains and introducers she had connected to Falk's skin. He winced slightly as she pushed a trocar into a cannula.

"Let's go," said Apfel, steadying his arm. There was a sort of cage frame to hold on to. An electric motor started. Falk felt himself beginning to sink into the tank, felt the pleasant warmth of the fluid swallow his legs. The motor stopped when he was waist-deep, and Ayoob fitted him with ear plugs, a face mask and, last of all, blackout goggles.

The final thing he saw was Ayoob grinning and giving him a thumbs-up.

The final thing he heard, after the muffled noise of the motor restarting, and the lap of the warm tank water climbing up his chest, was the clunk of the hatch closing overhead.

ELEVEN

There was a clunk as the hatch opened, and light flooded in.

Heel on the step-rung, he jumped down out of the Fargo. Grit dust underfoot. The dawn sky over Camp Lasky was the proud blue of a corporate logo. The camp was catching the sunrise, side walls washed luminous white. The floods were off. The compound was buzzing with personnel dismounting rollers. He was already inside the gate.

He walked in through the assembly area. He didn't know where he was going, but that didn't seem to matter. His feet did. He walked with confidence, a swagger. His head was muzzy, like the greyscale hours that follow a migraine, but he hadn't felt so lithe, so physically able, in years. It was like idling in a high-performance vehicle. He knew, he just knew, how rapidly things would accelerate if he gunned the throttle.

But something was off. He tried to work out what was disconcerting him. Something sat badly, ill at ease. Other troopers grinned and fist-bumped him as he walked in. He knew their names. He knew who he could banter with and who to steer around. He knew exactly how to needle some of them: the right words, names, references. Playful, mostly, sometimes the snap of rivalry, sometimes a verbal cuff to keep someone in their place. He thought he saw Selton, but she was heading somewhere.

Even so, he felt he should avoid her.

He stopped and dropped down to adjust the laces of his left boot. Into view: combat boots; a leg, kneeling, brought up to his chin, wearing tundra-pattern kit; strong, subtle hands, tanned from outdoor work, from dusty sunlight. He re-laid the tongue of the boot, re-laced, tied off. He realised he didn't know he could work that knot and lacing pattern.

SOMD personnel were queuing up out through the dust screens of the stores block. He'd take his turn, but he had little desire to loiter in line. He crossed a patch of sunlight into the wash house. Restroom stalls down one wall, brick-bond tiled floor, the shower block opposite. There was a humid smell of bodies, of cheap soap, the locker-room funk of a forgotten sock or vest baking behind a heating pipe. He said hello to the two troopers heading out as he came in, swinging fieldpacks onto their shoulders.

Then he was alone. He took off his glares and went over to the sinks. Above the stainless-steel bowls, a long, slightly foggy mirror had been riveted to the cinderblock wall.

He looked back at himself. The clean, pressed tundra-pattern reg shirt, the digital brooch and the stitch-label tag over the left breast pocket, both stating the same name, the cuff-cut short sleeves revealing corded arms, muscles bunched as he leaned forward on the edge of the sink in examination. Dirty-blond hair, high and tight, like straw stubble. A face that was familiarly unfamiliar, handsome and strong the way a good piece of furniture or a landscape is handsome and strong. Blue eyes, blue as an Eighty-Six sky, a corporate logo. Blue eyes that looked into foggy glass and saw through to somewhere else entirely. A wry half-smile.

"Hello," he said, blue eyes looking right into blue eyes. "You should be able to hear me. They said you should. I won't hear you, so."

He shrugged.

"I don't know if you're in there, I don't feel you, but I feel something. Like a, like a something, an ache. Like when you have the flu coming. Is that you? I hope so. I don't want the flu. I have had shots, also."

He leaned closer, still staring.

"I just wanted to say hello, because the chances are we will not have a moment like this again. You talk to yourself in front of your guys, they tend to take your gun away and reassign you to food services. We're not going to be alone much from this point on."

He grinned more broadly, and held out a mocking hand to his reflection, as if to shake.

"My name is Bloom. Nestor Bloom. Pleased to meet you. Freek® alone knows what your name is. I don't get told that. But it's good to have you along. Just keep it down in there, okay?"

The door opened behind him. Two troopers came in.

"Hey, Nestor! My main guy!" said one.

"We are going for it," said the other, shorter, Hispanic. "Into the Hard Place! We gonna show those mothers our A game, man!"

Laughter. Palm-slaps.

He had too many questions. He had a sick feeling deep down, the nasty burn of adrenaline. He didn't want to turn away from the sinks, but he was turning away from the sinks. He didn't want to take a piss, but he was taking a piss. What the fuck? *What the fuck?* It was as if he was paralysed, *moving*, but paralysed. He was willing himself to do things and his body was doing something else. It was making him crazy, insane with claustrophobia.

With a final, titanic effort, he made a sound.

"You okay there, Nestor?" asked the Hispanic trooper, hosing a long stream into the metal trough, hands on hips.

"Yeah."

"You gonna puke, man?"

"No, I'm okay," he replied. "Just a little heartburn."

"Sounded like you were retching, Nestor. Like you were going to puke."

"Just freeking® heartburn, man," he replied, patting his chest, smiling. Not smiling inside. "I'm wealthy."

The little Hispanic came over. He knew his name before he read his brooch. Valdes. Valdes's expression was that of a long-suffering brother-in-law.

"You ever going to get that ling patch lifted out of you, man?" Valdes asked. "You know you don't have to worry about no harsh language where we're going."

"The Hard Place, Nestor," said the other trooper. "No dummy rounds, it's live language out there, you know?"

"I'm going to get it lifted," he said.

"Good, that's good," said Valdes.

"You're SOMD, you better cuss like a motherfucker," said the other man. "Not like some fucking adfomercial."

"You coming?" asked Valdes, heading for the exit.

"I'll be right along."

They left him alone. He turned and looked back into himself in the mirror.

"You do not pull that freek® again, you hear?" he said. "Whatever that was you did. You do not do that. You just ride along. Ride along. Do not freek® with me again."

• • • •

Glares on, he walked into stores, out of the hard light. It wasn't even 6.30am. The air was beginning to carry dust, like shot silk. The blue of the sky had faded, weathered. Out on the west side of Lasky, boomers were running ignition checks, making an unholy row like a fleet of brushcutters.

He'd worked out what was so disconcerting. His POV, his eye level, was about eight inches higher than he was used to. It was a small but significant defamiliarisation. It made him feel seasick.

There were about ten staffers managing the points of service. Each one was using a Mil-issue celf to swipe ID brooches and call up the spec-tailored requisites from the manifest. From initial swipe and confirm, it took about forty seconds for the plastic-wrapped kit sets, fieldpacks and webbing to come down the belt. Body armour harnesses and torso rigs came out on an electric rail a little slower, swinging and jiggling like funhouse skeletons.

His stores manager was a small Korean girl with a sarcastic smile.

"Nestor!" she announced, swiping him as he came up to her station. "Fuck's happening, man?"

"Fit me up, Chin."

"I so will, soldier boy. You're usually first man in."

"I got held up."

"Fuck that. You gonna kill someone for me, real nice?"

"Sure. You got blate for me?"

She did a little shimmy, elbows out, as the ablative/ballistic plate armour rattled down the rail towards them like clothes on a carousel at a dry cleaner's.

"Only best blate for you, hot boy," she said.

"You're a freeking® star, Chin."

"You gonna get that shit stripped out, Nestor?" she asked,

pointing at his mouth. "It's not good. I wanna hear you talk dirty talk."

"I dunno."

"Docs do it right now," she said. "You go ask. Takes like five fucking minutes."

"I figured I'd keep it, Chin," he said. "Let my piper do my talking for me."

"You badass!" she declared.

He looked badass. Ten minutes later, plated and blated, he caught sight of his reflection in the screen windows of the obs station. The body panels bulked his already tall, hefty frame to heroic proportions. The backboard contained rechargeable power packs for running any and all equipment, including the integral Limb Assist Exo Frame, an external servo armature buckled around his left arm, designed to help support and steady the M3A piper during extended operations. The inertially reactive joints uttered a soft purr every time he moved his shoulder or elbow.

He passed the misters, filling the doorway space with a fine fog of Insect-Aside.

Team Kilo was assembling on the decking beside its hopter in the dust-mote dark of the hangar. Their pipers, PAPs and thumpers were laid out on the ground sheets under the tail boom. The hopter was just one of eighteen set up for final check as its team gathered for prep brief and grace. There was a smell of petrochemicals and paint. Amped voices delivered echoing instructions across the hangar yard, and the air throbbed with starter motor test-fires, warning hooters from freight porters and the pulsed whoop of power drivers winding home hex-head screws.

Eighteen matt-grey boomers, lined up just so, like missiles in a silo cage.

"Good of you to join us," said Huckelbery, the staff sergeant, as he walked out onto the mat. Everyone else was there, apart from the sergeant. Caudel, Stabler, Goran, Jay, Preben, Valdes, Bigmouse, the rest. They were all on their knees, or squatting, making a half-circle around Huck. Some of them were still adjusting the fit of their fresh-issue harnesses, or re-lacing their boots.

"Was going to let you go on ahead," he said, dropping in beside Caudel, "but I knew you wouldn't last five minutes without me."

"Yuckity yuck," replied the staff sergeant. "Briefing's gonna be in the air, but so far we know it's Gunbelt Highway, Eyeburn Hill Junction, and we know it's Close Target Recon."

"But we know it's the Hard Place, right?" asked Valdes.

"The hardest," replied Huck. "Guaranteed hot pocket. This is no fuckabout. It's come down from the top, the gloves are off. We're going in live, so I do not expect you rat-ass motherfuckers to make me look like a pretard. Every day for months you've been telling me you want the real thing. Here we go, the real thing. You fumble this, so help me I will sodomise each and every one of you with a loaded PAP 20. Who are you?"

"Team Kilo."

Huck looked unimpressed, cupped a hand to his ear.

"Who?"

"Team Kilo!"

"Better. Let's take a moment, okay?"

They all bowed their heads. Some hands covered hearts, some clasped ID brooches. He heard several sets of LEAF servos purr.

"God of my personal conviction," Huck said. They all echoed the words. "Watch over me on this morning, and throughout this endeavour, and watch over my comrades in this unit, even if they are heathen sunbitches who believe in some other god than thou. Help me to maintain honour and courage, and uphold the great institution of the Settlement Office, and the constitution of the United Status, amen."

Amen. Heads came up.

"Let's go!" Huck said, clapping his hands.

He rose. Across the mat, beside the next boomer in the line, he saw payload specialist Renn Lukes. Lukes was talking to an air crew tech,

This was it. He felt his heart knot. Lukes knew him. It was all over. The whole thing was done.

Lukes looked over.

"Nestor!" he called, throwing a grin and a two-finger eyebrow stroke of a salute. He turned back to his conversation.

"Sup, Bloom?" asked Stabler. She'd come up beside him.

"What?"

"The look on your face," she said. Karin Stabler. He knew he knew what she looked like naked.

"I'm okay," he said. "I'm wealthy."

"Fuck, I hope so. You pulled something, Nes?"

"What?"

"When you walked up just now," she said, "you had a little pimp roll going on. Like you were favouring your left foot."

"No, I just need to get the lacing right on these boots. They're pinching."

"You'd tell me if there was something wrong, right?" she asked. "I mean, it's me."

"I'd tell you," he said. They fist-bumped. Then she squeezed his right buttock and walked away.

The boomers were named. Each ground crew team had stencilled on a little tag or sample of nose art. It was strictly taboo during normal ops, because the SO didn't like the press seeing that kind of sensitivity-adverse shit. The hopter to the right of them was called *Crap Salad*. To the left, *Fuck You Very Much*, complete with an image of a pretty, coy girl caught *déshabillé*. Team Kilo's boomer was called *Pika-don*. A diligent calligrapher had written a motto under the name. *"Ask not what the fuck your country can do for you – ask what you can fuck for your country."*

Sound filled the hangar, and everyone turned to look. In the vast slab of washed-denim dawn sky visible through the huge, cranked-wide doors, a flight of boomers was suddenly in sight, hammering away from them in loose formation, gaining altitude. It was the airborne force from Hangar Two, right next door. They were off and running. Everybody whooped and clapped and whistled as they watched the flock retreating towards the dust-blue skyline.

They reminded him of a swarm of blurds, buzzing up from a patch of long grass, disturbed by a footstep. Not fleeing, the way the harmless, lacey lamp-bumpers did.

Angry, like the vicious black-bodied predators.

The ones that could sting.

TWELVE

Cicero, the sergeant, was giving them the scoop. They were
cutting down through rain-fat ribbons of morning cloud,
broad and flat, and the airframe was bucking. His LEAF
locked tight as he looped his left hand through a wall strap.
He couldn't hear its purr because of the rotor noise, and
because he was ear-plugged into the sergeant's talk-
through. They'd just done their Mil-secure link check. There
was no central display for the brief. Cicero was routing the
visuals to their glares, and marking things out via his celf
using a stylus.

He volunteered a brief and unnecessary spiel about the
"paramilitary threat", which was too vague to be of use to
anyone, but sharp-edged enough to paint the opposition
firmly as the black hats. Two, maybe three times he used
the word *terrorist*, a piece of vocabulary that the SO, for the
most part, had strenuously avoided in all to-media state-
ments and interviews. It wasn't that the word was
sensitivity-adverse per se, just that it was incendiary. It was
the next gear up. If they held it back, it gave them a rhetoric
of mass destruction they could resort to later.

It was in play now, simply to get the blood up. The SO had okayed the word for use in field briefings. It was too loaded for media use, but it juiced the fire teams with a sense of righteousness.

"Gunbelt Highway," said Cicero, punching the next image to their glares. Orbital relief, real time, real colour. The highway was the continental coast road. Winding along the landmass shelf for two thousand miles, around the buttresses of headland and throats of inlet, it linked Shaverton to Antrim by way of half-a-dozen junction bergs. It was a long, hard route, even in the air-con module of a bulk roadliner. Its looped line was intersected by thousands of dead creeks, run-off slots spoking down from the rim of the upland caldera, dry for years on end. From the air, from orbital vis, it resembled ammo linked into the belt-feed of a crew-served weapon.

"Eyeburn Hill Junction is a weather station," said Cicero, loading the next image. "There's a fuelling depot, oceanic observatory and a horticultural fac. Select multiview to walk yourself around. Do it. Even you, Valdes."

Valdes made a *pft* noise.

"Valdes, how are you going to show them your famous A game if you don't pay attention?" Cicero asked.

There was laughter.

"Eyeburn went dead-air two nights ago, though this could be nothing," Cicero continued, "Several of the coast towns have been having uplink problems in the last month."

"Cause?" asked Caudel.

"Seasonal. Solar flares. That's what they're telling me."

"Just us?" asked Jay.

"Three booms. Us, Juliet, Hotel."

The three Boreals had broken from the pack together about five minutes earlier. He could just see Juliet and Hotel through the sliced cloud, in line astern, portside.

He sat uneasily, crouched down, his h-beam in a weathercase on the deck beside him. Everything was vibrating from the shock-rock of the ride. His skin was tingling from the quiver, organs sloshing with each air-pocket lurch.

Inside, a strange stillness. Taut, like something was stretched tight and rigid to the limits of its give. He felt the other him pulling against him, like an anti-him, equal and opposite, blocking his every urge, his every desire, negating his every move. He couldn't speak, and when he did speak, it didn't feel like it was his voice. It felt post-ictal, dismaying. It felt like he was wearing clothes the wrong size. It felt like the sudden onset of body dysmorphia.

He used his celf to tap out a text flash, let it trickle across the inside of his glares, one character at a time.

I need you to calm down or something, buddy. You're making me sick.

He waited, then erased rather than sending it. Then he wrote again.

If this is you, deal with it. Stop it. Relax or something. If this is the process, then we are going to have to pull the plug, because I can't handle this feeling.

Erase. Then: *Waiting.*

"Bloom?"

"What?"

He looked up.

"The sergeant is addressing you personally, Nestor," clipped Huck over the mic. "Wake the fuck up."

"Sorry."

Cicero was staring right at him over the frame of his glares.

"I want Kilo One to secure the weather station. Can you do that, or are you too busy looking out of the damn window?"

Cicero wasn't ling patched because Cicero didn't swear. *Damn* was as strong as it got, which made him using it shocking.

"I can do that, sergeant. Kilo One can do that."

"You certain?"

"Certain as, sergeant."

Cicero let it hang. He kept his eyes on him.

"You okay there, Bloom?"

"I'm good, sergeant. We're good."

"Yeah?"

"We're wealthy. We're golden."

Cicero nodded. He switched his gaze to Goran.

"Kilo Two gets the depot," he continued.

Looking down on the continental rim, it looked like a rutted mud track seen from the underside of a roller. The caldera bit deep like a pothole, its belly full of water. Fragments of water lay in other ruts and furrows, like slivers of glass, catching the light. The terrain was a moist brown colour flecked with white, like the ganache of a coffee cake. Only the fragile wisps of clouds whipping past lent any sense of depth of scale.

Pika-don rocked. A squall hit it crosswise, rain pelting off the canopy and ports like small-arms fire. It squirmed across the glass like worms of liquid diamond.

"Four minutes!" the payload officer called.

He started to glove up. His right hand was shaking. He clamped it in his left to halt the tremor. No one had noticed. He pulled on his gloves, then unpopped the weathercase of his M3A. He stared at it. Licorice black, hefty, like an implement for heavy construction or road breaking. Adjustable stock, billet lower and trigger grip, top rail and optics cluster, power cell, vertical grip and the long pipe of the muzzle sleeve, all black oil, a dull sheen.

He felt afraid of it. Too afraid to pick it up. If he did pick it up, he was afraid he wouldn't be strong enough to carry it. To aim it.

"Freek®," he said, under his breath.

"Nes?"

· His guys were looking at him. Kilo One. Stabler, Preben, Bigmouse. They were ready. Their expressions were stone, unreadable, but he could taste wariness. He could see someone else's face reflected in the espresso-black of their glares.

Stabler slid hers up off her face. Her eyes were grey.

"You okay, Nes?"

"Wealthy," he said, forcing out a smile that took as much effort as the last rep of a bench press. "Set?"

"Set," she nodded.

"Set," said Preben.

"Set," said Bigmouse. "I got a point of entry ready, referenced to the landing plot."

"You lead off, we'll disperse wide," he said. Close enough they wouldn't lose sight contact, wide enough that a thump round or an IED wouldn't scorch them in one hit. Jesus, that clinical? The full expectation that not all of them would make it to the first marker?

He ignored his inner whisper.

"You got codes for the entry?"

"I got codes," said Bigmouse.

"And if there's no power?"

"I got other skills," Bigmouse replied. He and Stabler fist-bumped.

"Two minutes!" the PO squawked.

They would be delivered first. They got up and shuffled to the hatch, bent low under gear weight like invalids.

"Don't fuck up," Huck told him.

"I'll bear that in mind," he replied.

Huck smacked him on the arm.

"One minute!"

They were low now, really low, wallowing drunkenly in the cold air, churning through a crosswind. The sound of their rotors was bouncing back up at them from the valley sides. Their guts were yanking up and down like yoyos with the pitch and yaw.

The PO dragged the side hatch open. Rain exploded in like spindrift, windblown. Air, noise, the howl of the blades and the downrate. Cold too, bone-cold air, hard like a wall.

They were in the doorframe, feet braced, hanging from the over-rail by their left hands. Any and all loose cloth on their bodies was flapping, whip-cracking. Rain in the face, needles.

"In ten!"

The PO's voice was strangled by the mic and the noise wash. The ground was zooming up, a mountain rising to greet them, a breaching leviathan ascending from the depths. Vibration was wobbling them so hard, he could barely see steadily. Below, huts, refabs, demountables, something cinderblock, weatherboarded. High ground, a track, a storehouse. Two parked tray-trucks. A forest of turbine masts, a windfarm, like robot daffodils. More refabs. Some crate-and-creates. A livestock pen.

A yard, a compound yard. Mud, coffee ganache, rutted with real wheeltracks. Puddles that were actual pothole puddles, not mountain lakes.

Wet mud dimpling, smearing out in concentric rings, planed and smoothed by the boomer's underblow. Spray pluming into mist, in a circle all around them, driven up in a ring. A rainbow as the sunlight cut the water in the air.

Down.

Down.

Go.

THIRTEEN

The ground gave under his feet as he landed, jetting brown water up his legs. The mud in the rutted yard was slush, like wet snow. It was not thick, sucking mire. Morning rain had hammered the hilltop so hard, everything was water-logged and saturated, loose.

The boomer's fan wash was pushing against his back, and he was soaked with driven spray, so his spine and shoulders chilled unpleasantly. The woodchipper howl of the engines pummelled him. Droplets of water coated his glares, even though the lenses were auto-vibrating to repel moisture.

He tucked his head down, and started to run. The M3A was as heavy as a length of box girder in his hands. As he began to move, his LEAF locked off to provide a stable plat-form. The armature distributed the weight across his body, allowed him to move more freely. The liberation came as a surprise, which in turn terrified him. He knew what a LEAF did. Of course he did. Active tours, weeks of conditioning and training: he knew what it felt like when a servo tension-enabled. What the hell was wrong with him that it came as a genuine surprise?

The steady heart monitor chime of the target sampler system entered his left ear via the audio plug. Like a metal detector, the pulse rate accelerated or declined according to the aiming field of the pipe. If he turned the muzzle of the M3A towards an open space, the chime decreased. If he swung it towards a shape that the sensors read as a doorway or cover point, the pinging grew rapid. Graphics zipped across the inside of his left lens, quadranting the target potential. Door frame, truck side door, underside of truck, low roof, side windows, barn dock. Each one flagged yellow, sometimes orange, depending on perceived threat intensity. Then the sampler identified a humanoid shape, and the flag went red.

Just a scarecrow, a weatherbeaten tramp Christ, crucified in the vegetable garden.

He kept moving. He was aware of his own tongue, his own breathless wheezing. Whenever the others crossed his field of view, the sampler recognised their aura code and didn't flag them.

Bigmouse was up ahead, Stabler wide to the right. Preben was behind him. They were coming up the track, leaving the mud lake in favour of a walkboarded pier, approaching the outbuildings of the weather station. The air was cold, rain-sweet. His cheeks stung. The hilltop sky was vast and white, splashed with rashers of grey cloud. Bigmouse was at the gate, two block-raised demountables to his right. They were bright yellow, used for off-site storage.

Behind them, the engine scream changed tone. *Pika-don* hoisted herself out of the mud, rump up, blizzarding water and mud spray with renewed force. The PO sign-off came as a rasp click in his ear. One extra-harsh buffet of cold hurricane wind, and the boomer was over them, clear, passing away over the roofs, behind the uplink mast. Its shadow, trailing behind, blinked over them.

Its rotor-beat became a hard clacking in the distance, rolling around the hills. The quiet it left behind was uncomfortable. He felt vulnerable. He wanted the roar back so he could hide in it.

A much softer range of sounds circled them. The flap of the wind, the patter of rain against mud and weatherboard sidings. The splashes of their footsteps. The labour of their breathing. The churning murmur of the big windmills down the hill. The fast, shrill flutter of the toy windmills stapled along the vegetable garden fence. Tiny, double-rosette windmills for children, whizzing and spinning in the breeze, their brightly coloured plastics faded by weather.

There was a shriek. He switched around, expecting a red flag.

Bigmouse had opened the yard gate, a repurposed rusting wire frame from an old feed pen. It squealed on its hinges. Stabler came up past him, the stock of her PAP tight to her cheek, first one onto the boarded pathway that led through to the main site buildings. Her boots made a sound like someone knocking on a door. The boards, sprung by the mud beneath them, jumped under her and Bigmouse, trampolining drops of water.

He reached the gate, waited a second, took a moment. The frantic whirl of the stick windmills was getting on his nerves. He was scared again.

He turned a full circle. The hilltop was big, rounded. It was called Eyeburn because, the presearch brief had claimed, on clear summer days the sun could come up over the brow so hard and big it could scorch out a man's retinas.

Hard to imagine on a day like today, grey and rinsed. The smoke-vague line of the caldera rose up behind the rain-bleached station buildings. In the opposite direction, beyond the forest of turning turbine heads in the windfarm, the coastline dropped away. Most of the settlement clung to the skirts of the hill, but the weather station had been planted up where the wind and rain could find it. The sea was a dark plain, frosted with morning mist. The sky came down to meet it like a sheet of sandblasted metal, a beaten panel, primed but unpainted. If he listened carefully, past the hypnotic masking throb of the turbines, he could hear the boom-hiss of the sea down in the bay. Crash-boom, *suck-hiss*.

"Get with it," said Preben.

"I'm with it. Just getting my bearings."

Preben scowled. Farel Preben had the face of a prepubescent boy, and the physique of a bodybuilder.

"You're fucking dreaming."

They went through the gate and up the path. The auto-vibe had shaken the droplets off his glares. The sun yawned out suddenly, hard and bright. Respond traffic was still nil. Bigmouse and Stabler were approaching the front door of the main station house. It was a hatch lock. The wind banged an unsecured window shutter. *Rap rap-rap rap rap*, a signal telegraphed in some unknown code. Preben lugged a piper, same as him. Stabler had her PAP, and Bigmouse had the extra weight of the thumper. He was beside the door, trying the code in the pushbutton panel. Bigmouse had been called that for a long time, christened because of his size and his informatic skills, even though no one outside a museum had used a mouse in twelve decades. Stabler said Bigmouse's nickname was *retro*, as though that was a recommendation. He was their techie. Strapped to his left thigh was the team's eFight pack.

Bigmouse was long-boned and without grace. His frame was functionally large instead of heroic. He had eyes like the windows of an unoccupied apartment, and a deep philtrum that made him look like a bad caricature of a real face.

The codes weren't working.

Falk hung back with Preben, sweeping the zone with their pipers. His heart was beating fast, like he was really sick or on a chemical rush. Cardiac blow-out. Cardio-pop. The fear was deep in him, lodged like a knife, nicking his ribs, his heart, his lungs, making them deflate so he couldn't draw a proper breath.

"Hurry it up!" he shouted.

"Hatch is dead!" Bigmouse called back.

"Power?"

"Power's out!"

"Just the hatch," said Preben. He nodded up at the roof. A little link dish beside the chimney flue was in the middle of an automatic re-alignment.

"Get it open!" he ordered.

Bigmouse put his thumper over his shoulder on its sling, opened his thigh pack and pulled out an electric driver, a little thing the size of a stylus. It zipped the screws out of the lock plate almost silently. Bigmouse let the die-cut plate fall off the key pad into his palm, then switched the drill for a juice stick, inserted it and powered up the lock assembly. It banged two or three times, whinnied, and then the hatch shunted open a couple of inches. Stabler got the snout of her PAP in the crack, and then forced the door wide open with her left hand and foot.

Inside, an entry corridor. Metal grille decking, boot bench, a wall rack for tools and lamps, a row of hooks. Weatherproof coats, all high-vis, rustled in the wind.

He took a step forward. Fear made him puke. He kept the swill in his mouth, sucked it back, swallowed it.

"The side," he said, throat rough from stomach acid. "Find the secondary."

Stabler looked at him.

"You and Preben. Go."

They took off around the end wall, down the lea side of the building.

He led the way in. It was tight. Everything was flagging his target sampler. He banged the end of his piper against the tool rack.

"Jesus, Bloom," said Bigmouse from behind.

Stupid. He knew better. Nerves were making him stupid. The taste of puke in his mouth was making him brainless. The beam piper was too much gun for close interior work. A PAP was the preferred clearance weapon. That's why Stabler had looked at him funny when he'd sent her around instead of letting her take point.

He made his pipe safe and locked it to the carry slot on the backplate behind his left shoulder. He drew his PDW, matt grey and heavy, armed it, got it comfortable in a two-fist grip. Bigmouse already had his out. The *Personal Defence Weapon* was an automatic (caseless) handgun manufactured under SO contract by Colt. Forty 2mil rounds in a disposable slot-in stripmag. An interrogator flashed up on the inside of his left lens. Did he want to mate the PDW's muzzle sensor with his target sampling system?

He selected *no*, killed all the eye junk jumping about on his lenses. He didn't need any more distractions.

He glanced back at Bigmouse. From the faint glow behind his glares, it was clear Bigmouse had selected *yes*. Of course he had. That would be the smart thing to do. That would be the approved thing. That would be SOP.

"Power to the door was cut from the inside," said Bigmouse, checking the interior side of the hatch lock. "Someone pulled a fuse."

The corridor headed away from the hatch to a cross junction. The hanging coats smelled wet. He put his hand on the shelf below them, felt the run-off of rainwater that had collected there. Somebody had been out, early, in the rain. How long had it been raining? Since daybreak? Since the small hours?

The overheads were motion-sensitive, a power-conserving function, but they didn't light up. Someone had stuck little strips of torn tape over the wall sensors.

Why was that? Was it for a good reason, such as the on-off lights had begun to annoy one of the long-term residential scientists? Was it for a bad one, such as the corridor had been prepped for an ambush?

The utility wall liner was covered in instruments, everything from modern hydrometers to antique barometers, even a skein or two of non-local seaweed, brittle and pungent. Among them were drawings done by children, skies at the top, grounds at the bottom, suns somewhere between the two, with square cabin houses and people in yellow and orange coats, and lots of windmills.

They edged on, sweeping left and right, training their PDWs. Here, old coffee tins had been left under a patch of leaking roof. They were full of water, overflowing. There, a signed SO flag with the logo of the Climatographic Division, framed behind glass like a picture. Old paper books on a shelf, damp from the air. Wooden boxes of unwashed root vegetables, still thick with soil, slid under a wall bench. The smell of turnips, of earth. A sun-faded kite hanging from a wall bracket.

He heard a noise, swung his gun up. A coastal-form blurd, the size of a man's middle finger, was bouncing off the tinted skylight overhead, trying to escape into a golden summer's day that didn't exist.

He lowered the weapon, tried to lower his breathing rate along with it. It was so damn airless. His chest was tight.

"Bloom."

Bigmouse had found the station hub. Through a hatch doorway to their left was a large monitor room, stacked with junk and equipment. Most of the consoles and boxes were off, but some still glowed on standby power.

"The heating pipes are warm," said Bigmouse, touching them. "Where did everyone go?"

"See if the answer's in one of those," he replied, looking at the consoles.

Bigmouse holstered his PDW, and sat down at the primary position. He looked the console over, then opened a fascia panel and wired in another juice stick. The box mounted above the console lit. Bigmouse drifted through weather patterns, temp charts, precipitation measurement tables.

He could still hear the blurd knocking against the tinted skylight.

"Look for a log," he said.

"I'm looking for a log," Bigmouse replied.

He went out, through a pantry where tinned and dried goods sat on metal shelves. Through a side door lay a washroom, with stalls, sinks and a mirror. It smelled of bleach that was intended to mask the aroma of damp and a brimming septic tank. The windows were reinforced with wire mesh, and formed rectangles of pale, luminous daylight. The mesh and window sills were crusted with dead blurds.

He ducked back out. A broad, unlit well of a passageway continued on into a machine shop, beyond which lay the generator plant. There was a background hum. He swallowed back fear and bile. He used the LEAF to keep the weapon rock-steady.

Tools hung on pegboards. Labels were handwritten. Hoist chains dangled over workbenches, and an inspection pit yawned like a freshly dug grave, heady with the smell of oil. There was an up-and-over hatch, currently locked tight, which allowed small or mid-sized vehicles to be brought indoors up a concrete ramp.

Despite the LEAF, his hands were shaking.

"Stop it," he whispered. "Stop doing this to me."

He flicked on his target sampler, lit the lens. There was something in the shop with him. The genny hummed, just running on reserve. Doorway: yellow flag. Lockers: yellow flag. Shadows of the inspection pit: orange flag. Side door: yellow flag.

Movement: red flag.

He was going to shout a warning, but he'd retched into his mouth again. He felt as though his heart was about to blow up.

He fired the handgun.

FOURTEEN

The PDW made two thunderclap sounds. The recoil punched his wrist. Blowback gases choked him, acrid, prickling his face. The muzzle flashes were so bright, his glares auto-tinted.

He hit something. The opposite wall detonated. A peg board shattered, one corner releasing so it swung down sideways onto the workbench. A noisy avalanche of wrenches and pliers, hammers, handsaws. Nails and washers pinged off the floor, rolled like coins, scattered.

He stood blinking for a second, gun gripped and aimed, ears ringing. Smoke fumed around him in the light from the skylight. A final rolling washer trickled to a halt.

"Bloom? Bloom!"

Bigmouse, over the audio. He could hear his voice too as he came crashing through from the hub.

He swallowed hard.

"Clear!" he shouted. He still hadn't lowered the gun.

Bigmouse ploughed into the shop, PDW out.

"Fuck happened?" he asked.

"Clear," he replied. It seemed like all he could say.

"Was it contact? Did you get a target?"

"Yes."

"What the fuck did you shoot at?"

The up-and-over shutter hatch clattered open, letting in daylight and the laundered smell of rain. Preben and Stabler stood there, framed in the square of light, aiming their main weapons.

"Clear!" he told them. They lowered their guns cautiously. He could smell burned metal where they'd sliced the padlock off the shutter.

"Hell's happening in here?" Stabler asked, coming in. "Nes?"

"He started shooting," said Bigmouse.

"I had a contact," he said. "I saw a contact. In the doorway."

"There's nothing here," said Stabler. She looked at Bigmouse. He saw Bigmouse shake his head at her.

"There was movement. Right in front of me. I saw someone. I saw a weapon."

He looked at the three of them. The fear was looping inside him like a snake biting its tail. He hated the looks on their faces.

He holstered his weapon and adjusted his glares. Review playback. Movement. Red flag. *Flash flash*, bright as an eye-burning sun. What the hell had he shot at?

Slow it down. Red flag alert. *Flash*. Back a little. That shadow blur, just before the flag. A nanosecond of movement. What was that? An apron, hanging on a pegboard, caught by a breeze? Enhance. Nothing, something.

A figure. A human figure.

"Someone came out of that doorway," he said, pointing, reading his glare display.

"Who?" asked Stabler.

He shook his head. "It's just a shape."

"Not real then," said Preben.

"It's a person. You can look at the playback. I'm running frame by frame. A shape. It red-flags."

"Were they armed?" asked Bigmouse.

"Yeah. I can see it. A pistol, left hand."

"What make?" asked Bigmouse.

"It's just a shape. A... silhouette. For a frame, no more than that."

"So where did they go?" asked Stabler. She was staring right at him. "Bloom, come on. Please. What the fuck's with you today? Where did they go?"

The audios crackled. Bigmouse turned away to report their sit to Huck on the secure link.

"Someone came out of that doorway," he repeated to Stabler. What was that look on her face? Pity? It made him want to scream.

"Fuck," said Preben.

They looked at him. He was staring down into the inspection pit.

He went and stood beside Preben.

A young woman was tangled at the bottom of the pit, face-down. Her head looked like it had been dipped in blood.

Best guess was she'd come out of the side room, the shop store, and fallen into the pit diving out of the way of his gun. His shots had missed her because she was already falling by the time he fired. He'd killed the peg board instead. He'd almost blown her head off.

She'd hit her hairline against the pit wall falling into it, almost scalped herself. There was a loose flap of skin, and blood everywhere, excessive amounts that had, at first, looked like a killshot to the skull.

They'd got her up out of the pit using a backboard from the medical suite, and Preben had cleaned and sealed her scalp wound. She didn't wake up. They made her comfortable.

"No name tag," said Stabler.

"The clothes are settlement standard," said Preben. "She's a local."

"Scared local," Stabler agreed.

They both looked at him.

"She had a weapon," he said.

"Yeah, where is that?" asked Preben.

The girl looked very pale, pale as death. Her breathing was so shallow, you could scarcely see it. They'd made her comfortable on a couch in a shelved alcove off the hub.

He bent down beside her. He could smell her blood, tacky on her weatherproof jacket, matted in her hair and along the sealed tearline. She was small, with a heart-shaped, symmetrical face and tight features. He wondered what her eyes were like. Her hair was dark, almost black, and thick, but cut back to a bob.

"No name tag," he said. "No brooch. You've looked in the pockets?"

"Nothing," said Stabler.

"The tag pocket's empty, too. See?"

He pointed at the small, plastic window pocket on the breast of her coat. It was empty.

"She could have taken the tag out," said Stabler.

"Maybe it's not her jacket," said Preben. "Maybe it's not anybody's jacket."

"Why would she take the tag out?" he asked.

"Fuck is going on?" asked Stabler. "Nes, what? You think you've brought down a paramilitary here? What the fuck? Is that what you're saying?"

"She's a station tech. A local," said Preben.

"We don't know that."

"We know you scared her so bad she fell in a hole and brained herself," said Preben.

"Cicero," Stabler began.

"What?" he asked.

"Cicero says he wants to talk this out with you as soon as Eyeburn's secure," she said, with reluctance. "May have to write up a formal. I mean, discharging a weapon at a local."

"You know it wasn't anything like that," he said. "Freek®, Karin! I showed you the playback. Red flag. She had a weapon."

"I didn't see a gun," said Stabler. "We didn't find a gun."

"You saw it!"

"I saw something. A shadow. Her hand, maybe. A torch."

She looked at him. It wasn't even clear from her expression that she wanted to help him. They could all feel how wired he was. It was as though they didn't know him. As though he wasn't himself.

"We don't even know who she is," he insisted. It felt stupid.

He got up and walked away, balling his fists to stop them quivering. He banged the door into the restroom, slammed it behind him. He looked at the windows, just soft slabs of colourless daylight, the mesh grilles choked with dead blurds. Except the end one. The blurds there littered the floor under the sill. The bleach-masked bad stink lingered.

He took off his glares and squared up to the mirror. It had a crack across it. His face looked back, drawn and white. His tan had gone, and the blue in his eyes had dimmed. He looked like a crazy person.

"Whoever you are," he said, "whatever your name is in there, stop it. Stop freeking® me up! I mean it. You've got to stop. I can't think! I can't centre! Freek® it, man!"

He took a breath, another, sucking hard, fighting panic.

"I don't get scared," he whispered. "I just don't. Not ever. I get pumped. I get ready. Not scared. Never scared. Freek® are you doing to me? Are you such a freeking® baby you're infecting me with your fear? It's in me, man! It's leaking into me! Is that you? Are you too freeking® scared for this? Get out, then! Get the freek® out of me! I mean it! Get out of me and leave me be so I can do this!"

Another breath.

"I need to do my job. If this is you, you're stopping me. You're freeking® me up. If this is the process, then that's got to stop. End of. Finit. Tell them. Tell them to yank you out of me."

No one answered, but the snake in his belly knotted again.

"I nearly shot that girl. I nearly shot her because you made me crazy. As it is, that head wound. She could die anyway."

Nothing.

"Freek's® sake! Are you hearing? Are you in there?"

"Fuck are you talking to?" asked Stabler. She was in the doorway of the restroom, holding the door open. The new look on her face he liked even less than the old one.

She took a step towards him.

"Who were you talking to, Bloom?"

"No one. Myself."

"What the fuck is up with you?"

"Nothing."

"Don't give me shit, Nes. I need to know. What is up with you?"

"I– Nothing. Nothing. I'm wealthy. I'm golden."

Stabler shook her head.

"I never thought it would be you," she said. "I never thought it would be you. They say sometimes people break when they finally get to the Hard Place, and it's often the last person you expect. But I never thought it would be you."

"I didn't break," he said. "I haven't broken."

"Then I don't know what the fuck this is," she said. "We've only just started, Bloom. We haven't even gone hot, and you're cutting loose at civilians."

"It isn't like that," he said.

"What the fuck is it like, then?"

"It isn't like that," he said. "I didn't break."

"You're fucked," she said. "You should have seen it this morning, and stepped out. You should never have got on the boomer. You were fucked up first thing when I saw you, and you're fucked up now. You had no right to do this to us, Nes. No right."

"I'm okay."

"Oh please! What is it? Is it drugs again? I thought you'd kicked that."

"It's not–"

"It's something. That freaky limp, that look on your face. You're not even talking to me the way you talk to me!"

"Karin–"

"Shut the fuck up, Nestor! I'm going to speak to Cicero. No. No. *You* have to talk to him. Get him on the secure. You have to let them evac you before you get one of us scorched."

"No–"

"Nes, you've got to, and it would go much better for you if it came from you. If it was voluntary. They'd probably get you assessed, sort you out and get you back on active. If I speak out on this, you're gone. Out of service."

Preben appeared in the doorway behind her. He eyed them both suspiciously.

"Bigmouse found something," he said.

• • • •

Bigmouse was sitting at the primary position in the hub.

"Personnel list," he said, nodding at the box. "It was tucked into one of the housekeeping files."

He splayed his fingers across the touchscreen and opened out four tiers of panes with small headshots and bio data.

"Seventeen residents," he said.

"It doesn't show children," said Stabler, "but there are clearly children here."

"So the list's not complete," said Preben.

"It may only show employees," said Bigmouse. "Here, see? AnniMari Tuck. Says she has two kids, but it doesn't show pictures of them."

"So do they live here, or does she just have two kids somewhere?" asked Stabler.

"I can sweep the station again," said Preben. "Count beds and cots."

"Where the fuck did they all go this morning?" asked Stabler, mainly to herself. "Why was it just her left behind?"

"She's not here," he said.

The three of them looked round at him. He pointed at the display with a jut of his chin.

"She's not there. She's not one of the seventeen."

"It could be her," said Stabler, tapping one of the panes.

"No, not if you look at it," he said. "The nose and cheeks are wrong."

"Her, then," said Preben, indicating another.

"Really not."

"It could be," said Stabler.

"It's not. She's not there."

He stared at them.

"Maybe that's why she isn't wearing a name tag. To make sure we can't compare it to the manifest."

"We already said this list doesn't show everyone," said Preben. "She might not be an employee. She might be a guest, a visitor. A sister. A girlfriend."

"Or something else," he said.

"Shut the fuck up," said Stabler. "Isn't it bad enough you made her crack her head open?"

He was going to answer, but a storm blew up outside. A boomer, swinging in.

They went out. The sky was bigger, clearer, but the rain was scattershot. Out to sea, the dark rumour of a real rainstorm loitered along the horizon.

Pika-don was descending, whipping up spray. It settled, gear struts creaking, in the middle of the station yard, aerosolising mud like a smokescreen. Then the rotors began to power down, the noise dropped and the spray fog began to waft away.

Ciccro dismounted through the starboard hatch, followed by the PO and a private called Martinz.

He strode across the mud towards them.

"Inside!" he ordered. "Except you, Stabler."

They went back inside. Stabler came to the gate and stayed talking to the sergeant.

"Doesn't look good for you," Bigmouse said to him.

"Shut up," he replied.

They waited inside, in the hub, then Cicero joined them, bringing Stabler and Martinz.

"I want a word," Cicero said to him, then got the others busy stripping out all the data they could locate in the station system.

"Stabler says you're a little rattled," Cicero said quietly, when they were face to face in the hallway outside the hub.

"I'm wealthy, sergeant."

"You looked off this morning," said Cicero.

"I'm fine. I was fine then. I'm fine now."

"Not what Stabler reckons. She's worried. Says you're jumpy."

"I'm not."

"Now's the time to say it, Bloom. Right now. She's looking out for you."

"I'm wealthy, sergeant."

"So tell me about this woman," Cicero asked.

He explained the incident as best he could. He let Cicero borrow his glares so he could review the playback for himself.

"It's not clear she did have a weapon," said Cicero. "*She's* not even clear. You looked for a gun?"

"Preben did. So did Stabler."

"You didn't, Bloom?"

"I wanted to get her out of the pit and patched up, sergeant."

"Look, Bloom, I think this is one of those things. Just one of those damn things that happens sometimes. From the replay, I can't see you did much wrong at all, unless you were already spooked or wired. But if she's a civilian, and it looks like she is, there will be a report. Write-ups. She may even file for damages, who knows? I'm going to need the medic to take a blood sample from you, and check you out. Are you on anything you shouldn't be?"

"No."

"Really no?"

"No, sergeant."

"Nothing in your system you don't want me knowing about?"

"No, sergeant."

"Okay, Bloom. We should take a look at her too."

He led Cicero over to the alcove.

The girl was gone. There was a faint smear of blood on the upholstery, and a whiff of antiseptic gel lingering in the air.

"Where is she, Bloom?"

"I... I don't know, sergeant."

"Nobody thought to watch her?"

He didn't know what to say. He went with, "We didn't, sergeant. We were trying to find out who she was."

"We'd better find her."

"I'll start looking."

Cicero shook his head.

"Not you, Bloom."

He turned and called out to Martinz, Preben and Stabler. He told them to mount a search.

"Go and sit down somewhere. Keep out of trouble," Cicero told him. "I'll get the medic in from the boomer to do your bloods."

He went back to the restroom so he could pace and stop his hands from shaking while he waited for the medic to come inside. An exam, any exam, would reveal things, the needle tracks and pinpricks from the biologic tests the corp's people had run on him. He didn't know what part of the process might show up in a blood test, but they'd shot him full of all sorts of shit to prep him for the reposition match, and some of that had to be detectable.

He was screwed. He'd gambled, and he'd lost. His career was in a place that smelt worse than the station restrooms.

It was airless. The stink of damp and excrement was nauseating. He went to open a window, let some air in. The mesh grilles, thick with blurd husks, were bolted in place.

Except the end one. The dead blurds were scattered on the floor under the sill because the grille was free. Someone had taken the bolts out so it could be lifted off to open the window. They disturbed the collection of blurd corpses every time they did it.

He lifted the mesh off and opened the window.

The smell was worse. Overpoweringly worse. The fear-snake squirming in his gut, he peered out.

The restroom windows looked out into a dead space, a blind gravel sump or run-off between the wings of the station. Directly under the window, five human bodies lay face-up, clothes plastered to them, skin like white cheese, draped over one another where they had been rolled out of the window and dropped. Black blurds were buzzing around pale, open mouths, clustering like sequins around unblinking eyes or the black-red punctures of hard-round entry wounds.

He lurched backwards, feeling the panic attack hitting him like a roadliner. The window banged shut, and he threw up down the inside of it, then again on the floor.

He spat. He moved towards the door. He tried the secure.

"Sergeant? Sergeant, this is Bloom. Come back. Stabler? Kilo One?"

He went out into the corridor.

She was right in front of him, the young woman they'd raised oh-so-gently out of the inspection pit. She halted in her tracks as he stepped out of the restroom in her path. Her face was set with purpose but a curious lack of emotion. Clotted blood matted her sealed scalp wound.

There was an SO-issue PDW in her hand.

She shot him with it.

FIFTEEN

Someone in the sky was smiling down on him. Maybe it was God. His mother would have told him that it was God, God smiling down from the sky and watching out for him, but his mother wasn't around and he didn't know where she had gone.

The smile was a big smile. It filled the sky up. It was a cheerful, happy smile, a smile full of big white teeth that were so big and polished, one of them was actually catching the light, like a cartoon glint. There were dimples at the corners of the mouth, smile dimples.

He wanted to know where his mother was.

Cold rain fell on his face, like dressmaking pins. The smile did not alter. He could hear voices in the distance. It was very strange. There was no sign of his mother.

He recognised that this was an occasion when he'd been really scared. He'd been scared because he hadn't really understood what was going on, and he'd got lost, and his mother hadn't been there to find him or explain any of it.

The smile was becoming a little unnerving. No one held a smile for that long. But there were periods of visual blackness, the durations of which he couldn't estimate. Each time his vision returned, the smile was still there. It hadn't gone anywhere, it hadn't stopped smiling, even when he hadn't been able to see it. It was all still there, the smile, the voices, and the rain on his face.

It meant something. All of it meant something. It had great significance, just not to him.

His hip hurt. His head hurt. He wondered where his mother was.

They'd come into the city together, leaving home early. She had put on her best coat, and he had been able to tell, though she had said nothing directly, that there was something going on. Putting on her best coat and leaving home early meant something. It had significance, just not to him.

They went on the rail instead of the bus. That had significance too. His mother said she wanted to be sure of being on time, and you couldn't trust the buses. The rail was much more expensive. His mother kept blowing her nose.

You saw the city a great deal better from the rail than you did from the bus. You saw it sprawl out, veiled by plumes of white steam from the processor factories, glinting in the sun, catching the sunlight like polished teeth.

He was hungry, but they had to keep an appointment. He wanted to stop at a ProFood counter and eat a chocolate stick or a Bill Berry Muffin. His mother held his hand and pulled him along. His mother said they had to see a man. She said orbital construction work was dangerous, a very dangerous occupation, and you had to be brave to do it, and they'd always known that, they'd always known the risk. She said it was a terrible thing, but they would be all right. The Office would look after them. That's why they were going to see the man.

It all meant something. He knew it meant something. It had great significance, just not to him.

The man was waiting for them in a brown building off the crowded streets. Sunlight outside, echoing halls inside, hushed voices lining the interiors like velvet. His mother had stopped on the steps outside the brown building and taken a breath, as if she was getting ready to sing. When she sang at church, she always took a moment to get ready and compose herself.

The man was nice, but it wasn't real nice. It was put-on nice. Making-an-effort nice. The man kept looking at him and smiling.

"And this is your son?" he asked.

His mother sat down. She pulled down the hem of her best coat. The man offered her a tissue from a box on his desk. Someone brought tea-effect. Through the windows behind the man's chair, the glass of the city twinkled in the sunlight like polished teeth catching the light.

The man talked about stuff that he didn't really under-stand, but the man was evidently worried that he could understand, that he understood too much, and kept looking at him, just to check. Another man came in. He was younger, and he wore a long black garment, and both his mother and the first man called him father.

But the man in the black garment wasn't his father. He wasn't even Father Ercole from the church where his mother went to sing, though the garment he wore was similar to Father Ercole's. Father Ercole was old, and nice. Genuine nice. Father Ercole would ask his mother to sing most Sundays, and give his mother a moment to get ready and compose herself before singing out in front of all the people.

This man, in his black garment, was too young to be anyone's father. He certainly wasn't his father. His father was older, and taller, and had big heavy arms, and worked in orbital construction, and they didn't see him very often because he was always away on contract.

They hadn't seen him for months.

The man in the black garment asked what kind of preparations needed to be made, and his mother said that her husband had never really been of the faith. It was her faith. She was the churchgoer. She liked to sing at the services. It was a community thing. Her husband, he'd never really been bothered with such matters. Even when he was home, he hadn't cared to come with her to church, even though he'd never stopped her doing it. He was a rationalist, she explained. That's how he'd described it. That's what the future was all about. God had only ever got people into wars and things. You didn't need God when you had space.

The man in the black garment had expressed some concern. On the deceased's form, it clearly stated his personal conviction as being the same as hers. Many aspects of the deceased's work with the Office had been predicated on this, including work placements, family and accommodation allowances, and holidays. The Office funded a funeral service based on personal conviction, as it was listed in the form. The man in the black garment was concerned that his mother was misrepresenting her husband's choices and beliefs. Perhaps she was upset, and angry at God because of the accident? If so, this was understandable, because of grief but, the man in the black garment insisted, he needed to get at the truth. She mustn't, she *shouldn't*, let her own feelings get in the way of her husband's wishes.

Besides, if it turned out that the deceased had misrepresented his personal conviction and registered false information, there would need to be an investigation to see if allowance and compensation had been wrongly administered.

Her mother said that her husband had been brought up in the church, just like her, just like their son here, but it had become just a notional thing. He had ticked the box for the want of ticking a box. These last ten years, his faith had declined.

His mother needed some more tissues to blow her nose on. Her tone changed. He knew this meant something. It all meant something. It had great significance, just not to him. She said she couldn't believe they were saying these things at a time like this, after what had happened. He'd given good service, devoted service. What did they mean, an investigation? If there had been overpayments or payments made in error, she couldn't afford to pay anything back. They had so little anyway, and particularly now. The man in the black garment assured her it wouldn't come to that, and that there would be full industrial compensation. But a few things might have to happen. They might, for instance, have to relocate to different accommodation. Smaller. There were only two of them now, and tied housing was in demand. This was especially likely if they had been receiving a faith-supported accommodation grant under false pretences.

His mother said, in a very quiet voice, that this simply couldn't and shouldn't be the case. It was her home, her family home. Her son's home. Her son, her boy here, his home. She was part of the community, the church. They had neighbours and friends. They'd been there ten years.

The man in the black garment suggested to the other man that perhaps the child would be better off waiting out in the hall while they talked. He might get upset. He didn't really seem to understand what was going on. He was only four, after all. There were picture books outside, and some toys.

His mother kissed him and allowed him to be led out of the room, away from the window with its view of the city, twinkling like polished teeth.

He was taken into the hall, which smelled of floorwax, and asked to sit on a bench under a window where the sunshine streamed in. A young woman brought him a juice box and a piece of fruit. She showed him the box beside the bench where there were picture books, and a woodblock puzzle, and a plastic tank with an SOMD logo on it, and a windup toy spinrad made of tin.

He didn't like the fruit much, so he put it on the window ledge. He was still hungry, though. After what seemed like a long time, the young woman was called away, and the toy spinrad lost its appeal. He wandered along the echoing halls, through patches of sunlight falling through the tall windows, brushed by the soft voices.

Outside, on the steps in the sun, he saw the ProFood counter that his mother had hurried him past on the way in. Workers were queuing for their beverage cups and chocolate sticks. He went over and looked up at the photograph menu displayed over the counter, the glossy coffees and sugar-dusted pastries and cheese-and-spinach slices.

Then the man at the counter told a woman in the queue that she had a sweet little kid, and the woman replied that the child didn't belong to her, so whose child was it? The little boy was lost. A lost little kid in the middle of a busy city street. Where were his parents? Oh, the poor thing. He must be so scared.

He wasn't scared, not until they started to fuss around him. They asked him where his father was, and he didn't know, and they asked him where his mother was, and he realised he didn't really know that either. She was in the big brown building with the steps at the front, but there were big brown buildings with steps at the front all around them, and he couldn't tell them apart.

So that was when he got really scared. He wanted to

know where his mother was. There was no sign of her. He didn't really understand what was going on, except that somehow he'd got lost, and his mother wasn't there to find him or explain any of it.

And neither was his dad.

The man who worked the ProFood counter came out, and took him round to the side of the stand, in front of the big, brightly coloured die-cut picture of Bill Berry the Astronut, and gave him a NoCal-Cola ice-pop to lick while someone called the police.

He ate the lolly, and gazed up at the die-cut picture of Bill Berry. Bill Berry, in his shiny silver suit, was holding out a chocolate stick and smiling his trademark Berry Happy Smile®.

The smile was a big smile. It filled the sky up. It was a cheerful smile, a smile full of big white teeth that were so big and polished, one of them was actually catching the light. There were dimples at the corners of the mouth, smile dimples.

"What's your mother's name?" the ProFood man asked him.

"Mrs Carmela Bloom," he said.

"Good, okay. That's good. We'll find her for you, don't you worry. We'll find her right away. So what's your name, son?"

"Lex Falk," he replied.

The blackness came and went again, came and went. A couple of times, during the blackouts, he was sure he could hear a slooshing sound, like someone moving around in a bath tub. Each time his vision returned, the smile was still there. Bill Berry's giant Astronut smile. It hadn't gone anywhere, it hadn't stopped smiling, even when he hadn't been able to see it. It was all still there, the smile, the voices and the rain on his face.

The rain was weird. He didn't understand the significance of the rain. Standing beside the ProFood stand, sucking his lolly, looking up at the Berry Happy Smile® and trying not to be really scared, it was sunny. It was hot. It was a sunny, sunny day.

Why was there rain on his face, cold and prickly like little dressmaking pins? Where was his mother? His hip hurt. His head hurt.

When the man from the ProFood counter had asked him his mother's name, he'd said it was Carmela Bloom, but that was patently ridiculous, because his mother's name was Elaine, and she'd died when he was two years old, and his stepmother, the woman who'd raised him, her name was Clare Chavest, later Clare Falk, and neither of them had ever taken him to a brown SO building on a sunny day to discuss funeral arrangements and industrial accident comp with regards to his father, because his father wasn't in orbital construction, he worked for Lowmann-Escaper, and he wasn't dead either. He was living on Twenty-One with a new family, a family he'd left Clare to create, a family Lex had never met because he'd never really been prepared to make the effort and ride a driver all the way to Twenty-One, even if they were his half-brothers and sisters.

Why was it raining in the sunshine? Why did he hurt? Why was he so confused?

He wanted to get up. He was lying on his back. He wanted to get up, but he knew that would be a really difficult thing to do.

However hard that was going to be, he knew it was going to be much much more difficult to remember exactly who he was.

Lex Falk opened Nestor Bloom's eyes.

SIHTEEN

The smile was a big smile. It filled the sky up. It was a cheerful, happy smile, with dimples at the corners of the mouth, smile dimples. The smile was full of big white teeth that were so big and polished, one of them was actually catching the light, like a cartoon glint.

No, not *like*. An *actual* cartoon glint, a deftly rendered *ting!* of dazzle.

Falk blinked away the cold rain. That smile. Though he was seeing it from a funny angle, it was definitely a Berry Happy Smile®. It was weather-faded, flaking in places, but it was positively the classic old Astronut brand image, not that shit, bland Rooster Booster thing ProFood had brought in about fifteen years back as part of their big corporate makeover. Fuck do they do these things for? Bill Berry, with his retro silver suit and his purple bilberry skin and his giant, cheeky smile, complete with cartoon glint, he'd had real character. The Astronut logo was a classic piece of commercial design. Booster Rooster was just a colossal cock in a suit.

The smile was looming over him, three yards across. It was a section of fibre sheet cut out of an old billboard and repurposed as a wind defender. It was part of a whole row of windbreak screens made out of old display hoardings, or adboards, or even the metal-skinned sides of bulk shipping containers, slightly corrugated and flecked with rust. They trembled in the path of a stubborn hilltop wind. The frames creaked slightly. The drizzle pattered against their slightly inclined surfaces.

The sky was low cloud, frothy white like retardant foam. He was lying on his back in the mud. His hip hurt, and so did his head. He was soaked through and cold. In the distance, behind the wind and the spatter of the rain, he could hear the low throb of spinning wind turbines.

Behind that, he could hear another sound: voices.

He craned to hear. He couldn't even move his neck. Opening and closing his eyes was as much motor control as he could manage. He felt trapped, completely claustrophobic, the way he'd felt when the reposition had first installed him as a powerless passenger inside Private First Class Nestor Bloom. He was paralysed. He was stuck inside a body that didn't obey his demands, no matter how frantically he willed it. And now, Bloom wasn't moving them both around.

Falk began to panic. He tried to control that, but it was virtually impossible. It was like being stuck in a lift with an incendiary charge. The combustion source was burning up, getting hotter and brighter and more fierce, and he couldn't get out to get away from it, and it would consume him along with itself.

He made a sound. He felt a raindrop pinprick his lip. He managed to make a sound, a moan, a murmur. He remembered being back at Camp Lasky, looking at Bloom's unfamiliar face in the restroom mirror while Bloom introduced himself. He remembered freaking out because of the sense of total paralysis, and trying to do something, anything. He'd made a sound then, just a throat noise, but he'd managed to wrest control away from Bloom for a split-second. Bloom hadn't liked that at all. He'd torn Falk off a strip over it. Well tough titties to you, soldier boy. Where are you now? Why have you left me lying here in the rain in the dead weight of your flesh when–

The girl. The mystery girl with the scalp wound and the curious lack of emotion. She'd shot him. Well, she'd shot Bloom, but it amounted to the same thing. Falk could remember the Colt in her hand, the action snap-snapping almost in slo-mo, the bright gas ignition of the discharge.

He couldn't remember feeling the rounds hitting him. It was just blackness until Bill Berry started to smile down upon him. Shit, he'd been lost there in the darkness, shut up in Bloom's unconscious mind, wandering blindly into memories that didn't belong to him. A memory of getting lost as a kid, being rescued by a guy at a ProFood counter. That had probably been triggered subconsciously by the old sign on the windbreak. The resulting experience had been very peculiar. The memory was acute, and clearly signifi-cant, but it had held no value for him. Bloom's recollection had adhered to Falk's mind. Falk had merely viewed the memory, like someone being shown a snapshot of someone else's childhood. The content, the detail, the meaning, they'd all been attached and complete. Falk had understood it all because Bloom understood it, and they were sharing brain function.

But it had carried no weight, no emotional content. Falk hadn't engaged. It was like being obliged to watch the latest episode of a situation opera you hadn't been following.

He couldn't remember the rounds hitting him. They must have hit hard. A Colt PDW was a high-powered weapon, and at that range. Fuck, maybe this wasn't unconsciousness.

Maybe Bloom was dead. He fucking ought to be dead. 2mil slugs at close range? Fucking dead as. Falk was trapped inside a fucking corpse! He was inside a dead body, just left there–

Wouldn't that make him dead too? Surely, the trauma would have killed him or, if not the trauma, the biological death itself? Wouldn't that shock have killed him? Clearly not, but why hadn't the link been severed? Why wasn't he back home, coming around inside Lex Falk's crappy physiology, with Ayoob and Cleesh winching him out of that fucking Jung tank?

Why hadn't they aborted and pulled him out?

Bloom had to be alive. Injured, maybe critically, but alive. His brain still had to be functioning. Falk was no fucking expert, but it stood to reason you simply couldn't maintain sensory reposition when something was dead and therefore had no senses or brain function.

But Bloom himself had left the building, and Falk was stranded inside a cooling body that absolutely refused to answer any voluntary commands, a body stricken by tonic immobility. Locked-in Syndrome. Falk had read about that shit. Total physical paralysis. Just the mind awake inside a shell of dead meat, unable to communicate.

The searing panic came back, squirming in his gut like a snake. Fuck, fuck, *fuck*–

Wait. He was able to blink. He'd made a sound, a croak. He'd made a sound when Bloom was still on board and in charge, overriden Bloom for a second. If he'd been able to do that, and he could blink and croak, for fuck's sake, he could do something.

Falk strained. He willed so hard he felt he might blow a blood vessel or rupture something. He felt like he was going to burn out all muscle memory. At the point where he could strain no more and he felt as though he was going to explode, he made a sound.

Another croak. A little gasping groan. Simultaneously, he farted.

The fuck? That titanic, superhuman effort had achieved the grand result of him cracking one off? Fantastic. Fan-fucking-tastic. That pretty much summed up the abject fucking head-on between effort and outcome that was Lex Falk's life.

It was so fucking tragic it was funny.

It made him laugh. He began to laugh. He laughed, seriously laughed, for almost a minute straight, until he realised what he was doing.

He hadn't tried to laugh, and he'd laughed. He was trying too hard. What was required was quite clearly something more subliminal.

He relaxed. He turned his head to the side. Nestor Bloom's head turned to the side. In extreme close up, he saw the mud he was lying on, splashing up little detonations as raindrops hit it. Right there in front of him was his SOMD-issue earbud, his link to the secure. It had fallen out. He could hear it. It was where the voices where coming from.

He strained to hear. A lot of fuzz and pop. A voice, repeating the same words.

"Mil-secure system is down. Mil-secure system is down."

Falk sat up.

There was a delay that felt like whole seconds, but was probably only the time it took for a synapse to fire, and Nestor Bloom's body sat up too.

Balance was an issue. The head lolled on slack neck muscles. Pain increased, in his hip and under his right eye. Falk felt woozy.

He gazed down at his legs, at Nestor Bloom's legs, stretched out in front of him. Rain fell, tapping at his field kit. His legs were straight and limp. His glares, broken in half at the bridge, were lying on the ground beside his right thigh. There was blood on his lap and down the front of his tunic, blood that the rain was washing into the fabric. It was dripping from his face, his nose. He moved his hand to wipe it. His left hand wouldn't move. His right came up into view, clumsy. He almost punched himself in the mouth. It took a moment of adjustment to manage the fine control needed to operate the hand, to use the hand to wipe his face, to test and probe his cheek and mouth.

Blood covered his fingers. It was Nestor Bloom's blood, and they were Nestor Bloom's fingers. Falk could feel damage to the face. It was sore, but numbed. Blood was coming from the nostrils, from the mouth, and from some kind of damage to his right cheek, under his eye. All of it ached and throbbed as he pressed: his cheekbone, his skin, his jawline and teeth, his sinuses, his nasal bone, his tongue, the orbit of his eye socket. He realised he was drooling blood and spit, and tried to wipe himself.

Falk tried to move Bloom's left arm. He felt as though Bloom's body had stroked out, that only one side of it was working. His head throbbed, the pain reignited by his inquisitive fingers. His hip hurt. Weird, *weird* that Bloom's hip should hurt precisely where Falk's had done. He attempted to get up. That was a tactical mistake. He slipped and went over on his side, his left side, his stroke-seized side.

He came face to face with Stabler. She was stretched out in the rain beside him, face-up. They were lying side by side, like lovers at the top of a hill looking at the clouds or the stars. Her eyes were open. The back of her head was gone. The rain was pink where it dripped off her hair.

Falk recoiled violently. He slithered and rolled away from Stabler's corpse, Bloom's body flopping loose and lumpen like a badly operated puppet, flailing in the mud. He made terrible, mewling, incoherent sounds, sobbing sounds.

He was saying her name. He was saying her name with a mouth that had been damaged and wouldn't work properly.

Falk fell still a few yards away from her, staring back across the dimpling mud at the side of her face. He'd simply reacted in disgust, the reflexive horror of finding oneself lying beside a head-shot corpse. The shock and pity and the despair hadn't come from him at all. It had come from Bloom. Bloom knew her. Bloom had been close to her, as a teammate and more. It had been Bloom sobbing her name in miserable recognition, not Falk.

Bloom, or some involuntary part of him, was still alive inside somewhere.

Falk tried to rise again. He spat out blood, and aspirated more along with spittle as he gasped and heaved himself up into a sitting position. He ended up sitting, leaning against one of the wind defenders, part of an advert for GM corn.

The best Falk could tell, they were in a little alley beside the weather station, on the ocean side of the hill. A gale and driving rain were coming up off the sea, and the view was masked with white fog and spray haze. It felt later in the day, afternoon, perhaps.

Below him, on the slopes, were store buildings and demountables, as well as several covered cultivation plots. They were all shielded from the weather's raw force by walls of wind defenders. The alley was a path, a mud walkway, leading through to a rear yard. Weatherboard sheds lined one side. The windbreaks, including the Berry Happy Smile®, lined the other, shielding the side of the station.

It was a nothing space, really, an out-of-the-way walk-through. Like the dead space under the restroom window, it had been a convenient place to drag corpses and dump them. Both he and Stabler had been dragged there from the main buildings. Despite the rain, Falk could still see the grooves of the drag marks in the mud. There was another corpse too, a third SOMD trooper. Falk could only see him now he was sitting up. The corpse was the other side of Stabler's, face-down. Falk wasn't sure, but he thought it was the trooper called Martinz. There were three tufted exit wounds in his back, like little volcanoes of gore.

Their side arms and main weapons had been taken, and there was some evidence that ammo pouches and pockets had been emptied.

He dearly wished he could control his posture and balance. With his left side frozen and his motor control fucked, he was leaning against the windbreak board at a tilt, like some hopeless invalid propped in a hospital bed, waiting for an orderly to come and plump up his pillows and resettle him. His right hand flopped slackly into his lap. He could feel the spit welling at his lip and stretching down in a long string onto his shirt front.

He sat for a while, then he made another attempt to get up. He discovered that the immobility in his left side was partly due to the LEAF armature, which was designed to take up tension and kept locking out. Everything took a half-dozen attempts. The patience infuriated him, but patience was the only thing that worked. Each move, each motion, he repeated over and over again until he got it right. His movements were clumsy and woefully imprecise. He couldn't have found his mouth with a spoon. As for threading a needle, he wouldn't even have been able to pick the needle up.

Because it kept locking around his slack, wayward left arm, the LEAF became an asset. It was a rigid prop that he could depend on, a limb that would remain firm, no matter what, instead of suddenly giving out. He crawled along to the downspout of the guttering and then used the pipe to haul himself upright. It took a few thousand years. Continents shifted while they waited for him to get vertical. The uncontrollable sway and nod of his head became so maddening, he squealed a wordless blast of angry noise.

Then he was upright, leaning but upright, rain in his face, pain in his veins, and every bit as helpless as he had been when he'd woken up.

SEVENTEEN

He walked like a zombie, like some lumbering, spavined thing that retained only the most rudimentary brainstem connection between impulse and action. He felt his way with his numb left hand, using the LEAF as a prop and a balance, scraping its cuff frame along the wind breaks, then the wall, then a doorway. One hand to the wall, legs set wide, he steadied himself like a rating on a ship riding a deep swell. He felt his borrowed body overheating from the exertion. Sweat flushed his back and chest, and then chilled in the rain and wind.

Still no one had come to open the tank and lift him out of Nestor Bloom. Not Ayoob, not Cleesh, not Bari fucking Apfel.

The rain eased. The wind dropped. The light turned yellow and the day turned sour. Everything went quiet, except for the sound of water gurgling down the spouts or dripping off the eaves.

He tried the door. It took him three goes to get his right hand around the handle. The door opened.

There was a noise, sudden and piercing. It was a sort of un-noise, a sound so loud and penetrating it existed on the very edge of normal hearing. He felt it rather than heard it, a shrill bark. It made him jump so hard he flinched backwards and accidentally slammed the door again.

The sound made other things start. A flurry of large white blurds broke into the air and beat away overhead, across the roof slope.

The sound came again. Even though he was half-expecting it this time, it made him jump again. He heaved back into the wall beside the doorway, involuntarily smacking the back of Bloom's skull against the weatherboarding. His right foot slid in the mire and he nearly went over. He shot out his left hand, grabbed the doorframe, and felt the LEAF lock up and hook him there.

Falk realised something. He didn't recognise the noise. It was simply a sharp, strangely modulated sound that was making him jump with its abruptness. But he was responding with greater trepidation and alarm than that. The recoil of his body did not match the simple curiosity of his mind. It was as though Bloom's body knew what the sound was. It was as though Bloom's muscle memory knew to be afraid.

The sound came a third time. Now Falk detected an odour of burning on the cold air. He pulled himself back, obeying the wary instinct of Bloom's body. He got himself into the doorway, using the alcove as cover.

He heard footsteps. Boots splashing through puddles at a jogging pace. Two figures, just shadows, flashed past the end of the alley, crossing the open yard of the weather station. It was the briefest glimpse, but Falk knew they were both carrying things, heavy objects.

Pipers. Hardbeam weapons.

He heard the noise again, this time accompanied by a slight blink of light from the direction the figures had gone in.

Now he knew what the sound was.

Weapons fire. M3A discharge.

He opened the door with a shaking right hand, got into the dark of the station's back hallway and shut the door after him.

Inside, the air was cool. He could smell stale, sooty burning, an aftertaste. He could smell burned blood and shit.

He started to lurch his way, steadying hand against the left-hand wall, into the base.

He got halfway down the back hall when he was tackled from behind. An arm locked around his throat. It felt like he'd been intercepted by a wardrobe.

"Not a word! Not a word!" a voice hissed in his right ear. Something else was in his right ear too. The cold snout of a PDW.

He let himself be dragged off the hall into a small dorm room that smelled of old socks and poor ventilation. The room was half-lit, untidy, a share unit cluttered with dirty clothes. There were clips of Shiona Kona decorating the wall above the left cot.

Bigmouse let go of his neck and pushed him away so he could look at him. The Colt stayed aimed at his face.

"Nes? Nes? Fuck!"

Falk blinked and swayed. He sat down heavily on one of the cots, banging the side of his head against a shelf on the way down.

"Oh, fuck! Nestor!" Bigmouse hissed, holstering his pistol. "Jesus, I didn't mean to hurt you! Jesus! Jesus fuck!"

He knelt down facing Falk, peering frantically at Bloom's face.

"What happened? Nes? What happened to you?" His voice was a strained whisper, desperate to make a noise, boxed in by terror. Falk hadn't seen Bigmouse act this way, and he knew Bloom hadn't, either. Stress was pumping Bigmouse towards a point of brittle disconnect.

Bigmouse reached up and grabbed Bloom's head, one rough hand either side of the jaw. Falk mewed and tried to resist, but Bigmouse twisted Bloom's skull, scrutinising it, trying to get it in the light.

"Oh shit, you're hit. You're hit, Bloom! Oh shit."

Falk tried to respond. Bigmouse wasn't letting go of his head. His thumbs were probing Bloom's cheek, under his right eye, causing pain to radiate back through his face.

"What happened?" Bigmouse asked. He wouldn't quit with the examination. "Shit, look at this! I got to get this patched! I've got to get you to field surgery!"

Falk made a sound.

"It's nasty, Bloom! It's right in under the eye! Listen, I'm going to get you out of this, okay? You okay? You wealthy? I'm going to get you out of this shit, okay? We're going to get out of this together and I'm going to get you to an extract and a medic. Okay? Okay, Nes?"

Falk managed another ugly sound and slapped Bigmouse's hands away.

"Stop touching me."

"It hurts, okay. I get that. I'm going to patch it."

"No."

"Fuck it, Nes! We're in shit here! Insurgents, Bloom! They've compromised the whole location! They were waiting for us! We walked right into it!"

"Who's left?" Falk asked. Each word was a husky effort. Bloom's tongue was too big for his palate.

"Fucked if I know! I don't know where Spierman went, or Cicero. They took off after Preben, Stabler and Martinz when the shooting started."

Spierman. Who the fuck was Spierman? The PO who'd debussed with Cicero?

"Is the boomer still on the ground?" Every word a struggle.

"Yeah. I dunno. I haven't been out front. The shooting, you know."

There would be aircrew on the Boreal. The medic Cicero was going to call in. Probably another fireteam too. Falk needed a medic.

"Stabler's dead," he said.

"What? Are you fucking kidding me?"

"No. Martinz too, I think. Someone else."

Bigmouse rocked back on his heels.

"Fuck!" he said. "Oh fuck! Are you sure?"

"I saw," Falk said. He let himself settle back on the cot a little, his shoulderblades sliding against the wall, dislodging some of the swimsuit clips of Shiona Kona. "They took our weapons. Ammo."

"Shit."

"I need to get out of here," Falk said.

"I know. I'm going to get you out, Nes."

"I feel really weird," Falk said.

"It'll be okay."

"Is there a link we can call on?" Falk asked.

Bigmouse shook his head.

"It's jammed. It's all jammed. Mil-secure is scorched."

"What about the weather station rig?"

"It's off."

"Can you turn it on again, Mouse?"

Bigmouse stared at him, shook his head.

"It's not secure. I light that up, they'll spot it like that."

He snapped his fingers. Falk could see how badly Bigmouse's hands were shaking.

"Stabler's really scorched?" Bigmouse asked.

"Yes."

"That's so fucked up," said Bigmouse. He was welling up behind his glares.

"We've got to do something," said Falk. He was getting sick of the effort it took to make Bloom's voice work, and sick of slurring like a stroke victim. His throat felt like it had been worked raw with steel wool. "I'm really messed up, Mouse. I need to get out of here."

"I know, Bloom."

"We can't wait. Maybe we should try the station rig?"

"No way."

"Least we should do is try to get a shout out. Operations may have no idea what's happening here."

"It's too fucking risky, Bloom!"

"We get a shout out, they can send people in. We could try the rig, send a shout, call in support and an extract."

"Fuck it, Bloom!"

Falk swallowed hard.

"Mouse, I need to get out of here. I need help. I don't feel right."

"You've been shot, Nes."

"I'm not feeling myself."

Bigmouse stared at him, then slipped off his glares and wiped his eyes on the sleeve of his fatigue top.

"I told you," he said. "If we send using the rig, they'll spot it."

"So we use it fast, get out a signal, then move. Move to another building. Off the site, maybe."

Bigmouse hesitated. There was an indefinite noise from somewhere nearby, maybe a door bang. Bigmouse's PDW came out of his holster in a fast-draw clatter of fasteners and safety toggle. He went from zero to aiming it at the door in about a third of a second.

They froze, waiting. The dinner-gong pulse in Bloom's temple ticked out the drag of time. After eternity and extra time, Bigmouse lowered the weapon.

"We can't stay here," he whispered.

"We can't stay here," Falk agreed. The snake in his belly was back. "They're all over this place. If we stay put, they'll find us. We need to send a shout, call in help and get clear."

Bigmouse got up, holstered his weapon and hoisted Falk to his feet, unceremoniously. He got an arm looped under Falk's armpit. Falk tried not to flinch. The sudden movement had flared pain in his head and his hip.

"I'm pretty messed up," he rasped. "I don't know how much use I can be."

"S'okay," said Bigmouse. "It's all wealthy. I'll walk you."

Now he had Bloom propped against him, Bigmouse drew his PDW again.

"I could take that," said Falk.

"Get real."

"You've got the thumper," said Falk. The chunky launcher was still locked to Bigmouse's backplate.

"That hit turn you into a fucking retard?" Bigmouse asked. Of course. A thumper indoors. Gigantic sense.

They shuffled to the door like two guys in a three-legged race. Bigmouse cracked the door, looked out into the hall, then led the way, shouldering Falk along. He had his Colt sweeping.

They arrived at the station hub. Bigmouse's eFight kit was still open on one of the desks where he'd left it, diagnostic leads wired up through a console panel he'd lifted off. Bigmouse settled Falk on a wheelie stool, braced against the side of one of the monitor stations, then went to retrieve his kit.

"Hurry," said Falk. His head was starting to swim again. Bigmouse disconnected his kit, closed the pack and carried it over to the radio rig. It wouldn't take long for him to discover if it had been de-powered or disabled.

The side door opened, and a man they'd never seen before walked in carrying a PAP 20.

EIGHTEEN

He was in his mid-twenties, with short brown hair and a lean face that looked like it was used to working outdoors. He was wearing dirty, dark-hued litex weatherproofs and heavy-soled boots. Raindrops beaded him like sequins. The PAP was SOMD-issue. At the start of the day, it had been somebody else's property.

Falk knew that, a gut instinct. He absorbed all the details instantly: the look of the man, his manner, his bearing, the fact his gun was stolen, the wet-cold air smell the man brought in with him, the moment of confusion sparked by finding two men in a room he had expected to be empty.

The PAP came up fast. The only thing that slowed the man down was the fact he had two targets, one on either side of the hub. There was a nanosecond of hesitation as he made a choice of which one to hit first.

He chose Falk. He chose wrong.

The Colt PDW was still in Bigmouse's hand, and Bigmouse was wired as tight as a hair-spring mantrap. He leapt up, sending his open eFight kit flying into the air, tools scattering, and unloaded. The burst bracketed the intruder. Two or three rounds smacked into the wall on either side of him. Three or four more went through him: sternum, shoulder, forehead, chin. The chin impact made the most mess going in. The lower part of the man's face buckled. He was already hammering backwards, slammed by the kinetic force, arms flying up, whiplash cracking his neck. His hair rippled. His eyes defocused and almost crossed, his face contorted. He hit the wall behind him, slid down it, rolled onto his side. The PAP bounced off his thighs and clonked onto the floor.

Gunsmoke wreathed the silence, threading the yellow sunwash coming down through the skylights.

"Holy shit," said Bigmouse, not even quite sure of what he'd just done. He rose to his feet, lowering the Colt.

Stunned, Falk moved awkwardly and the wheelie stool skidded out from under him. He crashed sideways off the console he was wedged against, and ended up on his back. The stool overturned, castors spinning. Landing smacked the wind out of him.

"Stay down!" Bigmouse ordered. Grunting and trying to rise, Falk heard Bigmouse cross the room to the man he'd just killed. Through the kneehole under the desk, he watched Bigmouse check the man, search his pockets and pick up the PAP. Bigmouse didn't want to touch him. Falk could see his reluctance, like the man was radioactive.

The gunshots had not gone unnoticed. Someone else came running in through the doors at the other end of the room. Falk heard a shout. Under the desk, he saw Bigmouse pulling himself down into cover. From the far end of the room, another PAP lit off. It made a noise like a food processor churning something wet. The room shook with the concussion of the impacts. There was a sudden blizzard of dust and micro-debris – splinters of wood, shreds of fibre, powdered brick – from the wall and furniture around Bigmouse. Loose papers billowed into the air like blurds. A coffee mug shattered. A pen pot cracked and spun, shedding pens.

Bigmouse was pinned. He had the PAP, but he was trapped in the little box of cover provided by the metal frame desks. The unseen gunman fired again, and console screens fragmented.

Under the desks, Bigmouse looked desperately at Falk. Falk was two desk rows away. The second intruder wouldn't have even seen him.

Still on his back, pathetic, stricken, Falk reached out his right hand, grasping at Bigmouse, gesturing to him. It took Bigmouse a second to notice and understand. He was balled up in fear as the shots ripped in around him.

He got hold of his Colt and gave it a hard shove, sending it gliding across the hub floor on its slide like a curling stone. It travelled under the desks and finally came to rest just short of Falk, stopped by a coil of power cable.

Falk rolled over. It took two tries to raise enough momentum to turn Bloom's body, and he knocked his chin on the floor tiles on the way over. He got his fingers around the muzzle of the gun, picked it up, pulled it back. He rolled back onto his side, and put the weapon down on the floor so he could pick it up again by the grip.

It felt right in his hand. Bloom's hand knew the grip. His thumb toggled the safety off.

With shuddering, superhuman effort, Falk got himself up on one knee under the line of the desk. He had to pull out a drawer to brace himself with his slack left hand. The LEAF locked. The snake in his belly convulsed. He used the barrel of the PDW to prop his other hand as he lifted.

Then he swung up over the desk and fired.

Every single shot missed. The kick of the PDW was so hefty, he almost dropped it. The barrel rose and skied most of the rounds. His left leg started to give out.

At the end of the room, a man holding a PAP 20 to his cheek turned in surprise, wincing from the crack and whizz of the sudden, wild shooting. He brought the PAP around.

Bigmouse's PAP 20 nailed him to the wall. The burst exploded him, painting the wall red, stippling it with chunks of meat and fragments of bone. As the human wreckage collapsed, it left a huge cloud of blood vapour drifting in the air behind it.

"Move! Move! Move! Move!" Bigmouse yelled, running around the desks to Falk. "Come on!"

There was a pervasive stink of innards that made them gag, a compost smell of meat and fat-shrouded organs exposed to the air, of burst stomach, of atomised flesh. Bigmouse had to put the PAP down to help Falk up.

"Gimme that," Bigmouse said, eyes on the PDW.

"No," said Falk, and holstered it.

Bigmouse was wired to the balls. The fear had lit him up, but there was glee too, the glee of a giant adrenalin hit.

"Score two," he said, his grin manic. "Fuck me, you see that pretard burst?"

Falk struggled to find the right words.

"In the Hard Place," he slurred. "Right in the zone, Mouse."

They managed a messy fist bump. Bigmouse began to move him towards the door, the front exit. Falk was doing quite a good job making Bloom's body shuffle that way on its own. Black hats were going to be converging on the hub space in seconds, drawn by the exchange of fire.

"I say front," said Bigmouse. "The yard. Maybe out and down the hill."

"Yeah," Falk replied. Pain was reaming his hip, and his legs were burning with lactic acid. He could cheerfully settle for simply being behind something large and solid. There were precast bunkers and silos around the station yard area, plus the windfarm just down the slope. They could duck down, get their breath back and their heads together.

They exited via the corridor he and Bigmouse had originally entered by. The hatch was ajar, letting daylight in. The breeze stirred the kids' drawings amongst the seaweed on the wall liner. Hanging coats loomed against the rectangle of daylight like loitering figures. Their footsteps on the metal grille made too much noise.

Bigmouse slipped ahead, PAP ready, checked the hatch, took a squint outside. Falk waited, leaning against the coats, panting hard.

"Come on," Bigmouse hissed.

They went outside, into the painful light. There was still rain in the air, and it was cold, but the sky was mustard-yellow and full of fat clouds that were crinkled like cauliflower or brain tissue. Falk gulped in the cold salt air in an effort to rid his nose and throat of the reek of particulated flesh.

Pika-don was still parked in the main yard, engines off, side slide open. They edged down the spongy line of the walkboards to the old metal gate.

Bigmouse beckoned him on. PAP ready, he led the way across the mud-lake of the yard towards the hopter. As they approached, Falk could tell there was no one aboard. That was wrong, in so many ways. Aircrew did not desert their mobile in the field unless there was no other option. They certainly wouldn't have abandoned it with the ports wide open.

He came up to the boomer alongside Bigmouse. The nearest engine pod was cool but not cold. Internal standby systems were still live. There was a scalene triangle of wet on the deck inside the open side door where the rain had blown in at an angle. It had evidently stood open for a while. Bigmouse pointed. There were a number of tiny but deep dents in the cabin's metal liner. Small-arms impacts, from something fired in through the door. Little squashed lumps littered the deck: caseless rounds that had virtually flattened out hitting the liner skin. There was blood too, several arterial sprays on the wall, and a pooling patch that had run between the deck slats.

Bigmouse glanced at Falk.

"Check the onboard comms," said Falk. Bigmouse nodded, and hoisted himself up through the hatch. Rain tapped against the boomer's port and laminates. Falk saw that the seat restraints in the pilot's position were tangled.

"Get a medpack too," he called out.

There was a pair of glares lying on the deck just inside the rim of the hatch. Falk had no doubt that they'd fallen off someone's face, not out of someone's pocket. He picked them up, and hooked them by one arm from the neck of his vest. Then he sat down gingerly on the step plate of the hatch to rest his hip.

"Radio's out," Bigmouse called. "Jammed."

"Totally?"

"I'm looking."

"Mouse?"

"Uh-huh?"

"Bigmouse?"

"Yeah?"

Bigmouse clambered out of the cab front and came to the hatch. Two men had come out of the weather station via the main hatch. A third followed them.

"Shit, shit, shit!" said Bigmouse as soon as he saw them.

None of the men were wearing SOMD kit. They were all armed. One of the men, Falk realised, was a woman. The girl. The girl who'd fallen into the inspection pit.

The girl who had shot him.

She opened fire from the walkboards with the PAP she was carrying. There was a little crackle of muzzle flicker, most of the sound stolen by the open hilltop. Rounds spanked off the hull beside them and flumed up angry splashes from the mud around the landing feet. Several shots chipped the forward screen, leaving little cracked stars in the ultra-dense polyglass.

Falk got down behind the side of the hull. Shots sliced the surface of the mud around him. There was a pair of unexpectedly loud bangs as rounds bounced off the engine cowling beside his head.

"Bag of suck," remarked Bigmouse. He had jumped down and snuggled in beside the boomer's fat, armoured nosetip. He lined up and began blasting back.

The three figures scattered. Falk saw Bigmouse's shots peppering the gate, the walkboards, the mud and the fence around the vegetable plot. Dirty water squirted up, and filaments of walkboarding fluttered like chaff. Parts of the fence broke. The blade-head of a toy windmill went spinning into the air.

Falk checked Bigmouse's Colt. The LED at the top of the grip told him he had eighteen rounds left in the clip. Bigmouse carried the spares. Neither of them had reloads for the PAP Bigmouse was hosing away with. It took the same 2mil round as the PDW, so they could strip out ammo from the PDW spares and refill the PAP's two-hundred-capacity box mag by hand, but that would take time to do right.

"Slow down!" Falk warned. Bigmouse was shooting at nothing. The black hats had found cover around the yellow demountables or the vegetable plot side of the station front.

Bigmouse stopped firing. The fast-approaching limit of the PAP 20's supply had just occurred to him too.

The insurgents rallied. They began to return fire. The two guys had M3A pipers. Falk suddenly heard that unearthly un-noise whine again, the shrill, edge-of-hearing bark of the hardbeam. He was on the receiving end. Little, local blinks of light occurred near the demountables.

Pika-don shook hard like she'd been rammed repeatedly by a truck. One of the hardbeam shots went by the nosecone, too fast and bright to be seen, but it left a searing idiot afterimage across his retinas. Then another one punched through the boomer's hull beside him. It had come clean through the hull, across the cabin space, and out the other side. It left a fused, super-heated hole the size of a large-denomination coin. The edges glowed. There was no light, no flash, no visible raygun beam like in the sit-ops, just a smeared blur of heat haze, like petroleum jelly on glass.

A second later, it happened again. Another bodyblow to the hopter, another through-and-through superhot hole. Falk remembered the fucktard from thInc, Jeanot, blah-blahing on about the boombird's hull armour during the ride to Mitre Sands. Dermetic-weave six-ply fuselage sheathing, a laminate construct designed to survive hardbeam damage through a combination of ablation, dissipation and cushioning. There were layers of reflective bead silicates between the armour skins, alternating with energy-soaking graphene membranes. It was pretty good at stopping the output of a man-portable pipe weapon. It certainly had a good chance of stopping a guy with an M3A from knocking a moving Boreal out of the sky.

But they were on the ground, a static target, and the M3As were firing at them from less than twenty yards away.

A shot went through the front canopy, gouging a huge molten tear out of the curved and tinted polyglass. The tint contained a polarising anti-laser treatment, but it was useless at close range. The glass bubbled and glistened like honey. Bigmouse swore and ducked down tighter.

There was a loud bang from underneath the hopter, and another smear of heat haze light. A pipe beam had struck and destroyed the forward pilot's side gear. There was a sharp smell of burning metal and oil. Debris blew out and the hopter gently sagged to one side, nose dipping, as the landing gear assembly collapsed.

"Bigmouse! Bigmouse!" Falk yelled.

Bigmouse dropped the PAP into the mud and unslung the thumper from his backplate clamps. It was fat, black, unlovely, a 1090 MSGL Rand Dynamik grenade launcher with an eight-shooter drum. He cancelled the airburst ranging, selected strike detonation and pumped two shells at the demountables. The thumper thumped, a solid, dead noise like a carpet beater. The chunk shells smacked into the side of the nearest demountable and blew the side off in a sheet of flame and a spray of whizzing tiles and weatherboard fragments.

Bigmouse tilted and put a third grenade into the vegetable plot. He glanced at Falk.

"Move your ass," he said. He paused to recover the PAP and they began to move away from the station as fast as Falk could go, heading across the yard, towards the slope of the hill, keeping the stricken hopter between them and the station buildings.

After a few seconds they heard the un-noise barking of hardbeams again, but there was no sign of impacts. Mud sloshed up over their boots.

"Head for those refabs," Falk gasped. He was panting hard. Bigmouse had him by the arm, frogmarching him down the incline towards an overgrown fence and a group of battered crate-and-creates behind the *whup-whup-whupping* windfarm.

They could hear shouting from behind them. The voices weren't speaking English.

"Bag of suck," Bigmouse repeated. He was struggling with Falk and the weight of the weapons.

Preben stood up behind the overgrown fence ahead of them. He rose like a pop-up target on the range. He had his M3A against his cheek, aimed up the slope.

"Get the fuck down," he said.

NINETEEN

Preben began firing. Close up, the piper made a noise like
a seal expressing outrage at being clubbed to death. Each
shot offended Falk's nervous system, jangled his bones and
aggravated the snake in his belly.

They got past him, around the fence and bushes, and
onto a paved pan beside the refabs. Large slabs of precast
walling concrete had been dropped flat and butted together
to make a solid apron for vehicles. There were plastic sacks
of fertiliser and carbon chips stacked along the refab wall,
tops tied up against the thieving wind. Springy saltgrass
weeds and tangled ash-heads nodded and swayed in the
steady ocean breeze. Now they had dropped down the slope
a little way, the acoustics of the windfarm had changed. The
chopping rhythm had deepened and developed an echo. It
simply added to Falk's confused discomfort.

Preben backed slowly away from his initial position
beside the fence. He squeezed off another couple of shots,
spitting heat-haze streaks up the hill towards the yard.

"We're so screwed," he said. "The fucktards are all over
this place."

"Insurgents?" asked Bigmouse. "Insurgents, right?"

"What does that even mean?" asked Preben. He shot them a meaningful look.

"Some fuck spent five minutes drilling at me down the farm just now," he said. "Swear to Christ he was using a Koba."

Koba Avtomat 90. Standard Central Bloc hard-round troop weapon.

"Fuck happened to you?" Preben added, looking at Falk.

"Bloom got hit," said Bigmouse. "We need an exit strategy here, and a medic."

"No shit," said Preben. "This whole op is a cluster. There's nothing friendly and organised in this zone. Just poor motherfuckers like us, loose and lost."

The top corner of the refab beside them exploded. There was a flash, and the painful bang of mass energy transfer. The exploded stub was left smoking and black, and secondary beam-heat ignition lit flames along the roofing felt and the weed-choked guttering.

It scared the shit out of all three of them. Bigmouse started swearing and dragging Falk towards the cover of the refab row. Preben turned back and began firing again, his piper barking and wailing.

"We're never going to get off this hill," said Bigmouse.

"Not at this rate," Falk agreed. "What about that?"

On the other side of the refabs was another little concrete pan slipway. There were two weather-battered vehicles sitting on it, side by side. They were both variations of the same basic model, one of the Smartkart family of civilian utility vehicles. Falk couldn't remember the exact name. *Porta*? *Mule*? Basic workhorse trucks with cabs and flatbed trays. One was undercoat-grey and the other was lime green with a white wing, offside front.

Bigmouse tried the doors on both. Both were locked. He took out the driver's side pane of the lime-green one with the butt of his PAP and reached in to pop the door.

"Get in!" he called to Falk. He was already at work behind the wheel, breaking the bottom off the dash. He'd left his eFight kit scattered across the floor of the hub, but he still had some pocket tools and a couple of power sticks. The Smartkarts were duel fuel, an electric standby supporting an omnivorous fusion plant. Bigmouse was attempting to light up the basic electrics and get it rolling.

Falk walked around and got in the passenger side once Bigmouse flipped the lock. He was feeling extremely woozy from the exertion, and the state of palsy is his left side was back, worse than ever. He felt as though the left half of his face was slackening, like melting wax. His foot was dragging on the ground, his arm bent inside the LEAF like the wing of an injured bird. It took effort just to get up on the bench seat.

"Come on, come on," Bigmouse said, talking to the starter.

Two shots came by, very, very close. Clumps of earth spattered into the air and pattered off the bodywork. Vegetation caught fire, like dry grass under a magnifying glass.

"Shit!" said Bigmouse.

They could hear Preben shouting. He came running down onto the slipway behind them, yelling his head off.

Bigmouse got the dash lights to come on. There was a low whine. Suddenly, loud music detonated in the door speakers, filling the cab. Fast, upbeat bubblegum, Shiona Kona's latest masterpiece.

Ignoring the blaring music, Bigmouse slammed the driver's side door and undid the brake.

The undercoat-grey Smartkart beside them took a direct hit. The impact made a deafening bang. The hardbeam cored it, explosively shredding and crumpling its chassis and bodywork. All the windows blew out. Flames gouted out from under the hood as the engine block lit.

Bigmouse swore. Preben leapt into the tray of the lime-green truck and pounded on the rear screen for them to move.

Another shot went by. They started rolling, gathering speed as they drove off the slipway and reached the slope of the track, accompanied the whole way by a pounding poplite soundtrack. They left the other Smartkart behind them, burning and slumped. Filthy black smoke was streaming off it into the sky.

Bigmouse didn't seem to know where they were going. They were gaining more speed, and bouncing and lurching down the track slope. The rough motion had thrown Preben off his feet and he was clinging on to the tie-loops in the tray. Bigmouse was wrestling with the wheel. The cheerful, irre-pressible music rendered the whole experience surreal.

Falk looked at Bigmouse. He realised that Bigmouse had bypassed the key mechanism to trick-start the electrics, but that the steering lock was still on. Bigmouse couldn't turn the wheel. They were accelerating down the hill on a steep winding track, and they couldn't steer. And fucking Shiona Kona was shrilling about how fine her boyf was.

Bigmouse started to stomp the brake, but that simply made the kart slip out on the wet mud, wheels biting and spinning.

"Watch it–" Falk began.

They hit a gatepost, the endstop of a four-bar metal fence. The collision took out the nearside front and ripped away part of the wheel arch. The force of the shunt caused the back end of the truck to swing wide, and threw Falk and Bigmouse forward.

The fusion drive fired. The gathering speed had finally tripped it into life. It rattled and roared like an industrial pump or some kind of poorly maintained production line machine. The kart shook and bucked. Grey, greasy smoke farted from the exhaust.

Once the fusion plant kicked in, the wheel lock self-cancelled. Bigmouse yelled in glee.

They sped away down the track, trailing music behind them.

Most of the Eyeburn Hill township was scattered around the skirts of the hill. Past the windfarm, the track became more significant, and ran down past irrigated field systems towards a hamlet of barns and houses. Once they were well beyond the windfarm, Bigmouse slowed down a little, and got an opportunity to find the button to silence Shiona Kona's warbling.

They drove into the hamlet. A United Status flag was flying from a mast attached to the front of the main barn like a bowsprit. There was no sign of anyone around. Blinds were closed in the windows of the houses. They pulled up between a long, low, pungent clapboard building that served as a hatchery and coop, and a narrow shed that housed a processor machine for converting vegetable matter and, Falk was sure, blurds into animal feed blocks.

Bigmouse and Preben dismounted to check the locale. Falk got out and waited by the kart. He expected to die very soon. There was something wrong with the sight in his right eye, and his motor control was worse than ever. He felt cold. He was going to die, or he was going to wake up being dragged out of that fucking Jung tank.

He walked around the utility vehicle several times to get his legs working. It was old, and had been refitted several times. Along the chassis line, below the bodywork, there were traces of the old tariff stamps. The vehicle, or at least its mechanical basics, had been imported to Eighty-Six. That suggested it'd been in use before there were any local manufacturing plants. Either that, or it had seen service on other settlement worlds. Some settlementeers were superstitious like that. If they or their dependants or successors moved on to a new site world, they often brought along vehicles or machinery that had served them well: a kart that had never broken down, an uplink that had weathered storms, an autoplough that had helped feed a generation or two of the same family. It was partly the frugal mindset, partly the need for tools a man could trust.

A large blue-green blurd, as big as his hand, droned down and circled him and the kart twice, a slow, lazy circuit. Then it lifted away into the sky, its body flashing like glass.

Falk started to cry. It wasn't lost-little-boy crying, the kind you might do standing beside a ProFood counter under the warm smile of Bill Berry. It was broken heart crying, the deep, seismic sobbing of the bereft. It was grief, and he couldn't control it. He couldn't choke it off and shut it down.

He couldn't, because it wasn't his. Falk was hurt, scared, upset and extremely vulnerable, and he probably could have cried well enough if he had the mind to. Falk's mindset was simply providing the right conditions for Bloom's misery. It all belonged to Nestor Bloom. It was all about mistakes and stupid choices, and a shocking realisation that he'd fucked up. He'd failed on most of the basic professional levels expected of him. He'd fundamentally compromised his performance as an SOMD soldier.

More than anything else, it was about a girl called Karin Stabler. Falk was weeping uncontrollably over a woman he'd never known. He was expressing Bloom's grief for him.

When it was done, when the grief jag passed away like a rainstorm moved on by the wind, he felt oddly better. He

felt more together than at any point since waking up in the
walkthrough under the smile.

Preben and Bigmouse emerged from the buildings. He
looked at them, and for a second the vice of grief threatened
to tighten again. The deep currents of Nestor Bloom's
subconscious stirred memories that didn't belong to Lex
Falk. Here were two men he'd only half-known for less
than a day, but Bloom had known for years. There was a
brief firecracker flurry of sparking memories, synapses
lighting and firing, glimpses of other moments, other jokes,
other operations, other nights on the town. Inexplicable
kinship, like deja vu over something that had never
happened in the first place, or nostalgia for a life unlived.

Falk shook it off.

"You okay?" Bigmouse asked.

"I'm wealthy," he said. "What did you find?"

TWENTY

Like the hilltop weather station, the hamlet was abandoned. Preben and Bigmouse hadn't done a thorough house-to-house, but the sample buildings they'd checked had all shown signs of being vacated abruptly. Lights left on, doors and shutters unbolted, systems running, beverages cold and half-drunk, a sandwich on a kitchen block, made but not eaten.

The hamlet was called Eyeburn Slope. Falk learned this from a noticeboard in the hallway of the meeting house. *Eyeburn Slope Residents Associations* it read, in the official blocky typeface of the Settlement Office, and underneath were lists of sub-committees, of yard-cleaning rotas, of church meetings, of classes for pickle and preserve making, of the harvest festival. Eyeburn Slope was a ward of the greater Eyeburn Hill parish. Eyeburn Junction, a slightly larger township, lay on the highway, about six miles east. That was where the fuelling depot was situated. They could see the dark shape of it rising above the field systems of the hortiplex. It was one of the vital way stations on Gunbelt Highway.

The rear part of the meeting house was a community hall, which doubled as an assembly room and a gymnasium. There were beeball court lines painted on the polished fibreplak floor, and two fold-out hoops, high up, one above the entry doors, the other above a small table that probably also served as an altar during services. From the kids' pictures on the wall, the hall was probably a school room. On side tables and shelves, half-woven garlands and papier mache tractors showed the work in progress for the harvest festival decorations. On a brown fibre plaque beside the doors, the names and dates of office of the community leaders had been recorded in gold. There was a column and a half of names on a space marked out to hold eight full columns. Far more future than past. That was the optimistic way of looking at it, anyway.

The front part of the meeting house was a collection of offices. A clerk's office, a production management office, and a pair of rooms for land registry and realty. According to another notice, this one laminated, a Settlement Office registrar visited every other month to process and review parcel claims and purchases. The room had boxes of mining contracts, metal cabinets full of large-format territorial maps, a satlink projector and lightboxes. A quick look at the core files showed how land claims and registrations were spreading out like a mosaic from the trunk of the highway. Large areas to the north had been reserved for the bulk mining developments around Antrim, Furlow Pits and, to the east, Marblehead.

Until the previous week, Marblehead had marked the limit of paramilitary encroachment into the US-held Northern Territories. Whatever had happened in Eyeburn Junction, and it wasn't completely clear to Falk what that was, it entirely revised the tactical map. The paramilitaries

– insurgents, Bloc-backed landgrabbers, home-rule inde-
pendents, whatever they were – had brought the fight into
the farming hinterlands of the Shaverton region, right into
US land. And it wasn't simply a response to the new SO
offensive, either. The insurgents had been on the ground,
in Eyeburn, waiting for them.

The cause and effect bothered Falk. The insurgent forces
had clearly taken, or at least entered, Eyeburn in a low-key
fashion. There was no sign of full-on assault. It had been
an inside job, that's how it felt to Falk. Neighbours had
turned on neighbours. Townsfolk had suddenly revealed
insurgent sympathies. Resisters had been executed and left
in out-of-the-way dumpsites. It seemed likely to Falk that
the same story had played out in junction towns and farm
hamlets right down Gunbelt Highway.

But this morning's SO offensive had been fast-tracked
because of the Letts bombing. If you were stealthily taking
farmsteads up and down the farm belt, why would you
provoke a major military reaction by bombing the territorial capital?

How many other incidents like the Letts bombing had
gone unnoticed?

"They were using Kobas?" he asked Preben. There was still
an unhealthy slur in his unfamiliar voice that he didn't like.

"What?" asked Preben.

"This morning."

Preben shrugged. He was boiling water in the kitchenette
off the registry rooms while Bigmouse looked for food.

"Yeah, Kobas."

"So, Bloc, then? They were Bloc?"

"It'd be fucking crazy if they were," said Preben. "The Bloc
so doesn't want to get into one with the US, or the SO. What
the fuck could be worth this kind of pain?"

"Fred?" Falk suggested.

"The moon? You've been listening to those mineral access conspiracy theories, Bloom?"

"What's your theory then, Preben?"

Preben shrugged. His boyish looks and smooth skin mismatched uncomfortably with his very adult muscular frame.

"The Koba Avtomat 90 is a cheap, hardwearing weapon," he replied. "Sort of thing you could buy in decent numbers through third parties alongside agriculture machinery. If you were isolationists who rejected SO values."

Bigmouse appeared with a medikit he'd found in the management office, but Falk refused to let him touch him. He went into the bathroom, locked the door and peered at himself in the little mirror beside the hand drier. Bloom's face was pale and dirty, and rinsing it by hand in the basin didn't help much. There was a little black hole under his eye, like a drill hole. His cheek and eye socket were bruising mauve and violet, with an odd patch of yellow around the cheekbone.

"I want to go home now," he said to the mirror. "Cleesh, why aren't you bringing me home? Get me out of the tank. Tell someone what's happening here. The SO needs to know they are losing people left and right. Tell Apfel, tell him he needs to take this to the SO and get them fully appraised."

"You all right in there?" Bigmouse called through the door.

"Yeah, yeah," Falk replied. He flushed and came back out.

"You look steadier," said Bigmouse. "Walking steadier."

"Yeah, I feel a bit more together."

"You should let me patch that."

"I know, but I don't want to play around with it. I just want to get out. Get out of here and get to SO medical. It feels like it's stable, and I don't want to aggravate it."

"Okay," said Bigmouse.

"We all need to get out of here," said Falk. "We need to get a signal out."

"Agreed," said Preben, appearing in the doorway. "So we'll eat, then we'll–"

"Talk like you're in charge there, Preben," said Falk.

"I am."

"Allow us to follow the logic of that," said Falk.

"You're hit, hurt. We don't know how much you're impaired. I'm next in line."

"I'm fine," said Falk, "so that's settled."

"It's not–"

"I call the shots in Kilo One," said Falk.

"There is no Kilo One," said Preben. "Just three fucking idiots left out on their own."

"There's a Kilo One all the while we're here in the Hard Place, you dumb fuck," said Falk. "Get used to the idea."

Preben glared at him and then left the room. Falk glanced at Bigmouse.

"Fuck happened to your ling patch?" Bigmouse asked.

He was feeling better, but he was still hobbling like a stroke victim. There was a sense, that Falk was perfectly prepared to accept, that it was his imagination, that he and Bloom weren't fighting for control so much. Maybe Nestor Bloom had relaxed his grip. He hadn't died, because his emotions and memories kept surfacing, but his grip had slackened. Bloom was like a full-body LEAF, a metal brace locking out and limiting motion. Whatever, something had disabled his ling patch along the way.

His hip was still as sore as hell, and Falk was pretty sure it was his hip, and not Bloom's.

There was a trace of a voice in his head. A voice, or maybe

voices. When he'd first woken up, he'd heard them, and attributed them to the default repeat of the earbuds.

But it wasn't that. Some memory, or function of the imagination, or damaged inner ear, was making him hear voices. Nothing tangible, just a muffled echo, like a recording of speech played backwards so that each alien mutter came to an abrupt, unnatural stop. He had to concentrate to clear his head of the noises, and then they'd drift in out of the silence again when his attention switched elsewhere.

Falk wasn't keen to speculate precisely whose memory, imagination or inner ear was responsible. He limped around the buildings, distracted by everyday objects that reminded somebody other than him of something else. A water jug, a hairbrush, a dresser drawer that opened to release the trapped scent of an empty perfume bottle.

He heard someone calling Bloom's name.

It was Bigmouse. Falk hobbled outside into what was fast becoming a damp, stone-grey evening. Level sensors around the hamlet complex had already brought some lights on automatically, and the generator hum was audible over the fresh wind and the spatter of rain falling on the plastic slope of the walkway roofing. Preben joined them from the other direction.

"I found a radio rig," said Preben, "but I can't raise anyone."

"Forget that," said Bigmouse. "Listen."

They listened.

"I don't hear anything," said Preben.

Falk did. He heard the voices, like a backmasked audio track. He didn't say anything.

"There," said Bigmouse, raising a hand.

Very faint, in the distance. Over aways, in the broad belt of field systems between the hamlet and the fuelling depot. The low-lying area was little more than a dark blue shadow in the failing light.

"You hear that?" asked Bigmouse quietly.

Gunfire, a faraway rattle.

Bigmouse and Preben both trained their glares. Falk thought he saw tiny yellow and white sparks dancing out in the murk of the fields. He remembered the glares he had retrieved from the boomer. He pulled them off the shirt neck and put them on, his hands cumbersome and fat-fingered. It took a moment for the glares to react to body heat and wake, and another few seconds for him to blink away the clutter left behind by the previous user. It was difficult. Difficult because of the state he was in, difficult because he was used to the simple functions of civilian-model glares, not the complex options of Mil-grade sets. Bloom had known how to manage it. There was so much eye junk: stored files, snaps, target playbacks.

He cleared it at last and keyed in the low-light enhancer and zoom.

There was a firefight ripping through the field system. He could peg hard-round bursts and pipe fire. It was hard to resolve clear contacts, but the SOMD viewer protocols were flagging the aura codes of friendlies.

"They're taking some," said Preben. "Being pushed this way."

"We have to get down there," said Bigmouse.

"Why?" asked Falk. They turned to look at him.

"Are you fucking serious?" asked Preben.

"What good would we do?"

"We could come in across the top there," said Preben, pointing. "Give them some cover fire. Let them know that the compound is clean and, let's face it, more defendable than a fucking field."

Falk swallowed.

"Fuck's the matter with you, Bloom?" asked Preben.

"This is the Hard Place," said Bigmouse.

"Yeah, the Hard Place," Preben agreed. "This is why we're here, this shit. And pardon me, but aren't you supposed to be Mr In Charge? Aren't you supposed to know what the fuck we're supposed to be about?"

"I didn't mean it like that," said Falk.

"Really?" Preben replied. "I didn't mean fuck you like that, but fuck you, Bloom." He looked at Bigmouse. "Let's go."

Bigmouse hesitated, his eyes on Falk.

"Yeah," said Falk, nodding. "Yeah, let's go."

They came out of the covered walkway into the yard and the rain. The gunfire was louder now. Hip burning, legs stiff, Falk waddled behind the others, trying to keep up. Preben was prepping his M3A. Bigmouse had unslung the thumper. Falk remembered the PDW in his holster.

"I need spares," he said. "I need spares. I'm almost out."

Preben ignored him. Bigmouse reached into a thigh pouch and produced two stripmags.

They approached the edge of the hamlet compound and followed an embankment that formed the north-western end of the vast hortiplex zone. There were walkboard lanes and accessways laid across the mud, and Falk saw some pipework sections of the giant irrigation grid that overlaid the field system and watered its channels and beds in the hot season. Some field lots were dense and in need of clearing. Others were bare and fallow, or caged with growing frames. Towards the central part of the acreage there were long rows of polytunnels and crop shelters, along with a cluster of refab storage huts. Bursts of gunfire were backlighting the crop rows and growing frames half a mile away.

"That's a Koba," said Preben, listening. "That's a damn Koba on auto."

"What do we do?" asked Bigmouse. He kept pursing his lips to blot the nervous sweat collecting on his philtrum, a stress habit.

"Come in around the top here, lay down some interference," said Preben. He started down the short flight of refab steps from the embankment onto the walkboards.

"Wait," said Falk, "wait."

"What?" Preben looked back up at him.

"We'll be coming up on the back of them," Falk began. "On the back of our own, I mean. They're falling back, on the run. How will they..."

"What?"

"How will they know we're with them? Bumping into them out of nowhere, out there... that's just asking to be shot at."

"We don't have a fucking choice," said Preben. "No secure, remember? With any luck, they'll tag our AC profiles before they scorch us." He turned and kept going.

Bigmouse lingered for a second, favoured Falk with a last glance, then thumped down the steps after Preben.

Falk took off his glares and studied them, turning them over in his trembling, unsubtle hands.

"Hey, hey," he called.

"Fucking come on, you pretard!" Preben growled back. "Come on, or stay the fuck here and shut up."

"The glares, our glares," Falk said, looking at them both. "To pick up profiles, they must have their own carrier fields. A separate field?"

"Fuck are you on about?" asked Preben.

"They're passive receivers, unless they're linked through a celf or Mil-secure," said Bigmouse. There was a look on his face that told Falk he was supposed to know that. Bloom was qualified on all equipment uses. He was being dumb.

"Cut me some slack, here," said Falk. "They shot me in the fucking head, okay? It's hard to concentrate."

"This is wasting time!" snapped Preben.

"Just help me with this," said Falk. "The black hats have jammed Mil-secure, but our glares are still reading aura code profiles, yeah? How? Remind me how."

"From our IDs," said Bigmouse. The brooches, the ID brooches they all wore. They generated the profile fields. Short range, ultra short range, independent. Passive recognition effect, separate from Mil-secure comms. Falk slipped the glares back on, blink-found the target sampler option. He got an immediate informatic view, and saw Preben and Bigmouse lit up with green flags. He ret-selected Bigmouse, which opened a data pane. It read *Mauskin, Private First Class Waylon Wakes, S.O.M.D.* A further sub pane folded out to display vital stats, blood type, medical notations.

Passive, short-range carrier field, generated by each brooch, read by the target sampler system.

"You stupid fuck," said Preben. "Stay here and keep your head down."

He swung around and walked away, picking up speed, Bigmouse shook his head, and followed.

On Seventy-Seven, Falk had covered a massive financial scandal involving Artine Pacific, four capital investment banks and two rising-star senators. During the bloody legal debacle of the inquiry and trial, Artine Pacific's lawyers had tried to control the news flow, delaying certain aspects of the story to allow their clients time to disengage and minimise the financial hit they would take when the markets found out. They tried gag orders first, then injunctions invoking corporate confidentiality issues. Finally, in desperation, they went hardball, and scorched all the celf and newsfeeds coming out of the state house using a system jammer, just to buy about ninety minutes of lead time to shed their liabilities.

Cleesh had seen that dirty pool coming. She said she'd anticipated it because it was exactly the kind of fucktard play she'd have tried. This was back when she still cursed, before the ling patch. No one, Falk included, could transmit out of the state house, but she'd made sure Falk had gone in with a jot pad and a stylus, the sort of passive field tool a waitress at a ProFood would use to write down a customer order so the till and the kitchen could read it. Then Cleesh had hired a bike courier to sit outside the state house gate with an ordinary, off-the-shelf base unit. Falk didn't broadcast anything. He wrote all the details down on the jot pad, and the courier at the gate read everything, copied it and, because he was outside the jamming cone, squirted it to Cleesh in her can. She broke the story forty-seven minutes before any other news source. Artine Pacific took a headshot on the market.

Falk blink-accessed his brooch, opened the priority medical awareness pane and used his celf to type in an update.

Then he descended the steps as rapidly as he could, Bigmouse and Preben about to disappear from sight along the walkboarded path. Hand shaking, he fired a single shot from his PDW into the decking.

Preben and Bigmouse jumped at the report. They both whirled around, weapons coming up, targeting him, locking up.

Then they both lowered their aim and relaxed.

"What the fuck?" said Preben. "What the fuck? How did you do that?"

"That's a fucking piece of genius," said Bigmouse.

He could only imagine what they could see, but his imagination was well informed.

Their target samplers had shown them Nestor Bloom, green-flagged as a friendly by his aura code. Across his body, like a virtual sandwich board, was an informatic pane, the priority medical awareness updater.

It read *Can you read this, you fuckhats?*

Preben and Bigmouse both raised their weapons again to relight the sampling flag, just so they could enjoy it a second time. They jogged back to him.

"How the fuck did you do that?" asked Preben.

Falk explained how.

"No, I mean how the fuck did you think of doing that?" asked Preben.

"It just came to me," Falk said.

Bigmouse had already tried it. When they pointed their weapons in his direction, they saw a pane that read *Fucking genius idea.*

"What do we write?" asked Bigmouse.

Falk shrugged.

"Kilo One friendly, in support to your rear?" he suggested. "It'll do for a start."

Preben's face dropped.

"Ah, I knew it was too clever," he sighed. "It's not secure."

"Doesn't matter," Falk replied. "It's only short range. Plus, they think we're jammed. They won't be looking for it."

"Yeah, but they can read it. If they see it, they can read it."

"If they see it," Falk agreed. "They like our weapons. They like our ammo too. But so far, I haven't seen any sign they've been lifting glares."

"They're old school," said Bigmouse. "Or untrained. The target sampler can be really confusing if you're not used to it. They're probably not bothering."

They adjusted their medic alerts and exchanged fist bumps. Then they moved off together.

The gunfire was getting closer. A wild pipe shot hissed through the crop rows and blew open the side of a galvanised reservoir full of rainwater. There was a shocked gasp of explosive steam, and a glugging rush as the tank emptied. The foliage the beam had cut through started to burn. Off to their right, hard rounds were hitting something solid.

Probably a wall, Falk decided.

TWENTY-ONE

It was getting scary. He was just playing at being a soldier. Then there was the matter of his hopeless coordination.

The cooking popcorn sounds of gunshots rippled through crop rows. There was a drifting sheen of smoke in the wet air, the distinctive burn smell of propellant. The target sampler kept throwing up yellow and orange flags.

Ten feet ahead of Falk, Preben suddenly turned to the right, cheeked his M3A and fired. A squeal and a blink of light.

Preben lowered his weapon slightly.

"Red flag," he said softly. "I believe I just scorched a sunbitch."

"More!" Bigmouse announced, and ran forward into the planting beds, ducking under training wires and rigged loops of irrigation pipe. He was squaring up to red-flag movement. Falk raised his PDW, a two-handed grip. Playing at being a fucking soldier, just playing.

Bigmouse adjusted for airburst, and sailed a pair of grenade rounds up over the crops. There were two big flashes followed by meaty, gritty bangs. Plants shook as if a wind had whipped through them.

Bigmouse jerked his head for them to follow. They left the walkboard, and pushed through the bed rows, ankle-deep in black loam, stooping to avoid the sprayer hoses. There was a strong smell of earth, of liquid fertiliser, of wet metal pipes. Overhead, Falk could see the low, grey evening sky through cages of irrigation gridwork and lighting frames.

They came out, crossed another walkboard aisle, then dropped back into the crop thicket again. Somewhere to the left of them, an assault weapon was clattering like a sewing machine.

Out onto another walkboard path. On the far side, the crop row was tented under a large polytunnel. There was no obvious entry point, so Preben drew his utility knife, and sliced through the side of the sheeting. They slid through the cut, into a warm, moist cave filled with the peaty smell of germination. Pre-packed sacks of fertilised soil mix were stacked up, ready for use. They were marked with the GEO logo. Preben cut a slit out through the far side of the polytunnel, and they emerged onto another run of duckboards.

There was a corpse on the path. It was lying on its back a few feet down from their slit exit. The man had his legs bent and spread, as though he was running. He was wearing dark clothes, no uniform. His head was tilted right back, as if he was offering his throat for ritual cutting.

The greater part of his torso was a mangled hole. The loss of tissue and bone, of general matter, was astonishing. It looked like something white-hot, the size of a beeball, had punched clean through him. The edges of the wound were shredded and mangled, fused into a smoking crust of burned blood and blackened flesh. Thick fluid, viscous as tar or expensive balsamic vinegar, drooled out of the astonishing yawn of the cavity, and there was a speckled haze of it across the decking behind him. That's what a hardbeam piper did to human anatomy.

"Fuck," murmured Preben, staring down, genuinely thunderstruck by the sight of his handiwork.

"Nice grouping," said Falk.

"Fuck me," Preben murmured. He'd fired live before, he'd done it up at the hilltop station, but Falk knew Bloom knew it was the first time Preben had been presented with proof of a killshot.

The smell was appalling. Faeces and toffee, cremated bone, melted meat, the inside-out body stench that no one who smelled it ever forgot.

"Sucks to be him," said Bigmouse.

Falk got red and green across his glares suddenly. He looked up, past Preben and Bigmouse, both still too startled by the actuality of the dead man to be aware of anything else. Three figures had appeared at the far end of the aisle. Three bright red flags.

Falk started firing, firing his Colt between Preben and Bigmouse, who both jerked back in dismay. The shots were wild. It was more to make a noise than anything. The red flags scattered. Preben turned himself around, and cut off with the M3A. The piper screamed in the direction of the end of the row.

The Colt PDW suddenly seized up in Falk's hand. He gazed at it for a second. The slide was clamped back and smoke was curling from the action. The *ammo out* LED was lit. Falk realised he didn't know what to do with it. He had asked for spare stripmags, but he'd never reloaded a weapon in his life.

Bigmouse shoulder-barged him. It was a full-on body-check, Bigmouse slamming into Falk, knocking him backwards. It hurt. It winded him. The force of the collision made him lose his footing, and he fell over against the wall of the polytunnel. The rain-beaded plastic was springy like a trampoline skin. He didn't tear through it, he bellied off it, and wound up on his side in the mud between the duckboards and the base of the tunnel.

For a very short time, he was stunned, unable to assess what had happened. The first coherent thing that occurred to him was that Bigmouse had tackled him and brought him over in some grandstanding stunt to save his life. But Bigmouse had fallen over too. Bigmouse was on his arse on the decking. He was groaning, whimpering like a beaten dog.

Falk registered a rapid *thup-thup-thup!* sound coming from above him. Automatic hard rounds were punching a diagonal line of holes through the polytunnel skin, creating puckered dimples in the plastic, each whorl stretching under the plastic's tension to form an indentation like a navel in the firm curve of stomach. Bigmouse had been hit by hard rounds. They'd struck him in the torso armour, clubbed him down, smashing him into Falk in the process. Falk couldn't see any blood, but he could see dents in Bigmouse's chest blate that looked like they had been punched with a hammer and an awl.

Preben was trying to drag Bigmouse into cover. He was fighting to manage the unwieldy bulk of the M3A with his right hand while attempting to grab the straps of Bigmouse's blate rig with his left. Preben was yelling. Bigmouse was yelling. Hard rounds slapped into the polytunnel sheeting, into the mud, into the walkboards, lifting little geysers of droplets and shredded fibreplak. One shot chipped off Preben's thigh plate, just a glancing impact, but enough to rotate him, to twist his lower half, to make him holler.

Falk had dropped his PDW. Frantic for cover, he scrabbled at the side of the crop tunnel. It was like trying to tear through a drumhead. Futile. Then the third finger of his right hand snagged in one of the bullet-hole belly buttons, and that afforded him purchase enough to tear. He wrenched. The plastic stretched and parted. He fell face-first into the tunnel, his hands still tangled in the sheeting.

Inside, on all fours, bullets were spitting through the transparent walls above him. Each puncture-hit sounded like a golfer driving off. As they passed through the poly-tunnel, the rounds ricocheted off the tunnel frame, off the sprinkler pipework, off the main props. They *thupped* into soil mix bags, destroyed racks of seedlings, shattered plastic pot trays, shredded mature plants. The already moist, suffo-catingly peaty air filled with the released sap stench of vapourised plant fibres. One shot shattered the casing of one of the sunlamps clamped to the tunnel roof.

Falk looked around wildly. Through the condensation-fogged wall of the tunnel, he saw Preben dragging Bigmouse off the walkboard into the plant row opposite. Falk started to crawl forward a foot or two and drew level with the slits where they had crossed through the tunnel earlier.

The corpse of the man killed by the hardbeam shot was right outside. His weapon, a compact grey assault rifle, had fallen into the gulley beside the duckboard path. Falk peeled back the flap of the hanging sheet, reached out, grabbed it, dragged it back in. Bullets zipped and tore through the tunnel above him.

He turned the weapon over in his hands. Koba Avtomat 90, the "A" version, modern, the latest upgrade. Clean, well kept, new. Twelve inch casehardened barrel. The stock was a milled finished plastic. Behind the angled foregrip, it had integrated connection polymer magazines, each holding sixty rounds of standard Central Bloc pattern 4mil cased. The bolt had already been pulled and the ambidextrous safety disengaged.

Falk took a breath, a deep one. He could hear the back-masked voices in the corner of his brain. He adjusted his glares and got them to maximum tint, then rose to his feet, using the nearest centre post as a support. A bullet *plocked* through the polytunnel and hissed right past his nose. Falk reached up, opened the relay box mounted to the post at head height, and gripped the paddle inside.

"Preben!" he yelled at the top of his voice. "Preben, close your fucking eyes!"

He didn't wait for a reply. He yanked the paddle down hard.

The sun lamps switched on.

They were mounted along each polytunnel row, and in the grow frames of several open-air beds too. Daylight lamp rigs were also set up around the walkboard junctions, and the access to the sheds.

The whole area suddenly blazed with painful white light. Black sky above, glare below. The firing faltered almost immediately.

Falk didn't wait. He dragged back the slit, swung out onto the walkway and opened fire. The Koba was sweet. Very little felt recoil, very little muzzle rise. It wasn't cued to his target sampler, because the Koba had no active sensor system that could be mated to it, but his glares were red-flagging shapes anyway. Human shapes in the crop rows at the end of the walkway, behind stacks of soil-mix bags, beside a rainwater tub.

He fired at the flags, a burst at each, loosing a stream of shots before switching to the next tagged target. Red and orange only. The cased rounds spat their spent, twisted plastic sleeves out of the ejector port like the sprayed off-cuts of some light industrial process. The torn cases rained onto the duckboards around his feet.

He hit one red flag squarely and saw a graphic enhanced human shape wallop backwards into a row of bushes, tearing some of them down. Other hits weren't so positive. One fell, but may have slipped or ducked. Another vanished, but could have been pulling back. Once the blinding surprise of the light had passed, the opposition began shooting back again.

But Preben had wrestled the thumper off Bigmouse. Supporting Falk's general fire, he pumped four grenades into the thickets of crops and watering frames. They blew the living shit out of the rear part of the row. Earth, stalks and debris spewed up into the air in a hot, gritty rush and rattled down on top of them like hail. Twigs and clods of earth drummed off the polytunnel roof. There were suddenly blurds everywhere, blurds flicking and darting through the air, swirling like confetti, drawn to the light, creating hard white blobs against the black sky where the lamplight caught them.

Falk fired several more bursts into the wafting smoke and swirling airborne vapour until he emptied the mags. A flick of the thumb ejected the mag casing. He tilted the whole weapon sideways as he did this so the flying case would spit out sideways, away from him, then bent down to search the corpse for reloads.

He stopped dead. Crouched down, his hip didn't hurt. Where had that little learned habit of tilting the weapon at ejection come from? What about the confidence and ease with which he'd checked and then used the Koba? Where the fuck had any of that come from?

Preben came out onto the walkboards, the thumper in his hands, the piper clamped to his back plate.

"You got reloads?" he asked, the launcher up and covering the far end. Blurds swirled around them both.

"Think so," said Falk. He found two more integrated pairs in the corpse's hip sack. Two hundred and forty rounds total. He tucked one into his thigh pocket, and slapped the other one home, then worked the bolt to cock the weapon. A satisfying, lubricated mechanical double clack. He got up.

"Nice. With the lights," said Preben.

"Uh-huh," Falk replied. His hands were tingling. He saw the PDW where he'd dropped it, slide locked open. He bent to pick it up, putting the Koba down for a moment.

"Is Bigmouse alive?" he asked. He wiped and blew flecks of soil off the Colt, ejected the empty disposable strip and palmed home one of the spares Bigmouse had given him.

"Yeah," said Preben, hunting for flags with his glares and the raised thumper. "Fucking lucky. Three hits, all on his body boards. They stopped them, but I think he broke some ribs. He's having a lie down and a cry."

"You shoot him up?" Falk asked, referring to the one-use painkiller spikes they carried.

"He refused it," replied Preben. "Says he'll get over it in a second. Good call. We don't want to waste that shit."

Falk finished checking the Colt. The reload had brought the ammo counter back to forty. He racked it to put the first one in the pipe, and then toggled on the safety and holstered it, buttoned down.

So sure, so practised, so expert. How did his hands know to do any of that shit? That wasn't playing at being a soldier. That was knowing what the fuck you were doing. That was handling and setting weaponry with skill and minimal fuss.

He stood up, the Koba back in his hands.

"Get Mouse upright," he said. "We're pretards if we hang around here."

"Yeah," said Preben. He brushed away a large green blurd that was fussing at his face. "Should kill the fucking lights too, I guess."

Preben went to get Bigmouse but stopped. Someone was coming. Movement, flagged shapes, from back down the walkboard path behind them.

Green flags.

SOMD troopers. Two of them. Then five more behind them, moving fast, moving low.

Falk got aura code tags on the first two before he could see their faces. Private Goran. Staff Sergeant Huckelbery.

"Preben? Bloom?" Huck called out. "Aren't you a fucking sexy sight!"

"Yes, chief," said Falk. "Who's with you?"

"Most of Two, plus Masry, plus Hotel Four," Huckelbery replied, coming up to them. He was dirty and wet, his skin feverish white in the lights. Ty Goran, the leader of Kilo Two, had blood on his left cheek.

"How the fuck did you do that thing with your aura code?" he asked.

"Bloom thinks outside the box," Preben declared.

"It's smart thinking," said Huck. "We were hosing at everything."

"I just used the medical awareness updater," said Falk.

"It's a fucking piece of genius," said Bigmouse. He was on his feet, looking ill, looking like he was holding it in and working extra hard. There was a sallow cast of pain in his face.

"Nestor! My main guy!" Valdes cried, raising his hand to palm-slap Falk. "This is the Hard Place, right? The fucking Hard Place, huh?"

"The hardest."

"What happened to your face, Nestor?" Valdes asked.

"I got shot in it."

"Fuck, man."

"We've got to move," said Falk to Huckelbery. "They are all over this. All fucking over it."

Huck nodded.

"What's that way? The hamlet, right?"

"Eyeburn Slope," said Falk. "It's not great, but there was no one there except us half an hour ago. You leave anyone behind?"

"Not alive," said Huckelbery.

"This is all you got?"

"They hit us about half an hour after we'd dropped. I had Kilo Two and Three with me."

"We never saw what happened to Jay," said Goran.

"Never saw him go," agreed Valdes.

"Then Caudel and Caudel's whole team got scorched in like thirty seconds trying to get cover."

"All of them?" asked Preben. "Fuck, Caudel?"

"Dog food," said Huckelbery. "Then we saw the Hotel boombird get taken down coming in for extraction. We got Masry out of the boomer just before they shot the shit out of it, met these boys from Hotel a while later by the lake."

"This was where?" asked Falk.

"The depot," said Goran. "We were dropping at the depot to support Hotel."

"They've got the depot then?" asked Falk.

"The depot, the junction, the whole freeking® highway," said Masry, the payload officer.

"What about Juliet? Where's everyone else?" asked Bigmouse.

"Fuck knows," said Goran.

"All I know for sure is where we are," said Huckelbery.

"Where's that?" asked Falk.

"Deepest shit," he replied.

TWENTY-TWO

As the night deepened, the backmasked voices grew louder.

With Huck and the newcomers, they struggled back through the hortiplex, scaled the embankment and took possession of Eycburn Slope, specifically the meeting house. They left the lights on over the field system to make it harder for anyone to approach that way unseen. By the time they were up the embankment, the illuminated air above the fields was hazed with smoke from the firefight, and shimmering with billions of blurds that had been drawn to the light. Every now and then, fat, blundering blurds bounced off their faces or sleeves.

The Slope hamlet was as they had left it, empty and lit by photoreceptive lamps in the yard and porch areas. Masry, the payload officer, was all for avoiding the settlement, and striking out into the black, non-arable country behind it, to lie low out of sight. The notion had a certain appeal. It was clear there were terrorists (Huck was using the term freely now, often hitched to the qualifier "fucking", as in "fucking terrorists") in the depot zone, and up at the hilltop station: in effect, either side of the lonely little farming hamlet. Following the firefight in the fields, those terrorists also knew that there were SOMD foot strengths still active in the area. They would come looking, before dawn most probably, and the little hamlet of Eyeburn Slope, with its genny and stores and shelter and lights, was the most obvious place to begin. Running and hiding in the dark seemed like a wise idea.

But it was also clear that Masry was pretty traumatised. Falk could see the tremor in him, the darting glances, the over-reaction to sound. Masry was trying to hide it. He didn't want them to think he was scared. But no amount of self-control was going to cover those ticks.

He had been payload officer on Hotel's boomer, *Gone With The Wendigo*. Crew specialists were all solid troops, trained to the same basic levels of combat proficiency as their footslog counterparts in addition to their specialisations. Fireteam members did not look down on them. Indeed, they often had an infallible reputation, a balls of steel rep for not blinking or thinking twice when it came to supervising a drop or extraction under fire. POs were unflappable. They were the guys that the guys on the ground could always count on.

However, as it seemed to Falk, Masry couldn't conceal the fact that he had not expected to be facing the sharp end of things. He had not expected to experience the Hard Place this way. The Hard Place was what the fire teams did, which is why God gave them h-beams and thumpers and feeble imaginations. POs were sky boys.

Masry had extremely fair red hair and a complexion to match. His hair was so blond, his eyelashes were virtually invisible, and in the hard, yellow light of Eyeburn Slope's yard lamps, he looked like he was a sand sculpture. His ling patch robbed the force out of all his comments, and made him sound like a pathetic, whining bitch.

That was unfortunate, because Masry deserved some sympathy. He'd come close to dying. Huck said they'd pulled Masry out of his boomer at the depot. He'd lost his crew. There was blood on his kit and combats, and it wasn't his. More significantly, Falk believed, Masry had lost his boombird. That was the real trauma. Crew bonded with their machines, and Masry had seen his die. He was bereft, and he was also stranded.

Ergo, he wanted to hide in the dark.

Huckelbery overruled him. Though the location was obvious, Eyeburn Slope offered them a lot of things. Resources, warmth, dry conditions, the chance for all of them to eat and some of them to sleep. More particularly, the walls and structures gave them a defendable position. Out in the scrub, it would be dark and cold and wet, and by dawn, they would be tired and shivering, strung out, cramped and aching, jumpy. If they were found in the meantime, they would be found in the open. A night in the hamlet might recharge their batteries a little. A night in the open would certainly drain them.

Huck suggested they use the end house as a strong point. It had the best vantage and the best position. From the front, they could watch the hortiplex, and from the side there was a clear view of the yard, the pens and the hill track.

Preben had a suggestion of his own. The meeting house. It stood among a cluster of buildings, and thus the lines of sight weren't as good. But it was surfaced block where the farmhouse was a weatherboard skin over a frame. Preben had checked under the lapboarding. The walls and floors of the meeting house would stop most hard-round fire, anything short of a piper in fact, and it would also soak up the blast wash of rockets or grenades. The jumble of buildings around it, though they made access more diffuse, also multiplied possible exit strategies in an emergency. They could slip out, covering their asses, a number of different ways. Preben had made a few sketches. He showed Huck. He'd thought about it.

Huck was impressed, and okayed it. Falk was impressed too. Preben was a solid professional. Falk wondered how well Bloom would have done it. Would he have seen those things, made those recommendations? How much were they missing Nestor Bloom right now? How much deader, or more alive, would any of them be if Bloom had been running things, and not someone wearing Bloom's face?

Masry went along with it, and followed the group towards the meeting house. He twitched, eyes staring, hunting, every time a blurd tapped against a lamp cowl.

Ty Goran's team, Kilo Two, was Valdes and a quiet black guy called Clodell. Jay, the lost member of the team, was spoken about. The usual, positive mythmaking was already at work. Jay wasn't dead, he was alive out there somewhere and they'd find him eventually. Fucking Jay. What an idiot, always getting into shit. Falk had a clear mental image of Will Jay. A memory. Someone else's memory.

Hotel Four were Lintoff, Barnard, Estmunsen and Rash. Bloom hadn't known any of them well, so they weren't even afterimages on Falk's mind. Rash was the leader, stocky and angry, shimmering with musclepower and discontent. His skin was actually black, far blacker than Clodell's. He was well spoken and extremely precise. It was a long time since Falk had met anyone so tightly wound as Rash: nothing to prove but absolutely hell-bent on proving it. Hotel Four had been one of the tactical squads charged with securing the fuelling depot. For clearance purposes, they were all equipped with PAP 20s that had been fitted with underbarrel shotgun mounts. The shotgun section could take a variety of shells, including a small-calibre grenade. All four men had belts of cartridges around their bodies, like bandits.

"Did you get any kind of look at the terrorists?" Falk asked Rash. He was still getting used to using the word.

"Insurgents," Rash replied, with a little shake of his head. He stuck out his chin and pursed his lips in an expression that indicated distaste. "I believe some of them may have been local settlementeers, converted to a cause, supplied by external agitators."

"Like the Bloc?" Falk asked.

"Not for me to say," said Rash.

"If you won't say, nobody will. You saw them as well as anyone. Did they fight like farmers or frontline troops?"

"I can't say," said Rash.

"Well, they fucked Hotel and Kilo up pretty good, so I'm guessing better than farmers," said Falk. "Wouldn't you?"

"I don't like your tone," said Rash.

"I don't either," Falk agreed. "Still, probably best we talk about these things if we want to, you know, live."

Rash looked at him contemptuously.

"They were well disciplined," said Lintoff. "They had the ground first, so that gave them an edge, but you could see by the way they coordinated. Extreme training. Proper fireteam skill sets."

"No uniforms, but good-quality hard-weather gear, plus clean new weapons," said Goran. "Nothing fancy. But proper workhouse shit. All Bloc-made."

"I heard some of them talking," said Huckelbery quietly. "Sounded Russian."

"I heard another language too," said Preben. "Don't know what it was, but it wasn't English."

"So, have we got Bloc infiltrators?" asked Bigmouse, "or locals militarised by Bloc-sponsored specialists and trainers?"

He was sitting to one side, stripped to the waist, wrapping his bruise-blackened torso with an elasticated support bandage and analgesic patches. Every couple of words, he winced.

"Plenty of room in these freeking® hills for training camps," said Masry. "Plenty of room to hide and work out and practise. Indoctrination camps, you know. Promise the local freekers® anything. Better subsidies, better support, play on their fears of big government, their expectations of religious freedom and liberty."

"Were any of them fat?" asked Falk.

They all looked at him.

"What now?" asked Huckelbery.

"Were any of them fat?" Falk repeated. "Or old? Any of them out of shape?"

"They're fucking farmers," said Valdes. "You live this kind of life of toil, you don't get fat, man."

"No, but you get old," said Falk. "And actually, I've seen plenty of tractor operators or battery farm workers who carry too much weight because they sit down all day. Plenty of weather station personnel who sit at a box all hours scarfing choc-effect bars and NoCal-Cola. So my question stands, were any of them fat or old?"

Rash glanced at Lintoff.

"Not that we saw," he said.

"We saw young, we saw female," said Falk. "But no fat or old. I've seen militias on other settlements. All manner of fuckers get involved. Beardie weirdies, fat hippy bitches, old fucks. You militarise a community like this, you recruit all sorts. These people–"

He paused and looked at Huck.

"–these *terrorists*, they are fit and trained and in the right age catchment for military service. SOMD or otherwise.

Besides, I saw a dump site up at the station. Civilian bodies. A few of them. Executed. Surplus to requirements."

"You never told us that, Bloom," said Bigmouse.

"We've been rather occupied," said Falk. He didn't want to expand on that. Truth was, that discovery had been partly wiped by the trauma and stress that had come on its heels. He was only just remembering, and he didn't want any of them knowing how frail his mind was. The back-masked voices were whispering things that he was sure were questions about his basic ability to function, and his hip was beginning to feel sore again. Lex Falk's hip, not Nestor Bloom's. Nestor Bloom was the one with the dull, toothache throb radiating from the middle of his face.

"When the fuck did you ever see militia on other settlements, man?" Valdes asked.

Falk avoided answering.

"Major Selton has mentioned, several times and strictly off the record, that the Bloc might be involved in this one," said Huckelbery quietly. "Don't any of you pretend to look surprised. We all knew this was part of the profile on this one. Looks like it's true."

"I think the Bloc had people on the inside in this community," Falk said. "Other communities too. They'd infiltrated. Long term, well planned, well resourced. When they got the go, probably when they realised we were mobilising, they activated their sleepers to prepare the ground for their main force. Cleaned house, got rid of everyone who objected or was in the way. Maybe they sent rapid-deploy squads in to assist with that. Fast and effective, ready to greet us."

"That's a lot of planning and preparation," said Rash.

"It really is," agreed Falk. "Which tells us something else."

"What?" asked Rash.

"Whatever's at stake has got to be really fucking important to make all this effort worthwhile."

Fred was up. Falk could see the little tallow disk over the battery pens. The rain had stopped, but the wind was up, and it sent little dark thumbprints of cloud scudding across the moon. It was so quiet, Falk could hear the Chinese whisper of the windfarm up the hill, and the ocean beyond it, trying to shush the whirring mills.

On and off, the voices kept him company. He got used to their unnatural, blunt-ended word-sounds, then suddenly became sick of them again. He wondered if it was Bloom, hurt and bewildered, chuntering on in the back room of his head. During the fight in the fields, Bloom's training and skills had come to the fore and taken over, like habit, like muscle memory, unbidden. They had been right there, under the surface, waiting for the extreme stresses of a firefight to provide the perfect trigger conditions. Stress and adrenaline had made the conflicted relationship between his body and minds switch to pure instinct.

Luckily, those automatic instincts had come from Bloom, not Falk.

Huckelbery had organised a rota to watch the post's perimeter. Mindful of Bloom's wound, he had put Bloom in the first set to catch some sleep, but Falk couldn't lie down.

"You should rest," said Huck, man to man, aside from the others.

"I'm too buzzed," Falk replied. "I'll just take it slow and quiet for a bit, see if that brings me down to a place where I can catch some zeds."

Huck nodded.

"Headshot or not," he said, "you're no fucking use to me if you're spazzed out with fatigue, okay?"

He said it like a joke, but he wasn't joking. Falk wasn't about to explain that he didn't want to sleep because he wasn't convinced he'd ever wake up again.

He wandered around the meeting house and the adjoining rooms for a while. In the land registry office, he turned on a desk lamp, made a little pool of yellow light and studied the satlink projector for a while. He had a half-cocked notion that it might run off an entirely separate communication net, and therefore afford them the means to bypass the jamming and get a call out. The system was live and separate, but there was no signal. Either the weather or the opposition had thoroughly closed down all link systems – radio, digital, orbital direct – and Falk's money wasn't on the weather.

He opened one of the metal drawer cabinets and selected some of the big format territory maps for the Eyeburn area. He wanted to get a feel for the lie of the neighbourhood, and it occurred to him that the local surveyors and developers might have more up-to-date mapping than the files they'd been given at Lasky. He looked at composite views of the whole area. Large-scale, from ocean up to the caldera, the length of the highway, the limits of Antrim, Furlow Pits and Marblehead. Furlow Pits was another township, maybe four times the size of Eyeburn, up in the geo-belt of the coastal range and the caldera. Antrim was a proper town, a mill and pressing town, the bullseye of a dartboard-dot cluster of mining complexes. It was also the best part of six hundred miles away at the end of the highway. Might as well have been the moon.

Marblehead, then, was a distant galaxy, all the way over to the east. Going to Marblehead on that excursion had been one of the most insulting wastes of time Lex Falk had ever had to endure, on top of which it had been a depressing, crap-hole dump. He felt pretty certain he was currently prepared to kill in return for being transported there immediately.

He pored over more local, larger-scale maps on a lightbox, studying the layout of the station, Eyeburn Slope, the field system, the depot, the junction and the intersection of the highway. There was an open-cast mine to the east, in the foothills, and another, a smaller one, just north of it. There were also individual farms and dwellings away from the main settlements, isolated private estates on private purchase land, all part of the greater community.

He took out his glares. It seemed sensible to record the maps to be on the safe side. Once again, the Mil-grade functions of the glares befuddled him. Bloom wasn't around to show him how to work them. Falk was on his own, fumbling around with only his familiarity with civilian models to guide him. How could snapshot be so difficult to select?

The glares had belonged to somebody else. He hadn't really thought about that before. He'd found them on the deck of the boomer where they had been left or, more likely, dropped. They had belonged to another member of Team Kilo, or to one of the bird's crewmembers. He remembered having to clear all sorts of saved snaps and eye junk away when he first used them, the residue of the previous user.

Here it all was again. All the crap he'd shoved aside. When he finally found *snapshot*, it opened the images that had been saved. Dozens of them: candid shots of SOMD buddies clowning around, laughing, toasting, posing with weapons while looking mean and moody, in groups at parties. He found the folder heading. Username *Smitts, Lemar*. Lemar Smitts was a member of Kilo Three, and Kilo Three had definitely been on the bird when Cicero brought it back to the weather station, because Martinz had been a member of Three too.

Falk looked at the snaps again. There was Martinz, beer-effect in hand. There were Valdes and Goran, Caudel looking tough with a thumper, Jay and Clodell. There was Bigmouse, and there was Preben, laughing in sunlight, a laugh Falk had yet to see. There were Stabler and Bloom.

His own face, but not his own face. Nestor Bloom and Karin Stabler in a bar somewhere, happy together, acting up for the camera, Bloom's arm around Stabler's shoulders, both of them alive. The sight of Stabler hurt. It put a little cramp in his belly.

Falk swallowed hard, felt Bloom's subterranean pain stirring. He flicked on to the next frame, the next, the one after.

Along with the snapshots, there was a video file. Forty seconds long. Falk keyed play.

The interior of the boombird cabin, the view saturated with daylight because the POV was low down, on the deck, looking up sideways towards the side windows and one of the open side hatches, all of them blinding, Rothko-esque slabs of white light. Zero shake. The user was not moving, and neither was the bird. The bird was on the ground. Two figures got into the cabin using the hatch, crouched down, spoke to each other. They gave a better idea of the user's position. To have recorded this, Smitts must have been lying down on the cabin floor, lying down on his back, turned to the side.

The clip was nothing. Forty seconds of overlit nothing, where nothing happened, the focus was poor, and the ambient noise on the soundtrack lousy. The crouching figures, silhouettes, spoke to each other for about twenty seconds, then got up, turned to camera, came towards the lens. Then there was a quick, confused motion and the playback ended.

Falk selected erase to dump the clip, but there had been something about it. He played it again. This time he paused when the crouching figures got up and turned to camera. For a second or two, they blocked the overwhelming white light of the doorway, eclipsing it, and became more than silhouettes. One was larger than the other. It was fuzzy, but the resolution was improved. A man and a woman. Neither of them was wearing SOMD kit.

Falk didn't know the man. But the woman was the girl who had shot him.

The cramp came back. It kicked him in the belly so hard he gasped out loud, doubled up. It was fear, the twisting snake, but it was physical hurt too. Clamped with an inexpressible discomfort that made him feel like he was going to vomit, he pushed back from the lightbox, fists balled, mouth wide, no sounds coming out. He dislodged one of the map folders and it fell on the floor. He couldn't call out.

He managed to get to his feet, folded over. There was a small couch in the corner of the office, covered with a threadbare throw. He shuffled over, fell on to it, rolled onto his back. The cramp squeezed again, then ebbed, and his knees relaxed, dropping his legs flat.

The pain wasn't really in his stomach. He realised that. He lay on the couch, flat on his back, almost paralysed, understanding full well that the pain, the real pain, was in his head. His cramping, spasming body was just another symptom of his brain dying. Bloom's physical brain, with his mind overlaid, dying together. Maybe from a bleed, maybe from a brewing infection, maybe from some kind of feedback shit storm cocktail mix of the gunshot trauma and the remote position transfer.

The reversed voices gossiped in the shadows around him, muttering, bickering.

The office door opened and light slanted in. Huckelbery peered around the door. He'd heard the folder hit the floor. Falk couldn't move. He couldn't speak or lift his head. Huckelbery looked in and presumed he saw Bloom finally catching some sleep. Satisfied, he went back out and closed the door quietly.

The pain and the tonic crash drifted away over the course of about an hour, during which Falk may have slept briefly. He sat up when he finally realised he could. He was thirsty, and he could smell coffee or hot chocolate being prepared nearby.

He played the clip again on his glares, slowed it down, replayed it, zoomed in, enhanced it, replayed it. Smitts, he became convinced, was dead or dying when the clip was recorded. He had been sprawled on the deck of the boomer, in the doorway. He'd probably been shot. The glares had started recording accidentally, or Smitts had been trying to record something surreptitiously, playing dead.

Even enhanced, there still wasn't much to see or hear. The man and woman got in, crouched down. They spoke to each other. It was hard to resolve the exchange because of the ambient background. A few words, not English. The girl was definitely the one who had shot Bloom. Falk played and replayed the moment she got up and faced him against the light. He could see the patched tear along her scalp, the dried blood. If someone had told him she was Central Bloc, he wouldn't have been surprised. There was something about her features, her hair, her manner. She was petite but strong, forceful, undaunted. The man was big, dark-haired, his face not clear in any shot or partial. From his build, he was military. There was density, a core strength to him.

He listened to their conversation four, five times. She was telling him something. Falk tried to discern the actual words, tried to fish them out of the hiss-murmur soup of the open-air recording. What was she saying?

The business at the end of the clip, on repeated play, became more apparent. They were getting up and coming over because they had realised that Smitts was alive and watching. The last jumbled seconds of the clip were the motion and disruption of them grabbing hold of Smitts to pull him out of the boomer. It shook the glares off. End clip. That must have been how the glares wound up on the cargo deck.

What were they saying? Falk could almost lip-read, except they weren't speaking English.

He got up, and went off to trace the coffee smell. Stepping out of the office, he found Preben and Rash in the hallway, talking with Masry.

Preben looked around at him.

"We think we've got a plan," he said.

TWENTY-THREE

"We're not walking out of here," said Masry.

"No one's walking anywhere," replied Huckelbery. He was eating soya beans out of a self-heating can using a plastic fork. He was standing too. Soldiers did a lot of standing-up eating.

"That's not what I mean," the PO replied. "Come dawn, it'll be a whole day since we inserted. How long before SO Command considers us overdue? How long before they realise this is all freeked® up?"

Huckelbery shrugged. Masry looked around the room at the faces of the other men. Falk didn't say anything. There was the leftover chill of a long night in the community hall, a pre-dawn dampness with a thin after-scent of Insect-Aside. Small blurds had found their way in, and were clumsily orbiting the lights.

"Another day? Another two?" asked Masry. "A week? Then what will they do? Send more teams in to find out what the freek® happened to the first lot? Doubtful."

Valdes made his dismissive face.

"The SO won't hang us out to dry, man. No way," he said. He was leaning against the wall bars, arms folded. "They'll get full-gain sat overview, a good look-see, then punch in a payback assault to scorch these motherfuckers. Show them our fucking A game. No messing."

Goran and Clodell nodded. Rash was impassive. The other members of Hotel Four were outside watching the perimeter, but Falk was pretty sure that if they'd been present, they'd have been doing their best to mimic their boss's expression. Hotel Four was a tight-knit pack. It wasn't clear whether that was due to trust and cohesion, or a painful lack of individual imagination. Rash was clearly a demanding squad leader.

"Suppose you're right," Masry said to Valdes. "How long will that take? Three, four days? We won't last that long. We've got to get out of here, and we can't do that on foot."

"So what?" asked Huckelbery. He licked bean sauce off his lip and twirled his fork absently, describing the spin of rotor blades. "We fly back out?"

"My boom's junked," said Masry, "and we don't know what happened to the Juliet ride. But Kilo's is right up the hill here."

"Up at the station," Preben said.

"It's taken hits," said Falk. "Mouse and I were there when it got shot up. Hardbeam hits."

Masry nodded.

"Yeah, it's dinked. But it's not dead."

"I told Masry about the damage we saw it taking, Nes," Bigmouse said. "I told him, some hull and screen smacks. The landing gear was the worst bit."

There were big, dark circles under Bigmouse's eyes, rings left behind by pain that was as clear as the marks a coffee cup left on a tabletop. The blunt-force trauma he'd taken to the chest was clearly sapping everything he'd got. Falk could see bruising spreading up his collar bones and throat, beyond the limits of the elasticated bandages and press-on analgesic patches.

"Boomers are built tough," said Masry.

"It took hits," Falk repeated.

"They're tough," Masry said. "There is good reason to believe the Kilo bird can get us in the air and get us home. A freek® of a lot faster than on foot. Faster than any ground transport we could rustle up."

"And you'd be flying it?" Falk asked.

"Yeah, okay, I'm not a pilot," replied Masry. "But I've been on boomers six years. I know my way around. And all POs are air-grade rated on control systems in case of emergency operations. Like if they have to take over as a second seat, something like that. I think this qualifies as a freeking® emergency, don't you?"

"I guess," said Falk.

"So, yeah, I can fly the thing. It may not be the smoothest ride you've ever taken, but I can do it. Good enough?"

Falk looked away. The high windows of the community hall were turning very slightly pale. Dawn in under an hour. They were going to rush this decision. There was no time to think it over.

"We need to do it," said Preben. "We need to try it."

"Shut up," said Falk.

"What the freek® are you so afraid of?" Masry snapped at Falk. "What is your freeking® problem?"

"You," replied Falk. He felt a twinge of cramp for a second. It passed. "You're clutching at straws, Masry. That doesn't make for good choices."

"What? You don't want to get out of here?" Masry asked.

Falk had been leaning against a stack of chairs. He straightened up, faced Masry and pointed to the black drill-hole in his bruised cheek.

"What do you suppose this is, Masry?" he asked. "How badly do you suppose I need medical attention? How completely do you suppose I want to get out of here?"

Masry held his gaze for a second, then, uncomfortable, looked away.

"I want to get out," said Falk. "I do not want to mount some kind of half-assed raid on a position we know is under insurgent control just on the off-chance they'll let us borrow a fucking Boreal."

"What do you suggest we do then, Bloom?" asked Rash.

"I don't know," said Falk. "I don't know what I suggest. Stay low and keep out of trouble? I have no idea. I'm keen to hear any viable alternatives. I just know I don't want to go charging into a guaranteed firefight just because Masry thinks he can magically fly us away home."

"Yeah," said Huckelbery, slowly and quietly, deep in thought. He put his can down on a table, fork leaning out of it. "We've got to be sensible. We've got to be smart. There aren't enough of us to go doing something rash. No offence, Rash."

Rash had clearly heard that gag a billion too many times.

Falk waited, rubbed his eyes. He looked at Bigmouse, and saw that Bigmouse was staring right back at him. Falk could read the fear buried in Bigmouse's features, the stress of simply staying upright. Private First Class Waylon Wakes "Bigmouse" Mauskin was counting on Nestor Bloom. He was counting on his team leader to get him out of the shit and back to safety. Bigmouse wasn't going to ask. That wasn't his style. He wasn't going to say it out loud. But he could hope and he could will it to happen. He needed it.

"Fuck it," Falk said under his breath. He limped across to Huckelbery.

"Look," he said, "maybe if we do it really tight. Keep our options open. Move in slow, take a look, size it up. Have ourselves a fallback position in case it turns to shit. Go in that way. Get the fuck out if it's not viable, go to ground. No heroics."

"No heroics." Huckelbery nodded.

"We get the fuck out if anything, I mean anything, feels off. Even a hair off. No pretard plays. None of that pressing on no matter what."

Huckelbery looked at his toecaps for a moment. Then he glanced up.

"Goran? Rash?"

"I'd go with Bloom's suggestion," Goran said.

"No heroics," said Rash. "Back right off the moment it looks compromised."

"Okay," said Huckelbery. "Okay."

He checked his wristwatch.

"Prep and ready. Fifteen minutes. I want us on that hill while it's still dark. I'll work ahead with Three, scout in, make the call, yes or no. Rash, you and your boys get to run support. Go tell 'em. Bloom, you and Preben escort Mouse and Masry. I'd like a look at a hard-print map of the hill and the station. Can we get one?"

"Yeah," said Falk. "I'll pull one from the registry."

"Fifteen minutes," Huckelbery said. Everybody started moving.

Falk headed back to the office. Backmasked voices whispered to him out of the shadows. He found the best detail map of the area, snapped it with his glares and then tore it out of the folder. While he was at it, he took some copy snaps of the other area maps too.

Bigmouse came into the room.

"Thanks," he said.

Falk held out the map sheet.

"Go give this to Huck."

Bigmouse nodded, took it and shuffled back out.

Falk keyed playback and watched the recording again. The figures crouching in the doorway against the light, murmuring something, then rising and approaching. End.

He played with the sound balance a little, and washed it through a modulator option he found on the audio menu. A few words, or partial words surfaced. The girl was clearer than the man. Falk listened to the brief scraps of sound three or four times over. She was speaking Russian, so although he could make out some of the words, it was still useless. Useless. With a linked celf, he could have translated it in under a second.

One word stood out from the others. It stood out because it wasn't Russian, or at least it didn't sound like a Russian word. She said it twice, close together. It sounded like she was saying "calico" or "heligo". Something like that. What did that mean?

The cramp ambushed him again, made him grunt in pain, made him grip the edge of the lightbox to stop himself falling. The snake in his gut, the snake of fear, bit its own tail and squirmed around, sliding him along on its sheer, dry scales, bearing him on towards death.

He waited for the pain to let go of him again, for the snake to glide away. Slowly, he straightened up, took a breath. He unclamped his fingers. Pressure and perspiration had made the tips adhere to the lightbox. He peeled them away, and saw that he had gripped so tightly, he'd actually created a stress crack across the surface of the lightbox, a hairline fracture like something ominous showing up on an x-ray.

Falk buttoned up his jacket, tightened up his blate and picked up the Koba.

They would be waiting for him.

• • • •

They assembled in the yard outside, under the plastic roofing. It was still dark, but there was a pearlescent stain in the corner of the sky where the sun was due to arrive. Rain was tapping off the roof, and rippling the puddles in the yard. The hill and the hilltop station were black on black.

Huckelbery was still studying the map that Falk had procured. He got everybody grouped in under a lamp, demonstrated the route he wanted to take, the spread he wanted, the point of angle and entry at the hilltop. He got Bigmouse and Falk to confirm the location of the boomer. Everybody took snaps of the map and Huck's pointers with their glares. Huck finished his brief by indicating the fall-back options, in order of preference.

They had everything with them, everything they could carry. Fastened up against the rain, they checked each other's blate, front and back, and readied weapons.

"Now let's take a moment," said Huckelbery.

They bowed their heads. Hands slid over hearts, or clasped ID brooches. Falk heard several sets of LEAF servos purr.

"God of my personal conviction," Huck began. If any of them was repeating his words, they were doing it silently. "Watch over me on this morning, and throughout this endeavour, and watch over my comrades in this group, even if they are heathen sunbitches who believe in some other god than thou. Help me to maintain honour and courage, and uphold the great institution of the Settlement Office, and the constitution of the United Status, amen."

Amen. Heads came up.

"All right," Huck said. "Don't balls this up. If I say pull out, we pull out. Understood?"

They all murmured assent.

"Then let's go execute this fucked-up plan, shall we?" he said.

They bumped fists and swiped knuckles, and headed out into the rain, into the last sigh of the night wind, across the yard and into the darkness.

The automatic lights of Eyeburn Slope fell away behind them. Up ahead, in the black, the windfarm uttered its steady, threatening chop, like a disapproving slow handclap.

It was hard going. Within minutes, Falk was wet through and cold to the core. His face was numb, fingers too, and he kept slipping and turning his ankles on the blind terrain. He and Preben stayed tight to Masry and Bigmouse. The other two teams were just ahead of them.

The slope grew steeper. Falk started to sweat, hot wet against the cold of his skin, chilled by the wind despite the insulation of his kit. The wind noise, and the increasingly loud *whup-whup-whup* of the turbine farm, were blending to fill his ears with a dull roar, like the hush of the ocean meeting a beach, like the ambient background on a poor-quality playback.

Calico? Heligo? Helical?

The Koba got heavier and heavier. He adjusted the strap, but his hands were cold. He climbed the track, terrified that the cramp might come back and bite into him.

By the time they reached the first agreed marker, it was alarmingly light. Falk knew that was mostly down to his eyes getting used to the low light levels, but the sky was growing paler all the time. They could see the texture of the land, the grey distance of the sea, the silhouettes of the turning turbine heads. In the valley behind them, Eyeburn Slope and the hortiplex fields seemed ridiculously over-illuminated.

Ahead of them, up the steep mound of the hill, there were lights on in the weather station. They moved up to the next marker, a rusting demountable that had been

butted up alongside two refab sheds. Falk could smell tar
paper and cold metal. Weeds in the shed gutters danced in
the wind.

This was the point where they'd divide. Huck was
moving ahead with Three to scout, Hotel Four pulling wide
to cover them. Falk, Preben and Bigmouse were staying put
with Masry.

"I need to see the boomer," said Masry.

"You will," said Huck.

"I need to assess it."

"We had a plan," said Huck."Fucking stick to it. Stay here
until we tell you to follow us in." He glanced at Falk and
tapped his brooch. "Keep reading us," he said.

Falk nodded.

Kilo Three broke cover and moved off up the hill, heads
low, shadows amongst the black undergrowth and bram-
bles. Hotel Four split to the right, working around the hill
a little way. Falk adjusted his glares, tracking their aura
codes in the darkness. Four this way, four that. They could
message via their medical updater panes.

"Where is the bird?" Masry asked.

Falk pointed.

"Up that way, the other side of the sheds, in the yard. It's
pretty exposed."

Masry only had a PDW for armament. He had suggested
taking the thumper or the recaptured PAP 20 with its dregs
of ammo off Bigmouse, because Bigmouse wasn't well
enough to use them, and he'd been told "no" several times.

Preben had his M3A up, sighted to his face, tracking the
codes of Huck and Three through the target sampler. Falk
looked to Bigmouse, who was leaning his weight against
the side wall of the demountable so he didn't have to carry
it. In the twilight, he looked like he was made of snow.

"Okay?" Falk asked.

"I'm wealthy, Nestor," said Bigmouse. "I'm golden."

Falk grinned.

The wait time became unbearable. Masry couldn't keep still. Out on the horizon, the pale band of sky spread, and low cloud banks were edged with silver, like their paint had been buffed back to bare metal. Daylight was going to overtake them.

"Got it," said Preben. "Let's go."

Falk took a quick look, and picked up Huck's medical alert pane.

Move in.

They started to move, coming around the demountable and up through the angled undergrowth of the bank. Big spots of rain started to fall, cold and heavy. Bigmouse could only move so fast, and Falk kept with him to support him. Masry's eagerness swept him ahead.

"Slow down!" Falk hissed.

Masry didn't answer. Preben glanced back at Falk quickly, then made an effort to stay with Masry and keep him on a leash.

"Sorry," said Bigmouse. "Sorry I'm slowing you down."

"Shut up," said Falk.

He knew the snake wasn't far away, knew it was just waiting to loop its coils back into his belly, drawing the cramp with it. He swallowed the spittle building in his mouth, tasted the blood in it. Sour, metallic. A man's spit shouldn't taste like that. Not a healthy man's.

He heard Preben hiss, "Fuck it, Masry."

Masry was almost running.

Falk and Bigmouse followed them up into the yard. The station was off to their right, a bundle of black oblongs against the sky, lit by internal lamps. *Pika-don* sat to their left, tilted slightly on the muddy slick of the yard like a sleeping bird, head tucked under one wing. It was just a black shape, the silhouette of a piece of sculpture, stark and angular with the slate-grey sky behind it. The sky was pale enough to appear reflected in the yard puddles, pieces of gleaming off-white.

Weapons up and hot, Huck and Three had the yard covered. Two pipers, two PAPs. Valdes's pane, misspelled, reported the sound of voices and the smell of cooking from the main buildings. Rash's team was out of sight but close.

Masry was all but sprinting towards the boomer. Preben was with him, and Bigmouse and Falk followed. Huck's team held position, watching the angles, looking for movement or discovery.

Masry circled the Boreal, assessing it. He bent down, trying to see how much damage had been done to the undercarriage, tried a different angle, knelt down in the mud and got his head and shoulders in under the nose to look. Preben stood point.

"Here," said Falk when Masry reappeared. "Here, and here." He showed him where the other hits had struck, the hull impacts, the through-and-throughs, the h-beam that had sliced an ugly hole in the front screen. The blister had cooled, hardened off.

"It's okay," said Masry. "It's okay. It's not structural. The bodywork will hold together, good enough. The gear's shot out, which isn't great, but I can compensate on lift-off and we'll just be setting down with a bump."

"You sure?"

"Yeah, yeah."

"Masry?"

"It's fine. She's wealthy."

"Okay."

"I've got to get inside. Prep. Get her set and started."

"How long?" asked Falk.

"Five minutes."

"Masry, can it be less?"

"Maybe."

"Masry, listen to me. Listen to me." He forced the PO to look at him.

"Start the prep, fast as you can," said Falk. "You listening to me? Start it and prep it. Do not fire anything up without you warn us first, okay? Okay?"

"Okay, Bloom. Jesus."

"Masry, if you're going to make this baby make a noise, if you're going to power up or start an engine, warn us. It's going to bring them running, and we need to be ready."

"Okay."

Masry opened the side door and climbed into the pilot's seat. He started to check over the instrument display.

"Get on board," Falk said to Bigmouse.

"What?"

"Get aboard," Falk repeated. "Don't wait around."

Bigmouse nodded and started to haul himself up into the payload space. Preben saw he was having trouble, and helped him.

Falk waited. Day was straining to break. Before it could get there, the snake bit him.

The cramp came back, in his throat and the back of his neck as well as in his belly. Falk made as little noise as he could, a muffled snarl, but still it felled him, dropped him to his knees in the mud beside the boomer's slide door. He heard Bigmouse call his name, heard Preben moving to him, heard Huck.

Heard rain. Heard the chop of the windfarm.

Heard himself gasping, his blood pounding.

"Get him up, get him up!" Huckelbery said.

Hands on him trying to lift him, stretching out the tendons that attached the pain to his bones.

"What happened to him?" That was Preben.

"Just get him up!"

Madness. Coiling pain, hissing like a kettle, like a snake, rushing up from his belly, up the pipeline of his spine, into his brain, too much pain to live through.

"What's wrong with Nes, man?" That was Valdes, behind him.

"Keep scanning!" Huck replied.

"Is he dying, man?"

Yes, I'm dying, Falk thought. This much pain could only be dying. This was the snake-pain, the hate-cramp, that came to get you when your time had come.

"Keep watching the station!" Huckelbery snapped. "Preben, help me get Bloom in the cabin."

Hands hoisted him. He saw the boomer's door sill close up, raindrops on it like diamonds, the worn, bare metal of the deck grille, then Bigmouse, stiff with his own pain, looking down at him with frightened eyes.

Someone started screaming. A low, guttural complaint that grew and rose into a whine, a scream, a howl.

Not someone. The engines. Masry had fired the boomer's engines. The fan jets thundered into life. Blown mud-spray lifted in a halo around the hopter.

Falk was on his side, tight in a foetal curl, on the cabin deck, with Preben trying to pull him further inside. Masry had started the engines. No warning. No countdown. No cue. The airframe was shaking. Over the jet roar, Falk could hear shooting. He tried to see. He got one hand on the hatch pillar and tried to look out.

Gunmen were spilling out of the station. Gunmen, insurgents, black hats, terrorists. Falk didn't know what they were, what name they wanted to be known by. The pain made certain he didn't care. He barely cared for the SOMD men outside, the men whose fate he was sharing. About the only emotion that was bright and sharp enough to pierce his shield of pain was his hatred of Masry, of Masry's selfish panic and thoughtlessness.

The gunmen were in their drab, dark all-weather gear, like mountain hikers or hortiplex labourers, like the people who had tried to kill them earlier. They had Kobas and a few appropriated SO weapons. They came from both the front and side of the station, moving low, weapons up, firing tight bursts. They were professionals. Falk, just playing at being a soldier, could recognise real ones. It was the way they moved, carried themselves, used cover, blocked for each other, fired their weapons.

Goran, Valdes and Clodell were returning fire, backing rapidly towards the howling transport. Huck was firing from the door. Preben had given up trying to drag Falk any further inside and was lining up with his M3A. There was no sign of Hotel Four.

Falk wanted to shake the pain off, get up, add his Koba to the fire they were laying down. The cramp wouldn't let him. It wasn't done with him. The snake constricted around him, kept him pinned and scrunched up. The only thing he could do was hold on to the door pillar and make noises through his teeth.

"Fuck you, Masry!" he slurred. "You fuck! You *fuck*!"

Masry said something from the front. Falk couldn't hear it over the fan wash. *Pika-don* lurched a little, as if actually about to lift, like a big animal shifting in its sleep.

"Hey! Hey!" Preben yelled.

Hard rounds spanked off the hull. Huckelbery started to move away from the bird, firing, yelling.

"Fuck's he going, man?" Valdes shouted.

"Chief!" Goran bellowed. "Stay here! Stay with the bird!"

Huckelbery was trying to make an opening. He was yelling for Rash and the rest of Hotel Four. He was yelling at them to close in, to head towards the bird, to get to the dust-off. Maybe they were pinned down around the side of the station. Maybe Huck was trying to punch a hole and let them through.

Pika-don lurched again.

"Masry, you fuck!" Falk gasped. "You've got to wait! You've got to wait!"

It was too late for Clodell. Hard rounds felled him, bouncing off his blate. He went sprawling in the mud, alive but winded, dented, bruised. Falk heard another round crack one of Clodell's blate panels, actually fracture it. Clodell started to rise. An h-beam took his head off. It just scorched it off, vapourised it. There was a bang, a puff of smoke and a little shower of black debris, a brief, intense smell of burned bone, and Clodell's body tipped back into a puddle with just a smoking, fused stump sticking out of the neck of his blate. It was a gnarled lump, charred, steaming, that looked like a bad barbecue cut, a chunk of flesh and a piece of jaw with a couple of teeth still sticking out of it.

Valdes and Goran went crazy, pouring weapons fire back at the station. Falk had no idea if they hit anything. The boomer shifted again, properly bumped a little.

"Don't you dare, Masry!" Falk yelled. He had fought the snake back enough to half-rise. He screamed over the seat backs at Masry in the pilot's seat.

"Stay on the ground!"

"We've got to go!"

"Stay on the fucking ground, Masry! We're not all here!"

"We've got to freeking® go, you freekhead®!" Masry yelled back. "We're dead if we stay here! They're on us! They're freeking® on us!"

"Stay on the fucking ground until Huck gets Hotel Four aboard!"

"Freek® you!" Masry answered. "I'm not going to sit here!"

The Boreal rose slightly, engines shrilling, then dipped back into the mud. The lurch threw everybody about. Valdes had been half in the door and he fell out, onto his back. He got up, slithering around in the mud, and tried to climb back in.

"Chief! Chief! Come on!" Preben yelled from the side door. Huck turned, saw them, saw there was no time left, and began to run back. Goran knelt down to give him covering fire.

Rash appeared. Rash, then the other members of Hotel Four. They came out of the undergrowth on the far side of the yard, out from behind a refab, firing as they moved. The urgency had forced them to abandon cover and risk the dash across the yard. It was that, or be left behind.

Barnard only made it a couple of steps. He folded sideways in a puff of blood mist, then tumbled over, rolling and rolling. A hardbeam cut Lintoff's left leg mid-shin and he fell over before he realised why he could no longer run or even stand. Estmunsen skidded to a halt, then rushed back to help Lintoff. Rash turned too, yelling Lintoff's name. Estmunsen got his wrists under Lintoff's armpits, started to drag him, Lintoff shrieking an inhuman kind of squeal. There was a bang. A second hardbeam shot went through both of them, both torsos, clean through, leaving a cauterised tunnel the size of a porthole. They fell as one, Lintoff suddenly mercifully silenced, hitting the yard in a splash of rainwater.

The boomer's tail came up. The fans thundered. Huck grabbed the screaming Rash, dragged him back towards the floundering aircraft. Hard rounds and the occasional hardbeam ripped around them, splattering mud, steam-blasting craters. Rash was fighting Huck, and fighting Goran too when Goran tried to help Huck. He tried to push them away, resist their efforts to get him aboard so that he could stay in the yard with the mutilated bodies of his team members.

"Fuck it! Fuck it, man!" Valdes yelled from the door.

Like a cop restraining a violent offender, Huckelbery got Rash in an armlock from behind, turned him around and bundled him into the hatch. Preben grabbed him, Valdes too, Goran and Huck frantically posting Rash up from behind. Rash's head was back, eyes clenched shut, mouth wide open and bawling at the sky. Preben and Valdes got Rash inside, almost threw him down on the floor. They heaved Goran up and in, Huck right behind him on the kick-step.

Masry took the hopter up. No warning again. Just a sudden, violent ascent, overpowered, unskilled, woefully inept. *Pika-don* rose hard, twenty or thirty feet into the air, turbines protesting. At the same time, she yawed to the side, desperately unstable, tipping, swinging.

The ugly combination of violent rise and spastic dip took them all by surprise. Rash rolled and smashed into the cabin partition. Falk lurched forward, smacking his mouth into the door pillar. Goran lost his grip entirely. He fell backwards off a deck that was tilted at forty-five degrees. He fell back into Huckelbery, who was still clinging to the outside of the open hatchway.

They vanished together, out and away, falling face-up out of the side of the boomer.

Masry got the bird level, turned the nose.

"You've got to go back down!" Falk heard Preben screaming at Masry over the hammering roar of the jets and the wind. "Go back down! Down, you fuck! We've got to pick them up!"

The Boreal's tail rose, the chin tucked in. Climbing steeply, Masry accelerated them away from the hilltop yard.

TWENTY-FOUR

They climbed away, fast and urgent, but stability and control were all over the place. The bird, perhaps more significantly damaged than Masry had reckoned, shook wildly, as though it was juddering across an uneven surface, or simply untameable. The vibration became so intense it was all any of them could do just to hold on. The wind noise and the engine roar assaulted them, urging them to let go.

Falk wondered if the atrocious ride quality was entirely due to damage, or if Masry had vastly over-rated his ability to fly the thing. Even with equality compensator systems, multi-fan machines took skill and delicacy to control in terms of pitch and balance. They required experience, extensive simulator time and hundreds of logged flying hours. Masry came with nothing except second-hand exposure and a basic understanding of the principal controls.

Masry had left Huck and Goran at the station. The image of them falling was all Falk could see. Why hadn't Masry gone back? What the fuck would have stopped him going back? Terror, cold-blooded pragmatism, or just the fact that he was panicked and didn't have anything like enough skill to set the boomer down again once he'd got it up?

The engines were making a brutal noise, an uneven, grinding clatter, especially the rear starboard unit. Falk tried to rise. He had fresh blood on his lips and chin where he'd head-butted the pillar. He was pretty sure that if he got the opportunity, he was going to shoot Masry.

Pulling himself up a little, bracing against the constant shake, he looked out. It was freezing cold. Clouds slashed past them. It felt like they were miles up in the air, but it was only a thousand feet or so. He could see the valley below them, the thin white vein of the highway. He got his bearings a little. There, the highway, the rising bulk of the mountains, the caldera rim. The ocean, that had to be behind them.

"Masry!" he yelled, gripping the headrests of the front seats for support. "Masry, where the fuck are you going? What are you doing? We want south! We want to go south! This is east, you fucktard! Where the fuck are you going?"

All of Masry's effort was focused on fighting with the stick. The instrument panel was lit up with red warning lights and flashing yellow alerts. Falk realised it was pretty much all Masry could do to simply keep the boomer aloft. Navigation, headings, all of that shit had gone right out of the window. Discarded. Non-essential. Remaining in the air was the only thing that counted.

"You've got to turn!" Falk yelled."Turn that way! South! South, you get it? Masry?"

Masry glanced up at him, just for a second, just a second, just long enough for Falk to see that there was no more reasoning with him. Masry was beyond argument or persuasion. He wasn't even really hearing Falk. His mind was locked. There was nothing in his face at all but some blind flavour of craziness. Falk saw a man who had swum way out beyond the safety markers and the life guards, a man who knew he'd embarked upon something he should never have attempted, something he couldn't hope to finish.

Masry turned away, returned to his struggle.

"We are so fucking dead," said Falk.

The rear starboard engine decided it wanted to die first. Just before Falk finished uttering the words, there was a painful metallic bang, like a ton of scrap iron being dropped into a skip. The boomer bucked savagely. Pieces of broken rotor head exploded out of the case and punched into the main hull like porcupine quills. Black smoke, as dark and gold-shot as expensive silk, spilled out of the engine housing and trailed into the slipstream in a long and slender ribbon.

A klaxon started to whoop. Hazard panels flashed battenburg patterns. The awful, juddering vibration suddenly became something a whole lot worse: a feral, pummelling fury.

They were descending rapidly, planing down in an easterly direction. Once again, Falk wasn't sure if this was something that Masry intended, or a result of the boomer's increasing inability to avoid the ground. The cold highlands loomed ahead of them, grey and wet, scribbled on with chalk-mark clouds. They were crossing the line of the highway, leaving Fyeburn Junction and the depot behind over their right shoulder. The landscape below was unworked, wild. Scree slopes, grass meadows, thickets of gorse, thorn and salt bramble, pale and rusty like a stain of lichen on a boulder. Beyond that, stands of trees, then beards of denser forest, tangletree and snowgum and the fat, starchy genus that looked like rubberwood. The forest coated the escarpments of the rising hills, and lined the dark clefts and glens, the steep slices in the rock where mist hung like net curtaining, veiling private darknesses and secret streams. It felt as though they had some destination, as though the wounded Boreal was pressing on, down towards one of the forested gaps, drawn by an instinct or a navigation program.

Despite the icy, wet wind blasting in through the open slider doors, they could all smell burning, an overhot stink of frying plastic that was welling out of the drive compartment behind the cabin space. Debris from the exploding engine had punched into the main fuselage and done untold harm, splintering and tumbling and spreading like hollowpoint rounds inside a target body. What systems had been destroyed? What was burning? Hydraulics? Fuel lines? Electrics? Fucking fire suppression?

"Can you land this?"

Falk looked up. Preben was braced beside him, holding on to the overheads, shouting forwards at Masry in the nose.

"Masry? Can you land this?" he called.

Masry said something.

"I can't hear you, Masry," Preben yelled. "What did you say? Can you land this or not?"

Something. Something like a yes, maybe?

Preben flicked his eyes at Falk for a second, saw he was watching. Falk wiped blood off his mouth.

"Masry?" Falk shouted. "Masry, where are you going to set down?"

"Masry, answer Bloom's question," Preben called. "Where are you going to set down? Masry?"

Nothing. Preben looked at Falk.

"I should just fucking shoot him," he declared. "We wouldn't be in any worse shit."

"Masry!" Falk shouted.

The engine note changed suddenly. Briefly, Falk thought everything had cut out, but then he realised that the ground was beginning to rise quite significantly beneath them. It was rushing closer. The tree cover was soaking up the reflected roar and clatter of their engines, suddenly giving little of it back. The roar became a buzzing and whirring. The airframe kept jolting and rattling.

"Oh fuck, man," Falk heard Valdes moan.

"Masry!" Falk yelled. "Steer towards the flat ground! The open ground, Masry! Over that way! Don't take us down into the fucking trees! Masry!"

It wasn't going to happen. There was an ocean of tree tops skimming under them, a grey treescape. Falk willed them to stay above it. It was just leaves. Just leaves and twigs. It should be soft, it ought to give. They could almost bounce right off it, like a coin springing off a corner-tucked sheet, like a stone skipping across a lake.

Turned out it was like hitting a wall.

There was an impact, like striking rock. Noise again, roaring, clattering, engines shrieking. Klaxons. The whole machine shaking and rattling with homicidal rage. Squeaking, scraping, ripping, cracking, scratching sounds as they tore through the tree cover, broken branch ends knifing the hull, leaf debris in the air around them, driven in through the side doors.

Then something bigger, heavier, more ungiving, smacked into them and turned them hard, like a right hook breaking a jaw, turning a skull aside. Then another, a blow to the ribs that almost rolled them to the left. Headlong still, demolishing canopy and splintering solid boles. Needles of wood and chips of bark in a blizzard, motion too blurry to control.

The final sledgehammer hit. Falk was thrown forward, bouncing off the back of the cab seats and the cabin divider.

The shaking wouldn't stop. There were sounds all around him. The hull yelped like a whipped dog as it buckled and cracked, laminates crumpling like foil, metal screeching and shredding, dermetic alloys protesting. Falling metal versus trees and ground.

Then nothing.

Falk wasn't sure which way up he was. He wasn't sure if any parts of him were missing, if any parts of him had been torn off. He was reasonably certain he was alive, which was, in itself, a major miracle. It wasn't clear how survival had been at all possible.

Denying all of the pain that would inevitably follow, he allowed himself a tiny moment of triumph, of joy at the randomness of fortune.

Then the snake struck, and the cramp hit him, and he was gone anyway.

TWENTY-FIVE

"Falk."

His name was unfamiliar. He hadn't heard it spoken in a while. Backmasked voices and upside-down sounds hummed inside his head, coming in and out, first soft, then louder, then soft again.

His name emerged from the sounds, briefly, like some small, deep-sea creature coming up for air and breaking the surface. It was the right way around, his name appearing intact out of the reversed nonsense of the voices.

"Falk."

There was no pain. This was either merciful good news, or an early indication of fundamental spinal calamity.

"Falk."

He opened his eyes. Bloom's eyes. Above him, a canopy of leaves and branches, a dark grey, cavernous space under the spread of the forest, where the light was soft and slate-coloured, like snow light, like the hue of the sky before a blizzard came in.

He was on his back, looking up at a roof of gum branches, tangletrees, leaves the colour of ash and chalk, bark like untanned skin. Succulents wrapped every limb and trunk like external circulation. The looping ropes, which reminded him uncomfortably of snakes, were weighted with white berries like milky pearls, and little dot flowers of yellow. Some of the vines had intertwined so enthusiastically, they resembled sheafs of electrical trunking or cable-tied wires.

Daylight, tiny triangles of daylight, peeked through the gently moving roof.

Faces loomed. People were bending over him, looking down at him, into his face. Expressions of concern. Rash, Preben, then Valdes. They were all grubby, their faces smeared with dirt and sweat, and speckled with blood and oil.

"Falk?" said Rash. "Can you hear me? If you're alive, make some kind of sign."

"Falk," said Preben. "You're hurt. We have a serious problem. Unforeseen. We're trying to solve it. Falk? We're going to help you, okay?"

He wondered how they'd found out his name. How had they done that?

"Falk," said Valdes, eyes wide as he peered down. "Please. We've been trying to reach you for hours. Please respond to me."

They all had the same voice, he realised. All three of them had the same voice, and it was a woman's voice.

"Please, Falk, please respond," said Rash. No, he wasn't saying that. He wasn't saying anything like that. His lips didn't match the words. He was saying something else, saying something to Preben. The voice Falk could hear was merely speaking at the same time. Overlap. It was like bad dubbing on a movie.

Falk closed his eyes so he could hear the voice better. It was coming and going out of the backmasked track, but many of the words were now the right way around.

"Falk?"

"Cleesh?"

A pause.

"Falk? Oh my God! Oh freek® me! I've got him! I've got him! Falk, can you hear me?"

"Yes, Cleesh. It's nice to hear your voice."

"Oh, Jesus, Falk! You freek®! We really thought we'd lost you! I have been going crazy here!"

"Can you calm down a little, Cleesh? Can you? It's a bit weird here. I need you to talk slowly and more calmly, so I can understand you."

Her voice receded into the blackness for a moment then came back.

"...I can, sure. No problem. It's just good to hear you, that's all. Listen, listen to me, Falk, we're trying to dig you out of there. We're trying to disengage you from the soldier."

"His name's Bloom."

"Bloom. Right, okay. I knew that. Look, it's complicated. Ayoob says it's complicated. Things have happened that they weren't expecting."

"Like what?"

"Just things they couldn't predict, things they couldn't prepare for. We're working on it right now. They're–"

"Like what?"

A pause. It gave him a moment to get used to the blackness around him. With his eyes closed, it was almost as if he was floating in a lightless tank full of warm water and not lying on a forest floor at all.

"I've been talking to you all the time, since you went under, Falk," Cleesh said. "Have you been able to hear me? I've been with you all the way, like I promised I would."

"Thanks."

"I said I would. Like old times."

"I know."

"Okay."

"Cleesh, can you tell me what the problem is? Why am I still in the tank? Why haven't you pulled me out?"

"Bari says–"

"Bari can go fuck himself. Sorry, but I want you to explain it, Cleesh. I want you to explain it without any fucking around."

He waited. He could hear the warm water gently rocking in the darkness.

"Turns out," said Cleesh. "Turns out you weren't properly fit. Underwood was right. We should have done a lot more tests. A lot more. We rushed into it. I told you it would be okay. I'm sorry, Falk. I shouldn't have done that."

"It's okay. What's the problem?"

"You had underlying medical problems, which mean you're weaker, your immune system. Uhm, there was way too much alcohol and stuff in your bloodstream too. That's freeked® things up a bit. The biggest problem is your hip."

"My hip?"

"Yeah. The bone density. Too much time on drivers. Underwood said the bone density was a systemic problem, but your hip is the worst place. The bone strength there is so weak, you've actually broken it."

"I've broken my hip?"

"It's a hairline fracture, but yeah, basically. You had so much alcohol in you it was masking the pain, but the fracture, it's new. Looks like you might even have broken it as recently as the night we put you in. Falk?"

"Yeah?"

"Why did you laugh?"

"The chances are I broke my hip engaging in vigorous and empty sex that I was too old for anyway."

"You dog," she said. "That'll teach you."

"It will. So I've got a fucked hip. How does that alter anything?"

"It's infected. Remember what I said about your immune system? You're sick. Fighting it, running a temp. Underwood's trying to treat it with broad spectrum, that kind of stuff, but you're sick and it's affecting the interface. We're trying to disengage you, except Ayoob's worried that pulling you out might freek® your system up."

Warm black water slapped in a lightless womb.

"And when you say that you mean 'kill me'," he said.

"There's a range of stuff that Ayoob's concerned about," Cleesh said. Some of her words, if not actually backwards, sounded side-on. "Paralysis, brain damage, organ failure… Basically a whole bunch of things, none of which you want."

"You know me so well."

"So we're working on it. Just being able to get through to you is a huge step forward and a really good sign."

"There's the other problem as well, isn't there?" he asked.

Water, rolling in darkness. Backwards whispers.

"Yes."

"Bloom's dead, isn't he?"

"Yes, functionally."

"Tell me what you know."

"Underwood's monitoring his vitals," said Cleesh, "but the data is patchy. We haven't got the whole picture. What we've seen so far is the effect of the headshot. All higher function's gone. If he was on his own, he'd be dead."

"There's actually a surprising amount of him still about in here," said Falk. "Emotions. Memories. Under stress, his muscle memory takes over. It's done that a couple of times."

"Interesting. I'll talk to Ayoob."

"I keep getting bouts of pain, Cleesh. Crippling pain. Cramp in my belly and head. It comes on, no warning, and I'm helpless, then it fades."

She said something. The words were backwards, whispers.

"Cleesh?"

She'd drifted out, her speech just backmasked loops.

"Cleesh?"

"I said, that's us, Falk," she said, suddenly loud and the right way around again. "The pain is us. Our fault. I'm sorry. It's the attempts we're making to physically remove you from the Jung tank and disconnect. Each time we've tried, the trauma you've suffered has been so great, we've been forced to abort."

"What about Bloom?"

"What about him?" she asked. Unseen water lapped.

"What happens to him if you get me out?"

"We don't know. If there was decent medical support for him…"

"Cleesh?"

Quiet.

"Underwood thinks you're keeping him alive. Your mind is keeping the autonomic functions of his body running. You're kind of like his life support. You're what's keeping him going."

"So if you pull me out, he's definitely dead?"

"We think so."

"Okay. Okay. You know what's going on here?"

"We've got a partial picture. We've been listening via you. And we've been watching developments here. Apfel is going through channels via GEO's links to the SO, but there is no official line. SOMD issued a statement that an operation is underway, no other details. That whole zone is still communication-dark. Via you, we can see the problem on the ground. Have you got confirmed Bloc forces?"

"I haven't got confirmed anything. But if you wanted me to make an educated guess, I'd say yes. Central Bloc special forces."

"Apfel wants to know–"

The words suddenly inverted, became a blur.

"Cleesh? Cleesh?"

"–hear me? Can you still hear me, Falk?"

"Yes."

"Apfel says he wants to know what kind of hits the SOMD taskforce is taking there. We haven't been told anything official, but the SO is clearly gearing up to send serious support in. We think they're getting quite spooked about the total loss of contact."

"They should be," said Falk. "I don't know much. Of the three teams I went in with directly, there's about four of us left. Four people. The insurgents were waiting for us on the ground. Plus, they had expunged most of the local pop too. Whole settlements cleared out, executed."

"Are you serious?"

"They knew we were coming, or they knew we would *be* coming. Cleesh, there's something in play here that no one can see. This whole extro-transition element thing is beginning to make more sense. Scary sense. There's something so valuable, the Bloc is prepared to turn the Cold War hot for the first time ever. But listen, listen to me, Cleesh. Everybody says it's because of Fred, but I don't think it's about Fred at all. Fred might just be the icing on the cake. I think it's actually about something down here. This whole thing here at Eyeburn, this whole situation, it's really geographically specific."

"Like what?"

"I don't know. But I've got a clip. A playback. I need to translate some Russian. If I play it back and sound it out?"

"Yeah, I can work with that. Translation should be no problem."

"Okay. Give me a few minutes. Give me a second to sort myself out. Cleesh?"

Water moved softly, in hiding. A reversed whisper hid just beneath its lapping surface.

"Cleesh?"

Nothing.

Nothing lasted for a while.

He opened his eyes again and sat up.

"Shit!" Valdes cried. "Shit, man! Nestor's awake! He's with us!"

Falk looked around. The forest clearing was bathed in grey light, a haze. The trees were close-packed around them, heavy with cables of tendril creepers. The underbrush was a thick carpet of grey-green leaves and thorns, a foot or two deep. There was a smell of damp earth, of plant resin, of loam. It was cold, the wrong side of damp and unlit.

Preben and Rash stood over him, Valdes crouched to his left.

"We didn't die, then?" Falk asked.

"Not all of us," said Preben.

"Thought you had, though, man," said Valdes. He grinned. His face was bruised under the dirt.

"Where did we come down?"

"A way back that way," Rash said, gesturing over his shoulder.

"You carried me?"

"Had to," said Preben.

"We thought the fucking thing might explode," Valdes said. He shook his head. "Thought the whole fucking thing might go up in a fucking fireball."

He looked at Falk, grinned.

"It didn't, though," he added.

"Where's Mouse?" Falk asked.

"Here," said Bigmouse, from behind him. Falk turned. Bigmouse was sitting propped up against a tree trunk. He tried to smile, but he looked like death. The half-light of the forest was making his skin look particularly ashen and sickly.

"Masry?" Falk asked.

"Fucker," said Preben.

"He wasn't so lucky," said Valdes. "Not so lucky at all."

Falk got to his feet. It wasn't a stable, steady process. Valdes rose and helped him.

"Where are we?" Falk asked.

"In a fucking forest, man," said Valdes.

Falk looked at Preben.

"What he said. The middle of a fucking forest," said Preben.

"We're going to need to move. Find decent shelter," said Rash. "It was hard to carry you anywhere. But now you're awake."

"What would you have done if I hadn't woken up?" asked Falk.

"We would probably have had to leave you," said Rash.

"Shut up," said Valdes. "You shut up. He doesn't mean that, Nes. He really doesn't."

"It's what we talked about," said Rash. He shrugged.

"I hope it was," said Falk. "Seriously. This is the Hard Place and a lot more besides. If it's a choice between ditching me and making yourselves secure, you know what you have to do."

"Exactly," said Rash. "We can't be weak."

"I ain't weak," said Valdes.

"Where are my glares?" Falk asked.

"Didn't see them," said Rash.

"They weren't on you when we carried you clear," said Preben.

"I need them," said Falk.

"Borrow mine," said Rash.

"I had good copies of area maps," said Falk. "Not just Eyeburn, this whole zone. I copied them from the land registry. Probably need them. Probably be really handy."

"They must have fallen off you," said Preben. "Maybe at the crash site."

"I need to look," said Falk. "I need to find them. Try, at least. Where's the crash?"

"I'll show you," said Rash. "Rest of you stay here. We won't be long."

Someone had brought the Koba along. Falk picked it up.

"Let's go, then," he said.

They walked back towards the crash site. Rash led the way, stopping now and then to wait while the slower-moving Falk caught up. The forest was quiet, wisps of mist drifting like smoke, like steam.

"Who's Cleesh?" Rash asked.

"Who?"

"Cleesh?"

"Why do you ask?"

"You were talking. After the crash. You were talking like you were having a nightmare. In your sleep. It was the main reason we decided not to dump you. It was as though you were talking about someone called Cleesh, or *to* someone called Cleesh."

"Just someone I used to know. Years ago. I haven't thought about them in a while. My mind must've gone there."

"That must be it."

They moved on in silence. Falk began to smell a waft of petrochemicals. The backmasked voices drifted around in the shadows behind him.

"Here," said Rash. "Just here."

The crash site was a little way ahead. They were approaching a glow, a luminosity cupped within the forest gloom. Daylight was streaming down through the ruptured canopy, through the grey mist that was gathering under the spectral snowgums. *Pika-don* was dead, a tangled black carcass driven up against a stand of robust trees, front end crumpled in like a boxer's nose, flanks dented from motion impacts and scarred down to base metal. Its tail boom was up, partly propped by a slumped tree trunk. Vines and ropes of succulent creeper were draped off its edges and stub wings, dragging like streamers, like lilac ribbons off a wedding car's bumper, like the running cables of multiple harpoons stretching out behind a whale that had finally been slain. There was a great carved wake behind it, a giant furrow of splintered tree trunks, ploughed soil and shredded vegetation that stretched away through the forest ranks, a deep incision bleeding green sap and pulped wood. The ground was littered with debris: pieces of twisted hull plate, fragments of glass, chips of plastic, unidentifiable component parts trailing wires or cables. An entire engine mount had torn off and lay half-submerged in the undergrowth. There was a lingering smell of burnt sugar.

Falk limped towards the main hull and approached the port cargo door. The door was missing, wrenched off its sliders, leaving only the buckled runners and the slot it had fitted into. A large piece of tree branch was wedged into the upper corner of the door space, like a lump of gristle stuck between teeth.

Rash came up behind Falk, weapon clutched low across his belly.

"See them?" he asked.

Falk shook his head. He looked around, parting ground cover stalks. Then he got up on the exposed kick-step of the hull and leaned into the cabin. Leaves, twigs, glass and stones had gathered at the foot of the sloping deck. There were blurds all around: small ones buzzing around his face, larger ones circling the glade, catching the shafting light. Some, large and glossy, crawled and basked on the trunks of nearby trees.

He finally located the glares behind the pilot's seat where they had slid. He leaned in to retrieve them. One arm was slightly bent.

"Okay?" asked Rash.

"Yeah," Falk replied.

Masry was still in his seat, and his seat was still in the nose section of the boomer, but the nose section now shared, with a massive tree trunk, a space that had previously been occupied by the trunk alone. The compression damage was immense. The hull's metal skin had puckered and wrinkled like elephant hide as it crunched and folded. Hydraulic fluid was leaking out of fissures and cracks, beading the leaves of the undergrowth, stinking of lube oil and man. The enormous impact forces had crushed Masry into his seat, pushing him down into the footwell under the instrument panel and then squeezing that shut too, like an over-stuffed purse. Falk didn't really want to think about the physics required to pack a body up into a space so small and enclosed, the snapping of long bones that would have been required, the terrifying momentum. Masry had been jammed into a cavity designed to accommodate his legs. Very little of him was visible, just his right arm and hand, raised to ward off both the forest and the death rushing up to greet him. The arm was draped forward, limp and unmarked, over the top of the instrument panel, through the shattered front screen. It was pinned between the seat back and the dashboard mount that had shunted backwards to meet it during impact.

Falk was pretty grateful he couldn't see Masry to admire the compact form into which he was now packaged.

Blurds buzzed and chirred around the arm and found ways into the compacted mystery below. They settled briefly on the top of the dashboard and twitched, then buzzed away again. They landed on Masry's sleeve, his cuff and on the red-gold hairs of his arm. Falk found himself staring. The tiny touch of blurds against the fine arm hair made him itch. He kept expecting Masry's arm to move, irritated, to flick them away.

The blurds were the same kind of bottle-black ones he had seen on the corpses up at the weather station.

"Tucker," said Rash.

Falk nodded.

Rash stared at what they could see of Masry.

"If he had survived," Rash began. He cleared his throat. "If he had made it, I swear to God I would have shot him."

"That's been a popular sentiment," Falk replied.

"Uh-huh."

Rash looked up at the canopy around them, the grey-lime wash of the light, the spiralling blurds.

"We should go back," he said.

"Okay," said Falk.

"You got what you need?"

"Yeah."

They turned and started to pick their way back from the wreck, through the undergrowth and ground flowers. Rain, a passing squall, pattered on the leaves above them, and wind shushed the branches. A moment later, drips fell like glass beads out of the tree cover.

Falk took a last look back at *Pika-don*, dead in its forest grave. Masry's arm, hanging from the compressed cockpit, looked like it was waving them goodbye, a sad farewell.

Either that, or it was beckoning them back, urging them not to leave, encouraging them to stay.

Falk didn't want to stay.

They moved back through the forest, Rash going at Falk's speed, mindful of his injury. They didn't speak. Away from the gash the boomer had cut through the forest cover, it was dark and closeted. The trees, mostly snowgums, were pale columns like the legs of giant grazers. Shadows were deep black or emerald-green, pockets of darkness. The air was tinted grey-green, forest light, leaf-filtered.

Overhead, the canopy sighed and creaked in the wind, leaves hissing like surf on a shingle beach. There was a strong smell of leaf litter, and the sounds of their footsteps were magnified. Every now and then, a large blurd droned past, clattering like a wind-up wooden toy or buzzing like a saw.

Rash stopped.

"What's up?" asked Falk.

Rash looked at him, and didn't reply. His eyes were fierce. He looked pointedly off into the distance behind them, in roughly the direction of the crash site.

"What?" asked Falk.

"Something," Rash murmured. He raised his PAP 20, moved back a few feet, using a tree for cover. Falk followed, sliding the Koba off his shoulder.

"Just the trees moving," said Falk, conscious of how quietly he was speaking.

Rash shook his head.

"I heard voices," he said. "Behind us. I'm guessing a

search sweep, looking for the bird. Looking to find out where it came in. Looking to see if anyone walked away."

He fell silent, waited. Falk listened.

From far away, very far away, he caught the sound of voices. Men talking as they moved along, checking back and forth, an exchange of commands.

"They're coming this way," whispered Rash. "Probably not far off finding the boomer."

Falk nodded. They started to move again, more urgently, heading towards the camp. Falk tried to go as fast as possible so as not to slow Rash down.

He paused, and took one last listen to the sounds of pursuit.

Very far away.

But nothing like far enough.

TWENTY-SIX

Falk accessed the images stored in the glares. The maps were intact, but the glares had suffered some wear and tear. The power cell seemed to be faulty, or there was a bad connection. Images flickered occasionally, for no reason.

Rash got the group moving at once. He aimed to put some distance between them and the searchers before getting too concerned about precise location. As they wound through the trees in the trackless forest, with Bigmouse determining the rate of movement, Falk tried to pinpoint their position using the stored maps.

It occurred to him that Eyeburn Junction, like so many small towns and communities in that part of the continent, was still coming to terms with what it was, and what it would become. It was a classic early-stage settlement, with a population that was original generation, or not many past it. It bore the affirming boldness of land stakes, of first principles, of community foundation. The spirit of that process had been part of the human experience since before man expanded out from his cradle. As a trope, it recurred on every settlement world. People finding some new ground, some new land, and deciding, almost arbitrarily, that they would connect with that particular place, that this was what they had been looking for. They had brought a curious, portable sense of belonging with them, a ready-to-use ownership, and they had planted it in the first suitable place, declaring that this was what anchored their lives now. This determined them, and would determine their children. This particular patch of land defined them.

Falk had never felt that way. He'd never felt connected to anywhere, not even as a child, certainly not as an adult. His profession, tailored by his character no doubt, required him to be a guest, visiting places and people, looking in, informed by the contrasts and details revealed simply by his lack of familiarity. He was an observer, and he never stayed anywhere long enough to get bored with the view.

He liked to drift. To look in through other people's windows. Or, in this case, out of other people's eyes.

His father's life had been shaped by a long career in propulsion. He designed engines, very successfully. This talent had literally propelled him around the worlds of the Human Settlement, and he acquired as he went the habit of travel that inspired his work. Indirectly, brought along for the ride, his family had learned the behaviour too.

When his father finally, and without much notice, dismantled his starter family, and decided, obdurately and in the face of an entire lifetime of far-flung work postings, to settle somewhere and make one place his permanent location, Lex Falk had simply not been prepared to stop as well. Part of it, of course, was resentment at his father's actions and towards his new half-family, but he had also acquired an addiction. Moving, never stopping, always driving on to see whatever was next. Never settling for settlement. He had learned it from his father, contracted it through contact with his father's demanding career.

And he had always been grateful to his father for it. He had always believed it made him somehow more sophisticated. He was not satisfied with one, static experience. He was not one of life's fence builders or roof raisers. He was not filled with a desire to make neighbours out of anybody. His father's late-onset shift into this fixed state had made him anxious. Or rather, disappointed at his father's sudden change of heart, and anxious that one day, without warning, his genes might pull the same dirty trick on him.

If they were going to do that, he had always presumed, it would be a sudden change, sudden like his father's change to changelessness had seemed to be. But Falk had a sneaking suspicion, one that had quietly developed over the previous few years, that the change was in reality rather more subtle. It was creeping up on him, very slowly decelerating his forward velocity, an imperceptible shift, just like a spinrad driver could use the gravity well of a sun to gradually arrest his craft and turn it without expending any of its own power. Something in his life was transmitting just such an effect to him, bringing him progressively to rest.

When people came to rest, voluntarily or deliberately, they often didn't immediately know where they would end up. First principles of survival – a roof, a supply of power and food and water – gave way to a much more interesting period of determination. Much of Eighty-Six was doing that, not the cities perhaps, but certainly the great colonial plots, the settlement territories, land parcels like Eyeburn Junction. It was possibly why settlement worlds took so long to arrive at a formal name. It took a while for them to find out what they were going to be.

Falk didn't know why Eyeburn Junction had originally been planted. Perhaps the weather station because of the vantage, or the fuelling depot because of the range of freight liners. Either one would have brought staff, and staff would have brought families, and families would have made a community like Eyeburn Slope, and that would have required the farming infrastructure. But agriculture was simply there to provide. It would never become a major off-world export. The hortiplex belts would feed communities, ship produce to towns, supply cities like Shaverton, maybe even become a mighty industry in domestic terms. But it wasn't the thing. Mining was the thing. The rich and precious resources of Eighty-Six's mantle and crust, that was what it was all about. Mining would be the cornerstone of Eighty-Six's trade and export. Mining would make Eighty-Six a prosperous world in the Settlement. Not for a few generations yet, but soon. Maybe one day, it would earn Eighty-Six a formal name like Prospect or Orpheus, or even Greenstone, the name that Fifty had been given. Maybe mining would decide what Eighty-Six was going to be.

In miniature, this was what was happening to Eyeburn Junction and the territory surrounding it. The land registry at Eyeburn Slope attested to this. The distribution of land parcels for homesteads and agriculture required careful record, but it was a service often performed by a central SO registry. The land office at Eyeburn Slope was not for farming purposes. Its detailed charts, deep resonance mapping, satlinks and surveyor records were evidence of people who were interested in the substance of the land. The settlementeers – and bigger corporations, no doubt – were prospecting the region to see where their fortunes might lie. A man could come and acquire a parcel of land in the Eyeburn belt for his family to live on, then spend the rest of his life studying parcels of land in the nearby hills to find the one that would turn his family into a rich dynasty. The area looked promising. In fifty or seventy-five years there would probably be glass masts in the city of Eyeburn, maybe a ferry port and a Hyatt, and Gunbelt Highway and Eyeburn Slope and Depot Street would be the names of roads and boulevards.

He wondered what the grey, silent woods would be called. A residential area known as Snowgum Heights, perhaps? The Tangletree Halls Campus at the University of Eyeburn?

They stopped so that Bigmouse could rest. They were still deep in the trees, submerged in the murky, sea-green light. They could hear the rain coming and going above the canopy, and smell the fresh, renewing damp after every shower.

Falk moved away from the resting group. He tried playback a few more times, then closed his eyes and waited.

The leaves rustled above him, stirred by the wind, sounding like backmasked voices.

"Cleesh?"

At first, she didn't seem to be there. Then Falk got the distinct impression that she was, that she was struggling urgently to get through. Little sideways half-words seemed to reach him, the sounds of words and phrases rotated in such a way as to render them nothing more useful than noises.

"Come on, Cleesh."

Still nothing, just a whisper, like a voice muffled by a door or a baffling conversation heard through a party wall.

"Cleesh, if you can hear me, this is what I need a translation for."

He spoke out the words the couple on the playback said as best he could, sounding out each part as accurately as possible. Then he did it again, breaking each part down, doing the lines one at a time, watching the playback and speaking along to it.

"Where have you gone, Cleesh?" he asked. "I need to hear from you."

"Talking to yourself?" asked Rash.

Falk turned.

"Yeah, it's a bad habit, I know."

Rash nodded.

"You find anything on those charts?" he asked.

"That's what I was just checking," said Falk. "I think I've got us pretty much locked. Of course, this territory is so young, nowhere has much of a name."

He blinked up a map, and then handed the glares to Rash so he could look.

"Copy it across," Falk suggested, and Rash touched Falk's glares against his own.

They put the devices back on, studied the results.

"Yeah, that's convincing," said Rash.

Falk had focused on an area that was called Twenty Thousand Acre Forest on the registry map, which encompassed the mouth of an unnamed glen and straddled a stream network that simply owned a serial number.

"I used the glares to run comparative mapping," said Falk. "Of course, there's a broader margin of error, because the source is a copy of a hard-print map and not a loaded chart. But it looks likely."

Rash nodded again.

"What's this here?"

"I think it's a barn complex, for lumber storage. It's about five miles west of us, towards the highway."

"And this? A farm, right?"

"Yes, and so's this. Both a good distance south-west. Those two triangles I think are markers for undeveloped or unclaimed parcels. That is some kind of livestock structure, maybe a gross battery pen or an automated bier."

"And this thing? Here, close by. No more than two miles north-east. It looks like a property."

"It does, but I think it's another plot. It's the registered proposal for an intended structure, a planning proposal. I'm not entirely familiar with all the registry notations yet, but the outline is pale blue. It looks like a residence or a structured plot, but there's no orange property outline so the parcel isn't registered to an owner, individual or corporate. I think someone's filed a proposal for land use, and if they get approval, they'll purchase the plot. At the moment, it's just the record of an idea."

"But you're not sure?"

"No, not absolutely."

"Shame," said Rash. "Looks like it could have been a big place. Decent shelter, resources."

Falk looked at him.

"We certainly need something," he agreed.

Rash took off his glares. His expression was solid, frank.

"We do. Your man, Bigmouse. He's in trouble, Bloom. And that means he could be trouble for all of us."

"We're not ditching him, Rash."

"Interesting. When you came around after the crash, you were all for pragmatic decisions. Very eloquent."

"That was about sacrificing myself," said Falk. "Not Bigmouse. He's one of mine. He's my responsibility, and he's depending on me. I'm not ditching him."

"We could move faster without him. Nothing is safe out here. Nothing is guaranteed. We're probably dead already, but we're more likely to be dead if we're weighed down by someone who is too hurt to fight or move. Our only chance is to stay mobile and keep out of the way of these bastards."

"So as far as Bigmouse is concerned, shelter is helpful?"

"Of course. We could maybe get him more comfortable. We could defend a location. Hell, if it came to it, I'd rather ditch him where he could stay warm and fed rather than leave him out in the rain. Give the man some possibility of survival."

Falk thought for a moment.

"We try this farm, then. This residence."

"You don't think it's real."

"If it's not real, we review. If it is real, it buys Bigmouse some time."

"Okay." Rash seemed unconvinced.

"Rash," said Falk, "if you'd had any choice in the matter at all, would you have left any of Hotel Four behind?"

"Point," said Rash.

By the time they had reached the skirts of the forest's densest section, the rain had eased and the sun had come out. The temperature climbed rapidly, a shift that felt unnatural from a human standpoint. It reminded Falk yet again of his first, uneasy impressions of Eighty-Six as a forced fit for settlement. It only took a few minutes of hard sunlight lancing down through the canopy before they were uncomfortably hot. The yellow light was dappled, filtered by the shifting mesh of the leaves, turning the forest interior into a dazzling, leopard-print palace. When Falk looked up, the light flashed and glittered beyond the trees like reflecting water.

They reached the edge of the trees, less than half a mile from the plot on the map. It was a building after all, a structure of some considerable size. They could see it clearly from where they had stopped. It was on the far side of a large, banking meadow and beyond a brake of trees. To their right, the meadowland curved up to meet the hem of the woods, which extended up and away in luxurious folds into the hills. These uplands were massive. Falk had seen them from the boomer and from the east side of the weather station site, but now he was at their feet and properly understood their scale.

To their left, alternating expanses of meadow and clumps of woodland patchworked the long slope of the land down to the distant and invisible course of the highway. In that direction was haze, the smoky heat and light of an afternoon stretching away towards the ocean under the sun.

The sky was clear, the powder blue of ground ore. The sun had burned all the clouds away.

Falk took a look at the building, using the zoom function. It was an impressive building, a massive two- or three-storey house of modern, rectilinear design, surrounded by small annexes and outbuildings. Preben made a passing reference to it as a ranch, but it didn't strike Falk that way. The outbuildings looked like simple service or storage buildings, not the infrastructure of a working farm station. It was a high-status house, a mansion, a country seat.

"Real," said Rash.

"Apparently," Falk replied.

"I can't see no one around the place," said Valdes. He was adjusting the pan and zoom of the powerful optics on his M3A, like he was going to take a shot at the place.

"Let's move in," said Rash. He glanced at Falk for an okay. There was a slight awkwardness between them. They were the two senior men in the group, both squad leaders. Falk – Bloom – technically outranked Rash because there were more of his original section in the remainder, but Rash had the edge because he was intact and Falk was carrying an injury.

"Let's move," Falk agreed.

The meadow was thick with tall nodding grass, stiff and pale gold like straw. Each stalk had high leaves and little white flowerheads that were husking into seed cases. The grass was waist-high, a lake of dried yellow. They waded into it, fording it. The sunshine was raising evaporation from the ground, shrouding the meadow in a fuzz of white fog, like the air in a steam room. It clung on tight, in a layer no more than a foot deep above the grass. Billions of tiny moth-like blurds, green and white, billowed in the blanket of mist, wildly active in the heads of the grass. Hectic and busy, none of them rose more than an inch or two above the layer of drifting steam. The light, the warmth, the ghost smear of mist, the confetti blurds, it made everything dreamlike. There was an equanimity.

Falk tilted his head back, closed his eyes, felt the sun on his wounded face. He felt a welcome heat in his blood, not a clammy sweat flush on his spine. For the first time since the weather station, he felt as though he was inhabiting a living body rather than shuffling around in a borrowed suit of dead flesh.

They were halfway across the meadow, heading for the brake of trees, when noise boomed up the valley. There was a jetrush whoosh, a spear of sound that sliced the air north to south, in line with the highway. Right on its heels came a series of deep, bass booms.

They all started, looked west. Nothing to see at first, nothing to see except a clear warm day. And then something. Bristling domes of smoke and ash, burned brown, thick, rippling, rising from the ground five or six miles north-west of them.

They were still staring at the smoke blossoms when the jetrush sounded again. This time, they were looking, so they saw the black dot streak by, low, horizontal, ultrafast, coming from the north, zipping towards the south, the powerburn of an attack run. At the far southern end of the pass, they saw the dot turn, bank, come up and over before climbing away, a flash of sunlight on a wing face or a canopy. By then, more smoke blossoms had boomed into being, overlapping the first, bigger and fiercer. This time, they witnessed the core spark of the detonation, the flash that the blast followed.

"Fuck," said Valdes.

"Airstrike," said Preben.

"Hitting the valley," said Rash. "Hitting the valley hard. The highway."

"But, ours?" asked Bigmouse, asking the question so obvious none of them had thought of it.

"Didn't get a good enough look," said Preben, "some kind of GAP."

"Standard US GAP is the A6, the Thunderdog. Dogs have eight ducted LA TF6 engines. They're fast."

"That was fast," said Valdes.

"No, *fast*," said Falk. "If they were providing a little close air support, we wouldn't even see them."

"Since when d'you know so much about it?" asked Preben.

Since the father of the man lurking behind Nestor Bloom's eyes worked for USCAM Propulsion in Fallowmal, Falk wanted to say.

"Standard Bloc ground attack platform is the Sukhoi 41," said Bigmouse.

"The Frogeye," said Falk.

"That's the one," said Bigmouse. "Do you think that's what we were looking at?"

"It seems more likely," said Falk.

"We need to get over to the trees," said Rash.

They all glanced at him. Rash was staring out into the distance, across the sea of mist and grass heads and swirling blurds. Down the line of the valley, where the clouds of smoke were growing and spreading in the sunny air, black dots had appeared. Three... no, four of them. Tiny to begin with. Peppercorns.

On the wind, intermittent at first, they heard the chop of rotors.

"Rash is right," said Falk.

They started to move, picking up their course, hurrying with a new urgency. They crossed the field towards the dense stand of snowgums and bleakwoods. The dots were getting closer. Their chop was a loud, air-cutting ripple, rolling out across the meadows like the clatter of distant lawnmowers.

Bigmouse was lagging. Preben and Rash got hold of him and almost picked him up, running with him through the standing grass. The stalks swished around their legs. Blurds flew up in their faces, as insubstantial as dusty feathers.

They reached the emerald shadows of the trees, clambered in amongst them, getting down amongst the thick, exposed roots in the undergrowth.

The black shapes moved down the valley towards them, low over the golden, sunlit meadows. The lines of the flying machines, and their glossy black bodywork, made Falk think of fat scorpions, except the form was reversed. The raised pincers were to the rear, spread, the hooked metasoma to the front. Falk knew what they were. Kamov Progressiv 18s, the Bloc's best rotorcraft gunship. The "pincers" to the rear were the distinctive paired mounts of the tiltrotor system. In their bulk abdomens there was crew space for a fireteam squad, but they also packed a significant amount of ground-attack armament. Not as large, or as fast, or as versatile as an SOMD Boreal, but considerably more vicious.

The gunships were moving down the valley, following the line of the highway, quite clearly hunting the terrain for movement or heat tracks. They were staying together as a loose pack, but every little while one of them would halt and divert, circling a ground target before rejoining the general formation.

As they began to draw level, one of them peeled away and began to skim up the meadow slopes towards the stand of trees.

"Oh shit," whispered Valdes. Preben prepped his M3A, perhaps actually believing he could swat a Bloc gunship out of the air if it came to it.

"Kill your aura codes," said Bigmouse. "Switch the fuckers off, fast!"

The Ka-18 approached. The distinctive interchop noise of its fat-bladed proprotors didn't get louder, but they could feel it in their chests more deeply. The chop made the trees tremble, made their leaves vibrate. As it came low over the meadow, the engine nacelles began to angle more vertically, and the black craft created gusting eddy patterns in the grasses below it, swirling them into a circle track, spinning the mist up like columns of smoke.

It came closer. They could see the sunlight flash off the brown-tinted glass of the bubble canopy, see the red lines edging the intakes of the turboshaft engines. The front end, that inverse scorpion's tail, bristled with hardpoint mounts, enough firepower to fell all the trees and turn them into wood pulp, and still puncture tank armour at four miles.

"Keep the fuck down," said Rash.

The Ka-18 swept past them, swirling up streamers of mist. They felt the proprotor wash like a winter wind, smelled the exhaust, the clinical metallic output. The trees bent and flexed, branches creaking.

The Bloc bird approached the country house, getting lower and lower as if it was trying to bend down to peer into the windows of a doll's house. It had come to investigate the structure. Close to, the rage of its engines was not just a roar. It was more complex. The deep, volcanic pounding was decorated with light, delicate jingling of swashplates and pushrods.

The main part of the house was an elegant rectangle faced in white fishscale shingles. There were long black ribbon windows in the front aspect, and the side that Falk could see. It was a good-looking house. It reminded him of a proposed retirement place an older colleague had once shown him pictures of. Neosettlement Revival. Good lines, and square angles. Minimal yet extravagant.

Falk watched the rapacious aircraft circle the place, saw the black shape reflecting in the ribbon windows, like a shark gliding in a darkened aquarium. Its downwash whisked and frothed the grass around the plot, whipping up the mist like candyfloss. Falk noticed that the long grasses extended right up to the edges of the plot, and grew in between the house and some of its outbuildings. There'd been at least a few weeks of growth since anyone had tended the outside of the place or taken a mower to the grounds. The house was sitting in the wild meadow as if it had just been elevated in position out of the ground.

Nothing stirred in the house. No one came out to wave at the hovering predator, no one fled from the back doors and tried to make a run for the wood. No dogs barked.

The Ka-18 made one last circle, rotating oh-so-neatly on its twin engines, which were upright like parasols, and then sped off again, nose down, proprotors tilting, throttle open in an abrupt blast of power and noise. It hammered away down the meadow slope and turned south in pursuit of its own kind.

They waited a while, until even the lingering chuckle of its sound had gone away.

"You, me and Preben," Falk said to Rash. He turned to Valdes and said, "You look after Bigmouse for me here, man. Okay?"

"Okay, man. Okay, Nes, you got it."

"Switch your codes back on. We will signal as soon as we've scoped the place," said Falk.

Valdes nodded.

"You got it, Nes. Mouse'll be okay with me."

The three of them got up and moved away from the trees towards the house. The building was so plain, so minimal, there was something almost unfinished about it.

The first building they reached was a refab shed, empty except for some metal drums that might once have contained paint or a weatherproofing solution. The next shed, adjacent, was a more substantial storage structure, well made of lapped timber. Preben forced the door.

The shed was full of unused building materials. Pallets of hand-glazed tiles, rolls of underfelt and a tube of expensive carpet, spare packets of fishscale shingles, paint, a box of light fixtures. The fixtures were expensive brass examples, high end, Early Settlement style, possibly even the real thing. Refurbed antiques, not local. Rash tried the store's lights, but they were dead.

"The building next door's the generator," said Preben. "Self-sustaining plant with a solar soak. Probably wind too, but I don't see a mill. I could get it working."

"Let's check the house first," said Falk.

They came in around the side of the main building. The sliding doors, insulated against deep winter and armoured against intruders, were nevertheless unlocked. The frame was wired with complex security installations, packet-fresh, which had never been engaged. Even the door handle still had shreds of its protective shipping wrap clinging to it.

Preben opened the door. Rash went in first, PAP steady. There was an entrance lobby, a tiled boot room, then a giant kitchen, open-plan and worthy of a lifestyle pictorial. The surfaces were glass and enamel, and the stove the latest ceramic block multifunction. It had never been used. There were still packing materials inside its grill compartment. There was a space ready to accommodate a bulk cooler. No water, hot or cold, issued from the hand-turned wooden taps. There was a musty smell of vacancy and cold, but also a scent of chemicals, new paint, sealants, specialised preparatory treatments. Falk stroked one hand along a sleek glass countertop, and it came away with a tiny residue of dust, like the finest sawdust.

He went out into the hall beyond, keeping the Koba ready. The hallway was triple height, a cored-out space with a tinted skylight that made the blue sky bluer. There was no carpet or flooring at ground level, just the underfloor boarding and fittings, fibreplak baseboard expertly cut to size and still marked with the smudged red stamp of the supplier. The rough hem of insulation layers and cushioning still protruded around the skirting plates, unfinished and waiting to be cut back. In contrast, the staircase was magnificent, a great curved sweep of Neosettlement Revival grandeur with hand-turned balusters, and the upper and middle newel posts decorated with a pendant drop. The handrail was a beautiful slope of steam-bent timber, polished and gleaming, the colour of good caramel.

Through a broad doorway lay the heart of the house, a breathtakingly vast, open-plan living space, split-level. The dramatic ribbon windows, with photoreceptive glass, afforded a panoramic view over the meadow towards the distant coastal hills where the weather station lay. There was supposed to be a fireplace here, but it hadn't been fitted. The bulk of it lay in sections in plastic sheeting on the floor. It had lain there long enough to form deep, indelible impressions in the otherwise unworn carpet. The fireplace was another ostentatious piece of Neosettlement design, marble and slate, a genuine antique.

Falk knelt beside the packaged fireplace and examined it. There was probably more than a ton of material wrapped up on the carpet. He thought about the sort of person whose life required a statement like that. That person would have to be equipped with disposable money and a powerful notion of his significance. It was one thing to build a home this imposing. It was a declaration of new roots, of a commitment to the future: a good spot with a good view on a promising world, the foundation of a legacy, an ancestral seat in the making. But a settlement like Eighty-Six brought a service industry influx with it, a tide of craftsmen and specialists, plumbers, engineers, joiners, stonemasons, woodworkers, glaziers, roofers. Given the virtually untapped natural resources of Eighty-Six, a decent craftsman could have sourced, shaped and fitted a stone fireplace of equal magnificence for a fraction of the price. A grand staircase too, cut from local wood. And the factories of Shaverton should have been able to produce good-quality light fittings.

But the maker of this house had brought them all to Eyeburn. He had chosen them, and purchased them, and paid to ship them whole from other worlds. Falk shuddered to think about the mass-burden the fireplace represented, the payload cost, the freight charges for conveyance aboard a spinrad driver. It was an enduring habit of man to drag the status trappings of his past with him. It was a defiant assertion of permanence, two fingers in the face of the galaxy's dehumanising vastness.

The truly ironic part, of course, was that this sort of Revival furnishing was part of an ultra-fashionable trend for frontier chic. For a long time, it had been the thing to do to import furniture and fittings from Earth, to transplant classic homeworld style and substance to foreign soil, to have a fireplace or a rolltop desk or a slipper bath that had once lived in France or Argentina or Norway, to have hand-coloured tiles that had come from a Dutch farmhouse, or a woodblock floor salvaged from an Italian library. That was a pathology Falk could understand, a birthworld fixation, an obsession with the original and the authentic. A kitchen table of Earthborn oak made a spiritual connection that no other table could achieve, not even if it were hand-made from the many woods superior to oak that settlement had introduced to the human race.

But that fashion was now considered crass. The thing to have these days was a piece of genuine Early Settlement design, a sofa from Three, a sundeck from Nine, reclaimed brick from Seventeen. Architectural salvage from redevelopments and demolitions on First Expansion settlement worlds, often from crude structures that had long outlived their original purpose or aesthetic, were being bought up and shipped out, to capture the flavour of human settlement. People were paying a premium for it. Fireplaces and windows and doors that had been fabricated by whatever local means were available from whatever local materials were available, just to make do, because imports from Earth were so prohibitive in the early days, were now being exported at great expense to new settlements to capture that frontier spirit. Falk felt that it missed the point by such a margin that it went past being funny and came back the other way. Truly capturing the frontier spirit surely meant fabricating what you needed from the resources around you, not importing the results of similar labour by previous pioneers.

He looked up and saw Rash staring down at the fireplace.

"Probably cost more to lug this here than it cost to bring Team Hotel," he said.

"Some fuckers are mad," said Rash.

"Funny how they're the ones who end up with an artisan crafted Casman-style mansion in the oceanside wilderness foothills of a premium settlement, though, right?"

"I've always found that highly amusing," said Rash.

Falk stood up.

"Work on this place stopped dead months ago," he said.

"Agreed. Or longer."

"But it was intended to continue," said Falk.

"Ran out of cash?"

"They've got a barn full of expensive stuff just waiting to be fitted. Don't tell me someone with this clout couldn't have got local workers to keep going at it on a promise. I mean, if money was the problem, it would have been easier to finish this place to a retail standard, then pay off your crew with a slice of the sale rather than just stop dead."

"Something else happened then. Legal? A permit thing? You said the map designation was odd."

"Maybe."

"Maybe someone thought they'd bought this whole plot," said Rash, "started work, then found they didn't have regs approval. Or maybe the parcel sale didn't go through. Maybe it's in a state of suspension because of some kind of ongoing legal action."

"Yeah," said Falk. "Would have been a nice place."

The window changed softly as the light outdoors altered. The sun had gone in, chased away by new clouds. Falk watched the terminator of the bright sunlight retreating across the meadows towards the highway, bright gold grass turning khaki. A little flurry of rain pattered against the ribbon windows.

"At least it's a roof," he said. "We can get Bigmouse indoors, maybe warm up some food."

Rash nodded.

Preben walked in to the living space and beckoned to them.

"Someone's here," he said.

They followed him out, along a corridor that led to other vast rooms, a study, a dining-room. This wing of the house was slightly more finished.

"What have you seen?" Falk asked Preben.

"Down here," said Preben. "There's a small kitchen, a bedroom and a bathroom at the end. Like an annexe. I think it's for a servant or housekeeper."

"Okay."

"Someone's been living in it."

The annexe had probably been the first section of the house to be finished, perhaps to provide basic accommodation for a permanent foreman or supervisor on-site. There was carpet and proper tiling, and though there was no power, water came out of the kitchen taps. In all three rooms, there was evidence of life. Dirty clothes, an unmade bed, a fibreplak sheet pinned across the bedroom window in lieu of curtains. There were open, empty self-heat cans, food wrappers, dirty plates and forks, cups, junk. There were also plates and glasses with candles fixed into fields of wax, each candle lit and fixed in the remains of the last. In the kitchen there lingered a smell of cold, old food and yesterday's cooking, in the bathroom, a scent of stale soap, in the bedroom a musk of human body, unventilated.

"Someone's been here recently," said Preben.

"More than one person," said Rash. He picked up two litex running shoes from the mess on the bedroom floor and put them sole to sole. Neither of them was large, but one was a good two sizes smaller than the other.

"Whoever it was, they could have left here a week ago," said Falk.

Preben shook his head. He picked up one of the open cans from the counter in the small kitchen and handed it to Falk. There was a plastic spoon in it, a babyfood utensil. The can held a residue of some kind of rice-effect dessert. It was a self-heater: you pulled the ring, and peeling the lid off tripped the little thermal liner to speed-heat the contents.

The can was still warm.

They looked at one another.

A renewed flurry of rain drummed on the annexe windows.

"Go bring Bigmouse and Valdes in," Falk said to Preben.

"Yeah?"

"We'll sweep and see who's here."

Preben nodded and headed back to the kitchen exit. Moving together, Rash and Falk finished checking the rooms on the ground floor, and then went up to the first via the back stairs off the annexe. There was carpet in the hallway, but not in the empty rooms destined to be bedrooms.

They came to a room that had been painted up as a child's bedroom. The white walls were covered with bright cartoon faces and glossy coloured shapes, and the ceiling light had been given a lively shade, a mobile of moving planets and moons around a sun. Against one wall was a roller box with the smiling face of a cow painted on it. The box was loaded with brand-new nursery toys and vivid, large-format fabric books. There was no bed, no dresser, no desk or chair. The room had never been finished.

Next door to it there were two bedrooms in a row that were partially fitted. Rugs had been put down to line and cushion the floor, and makeshift curtains hung. Old but serviceable bedsteads had been put in, with mattresses and worn bedclothes. The beds were made. The rooms were cold, but Falk saw little portable heaters in both. Both rooms carried, in their chilly atmospheres, a fading hint of incense, of patchouli or rose.

Falk glanced at Rash. There was an en suite bathroom attached to one of the rooms, and Rash edged forward to check it.

Falk stepped back out into the hall. The backmasked voices had darted across his hearing again briefly, and he wanted a second of silence to check if they made any sense. He saw a box room opposite, a walk-in airing cupboard or drying room with a skylight in the roof and wooden racks for bedding and laundry. The door was ajar.

He approached it, raised the Koba against his shoulder, right hand holding the pistol grip and bracing the weapon's weight against his armpit, left hand reaching forward to push the door all the way open.

Nothing. Empty white linen sacks for laundry. The decorators had used the wooden racks to store their folded drop sheets.

"Come on out," he said.

She appeared, very slowly, from behind the furthest rack. Short blonde hair home-shorn into an elfin cut, a small, gymnastic figure, taut and lean. Her expression was fierce, defiant. Two other girls cowered in the shadows behind her, but Falk noticed them rather less than he noticed the large kitchen knife in the blonde girl's hand.

"You can put that down," he said immediately.

She kept it raised. The daylight catching the long blade showed it was trembling slightly, but from the tension of her grip rather than fear. The girls behind her were murmuring anxiously to each other. The muscles in the corners of her jaw were as hard as knuckles.

"Put it down," he repeated. "You don't need it."

She curled her lip, showed teeth, and then started to rail at him, a stream of venom and invective, a challenge, a curse, a spell to drive him back and banish him.

"Whoa! Whoa!" he called.

"You leave us alone! You leave me and my friends alone! Go! Get out! Go away!" she shouted. "Go away or I will cut your balls off!"

"Hey!" he said, lowering the Koba slightly. "Hey, it's okay! It's wealthy! I'm SOMD! I'm not going to hurt you! Just put the knife down, put it down! I swear I'm not going to hurt you!"

"You are Office? You are Settlement Office soldier?" she asked. There was a hesitation, a surprise.

"Yes, I am. Yes," he said. "Now put that down. No one's going to hurt you. Put that down and we can talk."

Falk felt something touch the back of his head. It was hard and cold. He froze. He knew that the muzzle of an automatic weapon was resting against his skull.

"Fuck," he whispered.

"Fuck is right," said Rash. Standing directly behind Falk, he let the PAP 20 press a little harder.

"What are you doing, Rash?" Falk asked.

"Well, I'm asking you a question, Bloom," Rash replied. "And the question is, since when did you start speaking Russian?"

TWENTY-SEVEN

"The fuck is going on, man?" Valdes exclaimed. "Rash, what the fuck are you doing, man?"

"Take his weapons," Rash said, his PAP still covering Falk squarely. He allowed Falk to turn around to face him.

"It's fucking Bloom, man, are you crazy?"

"Disarm him right now!" Rash snapped. "Preben, help me! Come on, there are three Bloc national females in that store closet, and our buddy Bloom was talking to them in Russian. In Russian! He doesn't get to touch a weapon until we get an explanation! Okay? Okay?"

Preben faltered, then came forward, leaving Valdes wide-eyed, with Bigmouse at the head of the stairs.

"This is wrong," said Bigmouse. "This isn't right at all." He sounded drunk, vague, disorientated. His skin colour wasn't good. He was holding on to the top post of the grand staircase for support.

"S'okay, Mouse," Valdes said, "It's okay. We'll deal with it, man."

Preben came up to Falk and Rash. There was a caught in the headlights look on his too-young face.

"Take his weapon off him, Preben," said Rash.

"There's no need for this," Falk said. "Come on."

"Take his weapon, and his side arm too," Rash ordered.

"What are you doing? What is happening?" the blonde girl cried out from the closet behind them.

"It's okay!" Falk called out to her over his shoulder. "It's all okay!"

He stopped, saw Preben's look, Rash's expression. He heard the sound of his own voice, the words he had just spoken. Not English. Not English at all. A fluent, effortless something that could have been anything for all he knew but sounded Russian.

"You fuck," said Preben, and wrenched the Koba out of Falk's hand.

"No, you don't understand," Falk protested.

"Not another word from you, Bloom," said Rash. "Not a word, until we're ready. Okay? Okay?"

Falk nodded.

Preben slung the Koba over his left shoulder by its strap, then pulled Falk's PDW from his holster. He also took Falk's utility knife.

"Cover the women," Rash told Preben. "Just keep them covered. Watch the blonde bitch, she's got a blade."

"Okay," said Preben. The women in the closet had gone quiet.

Rash gestured with his weapon and indicated that Falk should cross into one of the crudely furnished bedrooms. He did as he was told. It was the room without the en suite. There was no other exit, and the window was a sealed unit.

"Stay in here," Rash said.

Falk stared at him.

"I'll be back in a minute," said Rash.

He backed away, the PAP 20 unwavering, and then shut the door. Alone, Falk lowered his hands. He waited for a second. He heard voices rise in protest, the women gabbling in fear as Preben took the kitchen knife and checked them for other concealeds. He could hear Rash and Preben giving them instructions, slow and overloud, in English, the women replying in terrified Russian. The blonde girl was the most strident. None of them had any real English, just a few swear words and the phrase "please do not hurt". Rash kept telling them to be quiet and to sit down. He told Preben he was going to use the closet as a holding cell for them as soon as they were certain the women weren't hiding anything more dangerous than a carving knife.

Falk sat on the bed, listening to the two overlaid, conflicting conversations outside, two languages colliding. He understood both of them.

He lay back on the thin, worn bedspread and closed his eyes.

"Cleesh? Please be there. Cleesh?"

He was fully expecting no reply when she said, "We thought you'd lost us for good."

Her voice was skeletal and far away, but in his eyes-shut darkness, it came with the soft swell of enclosing warm water.

"What happened?" he asked.

"I don't know. We could hear you, but you clearly couldn't hear us. Ayoob says there was some kind of delay on the sensory reposition. Maybe a side effect of whatever the Bloc is using to scramble signals in that zone."

"Aren't they just jamming our comms?" he asked, enjoying the serenity of the warm darkness for a moment, the sensation of his limp body and limbs supported and swaying in the lightless womb.

"If they were jamming, how would they coordinate their own responses?" Cleesh replied. "It's a scrambling effect.

Very specific, very new. Our sources say the SOMD is busting a vessel trying to find the key for it."

"What else do the sources say, Cleesh?"

"Not much. Big storm brewing. Lot of activity at Lasky and Thompson Ten and Broadknot Fields, several other depots. Stuff going on at the Cape too. Commercial drivers are clearing out of parking orbit. A friend of a friend says that would only happen if something freek® ass big was inbound on an intersystem transit."

"Something big?"

"You know, Falk. Something US Fleet Arm spinrad big. A main battledriver."

"There goes the neighbourhood."

"And centuries of peace, let's not forget that."

"What happened, Cleesh? With the language?"

A tiny, embarrassed laugh.

"We could hear you, Falk. Once you'd got the glares. We could hear what you were saying about the translation. We ran one for you, sent it back, but you clearly couldn't hear it. So, I figured, we could at least allow you to translate it for yourself. Anyway, I got you ling patched. Russian language. Just basic level. I thought I was helping."

"That kind of backfired."

"I'm sorry," she said. Invisible water lapped.

"There is–" she said. Whatever the last word was, it turned sideways and became an unintelligible sound. A beetle click, a toad rattle.

"What?" he asked. "What?"

"There is good news," she said, coming back stronger and clearer.

"Yeah?"

"Oh yes. Ayoob thinks he can pull you out."

"Out of the tank?" Falk asked.

"Out of the tank, out of that guy."

"Bloom."

"Right. Bloom. Of course. Ayoob thinks he's worked out a, well I don't understand any of it, to be honest. Some kind of neural damper. It'll basically cushion and absorb any trauma you might suffer at disconnect. Basically, we can pull you out alive. Hooray, right?"

"You can get me out of here?"

"Yes, Falk. Were you not listening?"

"What about Bloom?" Falk asked. "Will he be cushioned by the damper too? If he isn't, the trauma's likely to fuck him up completely."

She didn't answer.

"Cleesh? Can you still hear me?"

"Yeah. Yes, Falk. I'm here."

"What's the answer, Cleesh? Will Bloom be cushioned or not?"

"We have to get you out of there, Falk. Bari knows it. The GEO lawyers accept it. We can't risk you any longer."

"So what? Bloom gets screwed?"

"Listen, Falk. It's not pretty. It's not ideal. We both know that. We also both knew this gig came with unassessed risks attached to it. Bloom knew it too."

Falk sighed. "But the bottom line is if you save me and pull me out, Bloom dies of the resulting bioshock."

"The bottom line," said Cleesh, "is that Bloom is dead anyway. I'm sorry. He's only still ticking because you're there. There's nothing left. Even if we could slide you out with zero trauma, he would fade and die without you keeping his autonomics working."

Falk lay in silence. He opened his eyes, and stared up at the pale grey ceiling of the bedroom, the running shadow blur of the rain streaming down the window. He closed his eyes again, re-entered the darkness and the salty warm suspension of the Jung tank.

"If I quit this life," he said quietly, "this body dies. Without me onboard to run it, Bloom is gone."

"Falk–"

"I'm keeping him alive. Theoretically, I could keep him alive until I find a medical station to treat him and support him, and you find a painless way to disconnect me."

"Neither of those things is especially likely, Falk," said Cleesh, "particularly in the time frame available to us. Yes, hypothetically, if Bloom was on full and systemic life support, and we figured out how to unplug you without traumatic feedback, then he might stand a chance. But that's a gigantic might. We have to play the odds, Falk. We have to exit you."

"No," he said.

"Falk?"

"You do not disconnect me unless you have my specific instruction, do you hear me, Cleesh?"

"Don't do this, Falk–"

"Do not fucking unplug me unless I tell you to! Okay? Okay? I'm counting on you, Cleesh! I am counting on you! Do not let them do it, not Ayoob, not Bari fucking Apfel! Do you understand?"

"Please, Falk–"

"Do you fucking understand me?"

"I'll talk to them, Falk."

"Do better than that. Do what I tell you to do."

The bedroom door thumped open. Falk opened his eyes and sat up fast. Preben was standing in the doorway, Rash beside him.

"Who were you talking to?" Preben asked.

"No one."

"Then start talking to us," said Rash, stepping past Preben into the cold bedroom. "And make it good. Really good."

"There's been an unfortunate misunderstanding," said Falk.

"Yeah, how's that?" asked Rash.

"I got ling patched."

Rash shrugged.

"So?"

"He did," said Preben quietly. "He got one of those language censorship things. We all took the piss because of it."

Rash kept staring.

"He's cussing pretty good as far as I see," he said.

"Head shot," said Falk. "I think it fucked the patching up."

"You're going to keep playing that card, huh?" asked Rash.

"Only when it's true," replied Falk.

"Fine. Explain the Russian."

"Seriously, Rash, I understand why that did a number on you. It came as a surprise to me too."

"Yeah, right."

Falk rose to his feet.

"In the wind-up to this, we all heard the gossip. We all heard the talk that the Bloc might be involved. No shit this time. So I went and got patched because I figured there would be a lot of media coverage, and I didn't want to shame my mother by turning up on a newsfeed, potty mouth. Our brave boys at war. SOMD covered the patching fee. You all saw the notices. Free patching."

"Most of us can mind our own language," said Rash.

"The guy who patched me," said Falk. "He said if I stuck my hand in my pocket, he could patch anything I wanted. Said I could get a basic Russian and Chinese language starter. For the price of a few beer-effects. So I took the Russian. Thought it might be useful. Hoped it wouldn't have to be. Swear to God, you guys, I'd forgotten it was even there. I'd never used it. No one had ever spoken Russian at me. I just answered. I didn't even realise what was happening until I saw your reaction."

Preben shot a look at Rash.

"Sounds pretty convincing," he said.

Rash scowled.

"Yeah. And it sounds exactly what some Bloc spy would say too," Rash replied. "We know they were deep inside us before this shit went down. We know they were in place and ready to move. Stands to reason they would've been in amongst us too."

"Oh, come on, Rash," said Falk. "Think about it."

"You're looking me in the eye and telling me you're not a Bloc insert?"

"Yes, Rash. That's what I'm doing."

"You're not a spy?"

Harder to answer. Much harder. No way to control affect.

"I'm not a spy," said Falk.

"You can't even lie to me properly," said Rash. "You bastard, I can see it in you. You can't even lie."

"Rash, don't be a dumb fuck about this," said Falk. "If I'm what you say, why would I have done any of the shit I've done this last day or so?"

Rash didn't answer.

"Would I have brought Kilo in shooting at the hortiplex? Would I have gone for Masry's whole insane hopter plan to get us out? If I was a Bloc insert, I'd have walked you into a hot pocket trap, or just sat on you and brought trouble your way."

Rash stared at him, then walked out of the room. Falk looked at Preben.

"What do you think?" Falk asked. "Is he just stepping out to get a long run up?"

Preben grinned. He dropped the Koba onto the end of the bed. The weight of it wobbled the mattress. Then he handed Falk his PDW and utility knife.

"You scared genuine crap out of me talking Bloc like that," he said quietly.

"Scared the crap out of me," Falk smiled. "What did you do with those girls?"

They were in the walk-in closet, hunched in the far corner.

"Come on," Falk said. "Come on out. We'll talk."

They looked at him, sullen and unwilling.

"It's okay," he nodded.

They got up.

"It's okay," he said again.

"That's fucking freaky," Preben whispered to him. "The way you're saying that stuff."

"I know," Falk whispered back.

"Where do you want to take them?" asked Rash.

"Where are Valdes and Mouse?"

"In the main room. The lounge."

"Let's take them back down to the annexe," said Falk. "That's where they were living. Let's offer them some food, something to drink, and make some for ourselves too. Maybe they'll talk more if they're more comfortable."

Rash nodded. They led the three women down the hall and descended by the back staircase. The blonde was clearly the boss. She was keeping the others together, one strong lean arm locked around the shoulders of the smallest, a redhead, like she was a baby sister. The other girl, a tall, too-thin brunette, was about the same age as the blonde, and kept in her shadow, head down. The redhead still carried a little adolescent weight in her face and body. The brunette would have been a catwalk waif if she only stepped out and put her head back. The blonde just had a dense power, like a fighter.

"What are your names?" Falk asked. There was a little fusion ring in the kitchen space of the annexe, and Preben boiled some water in a glass jug. On the counter, there was an open catering drum of coffee-effect. The girls sat on a little bench seat under the window and stared at him.

"Names?" he repeated.

"Ask them if they have any papers," said Rash. "IDs, brooches, documents, anything like that."

Falk repeated the question in Russian.

"They took them," the blonde answered, tilting her chin up to release the words, like her mouth had recoil.

"Who did? Who took them?"

"Popa," she said, more quietly. "Popa and the men."

"So you had papers, but they were taken from you? And these papers showed you all to be citizens of the Central Bloc?"

A nod.

"With travel permits to Eighty-Six via where? One of the polar fiefs?"

Another nod.

"But no visa, I'm guessing, or entry waiver for the US Northern Territories? The places where the good work and the real money is?"

She shook her head.

"What's your name?" he asked.

"Tal," she said.

"Hello, Tal. Someone, this Popa maybe? They promised they could get you into US territory, didn't they? They said they could get you and your friends over the border, line you up with some work, cash in hand. In return, you had to give them your IDs."

"Yes."

"How much?"

"Six hundred each. Well, four and half for Lenka, because she's younger." She indicated the redhead.

"They said we'd make twenty times that back in a couple of months."

"What kind of work did they describe?" asked Falk.

"Bar work. Waitressing in a small town. ProFood, you know. Maybe farm working."

"And what did it actually turn out to be?"

"You know what it turned out to be," she said.

Preben was pouring the hot water into mugs, stirring in the powder. The clink-clink of the spoon was somehow prosaic and irritating. Falk looked at Rash.

"They were trafficked," he said. "Brought in over the border in the north, maybe down through Antrim on the highway run. A promise of summer work. But it was forced sex labour."

Rash thought about it.

"Here?" he asked.

"This happen here?" Falk asked the blonde.

"We were at another place first for a few weeks, down in the valley by the highway, a farm. Then they brought us here."

"How long ago?"

"Four months."

"Why didn't they leave?" asked Rash. "Ask them that."

"Why didn't you leave?"

"We had no papers," said the blonde. "They didn't give us no money. We had no clothes for outdoors. We didn't know where we were. They also threaten us and beat us. Popa or one of his men were here all the time."

"Is Popa Russian?"

She shook her head.

"No, he is US, like you."

"Where is the guard now? Why are you here alone?"

"Four days ago, the man who was here got a celf message. He left in a hurry. He said he would be back in three hours, he said we had to stay here and there would be big trouble if we didn't stay here. He said Popa would find us, and cut our faces. But he never came back, and no one· ever came back. And we didn't know what to do."

"So you hid?"

She nodded.

Falk told Preben and Rash what she'd said.

"I've seen this kind of thing before," said Rash. "On Eighty. Migrants looking for work, trying to stay off the grid. No one misses them. I haven't seen it with Bloc nationals before, but it doesn't surprise me. They answer an ad, talk to some guy in a bar, next thing they know, they're a prisoner somewhere."

"Come on, they could just walk out. Run away," said Preben.

"Out here?" asked Rash. "This kind of edge is perfect. No one around for miles. Through traffic, mostly men. No questions. The drivers who come to the depot, the seasonal field workers? They want a beer-effect, a bed and a fuck. It's economics. Supply and demand."

"That old frontier spirit," said Falk. "Sweat and toil and rough justice. Good old-fashioned values."

"You don't think this is about girls, do you?" asked Preben.

"Think what is about girls?" asked Falk.

"This war," he replied. "You don't think the Bloc has come in mob-handed because a bunch of settlementeer farmers have got hold of some girls?"

"You're a fucktard sometimes, Preben," said Falk. "This is just normal shit that happens. The Bloc doesn't care about these women any more than the US does. They're victim statistics."

"There is a connection, though," said Rash. "The frontier between us and the fief is clearly pretty porous, at least in terms of the black market. It suggests pipeline routes that could be used to get other people over the line. The inserts. The Bloc forces were embedded in the region, waiting to go live. It's probably how they got in."

Falk nodded.

They established that the girls were called Milla, Lenka and Tal. Milla was the tall brunette. Lenka, the baby sister, didn't seem to want to do anything except cry without making a sound.

Falk took a coffee-effect and sat talking to Tal in the kitchenette for a while.

"Do you know what this place is?"

"Popa said it was going to be a house for an important man. This man, he had put a claim in for the whole area, for the land, and had gone ahead and started building. But the claim had been turned down, or something. So the building was left. The man was very cross."

"Do you know the man's name?"

She shook her head.

"I was never told, but we saw some documents when we first came here, and they had a name on that was Seberg."

"They used the house because it was empty?"

"Because it was empty, and it had some class. Popa said he could get more money bringing men to a better venue. I think the man who owned this house, he had been in business with Popa, and with the men on our side who had sold us over. They all worked in mining, and in shipping."

"So the men who came here, they were drivers? From the highway? Farmers?"

"Some, but most were miners. Mining engineers. You

know? Prospectors. They were working in the area. They came in for a month or two at a time."

"Bloc citizens?"

"Yes, and also US. From both sides."

Falk listened to the rain on the skylights.

"They bring in other girls with you?"

"I've seen some," she said. "Some brought in at other times. They didn't keep us all together."

Falk took out his glares, zipped through the playback, froze on a decent frame and handed them to her to put on.

"Do you recognise her?" he asked.

She looked strange with her head up and the glares on, as if staring at something invisible in front of her face.

"I don't know her," she said.

"Okay."

"But I recognise the man with her."

"You do?" he asked.

Tal nodded and handed the glares back.

"He came here sometimes. He was a customer."

Falk put the glares on and looked at the frozen image he'd shown her. A moment from Smitts's clip. The girl who had shot him and a big dark-haired man, crouching together in the open hatch of *Pika-don*, backlit by fierce white light. A second later, they would get up and come towards the camera.

"Definitely him?"

"Yes."

"Know his name?"

"No."

"Was he Bloc or US?"

"He was Bloc," said Tal, "but he pretend to be US. His accent was good, but I did not think it was that good. It was like yours. I could tell it was fake."

"He was ling patched."

"What is that?" she asked.

He shook his head as though it didn't matter. "So he was made to sound US."

"I heard Popa call him a business associate. I heard someone else say he worked on local farm. His hands smelled of plant food. Not nice."

"What was it Popa did? Do you know? Apart from running girls, I mean?"

"Popa said he worked at fuel depot. He work for RP."

She looked at him.

"You asked me about the girl first," she said. "Why?"

"She shot me."

"She shot you?" Her voice was tinged with disbelief.

"This is a bullet hole," he said, pointing at his face.

She leaned towards him, squinting, staring at the wound.

"A bullet went in there?"

"Yeah."

"How are you living still?"

"Beats the hell out of me."

She peered even closer, fascinated. "It hurts you?"

"Yes," he said. "Don't touch it."

She pulled back sharply.

"I wasn't going to," she said. "I don't touch a man again."

She got up and walked towards the counter.

"Do you want another drink?" she asked. "I want another drink."

"I'm fine," said Falk.

"What is happening here?" she asked. "We heard bombs earlier. And then this hopter came in very close."

"There's a war," said Falk. "And it's started for real."

Falk went out into the spacious living room. Valdes was napping on one of the plastic-wrapped couches. Bigmouse was sitting back on another. He looked asleep too, but he was stiff and awkward, and his skin was waxy. Falk knelt beside him, trying not to disturb him. His breathing was shallow and laboured, and when Falk listened close, he could hear an unpleasant crackling sound deep in his chest.

It was beginning to get dark outside, and the rain cover was steeping the advancing gloom. Outside, in the twilight, he could see Rash and Preben walking the edge of the house perimeter, looking down the valley at the highway area.

In the kitchenette of the annexe, Milla had lit a candle in a cup.

"Keep it away from the windows," he told her. Tal was asleep on the bench, with Lenka curled up on the seat beside her, her head in Tal's lap. Falk walked through into the small, scruffy bedroom they shared, and pulled the door closed behind him.

"Cleesh?" he said, quietly.

There was no reply.

"Cleesh?"

This time, there were a few sideways sounds, beetle clicks, amphibious burblings.

"Cleesh?"

He sat down on the unmade bed. The girls had presumably shared the bed for warmth. Things had accumulated around and under it: candle stubs, food wrappers, a few dirty clothes. There were books too, colourful picture books taken, he presumed, from the child's bedroom upstairs. He picked one of them up. He hadn't seen any other books in the house, but he presumed the girls had chosen it because it didn't have the impenetrable slabs of English-language text a novel might contain. Simple bold captions in block type ran across attractive and arresting photographs.

Our Great Adventure it said on the cover. The words were superimposed on an image of a man in a First Era space suit, performing an EVA, free-floating beside a capsule in near-Earth orbit. The Earth was partly reflected in the oversized, gold-tinted dome of his helmet. He looked helpless, adrift, like a bloated dead man floating in a rip tide. The red acronym of his launch agency was embossed across the chest plate of his obese, snow-white suit. The shadows were hard, the light was hard, there was a lack of diffusion, a kind of purity.

Inside, the words and pictures told a simple version of the first milestones of post-terrestrial expansion. The Space Race. Falk had forgotten it had ever been called that. Such a glib thing to call it, so cheerful and optimistic. As he understood it, there had been no gentlemanly fair play. Just three global superpowers locked in a ruthless, often reckless, competition to establish domains beyond the terrestrial limits. Two of them, the US and the Bloc, had essentially used the First Era to pursue and expand their Cold War rivalry through technological superiority and brash endeavour.

There were the great moments he remembered from his own childhood picture books, the building blocks that had led to the real acceleration into the First Expansion. Vostok and Gemini. Glenn and Leonov. Shepherd and Gagarin. The Soyuz, Apollo and Long March pro-grammes. The launches. The orbits. The spacewalks and the launch pad fires. The most memorable shot of all, the indelible image of the first man on the moon. Virgil Grissom, June 1967.

"Falk?"

He started, dropped the book.

"Cleesh? Where did you go?"

"Same problem as before, sorry," she said.

He closed his eyes, slipped into the darkness to make listening easier.

"I've got a little info for you," she said. "I've been listening. Sorry. Hard not to. I've located you on the SO land registry. Pretty sure I have, anyway. There was a Grayson Seberg working for Resource Provision here on Eighty-Six. He was an operations director. When the coast sections and Gunbelt Highway range opened up for development, he lodged about four hundred private purchase bids for land parcels in the area."

"That's a lot."

"It is, though it's not unusual for a senior exec who's close to retirement and wants to invest heavily in a developing settlement. Seberg was part of a little cartel, in fact. Private speculators, several of them with backgrounds in mineralogy and earth science. I think those thirty years spent working for RP in a developing market like this showed him the smart investments were mineral rights and mining infrastructure. He took his retirement fund from RP, and chose the Gunbelt Range. Set up a little company called Ocean Exploratory."

"This house?"

"A retirement place. A family estate close to the bulk of his investments."

Falk sighed. Water lapped.

"And then?"

"Until about two years ago, things were clearly going well for Ocean Exploratory. They were developing relationships with several large corporate entities, both US and Bloc, probably looking for the right tender to set up a co-venture and start to exploit the land Seberg and his partners had secured."

"So playing both sides?"

"Nothing unusual there, either. Seberg was feeling out Bloc and US mining companies alike, surveyors, extraction engineering firms. His company was also talking to two

Chinese processing consortia. They were auditioning for the best partners to get into business with."

Falk lay back on the dirty bed, listening to her voice.

"Two years ago," Cleesh said, "the trouble started. Small stuff at first. Several pieces in the Shaverton newsfeeds claiming Seberg had used propriatorial data acquired during his years at RP to inform his choice of territories. RP and two of the big US mining companies up at Marblehead were going to sue him for abuse of privileged information. Seberg went on record and said it was hard to stick a pin in a map of Eighty-Six and *not* strike something worth mining, and he was simply embodying the settlementeer ideal of entrepreneurial yadda yadda. But then it all gets weird."

"By which you mean...?"

"It all goes quiet. Ocean Exploratory shuts shop. Seberg disappears from the picture, and all the development in that area comes to a halt. If you lift the lid and inspect the records, like I just did, you can see why. The SO stepped in. First they accused Seberg and Ocean of developing parcels before formal approval and permissions had been granted or ownership formally transferred. Then they slapped a Strategic Development Order on the whole lot."

"Harsh. What do we read from that?"

"What would you read, Falk?" she asked.

He shrugged.

"The US bias on Eighty-Six is particularly obvious. Maybe Seberg was getting too friendly with a Bloc partner and various US rivals didn't like it."

"That sounds credible, right?"

"Well, there would be a lot at stake," he replied. "Trillions, perhaps, long term, from extraction? Depends what he had here. A couple of big US corps think they're going to lose out, apply a little pressure to the SO, which then comes down on Seberg. I suppose if Seberg and his partners hadn't filed their claims impeccably, the SO might have found some technicality to exploit, and turned that into grounds to formally disallow all of Seberg's pending bids."

"Which, on top of everything else, would leave a bunch of very disgruntled Central Bloc partners north of the border, grieving over their ruined deal and failed investment."

"Indeed it would," he said.

"It's a serious story," said Cleesh.

"It's a major, major story," Falk replied. "Are you kidding? The SO displaying blatant bias and using its powers and influence to favour US interests, and in so doing light off the first ever post-global war? Our names will look very good on the awards."

"They will. Bari says–"

"Listen, Cleesh. I think we have to tread very carefully here. Bari is GEO, and GEO is not without a vested interest. Can he hear me saying this?"

"No."

"It's true. GEO is very much a US corporation."

"Agreed, except that GEO is a principal investor in the Eighty-Six settlement, and has been since the early days, and has no particular interest in a mining remit. Even if the SO's bias was pro-US, a war on Eighty-Six is going to hurt GEO in fundamental ways. Bari wants this out there as much as we do. If it can do anything to break the dead-lock and bring this conflict back from the brink, we have his full support."

There was a distant thump, a hollow sound. Someone had knocked against the outside of the Jung tank, and the kettle drum echo had rolled through the water to him.

"It would be very useful to get some hard evidence this end," he said.

"What are you thinking?" she asked. "I'm filling some pretty fat files here. Seberg. Ocean Exploratory. The parcel bids. The business courtships. The Strategic Significance Order."

"Yeah, but that'll be official record. The SO and the favoured corps will have covered anything untoward very carefully. We'd need contract lawyers to comb the evidence, and even if we did find an irregularity, it would probably be some very subtle thing that lacked any newsweight."

"I can get a team on it," she replied. "Bari can bring in some specialists."

"Hold off for now. It will sell better if we retain an independent firm to do the searches. GEO's thumbprint would not be helpful."

"Well, gee, Falk, I don't know what a hotshot like you has got in the bank," she said, "but I can't afford that kind of retainer. We need Bari for this."

"No, we need an outlet. We need to decide how we're going to break this story and handle it. That means a really respectable agency or network. Give it some thought. Between us, we've got plenty of links."

Someone gently banged against the metal tube of his tank again.

"So the evidence your end?" she asked.

"I don't know. It would be useful to know if a specific or unusual deposit was at the root of the dispute. It would be good to find Seberg or any of his partners."

"Oh, about that," she said. "It may not be much, but the employment records for the Eyeburn depot listed an asset manager called Reed Popper. That's double-pee-ee-are. He'd been there two years and was still listed at the time the place went silent."

"He was RP?"

"No, he was a contractor, but he was paid through RP. I was wondering if he was your 'Popa'. Right place, right time, probably knew Seberg."

"Probably."

"I tracked him back, and let's just say his identity record is not great. It's not entirely clear who Reed Popper is, where he came from, or when he arrived on Eighty-Six."

"See what you can do to track down Seberg or any of his key associates," said Falk. "The real prize, I suppose, would be proof that a US corp is exploiting any of the resources that Seberg claimed in this area."

"Because they shouldn't be?"

"Exactly because they shouldn't be. The SO snatched all the land rights away from Ocean. Do we know the grounds of the Strategic Significance Order?"

"They're not obliged to disclose the terms," Cleesh replied. "I'll go through it closely to see if there are any hints. It's usually either to protect the security of a sovereign state, or it's about protecting an area of singular scientific interest or an exceptional natural environment."

"Right, so technically, all the parcels should have reverted to SO protection. Like they did with the western veldt on Seventy-Seven? The habitat of those herding grazers?"

"Yeah. And like that bulk refinery the Chinese tried to build on that island off the Bloc settlement on Twenty-Six. That whole fuss, Falk, remember?"

"I do. So, if there's a commercial US operator or operators at work anywhere on what used to be Ocean holdings, even in a preliminary fashion, it's smoking-gun evidence that the SO strong-armed commercial competitors out of the way, cleared the region and let US national interests in through a back door. It would be primary evidence of prejudicial misconduct."

"In that case I lay real money it's connected to the Heligo thing," said Cleesh.

"The thing on the clip?"

"Yeah. You've run the clip since I patched you, right?"

"No, I–"

"Freek®, Falk! Get in the game! The translation I got off your sound-for-sound version pretty much makes it clear that Heligo is the thing. Whatever Heligo is."

"Shit. Okay. I'm going to play it back now and–"

The booming came again. Somebody kicking the outside of the tank.

"Nes! Nestor!"

Falk scrambled up, eyes open. Valdes blundered into the bedroom, urgent.

"You gotta come, man! You gotta see!"

TWENTY-EIGHT

Outside, night had fallen, a cold, hard night full of mean-tempered rain. Falk followed Valdes through to the palatial living room. Everyone had gathered there to stare out of the expensive ribbon windows towards the west. Even Bigmouse, slumped on the couch, had opened his eyes and propped himself up a little.

Beyond the edge of the woodland, three or four miles away, the landscape was alight. Great shock flashes of orange glare lit up the low clouds, huge, trembling lights. After each, time-lapsed, came the distant thump of detonations. Each thump sounded like someone kicking the outside of a theoretically conceptual metal box.

It was an artillery duel, an armour clash of significant size, running down the line of the highway and across the area where the depot lay. The quick, flickering flashes, burps of combusting gas, were the signatures of main armour weapons firing. The bigger, slower blooms of radiance were detonations. The fireballs of hi-ex shells. The brief, vast explosions of something going up as its magazine or powerplant was hit. The neon-spark showers of detonating munitions or shattering armour hulls. Falk could see flurries of tracers and the occasional odd, jump-strobe blister of hardbeam fire.

"Fuck," whispered Preben. They could all see the amber reflection of their own appalled faces in the window glass, lit by the distant fires. The sealed-unit glass shivered in its frame with the more significant shockwaves. Tal had Lenka pulled tight against her.

"What's happening, Falk?" asked Cleesh.

"The SO counter-offensive has begun," he said. "Ground forces coming right up the valley and the highway run, meeting Bloc units head-on."

"We can all fucking see that, you moron," said Rash.

"Sorry, I..." said Falk. "Sorry."

Falk could see small firefly lights, dodging and darting around the boiling lightshow. Hopter gunships on ground attack, visible because of the glittering discharge of their weaponpods.

"The fucking forest is on fire," said Valdes, pointing. "The fucking forest."

Over to their left, two miles from the house, a large section of the treeline was burning hot yellow, almost incandescent. Falk could see the black stripes of tree trunks in the brightness of it, realised that streaming smoke from the fire, black on black, was masking a whole section of the malevolent night sky. Something had gone astray, hit the trees, or maybe something had shot at a target using the forest cover. H-beams, probably, roasting and igniting vegetation like that.

They were all staring at the forest fire when the big one came. They felt it shake the building, and the flash was so bright they all cried out and winced away. An immense sheet of flame spread up into the sky, seething and ferocious.

It was like some supervolcanic catastrophe. The blaze didn't die back, it grew. The night became a lurid, amber day. Flames rose half a mile into the air, wet orange fire that rolled and folded into hellish black smoke.

A few seconds after the flash and the earth shock, the blast wind reached them, thrashing the trees in the nearby woods, flattening the long grass of the meadow, peppering the long ribbon window with grass seeds, water droplets, grit and twigs. The pelting lasted several seconds before it subsided.

"The depot," said Rash. "The depot just went up."

"No way that was intentional targeting," said Preben.

"No shit," Rash replied.

The colossal fuel blaze filled the western sky like a sunset.

"We should get clear. Get out of here," said Falk.

"Where to?" asked Rash dubiously.

"Into the hills. Away from that."

"Yeah, how?"

"On foot if we have to."

"What about Bigmouse?" asked Rash.

"We carry him."

"We won't get far, then," said Rash.

Falk looked at him.

"I don't think staying here is going to be such a great option for very much longer," he said, and then gestured towards the light show. "Would you like to head that way?"

Rash returned his look.

"Right now, we're fucked whatever we do," he said. "I think we should try the comms again. See if we can raise some friendlies now they're close."

"Yeah," said Preben. "Good chance they've cleared this jamming shit by now."

"Hey!"

They looked around. It was Tal. She was standing beside the couch, looking down at Bigmouse. Her posture was uncomfortable, unsettled.

"What is wrong with him?" she asked.

"What did she say?" asked Rash.

"Shit!" said Falk. He went straight over to Bigmouse, knelt down beside him. The others crowded in behind him.

"He's not breathing," said Preben. Bigmouse had slumped back again, his eyes closed. Even in the firelit gloom of the room, Falk could see the shadow of cyanosis on Bigmouse's cheeks and lips.

"Oh fuck!" he said. "Don't you fucking do this to me, Mouse! Don't you fucking dare!"

"Clear his airway, man!" Valdes cried.

"Yeah, so fucking helpful," snapped Falk. He was struggling to loosen Bigmouse's blate and shirt. The pressure on Bigmouse's bruised torso should have caused a sharp pain response. Mouse didn't stir. He wasn't breathing at all.

"Fuck, come on," Falk said.

"What's happening?" asked Cleesh inside his head.

"None of us are medics," said Falk loudly. "None of us are fucking medics. Times like now, I really wish I knew what to do with someone who had stopped breathing as a result of severe blunt-force trauma to the chest."

"No shit," replied Preben, helping with the blate, "we've got to make him breathe."

"Stand by," said Cleesh. "I'm getting Underwood."

"You got to pump his chest, man," Valdes said, pushing in. "I've seen it. You've got to get his lungs going."

"We have no idea of the injuries," replied Rash. "We start pushing his chest in and out, we could be ramming broken rib down through his lungs. Could collapse them. Or he could have a what, a blood build-up."

"Haemothorax," said Falk.

"Yeah, that. I've heard of chest wall damage where whole sections of fucking ribcage become detached."

"Is there any first aid stuff in the house?" Falk asked Tal in Russian. "Anything at all? Anything you've seen?"

"There is a box in the outhouse. A first aid box for the builders who were here," she replied, eyes wide. "We sometimes took painkillers from it."

"Go and get it. Show Preben where it is," he said. He switched to English. "Preben, Tal's going to take you to get a medical pack from one of the outbuildings. Get it fast."

They left the room together, running.

"Mr Falk, this is Underwood," said a new voice in his head. "What can you tell me?"

"He took several rounds in the body-plating yesterday," said Falk. "Bad bruising, chest pain, now he's stopped breathing altogether."

"What?" asked Rash.

"I'm just thinking out loud," said Falk.

"You're probably looking at severe pulmonary contusion," said Underwood gently. "Is his skin blue? His lips?"

"Yes," said Falk.

"Yes, what?" asked Valdes.

"How long since he stopped breathing?" asked Underwood.

"How long since he stopped breathing?" asked Falk.

"Five minutes?" said Valdes.

"He was okay when we came in here," said Rash. "He spoke to me. Two minutes?"

"Two minutes, you think?" replied Falk.

"You've got four or five at the most before the damage becomes irreversible," said Underwood. Her voice sounded like she was standing on the other side of a locked door. "You need to clear the airway and get him ventilated. You can do CPR?"

"CPR is going to make his injury worse," said Falk.

"Right, right," agreed Valdes.

"Being dead is going to make his injury worse too," said Underwood. "Start CPR. Is there any way you can intubate him? Do you have any medical equipment?"

"Start CPR," Falk said to Rash.

"You think?" Rash looked dubious.

"Yes. Can you do it?"

"Yes," said Rash.

"We've got a medical pack on the way," said Falk.

"I know we have," said Rash, kneeling down beside Bigmouse and looking at Falk as though he wasn't making any sense.

"CPR is the best we can do until it gets here," said Falk.

"When the pack arrives, you'll need the endotracheal tube and a bag valve mask," said Underwood.

Rash had begun CPR. From behind them, Milla uttered a cry.

Falk turned to look.

"What is it?" he asked.

She was staring out of the window at the firelit night.

He got up, joined her. The depot fire still lit the valley, and the armour fight was still blinking and blistering along the highway line. A soft rain of burning cinders, glowing like coals was snowing down across the landscape, the consequence of the vast depot eruption.

But there were vehicles approaching, coming up the edge of the meadow, on the same side as the house. They were transport trucks, light utility vehicles, running with their lights off, but the glare of the depot flare was so huge, visibility was like a strong sunset.

There were three of them. Three trucks. Behind them, at a distance, two more.

"Are they coming here?" Milla asked him. It was the first time she addressed him directly.

"Yeah," he said.

"Who are they?"

He adjusted his glares, applied a touch of zoom and vision balance. The trucks were SObild carriers, pretty standard cargo ATVs, painted drab-black. They were the sort of military utility vehicle either side might use. But his money was on Bloc forces. But why were they coming this way? Were they fleeing the fight, or hunting for an objective? Were they simply looking for a fall-back position to defend in the face of the high-scale SOMD aggression?

One thing was certain. There wouldn't be any negotiating. From the moment they began taking Eyeburn down and eliminating the locals, the Bloc ops force had demonstrated zero interest in talking about anything. This was serious business, professional. There was no wiggle room whatsoever.

"We've got company coming!" he called out.

"How much?" Rash replied.

"Too much."

Valdes hurried over to the window beside Falk and the girl. He groaned.

"We've got to go, man," he said to Falk. "I mean, just go! I don't run from fights, but I don't mind running from stupid!"

"What about Bigmouse?" Rash said.

"I don't want to ditch him, man!" Valdes cried, turning. "He's my brother, and I don't want to ditch him, no way! But he's already gone, Rash! Look at him! And if we stay here for him, he will get us scorched!"

Rash stared at Falk. He was still applying CPR. Lenka was kneeling beside him, holding Bigmouse's head steady.

"I guess it's your call," he said to Falk.

"Is it?" Falk replied. "Is it really? That's fucking great."

Preben and Tal ran back into the room lugging a large green plastic medi-crate.

"We've got vehicles inbound!" Preben declared, slightly out of breath.

"We know," replied Falk.

Preben set the crate down beside the couch.

"We've got to exit," he said. "Absolutely now."

"Yes, we have," said Falk.

Rash was still applying CPR. Every time his head came up, he looked at Falk.

"You got a pulse?" Falk asked.

"No," said Rash.

Falk looked at Tal.

"Open the box fast," he said in Russian. "We need a throat tube and a bag mask."

She nodded, and swung the lid off the plastic case.

"What are you doing?" Preben asked. "We haven't got time for any of that shit!"

"We tube him. We bring him with us," said Falk.

"Fuck, he's dead, Bloom!" Preben cried.

"We tube him, we bring him with us," said Rash softly.

Preben gazed down at Rash.

"You're both fucking insane. Pretards. Total pretards!"

"You and Valdes," said Rash. "Go keep the back door clear. The back of the annexe. We'll have to leave that way."

He glanced at Falk.

"Right?"

Falk nodded.

"Right. Do like Rash said. Keep the area clear. Even if we don't get far, we want to get into the trees at least. Maybe get down in cover, wait for them to move on."

Valdes and Preben stared at him.

"What? Am I speaking Russian again?" he snapped. "Get the fuck on with it!"

"Jesus!" Valdes replied.

"Do it quiet! Quiet!" Falk insisted. "No shooting unless you absolutely have to. If we can sneak out, that's a better way to go."

They turned to leave.

"Preben!" Falk called. He picked up Bigmouse's hefty thumper and the bag of grenade shells.

"If you do have to start shooting, make it count."

Preben nodded. Fast and fluid, he clamped his M3A to his back plate, slung the shell bag around his neck and took the thumper. He and Valdes headed for the annexe. Valdes was still grumbling.

Falk glanced back at the view. The lead truck was less than a minute away. The burning soot was still snowing.

"Okay, we're going to intubate him," he announced.

"And you know how to do that?" Rash asked.

"There's probably no point if there isn't a pulse," said Underwood, like she was suddenly standing right beside him.

"We'll do it anyway," Falk said. Tal had found a mask with a rubberised bag valve. She was stripping the sterile plastic wrap off an intestinal loop of plastic tubing.

"This?" she asked.

"Yeah," he said, and took it. He looked at Milla. "Go take the plastic sheeting off that couch," he said. "Try not to rip it."

She hurried to obey.

"Tilt his head back," said Underwood. "You need to open the airway as wide as possible. You'll have to pull the tongue forward and down, most likely, to stop it getting in your way. Use a depressor, if you have one. Or your fingers."

Falk moved Lenka aside, and got hold of Bigmouse's head. There was frothy blood around the man's lips. He felt cold.

"I think," said Rash, "I think there might be a pulse now. Really far away."

Falk nodded. He took the tube that Tal was holding out.

"Don't slide the tube down his oesophagus," Underwood said quietly. "Don't force it. You don't want to jam it into the wrong pipe, and you don't want him to aspirate stomach contents into his lungs."

"How will I know if I'm getting it down his oesophagus?" he asked. He was fiddling with the floppy tube, with Bigmouse's lips and tongue.

"I don't fucking know!" Rash replied.

"Just slide it in," said Underwood calmly. "Do the best you can."

Falk began to insert the tube. His hands were trembling. It was like trying to feed a snake through a wet sports sock.

Was this how the snake had ended up in his own stomach?

He fed it in further. He felt a tremor that might have been a slight gag reflex in Bigmouse's throat muscles.

"Go on, go on," said Rash.

"Is it in yet?" Underwood asked.

"Almost," said Falk. He glanced over his shoulder at the girls. Milla had pulled a large sheet of thick, clear wrapping free.

"Lay that out on the floor," he said to her in Russian. "Lay it flat, then fold it over several times, double or triple layers, but keep the sheet long. We need to make a sling to carry him. Like a hammock. Yeah?"

Milla nodded. She and Lenka started to flatten the plastic and lay it out.

"Okay, it's not going to go in any further," said Falk.

"Fine," said Underwood. "Tape it off to his cheek or chin, then connect the end to the mask and start pumping the bag."

"Tape!" said Falk. Tal fished a roll out of the box, and started to peel off strips of it. Falk secured the tube end to Bigmouse's face. The tube pushed Bigmouse's mouth open in a half-gape, so he looked like a man gagging as he tried to either swallow or regurgitate an eel.

"Give me the mask," Falk said.

Rash handed it to him. It took a second to discover how the plastic connector mated, then he pressed it in place and anchored it with the strap and more tape.

"Squeeze it," he told Rash. "The bag, the bag."

Rash started to pump the bag. There was a nasty, sucking, crackling noise as air went in and out of Bigmouse's slack body. Falk checked Bigmouse's throat, pressed his fingertips in.

"That *is* a pulse," he said. "That's definitely a pulse."

He looked at the others.

"Okay, we're going to lift him. You and me, Rash. Tal, please, keep working the bag."

He realised he'd said it all in Russian.

"I got the gist," said Rash, getting his arms around Bigmouse's lower legs as Tal took over with the mask.

Falk got his hands under Bigmouse's shoulders.

"Support his head as we lift," he told Tal in Russian. She nodded.

"On three. One, two, three."

They got him off the couch, and shuffled him across the carpet until they were standing over the laid-out rectangle of plastic sheet.

"Down, gently," Falk said. They lowered him. All the while, Tal kept the bag pumping with her left hand and cupped the back of Bigmouse's skull with her right. Then he was flat on the plastic.

"You do this," Tal said to Lenka, demonstrating how to keep the pump going. "You do this and don't stop. Milla and me, we lift the feet."

"Okay," said Falk.

Rash saw what they were doing.

"I'll get the heavy end," he said to Falk. "You take point and walk us out."

"Sure?" asked Falk.

"It's your fucking show," said Rash.

Falk got up and retrieved the Koba. Rash clamped his PAP to his plate, then crouched beside Bigmouse's head and gathered in the hem of the sheeting and wrapped it around his right hand for grip. Milla and Tal did the same at the feet, pulling the plastic into a papoose around Bigmouse's form. Lenka kept pumping the bag the way she'd been shown.

"Okay, let's lift," said Rash.

Between them, Rash and the two girls raised Bigmouse in the plastic sling. It was heavy and unwieldy, but much easier than trying to carry him loose.

"Move," said Rash. "I don't want to just stand here."

Falk led the way out through the hall into the annexe, moving slowly so they could keep up, struggling along under the burden.

"What's the situation?" asked Underwood. "Falk? What's going on? Is he breathing?"

"Leaving is more of a priority," Falk replied quietly.

"What?" asked Rash.

"Nothing," Falk replied. Quietly, he added, "Put Cleesh back on."

"What did you say?" Rash called.

"Just keep it coming," said Falk.

Preben and Valdes had blown out the candles on their way through the annexe, but amber light was flooding into the darkness through the windows and skylights. Falk adjusted his glares for low light, kept the Koba up. He could feel cold, outdoor air on his face, smell the damp. He could smell burning too, the falling cinders. He edged down towards the annexe exit, with the carry team shuffling along behind him. The plastic sheeting was making so much fucking noise.

The back door was ajar. Amber night outside, cool, rain-storm air. Already, the scents of petrochemicals and smoke were evident. A few snowflake coals, glowing orange, floated past.

Behind the house there was a turfed area growing thick with invasive meadow grasses, a gulley, and then the dark woods beyond. To his right was the extension of the service block, a structure containing a bulk rainwater tank and filtration system, and several large composting tubs. To his left, a row of oil or grit drums against the wall, and the corner of the house. There was no sign of Valdes or Preben. Falk could hear engines, loud, approaching.

Did they have time to move? Could they get through the door and across the grass into the trees? Could they disap-pear before the visitors arrived?

He was actually going to try it, but Preben appeared, to his left, running back from the end of the house, shaking his head.

"They're already at the front," he hissed. "Two trucks, squads in each one. They're stopping, dismounting."

"Shit. Where's Valdes?"

"Fuck knows!"

The third truck suddenly came into view. Passing the others, it had swung around to the rear of the house. Its lights were still off. It came through the long grasses, rollering the brush and damp turf flat with its heavy, cross-terrain wheels. Preben and Falk ducked back into the doorway. The SObild pulled up almost opposite the door. Men jumped out. In the shadow of the house, headlamps came on, pooling splashes of blue-white light in front of the vehicle and across the outblock and water plant. They could smell the heat and fumes of the truck. Blurds began swirling excitedly in the headlights.

"Back! Back!" Preben whispered at Rash and the girls. They edged their cargo backwards down the annexe hall.

Voices raised outside. Falk tightened his grip on the Koba. The SObild driver, the squad leader, had jumped down, pulling an assault weapon into place on a shoulder sling, racking it. He was issuing instructions. The men getting out of the truck with him began to fan out. Some were coming right for the doorway. It was so matter-of-fact, so routine. The ordinariness of it made it so much more sinister. *Go in there. Look in the door. If you see anybody, shoot them. We've got things to do.*

"Get the doorway!" Falk heard the leader shout in Russian. "Stick a slapcharge in there! Get the place checked! Pera, go around the side!"

There was no hope of hiding. In a second, a concussion charge was going to come bouncing in through the door, bowled underarm.

This was what the Hard Place really meant.

Falk glanced at Preben. He could see how fixed and intent the man's expression was. Preben understood that they had entered, miserably, one of those non-negotiable states where even fear was no longer currency.

Falk tapped the thumper in Preben's hands, then indicated a direction to the right of the door, the outblock.

"Show me how to do this," Falk whispered. Preben nodded, but Falk had been talking to Nestor Bloom.

He stepped out of the door. The Koba was already at his shoulder. Coming right towards him were two Bloc troopers in rugged black blate and webbing. They had been advancing to take positions on either side of the doorway, to check and enter. Both had Kobas. One had a slapcharge in his hand, produced from his pouch.

Falk put the first burst into the other man's face, because slapcharge-man was fumbling. The other man's weapon was ready. It was intensely short range, no more than three yards. Falk aimed high because the man had decent ballistic plate. It was instinct.

His target's head pulped in a spray of pink meat and bone, like a watermelon smashing. His face disintegrated before it had time to register anything, surprise, alarm, anger. The man walloped down onto his back, his feet coming up as though they had been expertly swept and lifted.

Falk was already turning to fire a burst at the second man. Not so clean. The shots ripped across his chest blate, spinning him up and around like a street dancer executing a roll drop. The slapcharge sailed out his hand. He made a huge *oooff* grunt as the rounds struck him, like the comedy gasp of a winded cartoon character.

Preben almost pushed Falk out of the way as he followed him through the doorway. He was turning right, his boots sliding in the wet grass. The thumper cannoned two grenade rounds in the direction of the compost tubs and the outblock. The Bloc squad members who had been spreading that way wheeled around at the bark of Falk's first burst, surprised, horrified, guns coming into line. Two of them got off shots. One flurry zipped past in front of Falk, whiplash cracks. The other burst hit the doorframe and house wall beside Preben.

The grenades exploded. The first hit the outblock wall, and the compressed force threw three of the men across the yard as though they had been tossed from a speeding vehicle. The other grenade detonated as it struck the sternum of the man whose shots had just missed Preben. The blastforce drove him down into the ground like a peg, and left his upper body and arms mangled and burning. The Koba clutched in his scorched hands emptied its clip, crazy and jigging, killing the side of the house in a shower of masonry dust, plastic flecks and shattering shingles.

Falk kept moving. If a bullet was going to find him, it would find him. He wasn't going to stop and wait for it, or cower in the hope it would miss. Once he had emerged from the back door, he broke stride only once to shoot the two men face-to-face, then kept bolting, running towards the truck. The Bloc squad leader and the two other men with him could have shot Falk easily, but simple animal instinct made them turn and run. Falk was running, they should run too. They didn't even think about it. It was pure threat response. By the time their brains had processed the situation, a synapse *zap* later, they were turning away, out of position, all advantage lost. Falk shot one with a burst that split the man's back blate up the centre line and ploughed him down onto his face.

The leader made it to the truck's cab. The door was still open. He grappled to haul himself up and in, desperate for cover. Falk's shots hammered across his backside, his spine, the back of his thighs, the cab frame, the door panel. Metal sparked on metal. The leader cried out a sharp noise that had a right-angle of pain in it, and fell back out of the cab, loose, heavy, bouncing off the frame, the step rail, the wheel arch, shoulders, hips and elbows glancing off everything on his way down. He ended up with his back against the SObild's big front wheel, one leg folded under him, staring squarely at Falk as he came at him. Somehow, he still had his Koba. It had stayed on his body because of the strap. He fired. Falk never found out where the bullets went. It was wild, inadequate shooting. The knee-length grass around him hissed and cracked and bloomed with clouds of shredded fibre. Falk fired. He hit the seated squad leader in the face and chest. Blood went up the wheel and the wheel arch like it had been applied with a paintgun. The man's head banged against the wheel arch repeatedly, hammered by the impacts. His mouth was open in a silent yell. Somehow, involuntarily, he fired again. Falk felt a savage sting like a cane's lash across his left hip.

Falk kept firing. The top two-thirds of the leader's head ruptured and plastered the wheel with gore and pulp. Only the lower jaw and tongue remained intact, slack, disbelieving.

Falk fell down a few feet from the dead man. The pain in his hip flared like a furnace-white poker was jabbing into it.

"Fuck! Fuck!" he screamed.

The third man had split past the front end of the SObild, running for the woods. He turned, favoured by the half-cover of the truck, and aimed the M3A he was lugging. But Preben, moving out from the doorway behind Falk, had already adjusted, and pumped a grenade in the man's direction. It dropped into the long grass about five yards in front of the truck and blew grass stalks, roots and all, in every direction. The blast shock lifted the Bloc national, threw him into the SObild's front grille, broke his face, his ribs, his collar bones, his neck. He rebounded and tumbled over in the grass.

Preben reached Falk, and lifted him by his blate straps.

"Get up!"

"I'm okay! I'm wealthy!"

"We'll get out to the woods!" Preben yelled. "Come on!"

"Okay, okay!"

Rash and the girls were already bringing Bigmouse out through the back door. Blue smoke wreathed the whole area behind the house, gunsmoke and propellant fumes, explosive wash. The tangled corpse that had taken a grenade in the chest was still burning, like a neglected bonfire. Another few burning cinders drifted down.

"This way!" Preben yelled at Rash. Lenka was still pumping the bag valve. They were stumbling. The ground was uneven, and Bigmouse was getting heavy.

Falk checked himself. There was blood soaking his hip, and he could see a large chunk of abdominal blating had been chewed off.

He looked down towards the corner of the house, the direction the SObild had driven in from. The others were coming. The squads dismounting from the trucks at the front were hurrying around the side, drawn by the fierce exchange of fire. The first couple came into view, at the corner, beside the row of grit bins. Falk fired at them, but his Koba jammed almost immediately. Ammo out. He'd exhausted the second double mag.

Hardbeam fire screamed in from his right, from the treeline beyond the truck. In cover, Valdes had an excellent angle on the corner approach. The first beam from his M3A hit one of the tubs, exploding grit in all directions like a nail bomb. One of the Bloc nationals went down, blinded, dazed. Valdes knocked his companion over with his second shot.

Half-running, half-limping, Falk moved to the front of the truck, where blurds were swarming furiously in the noon of the headlamps. He tossed the empty Koba away into the grass, and retrieved the M3A that the third man had been armed with. He needed a replacement weapon fast, and he could tell, he could *feel*, Bloom wanted a piper, not a hard-round gun. He checked the weapon quickly and expertly for impact damage. The M3A was a robust piece of kit. This wasn't a captured SOMD model, this was the slightly older M3 used by the Bloc, the same basic design, fewer frills and extras. Falk pulled the pouch of spare cells off the battered, twisted corpse.

They were taking heavy fire from the corner of the house, despite Valdes's blasts and the grenades pumped by Preben. Falk was pretty sure that the other two trucks, the ones that had been lagging behind the first three, had now arrived. His little clutch of survivors could be facing upwards of thirty battlefield troops. The air trembled and buzzed with crossfire. A hardbeam shot lanced over, an invisible heat ghost, and ignited a snowgum in the treeline.

Rash and the girls had almost drawn level with the SObild, but they had been forced to put Bigmouse down and drop because of the shooting. Lenka was crying. Milla had her arms and hair over her, trying to shelter her. Hard rounds were pinging and flinting off the truck's bodywork.

Falk raised the M3, lined it up. He felt the LEAF lock tight to platform its bulk. He lit off a shot. The piper made its trademark bark, and vibrated firmly with the discharge.

"I can drive that!" Tal screamed at him. She was gesturing violently at the SObild. "Why are we running for the woods? I can drive that thing!"

Falk glanced at Rash.

"Go! Go!" Falk yelled. "Come on! The truck!"

He started to fire repeated shots at the corner area, trying to keep heads ducked down. Preben reloaded and pumped off some smoke charges. Valdes fired, again, moving in from the trees.

Rash and the girls lifted Bigmouse and hoisted him into the back of the truck. The SObild had a high wheelbase, and lifting him all the way up onto the flatbed took such immense effort, Milla yelled out in anguish. For a second, Falk feared she'd been shot.

They slid Bigmouse in. As soon as the flatbed had its share of his weight, Tal let go and dashed around to the front of the vehicle, climbing in through the cab door on the side away from the house. Rash, Milla and Lenka scrambled up alongside the casualty.

Falk heard the engine clear its throat and start. He fired the M3 again, two more shots, one of which bit a chunk out of the corner of the house wall. He shouted to Preben and Valdes, the smoke in the air sanding his throat and making his eyes water.

Valdes arrived.

"Get in!" Falk yelled, and the trooper scrambled up into the back, Rash grabbing his hands. Preben was close behind. As soon as Preben was clambering up, Falk ran to the cab, half-falling over the corpse of the squad leader in his effort to get inside. Tal was behind the wheel. She didn't even wait for his instruction. The SObild took off with a wild lurch, wheels churning and spinning in the damp grass. Everyone in the back cried out, thrown around. Falk grabbed the dashboard to brace himself.

Shots hammered into them from behind. The hard-round impacts sounded like someone with a mallet beating the back and side panels. A hardbeam shot kissed the weatherproofed litex back shroud, and melted a gash in it. The fabric, superheated, started to burn. No one in the back was steady enough to reach up and beat it out.

The ground was rough. They were bouncing, jumping. The world through the front screen was a white glare of hyper-illuminated grass and brush, and a blizzard of blurds sweeping in to be massacred on impact. Tal's manner of driving was ruthless and all-out. She was standing on the throttle, fighting with the wheel, crashing them over the turf, heaving to correct oversteer and skidding caused by hitting ruts too hard. They were plunging towards the woods, tree trunks filling the headlamp beams. She was driving intently for the thickets, and the trees were going to stop them just like they had stopped *Pika-don*.

It was going to hurt.

TWENTY-NINE

With what appeared to Falk to be a great deal more luck than judgement, Tal fitted them between the trees.

Snowgums and bleakwoods, some trunks a yard across, appeared like surprises in the short, bright frame of the SObild's headlights, and Tal avoided every one of them. They took glancing blows off several, impacts hard enough to crumple bodywork and jolt everybody viciously. Some of the turns she made to avoid trees were so radical, Falk felt as though he would be thrown out of the cab. He braced for the moment when they'd come upon two trees that were too close together to drive between.

"Slower! Slower!" he yelled. He was feeling very odd. His hip hurt like a bastard. The thrashing of the engine, the thump of every bounce and the impact cracks and scrapes of branches and stout scrub made it impossible to hear if they were still being shot at. Whatever the case, they would have to stop before long. The woods were only going to get thicker. They'd have to ditch the truck, maybe find a place to lie low. It was hard to think what to do. It was hard to clear his head. He felt like he was clenched, everything clenched.

"Can't see a damn thing!" Tal complained, jerking the wheel brutally.

He realised what she meant. The headlamps were bright, but their field only illuminated the immediate ground. Tree trunks, blindingly white, loomed with little warning. The swirling blurds were worse than a midwinter snow flurry.

He adjusted the low-light setting of his glares, took them off, and slipped them onto her face as she drove. She didn't pull away, though he could tell that, despite her intense concentration, she was confused.

Then he leaned in and killed the headlamps.

She made a soft, chuckling sound, delighted by the way the world ahead of her had resolved. In the green wash of the glares' view, she had depth and distance, a better perception of the tree spacing, of what had previously been coming up blind behind the immediate dazzle of trees. Her driving quickly became less feral.

He sat back for a second, and tried to force himself to shed the tension. The feeling of being clamped as tight as a fist was almost more than he could bear.

But the ride was too uneven. He had to hold on just to stay upright. His head swam. He was pretty sure he was about to be very sick. Images were pinned to the backs of his eyes, shocking and grisly, the two faces he'd disintegrated with gunfire, staring at him.

He considered what a hopeless cliché he was. Fucking pathetic, soft-centred moral outrage, the squeamish sensibilities of his safe, Old Settlement lifestyle recoiling from contact with ferocious actuality. But it wasn't disgust. It wasn't shock at what he had just seen and done. Nor was it, as the journalist in him would have been eager to confess with calculated sincerity, revulsion at the glee with which he had assumed his role.

He was experiencing an extreme adrenaline dump from the hyperstress of the firefight. It was that simple. He had gone face-to-face with men who had been prepared to kill him, and he had killed them first, and in order to navigate a path through that uncompromising state, he had taken a giant hit of adrenaline. He didn't give a fuck about the bastards he'd dismantled. It was just biochemical overload from the effort to push past normal, everyday brakes like fear and hesitation.

Cleesh said to him, "God, Falk, are you all right?"

"I'm wealthy," he said, so quietly, Tal couldn't hear him.

"You're right off the scale here, Falk," Cleesh replied. "Ayoob and Underwood are panicking. It's like you had a convulsion in the tank or something."

"I'm fine."

"What?" asked Tal, gaze fixed on the way ahead.

"Underwood says your brain chemistry and neural patterning are way beyond acceptable bounds," said Cleesh. "She wants to tranq you, bring you down."

"Fuck, no," he said.

"She says she absolutely has to, or you could stroke out and die. Just a basic stabiliser."

"No. Leave it. I'll settle. Leave it."

Tal took her eyes off the path for a second, glanced at him.

"What are you saying?" she asked.

"It's okay," he replied. He tried to show her a smile. "Just thinking aloud."

She risked another look at him, her hands see-sawing the steering wheel. "You look sick."

"I'm okay. Watch what you're doing."

He could feel Cleesh there, hear her breathing.

"Cleesh, I need to come down on my own. I swear to God, if she tranqs me right now, I will die."

"Okay," she said.

Falk could feel a burn in his heart, like acid was leaking out of something inside his chest. He could taste a sour metallic tang, the unhealthy, artificially coloured flavours of panic and terror. He swallowed hard. Despite the jarring ride, he felt a slight, slow curve returning to his spine.

"We can't go much further," he said.

"What?" Tal asked.

He said it in Russian this time.

"We can," she said.

"We needed the truck to get out in a hurry, but it's not practical. The woods, the hills."

"You wait," she said.

"For what? Tal?"

"You see."

And he saw. It only took another three or four minutes, and she brought them to what she had been heading for all along. The SObild bounced out of the trees, ripped creepers flapping off its roof rails, and swung around onto a track.

She stopped, the engine chugging.

Falk leaned forward, took his glares back and looked out. The woods were thick on either side, so thick they joined to form a roof of foliage over the trail. The track was rough, just mud worn back by the steady traffic of heavy vehicles. It ran east-west, roughly, inclined so it swept up into the hill slopes. The rain was softening the ruts, and streams of run-off were trickling down its length in rivulets.

Falk hadn't seen any trail on the map.

"What is this?" he said.

"Track," Tal said. "Mining road."

"Where does it go?"

She shrugged her shoulders. "Up and down."

"How did you know it was here?" he asked.

"We found it," she said. "One day, when we walk. We used to walk, when it wasn't raining, just to get outside. We walk around the meadow, or into the woods. Not far. One day, we find this."

He could picture them, the three of them, pacing the boundaries of their wall-less prison, after days of only their own company, hoping to see someone, afraid that they actually might. Finding the road by accident one day, thrilled by its implied promise. Two directions, and they were too scared to choose either of them.

"Which way, then?" he asked. He knew which way, but he wanted her to make the decision too.

"Up the hills," she said, pointing to the right. "Up the hills is away from the fighting. Down the hills goes into the war."

"Let's go up, then," he said. He leaned over into the back and told Rash, Preben and Valdes about the trail.

"Give me Mouse's glares," he said. Rash passed them across.

"Is he still breathing?" Falk asked.

"He's more alive than he was," said Rash. Lenka was devotedly squeezing the bag valve.

"That's a good job you're doing there," Falk told her in Russian. He turned back, and handed Mouse's glares to Tal. He'd set them to low light. She put them on, cocking her head and pouting like a covergirl in mirror shades.

"Okay," she said.

She found a gear, and the wheels spun for a moment in the muddy streams of the track. Then they were moving, following the track up the long, curving gradient.

The climb was steep, and the wet conditions tough. Rain had come on again, so hard it stirred the tunnel of trees overhead. But the SObild was up for anything. It was a simple, hard-wearing machine decently constructed to handle poor terrain.

Despite the canopy cover, there was still a red afterglow from the west, the glare of the burning depot. Falk wondered if Bloc forces were coming after them. Had they pushed the other trucks through the wood in pursuit, or had they waited for backup and new orders? He was pretty sure that if he'd been the force commander, he'd have given chase. Falk's band had hit them very hard. Quite apart from payback, he'd have wanted to know who the fuck they were, and what they had been doing there.

The trail wasn't on the map he and Rash had been using. The registry chart of Twenty Thousand Acre Forest had given streams serial numbers, and had even shown the mansion, which shouldn't have been there.

But no trail. And the trail was considerable. It wasn't just a track made by someone trekking through the landscape. It wasn't metalled or formally constructed, but it was wide and reliable. It had been created by heavy traffic, maybe even by caterpillar-tracked vehicles. Bulk vehicles, industrial machines. Traffic would have had to come and go along this road regularly to cut it in like this. Every few miles, the track broadened for short sections, suggesting deliberate passing bays where big vehicles could meet and slip by one another. A working route. To the west, behind them, what did it join? The highway? Probably. A work access that ran right back down to the main arterial, maybe to the depot. To the east, ahead of them, where did it go?

Simple. It went wherever they were going.

Tal had called it a mining road. It ran close to Seberg's property, his luxury Casman-style home. It ran right up through the area where all of his four hundred parcel bids had been made. All of the four hundred that the SO had yanked from him with a Strategic Significance Order. This half-made road, both literally and symbolically, marked how far Grayson Seberg's mining empire had got before politics had stopped it dead.

Falk adjusted his glares, and played back the clip. He saw the pair as Smitts had seen them, framed against the bleak white daylight of the open boomer hatch. He watched the mouth of the girl who had shot him, the mouth of the man Tal had known and despised. He heard their exchange with a mind now patched for Bloc national Russian.

"They don't know anything," the girl said, tired, dissatisfied. "They don't even know what they're here for."

"Then we need to secure it fast before they find their asses with both hands," the big man replied. He grinned. "Or maybe find fucking Grayson and ask him, eh?"

She said, "He can choke in hell. Heligo. Heligo is all we need."

"Yes, but which number is it? You find that out?"

"Not yet," she snapped. "Fuck him for using numeric codes. *Shit!*"

They were both looking at Smitts suddenly, rising out of their crouched stances.

"Fucker's still alive–"

End of playback.

Falk played it again. He played it again.

Heligo is all we need. Fuck him for using numeric codes.

Falk took a few deep breaths. He accessed the snap file, and went back through the folder of images he'd taken with the glares. He'd shot a lot of maps at the Eyeburn Slope registry, a lot of them. The one they'd been using had been the most local, a large scale area map, slap bang on the woodland where *Pika-don* had finished up. Others were older, more general, larger range, smaller scale, records of mineralogical scans, humidity, floodplain. They were records of different surveys at different times, all recording different aspects. SO databases would compile them and form a composite of all the detailing.

He zoomed out, started studying the edges of the maps for tag marks or identifiers. Some were missing. Some were handwritten on dotted blue lines. Some were serial stamp-printed by a process recorder. Falk had managed to crop some of them out of his shots altogether.

He found a general view of the highland area above Eyeburn Junction. Small scale, very little detail, just contour shaping. On the dotted blue line there was a stamp, a number followed by *Ocean Exp*. The centre of the mapped area, a vast region, was subdivided into vaguely rectangular sectors, all packed in close together, like wedges, like teeth, their precise outlines and structures altering depending on the underlying formation of the land. Each sector was indi-vidually numbered. The numbering started just below twenty-five thousand two hundred and went up to just past twenty-five thousand six hundred, sequential.

Fuck him for using numeric codes.

Land parcels. Something of the order of four hundred of them, consecutively numbered. Seberg's bids. The founda-tion of Ocean Exploratory's mining enterprise. SO claim rules required all land packets to be filed by a registry number. But a man, an ambitious man, who was already on the ground and trying to open things up, he'd give places names. He'd talk about them to his men and his friends, and to prospective partners, in terms of names. He wouldn't fuck around with numbers except on official forms.

What names had he given to those places? Which parcel of land had Grayson Seberg called Heligo?

They drove on for another hour, climbing further into the immense hills. Falk kept leaning out of the cab window and looking back to see if there were any signs of pursuit. Three times he made Tal stop and turn off the engine so they could listen for the noise of rotors or ground vehicle engines. All they heard was the sound of the rain, and the distant booming of the clash in the valley.

On the second stop, Falk persuaded Tal to switch out and let Valdes drive for a while. She was reluctant to relinquish the wheel, but he explained how he wanted her to rest so she could be fresh for another stint, seeing as how she was the best driver.

She agreed, but insisted on riding in the cab with them, perched on the cab seat between Valdes and Falk. Falk kept an eye on the dashboard display, but the SObild ran on a fusion engine, and had decent legs left in it.

They had just followed the track over a hump of an escarpment when Valdes threw the anchors out and reversed hard. As Valdes brought the truck back, with Preben and Rash calling out from the back to find out what the fuck was going on, Falk saw what Valdes had seen. A spur off the trackway to their left, a turning.

"Hold on," Falk said.

He hoisted the M3 and jumped out. Preben got down from the back and ran to join him.

With the truck waiting at the mouth of the spur, engine rattling, they walked down the short track side by side, boots munching on the wet gritstone.

In the thick undergrowth on either side of the track, they could see fencing, and piles of old, waterlogged fibreplak posts. They reached a gate, a heavy chainlink frame big enough to open for a bulk transport.

The gate was held shut by swathes of padlocked chain. Weeds were growing up between the gate posts, and covering the yard inside the fence like fine grey down.

Creepers had braided with the chain shackles. No one had opened up the site for at least six months.

Falk and Preben peered through the link into the compound beyond. There were two refabs, and a row of demountables, along with an old Smartkart that had been stripped down on blocks, its transmission and engine extracted and left to rust on the ground beside it, like an automotive autopsy. Rust also adorned the bindings of the refabs, and the windward faces of the demountables were verdigrised. The forest growth, driven back and stunted by weed killer when the ground was cleared, was staging a comeback. It was encroaching from all sides, reconquering a site that had been temporarily opened for preliminary geological testing.

Falk wandered the length of the gate to the fence.

"You limping?" Preben asked.

Falk had forgotten the hit. He wasn't really thinking about the pain in his hip, just living with it. He glanced down and saw how the clothing below the chewed-off blate was stiff and black with dried blood. He lifted it, saw a crusted black furrow in the flesh of his hip that looked like a thick smear of caviar. The skin around it was hot and bruised. As he touched it, blood oozed out of the wound, and pain stuck fingers in his pelvis.

"We should—" Preben began to say.

Falk shook his head and dropped the hem.

"It'll keep," he said. He'd just seen the sign. It was secured to the gatepost, high up, a large placard printed on luminous ply. The thriving branches of a snowgum had partly obscured it.

It read OE 25208.

"What's that?" asked Preben.

Falk didn't answer him. He started walking back towards the waiting truck.

"Should we stay here?" Preben asked, running to catch up.

"Not here," said Falk.

"But it's got buildings. We could dig in."

"No. We go further."

"Why?"

"Because pretty much nowhere is safe right now," said Falk. "We're better off moving. Better still, we'll be safer if we have something valuable."

"Like?" asked Preben.

"Like knowing what this is all about," Falk replied. "People might not be so inclined to kill us if we know that."

He kept walking, heading for the right-hand end of the mouth of the spur.

"It's easy to tell you've been shot in the head, you know that?" Preben shouted after him.

Coming up this hill, Falk thought. Coming up this hill, up this track, driving a truck. A transport. Bringing in supplies. Valdes had overshot. Of course he had. You couldn't see the sign on the gate from the track. All Valdes had seen was the turning, after he'd passed it.

Falk waded into the undergrowth, parting the hillthorn and tangle. You'd put a sign on the outside corner, where a driver could see it from the bend, before he reached the spur. Falk rummaged in the tanglevine. Small blurds flew up in his face out of the wet, peaty cavity. He caught a flash of something, of more luminous ply designed to catch and reflect headlamp beams.

The board had gone over and been enveloped by undergrowth. It was several years old, much older than the gate and the fencing. Damp had rotted out its stump and felled it into the loam, but it was still easy to read what it said.

EUCHRE EXPLORATORY SITE.

Euchre was 25208. When men named things, they did it to make them easy to remember. The moon was called Fred, for fuck's sake.

Sequences became easy when you named them in alphabetical order.

THIRTY

Thirty more miles and three side spurs on, they had cleared the forest cover and slogged up into the proper foothills, surrounded by crags and dark red earth, the bulk of the hills mist-shrouded above them.

They had found their way towards dawn too. The sun was rising, vaguely surfacing out of a grey soup sky, rain falling loose and intermittent from puffy, unobliging clouds. Below and to the west, what seemed like a spinrad passage away, the burning depot glowed like a hazard beacon, and put an inverted cone of black smoke into the air that filled the sky from side to side at high altitude.

They had stopped to take turns at the wheel several times during the night, sometimes halting to stretch their legs and walk about too. On clear stretches above the treeline, they had got out of the SObild and watched the depot fire burning in the pre-dawn gloom, and the twinkling stars of aircraft chasing and hunting across the wide valley and coast plain.

After Euchre, the next two site spurs had been minimal. They had almost missed one of them entirely. It had been neglected, or never developed in the first place, and the undergrowth was so heavy that there was barely a trace of a track. There had been no staked sign, just a roadside marker that Falk had been obliged to dismount to locate.

The second had been a turning to the right of the main track, leading to a clearing that had grown back with abundant tangletree. A small plot, there had once been three demountables there, but two had gone, leaving only their foot blocks, and the sole survivor was a gutted shell. There was no fence, no gate, no sign, no notice, but stencilled on the flaking side of the remaining demountable was the name Griseld.

Industry had been more extensive at 25211.

The approach was along a gorge in the steep hillside, a throat blast-widened and then shored up using wire gabions of blasting rubble and shot rock. The earth and stone up here were gritty and red, and permitted only the most hardy weeds any purchase. The track between the basket embankments had been marked by tractor tyres and caterpillar treads. The lip of the mighty caldera loomed over the surrounding cliffs like the buttress of Olympus.

The gorge opened out into a vast site of red cliffs and spoil heaps. Work had taken place to commence a series of open quarries. They reminded Falk of the industry he had seen outside Marblehead. The quarry pits were step-sided, cut by blade excavators and h-beam cutters. On the flat inside the gate were a series of yards, a complex of refabs and squat, precast and cinderblock buildings. There were also machines, big bulk excavators and dump trucks, all lined up and lagged down under vast coloured sheets of industrial litex. It had cost a lot of time and money to ship the equipment up there. Seberg hadn't realised how far he was jumping the gun. When the SO dropped their desist order on him, he had made his material secure, hoping to come back and restart work once a legal fight was done. Cheaper than moving bulk machines off a mountain.

Falk found this evidence of Seberg's stubbornness and entrepreneurial optimism almost touching. The man'd had no idea, no idea what sort of fight he was actually going to see.

Parcel 25211 had clearly been a much more promising proposition than other Eyeburn bids.

A heavy chainlink gateway and fence blocked the approach from the gorge, shutting off its gabioned throat before the space widened into the first yard.

Preben was driving. He pulled up, facing the resolutely shut gateway.

"Here?" he asked.

"Yes," said Falk. He'd been dozing for a while, but came sharply awake as they swung off the track. It was cold. He chafed his hands.

"Why here?" asked Preben.

"Look at it," said Falk.

"So? It's a bigger site. So what?"

Falk got out and walked to the gates. Tal came with him, and so did Rash. Falk wondered how much he should tell Rash.

"Facilities look better here than anywhere else," he said. "We all need to stop and rest."

Rash shrugged.

"Just a few hours," said Falk. "Eat, sleep, fuel up the truck. Then we can head on over the range, maybe make for Furlow Pits."

"That's a couple or three days, if the road's useable," said Rash.

"So we'll need decent rest."

Rash stared at him.

"There's other stuff, isn't there?" he asked. "I can smell it on you. You're looking for something."

"We're all looking for something, Rash," said Falk, smiling Bloom's smile.

Rash pointed back down the gorge towards the black smoke in the distant sky.

"You see back there, back there where the depot is on fire?" he asked.

"Yes," said Falk.

"Everything stopped being funny around about there. If you know something, you tell me. You fucking tell me."

"Okay," said Falk. "Lets get inside, and I'll tell you what I think."

Rash stuck out his chin, thought about it, then sniffed and turned to look at the gate. He held his hand out. Falk hesitated, then passed over his M3.

Rash aimed the piper at the main padlock and fired. A loud bang echoed along the gorge. Smoke streamed off the disintegrated lock into the wind. Rash handed the piper back, and then gingerly pulled the broken chain away. Fused ends were glowing red-hot. So were the ends of the sundered links in the mesh behind it.

Rash put his shoulder into the right-hand gate and dragged it across the mud. Falk and Tal swung the other half. Preben drove the SObild through the gap, and they pulled the gates together again behind it.

The cavity of the quarry site was attractive to the wind. It knifed across the yards, rattled the windows of the refabs, and agitated the tarps covering the big machines. All the puddles in the yard quivered as though they were being vibrated from below.

The wind had actually managed to pull the litex sheeting off one of the heavy dump trucks, and had repositioned it across a nearby refab like a shroud, like a discarded surgical mask.

They parked the SObild behind a storeblock, checked around and then broke into one of the main refabs. It was dark and cold, bone-cold, and smelled of damp. The wind whined through the roofing and around the window fittings. They found two offices, a kitchen, a locker room, a bedroom with bunks. Rash and Preben carried Bigmouse in and got him onto one of the bunks. Valdes went around lighting the small fusion heaters, and then looked to see if he could conjure a light source.

"Generator's in the next block over," he said. "I'll go look."

The water that issued from the taps was pale green and smelled of ponds. Falk wasn't confident that boiling it would be any help. Tal and Lenka found a cupboard and unearthed a stack of old biscuit boxes containing self-heat cans with ProFood labels, and a crate of NoCal-Cola bottles. They opened some, drank, said nothing. The refab lights came on, just a glimmer, then full power.

"Way to go, Valdes," said Rash, toasting with his bottle.

"Eat," said Falk. "We eat."

They all pulled cans off the shelf and strip-heated them. The can labels all showed Rooster Booster giving a cheery wave of the wing. Falk had macaroni cheese-effect. He was on his second can when Valdes returned.

"You started without me, man," he said.

"There's plenty," said Falk.

"Plenty," agreed Tal in English, and laughed. Falk smiled.

Heat began to creep into the block, though surfaces still felt damp. Having food in his belly helped a lot. The cola made him belch, but he opened a second bottle anyway. This one tasted of lime, quite foul. He looked at the label. NoCal Freek®. He smiled.

He began to sort through the offices. It was just junk. What paperwork had been left behind was simple excavation proposals and sheets of supply costings, payroll, worksheets. He found a clamp folder stuffed with geo reports and began to go through it. The pages were cold. It was lists of the composition densities of ores extracted from samples. The lists were dated. The oldest was twelve years, the newest two. Some bore a headstrap logo. Ocean Exploratory company notepaper.

He could see nothing unusual. The mine was productive, certainly. There were clearly big deposits in parcel 25211. High-gain stuff, rare metals, even traces of extro-transitionals. A decent, hard working outfit could make a decent hard working fortune out of a site like this. If Seberg's four hundred investments in the Gunbelt range had yielded just a half-dozen locations as productive as 25211, then Ocean Exploratory would have turned a very handsome profit within a decade, and a serious return for its investing partners in two or three. More than enough to get you mad as hell if the SO fucked you around. Enough to make you fight it in the courts, throw money at appeals.

But nothing like enough to drag the US and the Bloc into a shooting war. The good stuff had to be hidden, or classified. Like Fred and its rumoured riches, there had to be more than met the eye. Maybe he was reading it wrong. Maybe, via Cleesh, Apfel's people could explain to him what he was missing in these bald, percentile lists.

Maybe it was just politics? Deep-seated Bloc/US agendas that the SO was ringfencing? Maybe Seberg's little speculation was just a good excuse to settle something less material?

"Come on, then," said Rash. He had walked into the office behind Falk. He had another self-heat can of food on the go. It smelled like curry.

"I don't know," said Falk. "I thought I'd find something here, but I haven't."

"You thought you'd find the reason we're fucking killing each other?" asked Rash.

"Yes."

"You're more of a fucktard than Preben," he said, and took a spoonful of curry. "Why here?" he asked, chewing. "Why this place? You've got stuff you're not saying."

"I thought the fight was about mineral exploitation," said Falk. "I thought it was the Bloc getting pissy because the SO had shut them out of some big mining action."

Rash shrugged.

"It doesn't add up," said Falk.

"And you, an SO shavehead, can tell this, being an expert on such things?" Rash asked.

"I don't have to be an expert," said Falk. "Casus belli. It's always about stuff. What I've got and you haven't. What you've got and–"

"I get it."

"So, it's also got to be big, then, right? Not just any stuff. Big stuff. After all this time, to finally start a fucking fight? Come on, just frustration, you think? Just doing what we've secretly always wanted to do?"

"My reading of history," said Rash, taking another spoonful, "and understand I do not pretend to be an expert of any kind, Bloom. My reading is wars are always started for ultimately stupid reasons. Reasons just like you said, big reasons even, but ultimately stupid ones. They always look like they could have been avoided, if someone had shown the presence of mind to communicate the right notion. We put up with a lot of shit from each other. Why stop?"

"So you're saying it's stupid trying to look for a reason that makes sense?" asked Falk.

"I am. They'll blame this on minerals. Well, great. It isn't the fucking ground's fault, right? It's probably some giant domino effect. Some asshole somewhere said the wrong thing to another asshole at some fucking summit, and then some other asshole didn't get his preferential deal, and so he cut the profits on yet another asshole's contract and then... and then... and then... and it's a giant rolling ball of shit coming downhill and sweeping everything up. And that giant rolling ball of shit's called history, Bloom, and we were standing in its fucking way."

Falk wandered back through the rooms. In the other office, Preben was sitting at one of the planner desks and doing a takedown and clean on his M3A. Valdes was idly playing with an informatic console that was giving nothing back. The girls were asleep, except Milla, who was keeping Mouse's bag valve going.

He went outside. The rain was fresh and cold, and the wind was almost too uncomfortable to bear. He walked as far as the closest excavation pit. Most of it had filled with water, like a dirty swimming pool. Along the edge of the quarry there was a metal walkway with a rail, and evidence of a small pump house and pipe system, installed so that rainwater wouldn't become an issue. It hadn't run in a long time, and the rain was winning.

The surface of the flooded excavation shivered with each gust of wind and dimpled with the raindrops.

"What are you going to do, Falk?" Cleesh asked, her voice in the beat of the rain.

"I think it's way past time we devised an exit strategy," he replied. He folded his arms to keep his hands warm.

"You mean unplug you?"

"No, I don't. I mean find a way out. It was worth chasing

for a bit, but this is getting insane. You didn't see. You didn't see what happened, Cleesh. Fighting our way out of that house. It's not a fucking game, Cleesh. It's not a fucking assignment, either."

"Are you okay?"

"I'm wealthy," he said. "I'm golden, Cleesh. But Bigmouse isn't, and we can't keep him alive much longer. And the others don't deserve to be stuck in this shit if there's a viable way out. Can you talk to Bari? Can you find out if GEO can get a transport in to us?"

"Of course."

"We're at parcel 25211. We're right up in the caldera range, Cleesh, a decent way from the main hot zone."

He waited for her to answer.

"There's a no-fly advisory on that whole region," she said after about a minute. "Absolute. SOMD has stamped control jurisdiction across the whole western half of the Northern Territories."

"I thought they might have," he said, trying not to sound disappointed. He tilted his face up, let the rain hit it, eyes closed.

"This is getting bigger by the hour, Falk," Cleesh said, some of her words turned inside out or see-through by static. "Even with the com blackout, it's clear how hot things are. There are reports of major fighting at Antrim and Hall Valley. They can see the smoke from that depot fire at Furlow. Our SO source says that there is an expectation that the Central Bloc fiefs will issue a formal declaration in the next thirty-six hours. Which will be, you know, a red letter day in the history of our proud species."

"Yeah, okay. Well, what if we keep going? Take the track across the range, head east as far as we can get. It may take another day or so, but is there somewhere a transport can meet us? Somewhere closer? Just a hopter with a scrambled medical team."

"Whoa, whoa, lose the misery," she said. "I said it was no-fly. I didn't say it was *wouldn't-fly*. Bari's looking into it. GEO leases some private airfields in the west. He thinks they might be able to sneak a bird up to you in the next three or four hours. Strictly off the books, a look-the-other-way job. They wouldn't be able to file any kind of flight plan, and they'd have to move low and slow to avoid attention, but it's possible. Bari thinks he can get the fuelling and prep done under the cover of general contingency. GEO has told the SO that as things degrade, they will be implementing policy to extract GEO personnel from the zone. He also reckons he knows a few crews who are crazy enough to want the adventure."

"How certain is he that he can pull this off?" Falk asked.

"I kinda like the look on his face right now."

"Okay. Thanks. Thanks, Cleesh. Let me know how it develops."

"We'll know in an hour or so what's practical. You–"

"What?" he asked.

"You're drawing a blank with Heligo then?" she asked. He could hear her smile.

"Yeah. It looked promising, but it's a mess, a bunch of nothings. If I get out of here, you and I can probably put everything we've got together and come out with a good, solid series about SO bias and mismanagement. Something pretty damn ballsy. Just not the great bit I was hoping for."

"You will get out of there," she insisted.

"Actually, let's assume I'm not going to, Cleesh."

"Oh, yes, let's! Let's be really freeking® pessimistic!"

He blinked raindrops out of his eyes.

"I'm serious," he said. "Listen to me. There's a girl, an affiliate for Data-Scatter. Her name's Noma Berlin."

"Okay."

"She's got a place in South Site. She was the one who brought the Letts story to me. I was going to give her stuff from this in return. Get it all to her, Cleesh."

"Serious? All of it?" Cleesh asked.

"Yeah. Feed her everything. Help her like you'd help me. Help her get the story out. Tell her, tell her to use the contact she made. Jill Versailles at Reuters. We couldn't do much better than that."

"Okay, if you like. Is this girl that good?"

"I don't know," he replied. "She's a pain in the ass, actually. But she might be. Yeah, I think she really might be. But all that matters is she's in the exactly the right place."

"Is she the one you had so much sex with it broke your hip?"

"Ha ha. No comment," he said. He suddenly became aware that he wasn't on his own. Tal had appeared, hands in pockets, head down against the rain. She wandered along to the quarry edge to join him and stared down at their wobbling reflections in the pit water.

"Who do you talk to when you talk to yourself?" she asked.

He shot her a look.

"You talk to yourself a lot," she said, with as much of a shrug as having her hands in her pockets would allow.

"I just think through things," he said. "Talk my way through things."

She nodded.

"I do that," she said.

"Like how best to survive a situation," he said.

She nodded again.

"We'll probably have to keep moving," he told her. "Keep running. It'll be quite a distance before we're clear of trouble."

She looked at him. The wind pulled at her fringe.

"Running is not so bad," she said. "At least if you are running you are doing something. We should have learnt to run a long time ago."

"You had nowhere to run to," he said.

"Do we now?" she asked.

"I hope so. We'll vouch for you. If we reach SO protection, or get an extraction, we will make sure the authorities understand the situation you were in. We'll make sure they take care of you."

"For myself, I don't care so much," she said. "For Lenka, she never deserved any of this."

She looked at him. He liked the bones of her face, the lean strength. Her cheekbones were high and her jaw was tight and heart-shaped. She reminded him of the wind vanes at the hill farm. Relentless, driven by the wind, but never knocked down. She managed a half-smile, like it was something she was allergic to, or a movement that caused her pain. He could almost hear the *whup-whup* of wind turbines.

The chop got louder and became real. Tal glanced at him in alarm and they both turned and looked up.

The rotorcraft swept in over the cliffs surrounding the site, coming from the north. It was moving fast and low, its hull leaning to port as it banked in on a broad, passing curve. The moment it cleared the clifftop, the chop of its proprotors became painfully raw. There was no barrier between them and the noise source. The rock cavity of the Heligo site made a sound box that echoed and amplified the clatter, turning it into the noise of a hundred rotorbirds.

It passed over, and disappeared from view, taking its sound with it. Falk and Tal were already running back towards the site offices. Behind them, it returned. It had turned and powered back, much slower now, body upright, paired tilts rising to a support angle as it appeared over the cliffs. It drifted in above the flooded pits of the quarry complex, hanging, inquisitive.

From the very first moment, Falk had known it was a Kamov. A Bloc gunship, an 18, like the one that had buzzed them at the house.

"You," said Tal, as they ran. "You and trouble are great lovers."

THIRTY-ONE

In the refab, everybody was on their feet. Valdes was at one of the windows, pipe in hand, pulling the blind slats aside to peer up at the hovering rotorcraft.

"Time to go," said Falk as he and Tal burst in.

"No shit," replied Rash.

"Did they see you?" asked Valdes.

"Pretty sure, yes," said Falk. "We were out in the open, and they were just overhead suddenly."

"Fuck," said Preben.

"Just pick up Bigmouse and get him out to the truck," said Falk. "We'll blow and go, right now."

"That fucking thing'll scorch us," said Valdes. "Come on, man, that gunbird will chew the truck up."

"But a static target like a refab is much harder to hit," snapped Falk. "Come the fuck on!"

Outside, the Ka-18 rotated slowly, fifty feet up, its bellicose chin out-thrust. Without explanation it accelerated away north and vanished behind the cliffs.

"Fucking move!" Falk said.

Rash moved into the bunk room with the girls to

collect Mouse.

"Get the SObild running," Falk said to Preben. Preben ran out of the refab's side door.

"Valdes, we're getting the gate," Falk said.

They exited through the front into the yard and the angry wind. Rash and the girls were already shuffling Mouse to the back exit in his sling. Lenka was crying again. This time, Falk could hear her.

He ran across the yard with Valdes, both of them lugging their pipers. The rain hit them hard, coming down in big heavy drops. They reached the gate, grabbed a frame half-each, prepared to drag.

"Fuck it, man!" Valdes exclaimed.

Through the gate link, they could see down the gabioned throat of the gorge all the way to the track. A pair of SObild trucks just like the one they were using had just pulled up at the mouth. In daylight, they could see the little red star decals on the cab doors. Falk wondered if the truck they had been driving around in all night had red star decals on the cab doors too.

"No exit!" groaned Valdes. He let go of the gate.

"Why aren't they coming down?" Falk asked, more to the air than to Valdes.

"Falk? What's happening?" Cleesh asked.

Falk saw why the trucks had stopped. They were giving way. Something bigger came into view. Its drive plant was making big, throbbing, revving sounds. Even without the trucks getting in its way, it didn't seem feasible that the Bloc MBT would fit its immense grey bulk down the entrance gorge.

"Fuck! Fuck! Fuck!" Valdes wailed.

The tank throbbed out a huge grunt of power and acceler-ated into the approach towards them. It was a T-22, a massive

tandem-turret fighting machine. Falk neither knew nor cared
about its variant specifics. Its vast adaptive track systems and
hydropneumatic suspension gave it a running sound that was
almost a soft purr, like a beautifully oiled, antique wooden
escalator in a classy department boutique. The Uralvagon-
zavod fusion plant growled like an emphysemic demon. Its
aft turret, small and high, mounted twin hardbeam pipe
weapons. Its forward turret, the big main cap, was low and
flat and seemed to look at them down its giant coldbore gun.

"Great. Great!" murmured Falk. "And what the fuck do
we do now?"

"We show them our A game, man!" cried Valdes. "We
show them our fucking A game!"

"Get real, Valdes!" Falk spat.

They started to run back across the yard. They had almost
reached the refab when the SObild drove into view, Preben
at the wheel. He had everybody else on board.

"Back! Back!" Falk yelled at him.

Preben braked hard, curling up a fat wave of muddy brown
water, and began to reverse, swinging the truck around to
head back into the site. Falk and Valdes ran after it.

They heard the hopter coming back. It had brought a
friend. The two Ka-18s ran in over the northern cliffs in
formation, and began to descend towards the centre of the
biggest yard space. Their rotors were stacked almost vertically to bring them down. Valdes raised his weapon to shoot
at them.

"Don't be a fucking idiot!" Falk told him.

They ran for the line of the sheds, willing themselves into
a position where there was something between them and
the Bloc units.

Kissing the mud almost simultaneously, whisking up
counter-patterns of spray, the gunships opened their carrier

doors and men leapt out, dispersing wide. They were dressed in black blate, weapons high and ready. Bloc special forces. Scorpions, perhaps. Black Butterflies. As soon as the fireteams had deployed, the Ka-18s lifted off again, doors still gaping, noses down as they ascended.

The T-22 came through the site gates. *Through* them. The chainlink frames scrunched and collapsed like sugar icing under its tracks and armour skirts.

The first gunfire came from the special forces. Valdes and Falk heard the hard rounds and beam shots banging into the end wall of the refab as they came around the side heading for the quarries. One hardbeam cut clean through two fibreplak sidings and blew out the windows of the refab behind them.

Preben had made a bad choice. Instead of swinging right and running the SObild through the acreage of the machine park in the east of the site, he had kept going straight along the edge of the flooded quarries and therefore rapidly run out of places to go. The SObild was stopped at the end of a muddy causeway between a quarry pool and a row of storehuts, its route blocked by a semi-extended bulk conveyor. The conveyor had the head of its scaffoldwork processor sloping down into the dark water of the field quarry, so that it resembled a rusty yellow sauropod taking a drink from a lake.

"Fuck are they doing, man?" Valdes shouted. "Back up! Back up this way!"

The truck was three hundred feet away, a long, lonely run along the quarry edge. Valdes started towards it, but Falk grabbed him. As soon as the Black Butterflies, or whatever the fuck they were, came around the side of the site refabs, Falk and Valdes would be clean targets.

One of the Ka-18s appeared, banking tightly as it came around two rusty-green ore hoppers. It skimmed in across the quarry, summoning clouds of spray from the water surface.

Valdes shouted out. Falk dragged him into cover behind the storehuts. They scrambled along down a rough, wet gully lined with drainage pipes.

The Ka-18 had read the heat of the SObild. It pulled up halfway across the quarry lake and lit off its chin cannons. There was a harsh, grating noise, like a coffee grinder full of nails. The SObild began to shake, vibrating on its springs. Then it shredded. Torn metal fluttered in every direction, glass sprayed like water. Large, dismembered chunks of the truck's chassis, transmission and engine block lurched into the air, turning over and over, shedding debris, freed from the truck-shaped shell that had once confined them. Something in the heart of it all ignited and lit the destruction with a gas-jet puff of flame.

Pieces of the disintegrated vehicle rained down on the hut roofs, on the mud, peppered the quarry pool.

Valdes screamed. Falk wanted to scream too, but he knew it was far too late. He seized Valdes tight and stopped him from running out into the open.

They reached the end of the storehut row, passing through the dispersing cloud of acrid smoke spilling off the truck's wreckage. Valdes clambered under the support stand of the conveyor and Falk followed. They heard the gunship chopping away, repositioning. If it had painted their heat, it was holding off.

And if it was holding off, that meant the Bloc ground troops were close.

Two or three shots burned down the gulley and spanked into the heavy metalwork of the conveyor. The metal struts boomed like a gong. The wind, relentless, was keening around the upper framework of the huge machine. Falk glimpsed two or three figures in black, coming down the back of the huts the way he and Valdes had run. Closer and closer.

Falk and Valdes ran clear of the conveyor, across a small, muddy yard and between two refab workshops. Falk wondered where they were actually running to, in the end. Heligo was a finite area, surrounded by ancient cliffs. The best they could hope for was somewhere to hide.

Beyond the weatherboarded workshops, the site floor shelved down into a more significant cut in the red soil, where a broad shelf ran alongside a much deeper quarry beneath the overhanging wall of cliff. Metal duckboards paved the shelf, and a set of temporary metal steps linked the two levels.

The quarry pit where the SObild had been killed must have been a shallow, exploratory cut to have been so full of water. The one they were approaching was a huge, stepsided cistern, cut into the ground with a giant spade. Metal staircases and scaffolding platforms lined the side below the causeway. A giant ramp of packed earth, like something raised to aid the construction of pyramids, filled the western side, providing access for the heavy machines. Far below them, the bottom level of the pit was full of dark water. It was a vast excavation. Seberg really had been a good way into his work when the SO stopped him. They ran down the steps, clanged across the decking and onto the walkway of the shelf.

The cliff-overhang gave them a little shelter. Three Bloc soldiers appeared at the top of the steps and paused to snag off shots with their Kobas. Falk felt the rounds smack into the chin of rock above the walkway. He saw the puffs of dust that the hits drilled out. Valdes, boiling with inexpressible rage, turned and lined up, fast and fluid. He got an instant red flag via his glares and fired. His piper barked.

There was a wink of hot, distorted light and one of the Bloc troopers was knocked flying. Falk was sure he glimpsed sky through the hole Valdes made in the man's torso. The other two men ducked, fired some more shots. Falk had to tug at Valdes to get him running again.

The Ka-18 came in over the earth cut and the banked wall, and rotated into the airspace of the vast quarry. The chopwash of its rotors filled the resonating hole of the huge pit. Far below, the surface of the dark sediment of collected rainwater whipped and swirled.

The rotorcraft came in low, cautious, inquisitive. It was on a level with the main shelf, nose towards the cliff, hunting for targets. Falk kept running. The walkway had to fucking lead somewhere. He realised Valdes wasn't with him.

Valdes had stopped. He was standing up straight on the shelf walkway, making no attempt to hide or find cover, lining up his M3A at the hovering Kamov.

"Valdes!" Falk yelled, skidding and turning back. "Valdes, you're fucking crazy!"

The h-beam piper was a hell of a weapon, but a Bloc rotorcraft gunship was in another class. It had composite reactive armour, ablative plating, heatsoak laminates. It was a bastard killing machine, and something that a man on the ground with a gun, no matter how much of a gun, didn't have a prayer of bringing down.

No one, it seemed, had explained any of that to Valdes. He had three things going for him. Expert operator rating on all M3 weapons, ridiculously close range, and an almost incandescent fury. The Ka-18 was right in front of him, its rotors tilted upright and thundering, so close they could see the pilot and gunner through the smoky cockpit bubble.

"Eat it, motherfucker!" Valdes screamed.

He fired. The hardbeam punched a fist-sized hole in the bubble and decapitated the pilot. Control vanished instantly as the pilot's nerveless hand or foot spasmed. The gunship hurtled forward on full throttle.

It didn't hit Valdes. It drove head-on into the quarry wall directly below him, folding and crumpling and shredding the way the SObild had shredded. There was a huge pressure clap as a raging fireball expanded out of it. Debris whizzed through the air like glitter. Falk felt pieces striking the walkboards, the wall, the cliff shelf. The head of an entire rotor assembly tore off, spinning wildly, chopping the air like a lethal, unleashed wind turbine. It bounced once, off the shelf between Valdes and Falk, its blades ripping up metal walkboards and strewing them into the air. Then it splintered off the cliff overhang and whirled away into the quarry.

The rest of the machine, the bulk of it, on fire and deformed, fell back, slipping and scraping down the face of the quarry wall, ripping away walkway platforms and metal stair flights as it dropped. Most of the scaffolded superstructure lining the quarry side came down with it. And hit the dark, cold water in the base of the pit. Falk heard the suck-rush as burning metal met chilled liquid, like the crash-draw of an ocean hitting a shingle beach.

Burning scraps were raining down around them. Valdes got up off his knees.

"Fuck, man! Fuck it, Nes!" he shouted, immeasurably proud of himself. "Did you fucking ever see shit like that, man?"

The first of the Black Butterflies onto the shelf behind Valdes put three rounds through his head. Falk flinched and yelled as red mist blew out the side of Valdes's skull.

Valdes didn't buckle. It was probably the weight of his

piper. Straight and stiff, he just tipped forward and plunged off the shelf, head first, limbs limp.

Falk fired wildly along the shelf. He couldn't seem to hit anything. He loosed three shots before he made a contact, and then it was only the cliff overhang. He brought chunks of it crashing down, driving the special-ops team back a few steps.

"Come on! Get into cover, you fucktard!" Rash yelled. He got down on one knee beside Falk and loosed two bursts with his PAP, followed by a pair of AP grenades from the undermount. The grenades blew in amongst the hostiles, killing at least one of them with a storm of high-density shrapnel shot.

Rash grabbed Falk and dragged him back along the shelf. There was a cavity ten yards along, a square cut opening in the rock like a cave. Rash pulled him into it.

"How the fuck are you alive?" Falk asked.

"We ditched the truck," said Rash, "nowhere to go. We figured hiding was a better idea."

"All of you got out?"

Rash didn't reply. He didn't have to. Rash didn't leave people behind.

They ran deeper into the cave. It was a tunnel, a side spur drilled and beam-cut into the rock. An exploratory channel? A lot of effort had been put into it.

"What is this?" Falk asked.

"It's better than outside, is what it is," replied Rash. "It was the best option."

They ran on. There was no immediate sound of pursuit. There was a barrier ahead of them, a serious, heavy-duty glass door installed at great expense.

"What is this?" Falk repeated.

"I'm guessing work access to one of the specialist mines," replied Rash. He had already forced the lock of the glass hatch to let the others through. He held the hatch open for Falk. It was heavy, like an airlock seal. Inside the hatchway there was a ring of sensor panels.

"I think they found a seam of something pretty fancy down here," said Rash. "Extro-transition, something like that. They must have been scanning the engineers in and out to make sure they didn't exit with pockets full of the good stuff to make a little on the side."

There was no power. The cut had been abandoned and sealed with the hatch. There was still a lingering afterscent of Insect-Aside in the cold air, as if the place had once been pressurised and ventilated. Falk guessed that was to pump water out and clear the workface.

They caught up with Preben and the girls. Only Preben and Tal, wearing glares, could see them in the low light. Tal quickly reassured Milla and Lenka. They were struggling with Bigmouse.

Falk and Rash took over, taking an end of the sling each.

"Where's Valdes?" asked Preben.

"Not coming," replied Falk.

"Someone is, though," said Rash. Far away and behind them, they could hear activity.

"Keep going," Falk said, struggling with the weight. "We'll find a defensible position. Halt there. Maybe then we can find another route out. This place was pressurised but there was no pipework or venting at the mouth. There could be another duct in, maybe a service port for heavier machines or ore extraction."

"It gets bigger up ahead," said Tal. "A bigger space."

The square-cut shaft opened out into the bigger space, a natural cavity in the rock. There was a route through it, walkboarded, which led to an even larger natural cavern, a vast and echoey chapel of rock. In the entrance area, sorted and stacked neatly, was mining equipment, toolcrates, spoil carts and other excavation kit.

They carried Bigmouse in, set him down and made him comfortable. Falk had almost forgotten what Bigmouse's voice sounded like. He didn't expect to hear it again. He looked at the immense cavity surrounding them.

It was cool and black, with a faint hint of damp. Falk had never felt so hidden, so enclosed. He closed his eyes to escape the green glow of the low-light vision for a second.

He had found peace and security, if only for a few minutes.

"What the hell?" said Tal.

Falk opened his eyes again and looked for her.

She had gone further into the underground space, right up to a metal safety rail positioned to prevent workers blundering off the rock platform of the entrance area and falling into the bottom of the main cave.

He limped over to reach her. Rash came with him. They stopped at the rail alongside her and looked out into the body of the main cavern. They saw what was lying there in the cave, half-buried, half dug out.

They saw it, but they didn't really understand it. It took a moment before they realised what the thing they were looking at had to be.

"Oh my God," said Rash.

It was right there in front of them, in the rock.

Embedded.

THIRTY-TWO

"There's some fucking weird noises coming from up there," Preben said.

"What do you mean?" Rash asked, too preoccupied to be really interested.

"Sounds like a fucking firefight," said Preben. "A full-on shoot up. You didn't leave Valdes up there fighting a crazy fucking rearguard action, did you?"

"No," said Falk.

"Well, I'm telling you, there's something going on. What are you all looking at?"

"Well, that," said Falk.

Preben looked.

"I don't get it. What is it?"

"I'm not entirely sure," said Falk.

"So who the fuck cares? It's just rock."

"I don't think it's rock," said Rash.

"I think everyone's going to care," said Falk. "And that's the whole point."

He turned and looked at Rash.

"I'm going back up. See what's happening. Keep

everybody here."

"I can come with you."

"Keep everybody here, safe, Rash. And keep an eye on this. I'm going to do everything I can to get us all out of this."

"What, *now* you can do that?" asked Rash. "Why couldn't you do that before?"

"Because the game just changed," Falk replied. "Everything just changed. Now we know what's at stake."

He headed back up the long, sloping tunnel from darkness towards the light. There was probably, he decided, something terribly symbolic about the walk he was taking, something he could work effectively into a later account. He didn't honestly care.

"Did you hear any of that?" he asked.

"Are you freeking® kidding?" Cleesh asked. "That was all a joke, right? A freeking® joke. Right, Falk?"

"No joke, Cleesh. No joke. Feed it to Noma, all of it. Feed everything from me to her until I stop sending."

"Why the freek® do you think you'll stop sending, Falk?" Cleesh asked.

"Because I don't know what's waiting for me up there," he said.

He pushed through the glass hatch. He could smell outdoor air, smoke. He could feel a breeze. There was a square of pale light ahead. When he came out onto the shelf walkway over the pit, he felt the rain on his skin again, smelled the damp. Columns of filthy black smoke were pouring into the air from behind the refabs. Stuff had happened over in the site yards. Now and then, the flames were big enough to dance into sight above the line of the roof.

Falk heard chopwash. He pressed into the cliff wall, wary. In close formation, two boomers droned overhead. They approached through the curtain of black smoke, rippling it, unveiling themselves, and flew on over the quarry towards the southern part of the site. A third Boreal followed them a few seconds later.

SOMD troopships.

He was approaching the metal steps when his glares began to tag aura codes. Bodies were moving in, approaching him. He saw twenty or thirty ID tags, clustered, dancing, moving towards him from the yards.

"SOMD!" he yelled. "SOMD friendly over here!"

Troopers appeared, dressed like him, armoured like him, but all much cleaner and fresher. The first of them fanned out at the top of the metal steps, covering him with their weapons.

"SOMD!" Falk repeated, in case his brooch wasn't working.

Their aim didn't waver.

"Put the weapon down!" one of them ordered. "Put it the fuck down beside you, kneel, and raise your hands."

"SOMD!" Falk protested.

"Do it! Comply, or we drop you!"

He bent down, laid the M3 on the ground and settled onto his knees despite the pain in his hip. He put his hands on his head, his fingers laced against his wet scalp.

Some of the troopers scurried down the steps and surrounded him.

"SOMD," he repeated. "Private Nestor Bloom, Team Kilo out of Lasky."

"You alone, Bloom?" asked the squad leader. His tag identified him as Essley. "Anyone with you?"

"I've got people with me, Essley," he replied.

"How many? Where are they?"

"I want a guarantee of their safety before I tell you where they are."

"Fuck's he think he is?" asked one of the troopers covering him.

"I think I'm SOMD personnel, and I think I'm a little fucked off at the treatment I'm getting," said Falk.

"Should I pop the sunbitch?" one of the troopers asked. Falk tensed suddenly. There was no missing the fact it had a genuine suggestion.

"Don't be a dick, Benet," replied the squad leader. "There's a procedure."

"A procedure?" asked Falk. "What kind of fucking procedure?"

"The kind where you shut the fuck up," replied the squad leader. "This whole situation is in the control of SO Human Services, and that means it's a few trillion miles above your head."

"What's Human Services?" Falk asked. He'd never heard of it. But he could guess.

"Human Services is us," said the trooper, Benet.

"Back off, Benet," said the leader. "This is an ultra-high confidence operation, Bloom. It is Bloom, right?"

"Yeah," said Falk.

"Ultra-high confidence, you understand?" asked Essley. "There are certain matters at stake. Issues we have to deal with."

"I understand," said Falk. He risked a look up at Essley. The man was clean-shaven, thin-lipped, lean, anonymous behind his glares.

"I understand," Falk repeated. "I've seen what's down there."

The men around him muttered. The one called Benet swore.

"You've seen it?" Essley asked.

"Yes."

"You understand what it is?" Essley asked.

"I don't seem to be as retarded as some of the men in your command," said Falk.

"You seem pretty fucking dumb to me," replied Essley. "You've just talked your way into much deeper shit." He turned to one of the other men.

"We may need to arrange rendition here," he said.

"Why fucking bother with that?" asked Benet. "We should just clean house."

Essley looked back at Falk.

"How many of you are there, Bloom?" he asked. "How many have seen it?"

"Why? Are you going to silence all the inconvenient witnesses?" asked Falk. "Scorch all the expendables? I thought that was the Central Bloc method. I understand what this is, Essley. US-sponsored SO efforts to effect cover-up, thus protecting US interests. It won't stand, and it won't work."

"Really?" laughed Benet. It was not a humorous laugh. "But you're the one kneeling in the mud with a gun at his head."

"I know something you don't," said Falk. "So the faster you wake up to the idea that you need me alive, the better it will be for you."

"Start talking," said Essley.

"Not to you," Falk replied. He looked past Essley at the huddle of SOMD personnel behind him, hunting for the code he'd seen a few minutes earlier when they first approached. "I won't talk to you, Essley. But I'll talk to her."

"Who?" asked Essley.

"Her. Tedders."

Tedders pushed to the front beside Essley.

"He wants you," said Essley, frowning.

"Do I know you?" Tedders asked, looking down at Falk. "Bloom, yeah? I think I saw you at Lasky."

"I'm going to stand up," said Falk. Essley nodded. No one stopped Falk from rising. He faced Tedders. He realised he was seeing her at a different angle from the last time they'd met.

"I don't know you," she repeated. "Except by sight."

"So let's have a conversation," said Falk. "Get to know one another."

"Why?"

"Because I have a position to communicate," he replied. "It was going to be a hard sell, a really hard one. But seeing you gives me a tiny chance to make it easier."

Tedders glanced at Essley, then stepped away from the group with Falk. They walked a short way along the shelf, the members of the special unit waiting and watching them intently.

"So, you're Human Services, huh?" he said.

"What's it to you?" replied Tedders. "Human Services has no public remit. It is not an acknowledged department. No accountability."

He looked up at the rain.

"No accountability, huh?"

"That's right."

"How many times has this happened, Tedders?" he asked.

"This?"

"Yes."

"It's never happened. That's why it's a big deal. Now what can I do for you?"

"Humour me for a second. Seberg found it by accident, didn't he? Kept it hidden while he worked out how to parlay it into the best result for him?"

"Yes."

"How long ago?"

"A few years, as far as we can tell."

"And the SO found out because somebody let it slip, and wanted the whole thing secure. But some of Seberg's speculative partners from the Bloc had already got wind of it."

"That's not how I'd care to characterise it," she said.

"There was a counter-intelligence war to discover the actual location of the site, because Seberg had kept that detail hidden to protect his prize. That war escalated into a real war."

She stared at him, compact and unmoving.

"You remind me of someone," she remarked.

"I know I do. And I'm right, aren't I?"

"I couldn't comment."

He grinned.

"The SO is backing the US in a secret war against the Bloc to locate and achieve private control of the most valuable find in history."

"There's never been anything like it," said Tedders. "Three hundred years, hundreds of worlds, and finally we find proof of the one thing we no longer thought was possible. It changes *everything*."

She looked at his face. "Have you seen it?"

"Yes."

"Is it amazing?"

"I don't know. I don't know what it is," he said. "It's an artefact. Big. There's technology to reverse-engineer. Decades of study and analysis. Fuck alone knows where it came from or how long it's been down there. Yes, it's amazing."

She sighed.

"You can appreciate why this is high confidence," she said. "Something like this, it has to be contained, controlled. It's sensitivity-adverse. The implications…"

She looked at him.

"Even the Bloc understands that," she said. "They came in silent and ruthless for precisely the same reason. They wanted it contained as much as we did, just under their terms. They understand what's at stake."

"Everyone should know," said Falk. "Everyone. This is too big to swallow up and classify."

"That's a naive attitude."

"Not really. It's a matter of public interest, Tedders."

She shook her head.

"I've heard enough, I think," she said. "Sorry, soldier. I'm sorry about this situation. I can't pretend it's not going to get difficult for you. You simply don't get it. You're not seeing the whole picture."

"You just don't know me very well, Tedders," he replied. "Don't walk away. I've got six people down below. Three SO troopers, three civilians, Bloc nationals. All seven of us are going to be escorted out of here and looked after. We're not going to be rendered and silenced."

"I'm not in charge of anything, I–"

"You're going to have to persuade Human Services that it's just not in their interests to harm us," said Falk.

"Well, they won't see it like that."

"They will when they realise the story is already out."

"This whole operation is secure," said Tedders. She cleared her throat. "This zone has been unlinked for seventy-two hours."

"Not as secure as you think," he said. "The story's out, Tedders. Out and gone. It's too late to pretend you can contain it. So it's too late to bother trying to win or enforce our silence."

"That's not true," she said. She smiled and shook her head sadly. "Nice try. I can see you're desperate to help your people. But there's no way the story has got out of this zone."

"Reuters already has it."

"Bullshit," she said.

"No, actually. Do you know what I'm going to do now, Tedders?"

"What?"

"I'm going to show you my A game," said Falk.

She narrowed her eyes, stared at him.

"My name is Lex Falk," he said.

"What? Falk? More bullshit."

"Lex Falk. The sooner you believe it, the sooner we can deal. My name is Lex Falk."

"Shut the fuck up. I've met Lex Falk, and—"

"I'm connected by sensory repositioning to a location in Shaverton," he said. "The exact location is, as you fucks like to say, hardly material. Reuters has it. Reuters has the story. Even this conversation we're having is being relayed, word for word, real time."

"What the fuck is this nonsense?" asked Tedders.

She turned and began to walk away.

"It was a small, family-run place off Equestrian," he called out after her. "And the best part was, the chicken-effect parmigiana arrived during your lifetime."

She stopped walking away.

THIRTY-THREE

They gave him a cane, and after he had learned to walk with it, he kept it for effect. An unseasonable heat had descended on Shaverton. The windows of the glass masts glinted like mirrors. The bugs were swarming, and everyone smelled like they had been embalmed with Insect-Aside.

The sky was a spoiled cream shade of yellow when the car brought him to the veterans' hospital on the Cape Highway. The place was pleasant-looking, a sun-baked compound of white Early Settlement style buildings on a plot planted with snowgums. He showed his papers at the front desk, and then again at a guardpost outside the trauma ward. The SOMD staffers went through his press accreditation, and the embossed permits with the Human Services hologram tags.

"This way," said the nurse who came to meet him inside the ward. "It's just down here."

She looked flushed, but the place was quite cool. He thought it was probably a byproduct of her pink tunic and the beige walls.

"How is he?" he asked.

"Stable," she said. "Not out of the woods. I'm sorry, I meant to ask, are you family?"

"No."

"A colleague?"

"Something like that."

She led him into a small waiting area. A glass wall looked into a private room. Through the glass, he could see the figure in the bed, pale, still, linked to full life support. He could just hear the rhythmic ping of the monitors, the pump of the ventilator.

He saw the dressing covering the cheek. The memory was physical, like a bruise. He raised his hand involuntarily and touched his own cheek.

There was no hole, or trace of a scar.

Having come all that way, he felt he ought to go in. Say something. Anything. The reminder on his cell had pinged just before he arrived at the hospital. Diary update. His driver was scheduled to leave in four days and he was due to report to the Terminal in two hours. He didn't have long, and he was pretty sure he was never coming back. He could surely manage some platitude about how everything had changed, and they'd been part of it?

"Can I go in and sit with him?" he asked.

"I suppose so, Mr Falk," replied the nurse. She opened the door, then lowered her voice. "Please don't expect too much," she said. "Private Bloom has very limited periods of consciousness. He drifts in and out. He probably won't recognise you."

"I understand," he replied, smiling.

"To be honest," she added, leaning forward to confide, "I don't think he knows who he is most of the time."

Falk nodded.

"I know how he feels," he said.

ABOUT THE AUTHOR

Dan Abnett is a *New York Times* bestselling novelist and award-winning comic book writer. He has written over thirty-five novels, including the acclaimed Gaunt's Ghosts series and the Eisenhorn and Ravenor trilogies. His novels *Horus Rising*, *Legion* and *Prospero Burns* (for the Black Library), and his Torchwood novel *Border Princes* (for the BBC), were all bestsellers. His novel *Triumff*, for Angry Robot, was published in 2009 and longlisted for the British Fantasy Society Award for Best Novel. He lives and works in Maidstone, Kent.

Follow him on Twitter @*VincentAbnett* and online at *www.danabnett.com*

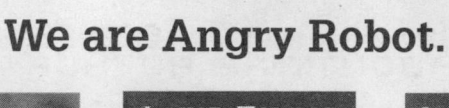

YOU WANTED THE BEST, YOU GOT THE BEST

Grab the whole Angry Robot catalogue

DAN ABNETT
- [ ] Embedded
- [ ] Triumff: Her Majesty's Hero

GUY ADAMS
- [ ] The World House
- [ ] Restoration

JO ANDERTON
- [ ] Debris

LAUREN BEUKES
- [ ] Moxyland
- [ ] Zoo City

THOMAS BLACKTHORNE
(aka John Meaney)
- [ ] Edge
- [ ] Point

MAURICE BROADDUS
- [ ] King Maker
- [ ] King's Justice
- [ ] King's War

PETER CROWTHER
- [ ] Darkness Falling

ALIETTE DE BODARD
- [ ] Servant of the Underworld
- [ ] Harbinger of the Storm
- [ ] Master of the House of Darts

MATT FORBECK
- [ ] Amortals
- [ ] Vegas Knights

JUSTIN GUSTAINIS
- [ ] Hard Spell

GUY HALEY
- [ ] Reality 36

COLIN HARVEY
- [ ] Damage Time
- [ ] Winter Song

MATTHEW HUGHES
- [ ] The Damned Busters

TRENT JAMIESON
- [ ] Roil

K W JETER
- [ ] Infernal Devices
- [ ] Morlock Night

J ROBERT KING
- [ ] Angel of Death
- [ ] Death's Disciples

GARY McMAHON
- [ ] Pretty Little Dead Things
- [ ] Dead Bad Things

ANDY REMIC
- [ ] Kell's Legend
- [ ] Soul Stealers
- [ ] Vampire Warlords

CHRIS ROBERSON
- [ ] Book of Secrets

MIKE SHEVDON
- [ ] Sixty-One Nails
- [ ] The Road to Bedlam

GAV THORPE
- [ ] The Crown of the Blood
- [ ] The Crown of the Conqueror

LAVIE TIDHAR
- [ ] The Bookman
- [ ] Camera Obscura

TIM WAGGONER
- [ ] Nekropolis
- [ ] Dead Streets
- [ ] Dark War

KAARON WARREN
- [ ] Mistification
- [ ] Slights
- [ ] Walking the Tree

IAN WHATES
- [ ] City of Dreams & Nightmare
- [ ] City of Hope & Despair
- [ ] City of Light & Shadow